WESTERN

Rugged men looking for love...

Fortune's Baby Claim
Michelle Major

The Cowgirl's Homecoming
Jeannie Watt

MILLS & BOON

Michelle Major is acknowledged as the author of this work
FORTUNE'S BABY CLAIM
© 2024 by Harlequin Enterprises ULC
Philippine Copyright 2024
Australian Copyright 2024
New Zealand Copyright 2024

First Published 2024
First Australian Paperback Edition 2024
ISBN 978 1 867 29968 4

THE COWGIRL'S HOMECOMING
© 2024 by Jeannie Steinman
Philippine Copyright 2024
Australian Copyright 2024
New Zealand Copyright 2024

First Published 2024
First Australian Paperback Edition 2024
ISBN 978 1 867 29968 4

Published by
Harlequin Mills & Boon
An imprint of Harlequin Enterprises (Australia) Pty Limited
(ABN 47 001 180 918), a subsidiary of HarperCollins
Publishers Australia Pty Limited
(ABN 36 009 913 517)
Level 19, 201 Elizabeth Street
SYDNEY NSW 2000 AUSTRALIA

MIX
Paper | Supporting
responsible forestry
FSC® C001695

Cover art used by arrangement with Harlequin Books S.A.. All rights reserved.

Printed and bound in Australia by McPherson's Printing Group

Fortune's Baby Claim
Michelle Major

MILLS & BOON

Michelle Major grew up in Ohio but dreamed of living in the mountains. Soon after graduating with a degree in journalism, she pointed her car west and settled in Colorado. Her life and house are filled with one great husband, two beautiful kids, a few furry pets and several well-behaved reptiles. She's grateful to have found her passion writing stories with happy endings. Michelle loves to hear from her readers at michellemajor.com.

For additional books by Michelle Major,
visit her website, michellemajor.com.

Dear Reader,

Do you like Valentine's Day? I've always had mixed feelings about the holiday. I love everything about love, but I don't enjoy the typical flowers-and-chocolate celebrations. So when I crafted Ryder and Esme's story, I knew I needed to give them a special way to commemorate the holiday. Especially since their relationship is complicated and enhanced by being new parents to two three-month-old baby boys.

Esme has dreamed of having a family of her own, and she gets that in the most unexpected way when she and Ryder Hayes, the last man she'd think a match for her, choose to raise the sons who were switched at birth together. She and Ryder both have past hurts to overcome, but together they find the love they both crave and the family that can make their dreams come true.

So I hope you'll enjoy their journey to happily-ever-after, along with a perfect Valentine's Day, as much as I enjoyed writing it. Please feel free to find me on Facebook and Instagram—I'd love to virtually hang out with you!

Happy reading!

Michelle

PROLOGUE

Esme Fortune didn't allow herself to believe in karma because that would mean she'd done something acutely awful to wind up in her current situation.

"You're doing fine," the nurse told her with a gentle pat to her arm before rushing out of the makeshift delivery room that wasn't a room at all—just a tiny alcove on the first floor of County Hospital outside of Chatelaine, Texas.

Another contraction started, bringing a surging wave of pain. At the same time, a flash of lightning followed by a booming clap of thunder shook the window next to her hospital bed.

The lights flickered again, something they'd been doing off and on for the past hour despite the various nurses who popped in and out to monitor the progress of Esme's labor and assure her that the hospital's backup generator was reliable.

At this point, she didn't trust anything—or anyone—other than her sister, Bea, who wasn't here yet. A fallen tree and downed power lines blocked the two-lane highway that led from Chatelaine to the hospital.

But she couldn't worry about her sister right now and instead concentrated on breathing through the pain that ripped through her. One, two, three, four. One, two, three, four…

The first thing she'd done after moving from Houston to Chatelaine a month earlier was to sign up for birthing classes with Bea as her coach. Esme, who'd spent her childhood dreaming of the sort of fairy-tale love that filled the romance novels she devoured, had failed at love and marriage, but she was determined to be the best mother she could.

Her baby would have a wonderful life full of laughter, happiness and no uncertainty about whether they were cherished and adored.

As the contraction subsided, a cold droplet hit her smack dab in the forehead, and she looked up to see water dripping from the ceiling above her. Esme sighed. Clearly, motherhood was not off to an auspicious start.

Who could have predicted that her water breaking would coincide with the late-October storm ravaging the region? It was the kind of storm that happened once in a lifetime—a hundred-year storm, the older neighbor who'd driven her to the hospital ominously reported, glancing at Esme like her situation had somehow predicated the lashing wind and pounding rain.

As it turned out, Esme wasn't the only soon-to-be mother whose baby seemed eager to meet the world in the middle of a torrential downpour. The frantic young woman at the admissions desk reported that four other women were already on the labor and delivery floor of the small hospital—a veritable baby boom in this sleepy region of Texas.

But now they were all crowded into a section of the hospital's OR with hastily constructed fabric partitions separating them after a burst pipe flooded the floor above them.

Esme cradled her stomach and tried to calm her nerves. It would work out. She could handle this. Her late husband might have believed she was weak and ordinary, but she was made of stronger stuff than Seth Watson had claimed.

And she'd do anything for the baby she already loved with her whole heart.

A woman's cries from the other side of the divider made Esme's anxiety ratchet up a few levels. But at least she could take solace in the fact that she was managing this unexpected turn of events with more calm than her neighbor, who had been swearing and screeching at staff and the man she kept calling "you big oaf" since Esme had been wheeled in.

"I don't want this," she heard the woman complain in a fierce whisper. "Make it stop. This is your fault, you big oaf! I'll never forgive you."

Esme couldn't hear the guy's response, but his tone was low and calm, especially given the venom being spewed his way. His words might not be comforting to her neighbor, but they had an oddly soothing effect on Esme, and she was grateful to the stranger.

Another contraction roared through her, so she concentrated on activating her own coping techniques once again. As the night drew on, the waves of pain came faster and more intensely, although the woman's shouting and cries drowned out Esme's soft moans.

She hated making any noise. It made her feel like she was losing the battle for control, but the pain slamming through her over and over felt relentless.

A new nurse checked her progress, assuring Esme it was all going according to plan, and she'd be ready to push soon.

No, she wanted to answer. *None of this was part of the plan.* Having a baby alone and raising her child as a single mother was not how she'd envisioned her life.

Was she as ill-equipped to welcome her son or daughter into the world as her neighbor loudly claimed about herself? The difference was the woman next to her had a big oaf at her side.

Esme imagined him broad, hairy and bearing a striking resemblance to the troll under the bridge from the classic children's tale.

How sad was it that even a potentially mean and hungry troll could comfort her now? Clearly, the fairy-tale life she'd imagined had gone very, very sideways.

She lost track of how much time had elapsed, but it felt like hours or days later when the curtain was yanked back to reveal another nurse and an older man who had the commanding air of a doctor.

As they entered the cramped space, tears sprung to Esme's eyes unbidden, but not in response to the pain or the exhaustion that threatened to pull her under like a riptide. She was simply so relieved not to be alone.

For an instant, her gaze was drawn to something over the doctor's shoulder, and she found herself looking into the most piercing set of green eyes she'd ever seen. Esme's eyes were green or hazel, depending on her mood, but the man staring at her had eyes the color of spring grass, vibrant and full of promise.

She had just enough time to register the handsome face surrounding those green eyes, a strong jaw and a full mouth that curved into the barest hint of a smile as he nodded and mouthed, "You've got this." He couldn't possibly be the oaf, or else Esme was delirious with fatigue.

But those three little words spoken silently by a stranger bolstered her resolve in a way that defied logic.

As the nurse pulled the curtain shut, Esme drew in the steadiest breath she could manage.

"Are you ready to meet your baby?" the doctor asked in a reassuring tone, then simultaneously winced and chuckled as another crack of thunder reverberated around them. "Because a child born on a night like this is bound to be special."

Esme swallowed around the emotion clogging her throat, then nodded. "I'm ready," she whispered.

CHAPTER ONE

"YOU AREN'T ALONE," Bea reassured Esme three months later as they sat at the small kitchen table in Esme's post-age-stamp-size kitchen.

However, she didn't mind the diminutive proportions of her house in one of the older neighborhoods of Chatelaine. There was plenty of room for her and baby Chase, and owning her own home meant the world to her. It was more than she could have imagined in the lonely, shocking months after her husband's death at the beginning of the previous year and the subsequent revelation he'd been cheating on her since the start of their relationship.

She and Seth had married at the courthouse two days after a doctor confirmed the results of the half dozen home pregnancy tests Esme had taken. But within weeks of the wedding, Seth turned distant, traveling almost constantly for his company and leaving her alone in a cramped apartment near the elementary school in Houston, where she taught first grade.

Then she'd discovered he'd been cheating on her since the start of their relationship. And although the betrayal hurt, she'd been determined to try to make the marriage work for the sake of the baby. She'd been scared but not heartbroken and Seth had agreed to go to counseling, but showed no signs of changing his behavior. And Esme had started to wonder if she'd be relegated to the same fate as her mother in an unhappy marriage and if staying the course was truly worth it.

When Seth was killed in a boating accident on the open water near Galveston the day before they were scheduled for their first appointment with the counselor, Esme felt heartbroken for her unborn child, who'd never know his father, but her heart had remained numb. She'd weathered another shock a few weeks later when she'd received a check as the beneficiary of Seth's modest life insurance policy.

He hadn't been the knight in shining armor she'd longed for as a girl, but she would always be grateful for how he'd taken care of her and their child.

"I don't know anything about Seth's family," she told Bea, as if her sister, who knew her better than anyone in the world, didn't understand where her trepidation about this moment originated. "He barely spoke about them, and it was never anything good. For all I know, they could be horrible people." She drew a finger along the edge of the envelope from the DNA testing company, 411 Me. "Remind me why I wanted to do this in the first place?"

"Because Freya gifted it to you, and you're curious." Bea squeezed Esme's trembling hand. "I'm curious as well. For all either of us know, Chase could be related to someone famous."

"Or infamous," Esme muttered and took a small sip of the wine her sister had brought over. "Why do you think Freya did it? Why has she done any of this?" The questions had been pinging around Esme's brain the past two weeks as she waited for the results of the DNA test her late great-uncle's widow, Freya Fortune, had encouraged her to take.

But to be fair, she tended to question every aspect of her life in the middle of the night as she blearily fed Chase, whose understanding of the difference between day and night had been wonky in recent weeks.

So it was difficult to know whether her uncertainty about Freya Fortune and the significant role she now played in the lives of Esme, her siblings and their cousins was justified or simply the workings of her tired and muddled mind.

Bea ran a hand through her flaming red hair. She was eight years older than Esme, and while their faces and eyes were the same shape, Esme had dark hair and green eyes in contrast to Bea's radiant red locks and blue eyes. Of course, Esme was also sporting some new-mom bags under her eyes, thanks to Chase.

"I like to think of Freya as a fairy godmother," Bea said with a smile. "Or our fairy step-great aunt." She drummed her fingers on Esme's table. "I'd always wanted to own a restaurant, but I never would have gotten a chance to open the Cowgirl Café without Freya's generosity. Neither Edgar nor Elias Fortune have the best reputation in Chatelaine—"

"That's putting it mildly," Esme said with a laugh.

Edgar and Elias had run the Fortune silver mine in town. But after overhearing a conversation between their estranged brothers, Wendell and Walter, they'd mistakenly believed their mine might also produce gold. The story Esme had heard after moving to Chatelaine was that the potential of wealth beyond their wildest dreams prompted the brothers to overwork their miners. Their greed led to the unsafe conditions that resulted in a tragic collapse of the mine that killed fifty men, including the foreman, who Edgar and Elias blamed instead of taking responsibility themselves.

She didn't want to believe her grandfather and great uncle had used their wealth to avoid being held accountable, but the brothers had left Chatelaine in disgrace shortly after the accident. They'd resurfaced hours away in Cave Creek, staying long enough for each of them to start a family before disappearing again.

Bea traced a finger along the rim of her wine glass. "If Great-Uncle Elias truly had a change of heart at the end of his life the way Freya claims, her financial support will go a long way in changing what people around here think about our branch of the Fortune family tree. I hope by her sharing what's left of his money with us, we can repair some of the damage our grandfather and great-uncle caused and hopefully make a positive impact on this community."

Esme sighed. "You always make me feel better, sis. Although you're doing much more good for this town with your plan to open a restaurant than I am with the money Freya has given me."

They'd each received a letter from Freya Fortune at the end of last summer explaining that she was their great-uncle's widow and extending an invitation to come to Chatelaine and learn more about their past in the town.

"Look at this little cutie," Bea commanded as she held Esme's phone aloft. The screensaver was a carousel of photos featuring baby Chase. One from the day Esme had brought him home from the hospital bundled in a blue blanket with a knit cap covering his wispy dark hair to several more recent photos documenting him sleeping and his first smile.

"There's nothing more important than devoting yourself to being a mother. You'll return to teaching refreshed and renewed next school year, Es. And the elementary school community will love you just like your former students. Chatelaine is both of our homes now. Asa's, too. He's bound and determined Chase will learn to ride a horse before he even walks."

Esme grinned at the thought of her older brother finally

owning the dude ranch he was working to purchase just outside of town.

"Still…" She tipped her wine glass in her sister's direction, then took another drink. "Don't you think it's strange Freya is taking such an interest in us?"

Bea wrinkled her nose. "Maybe, but I prefer to imagine thanking her with an amazing meal once I open my restaurant. And I'm certain that you're overthinking it right now as an excuse to avoid opening this report." She picked it up and handed the envelope to Esme. "Let's go, girl. I hope to find out my nephew is secretly related to George Clooney."

At Esme's raised brow, Bea clarified, "George circa hotter *before he was huge but he had great hair and the best broody stare.*"

Esme knew her sister was joking to ease the tension, and as always with the two of them, it worked. She slid one finger under the seal, tore it open and then pulled out the small stack of papers detailing her son's genetic family tree.

As part of the package, she'd also had an opportunity for her own testing, so she started with her results, which were exactly what she'd expected. There were plenty of skeletons in the Fortune closet, but most of those had seen the light of day years earlier—at least the ones that involved Esme's relatives.

She wondered what her grandfather and great-uncle would have thought of this kind of technological advancement if they'd lived long enough to see it. Her mom and dad had been killed in a plane crash five years earlier. While her parents hadn't shared a loving relationship for most of their marriage, she'd never expected to lose them so suddenly and wished they could have been here to meet their grandson.

Esme continued to read, but what the report revealed about her son didn't make any sense.

"What's wrong?" Bea asked. "Don't tell me there's truly someone infamous in Seth's family."

Esme shook her head. Her throat had gone dry as she tried to process what the DNA report meant regarding her son's background.

"There's not one Fortune or anyone from Seth's family listed. Several of them have the last name Hayes. I—I don't understand…"

"Maybe that was his mother's maiden name?" her sister murmured.

"No, her name was Williams. Lana Williams. She died when Seth was in high school, but he still used her name as a password for most of his online accounts. That's the reason I'm sure Hayes isn't right. *None* of this is right."

"Do you think 411 Me inadvertently gave you the wrong report for Chase?" Bea asked. "I mean, otherwise, how can any of this make sense when your results seem valid?"

"I can't explain it, but I had a weird feeling that doing the DNA test was a mistake."

"It has to be a mix-up." Esme's sister grabbed the papers from her. "They're based out of California, and it says customer service is still open. Let's call them and get to the bottom of it."

Bea had to be correct. It must be a technical error. She'd call, and they'd redo the tests, or maybe, as her sister had suggested, there had been a mix-up, and they would just send her the correct information.

"They better offer a refund for putting me through this headache," she said with a laugh that didn't feel humorous.

"You want me to call?" Bea asked. "I'd be happy to give those people a piece of my mind!"

Esme picked up the phone and punched in the number listed on the report. "Thanks, but I need to be the one to talk to them. I want to hear for myself that it's a mistake because the other option—"

"There *is* no other option." Bea hugged her, and Esme tried to channel her sister's confidence as she waited for someone to answer.

A few minutes later, she explained the situation to the cold and clinical-sounding woman on the other end of the line.

After double checking the results from their database, the woman curtly asked Esme if there was a possibility her child could have been fathered by someone other than the man she believed to be Chase's biological dad.

The question was almost as shocking as initially reading the report. While Esme hadn't been entirely inexperienced when she'd begun seeing Seth, her accidental pregnancy had still made her feel like a naive fool.

But she'd ended things with her only other serious boy-friend a year before meeting her late husband. Serious enough for that sort of intimacy anyway. The 411 Me representative didn't sound surprised or convinced by Esme's vehement denial.

Clearly, this wasn't the first call the company had received along this vein. After going back and forth several times, Esme finally persuaded the woman she was telling the truth, and the company representative's voice gentled considerably. Only the suggestion she gave Esme landed with all the subtlety of a lead balloon.

Her heart reeled and blood roared between her ears as she thanked the woman and finally ended the call.

"What did she say?" Bea grabbed her hand, but Esme

barely registered the touch. "Was it a mistake? Why do you look like you're going to puke? Tell me it's too much wine."

"She said I need to contact the hospital where I gave birth."

Her sister's eyes widened. "Why? Did they mess up something?"

Esme thought back to the chaos of the night Chase was born—rain lashing against the window, lights flickering and the kind nurses who seemed so discombobulated.

Still, the idea of what the 411 Me representative had proposed as an explanation was outside the realm of possibility.

At least, that was what Esme wanted to believe.

"She thinks it's possible that Chase isn't mine." Esme choked out a sob. "There could have been a mistake and…"

She met Bea's concerned gaze and tried to focus past the tears blurring her vision. It was obvious when her sister understood what she was trying to say because Bea grabbed her shoulders and shook them gently.

"No. Chase is *your* son. We'll go to the hospital right now."

"I'm not going to wake him." Esme wiped a hand over her cheeks. "It's getting late, and I need time to think. I'll call County Hospital in the morning and—"

"They'll have an answer for you," Bea assured her. "One that explains all of this. Do you want me to stay? I can sleep in the spare bedroom so you're not alone."

"Thanks, but it's okay. I'm fine." And even though Bea sat beside her, Esme had never felt more alone.

They talked for a few more minutes, then after another long hug, Bea left, and Esme walked up the stairs and slipped into Chase's nursery.

The crib was lit by the soft glow of a night-light plugged

into the wall, and she pressed a hand over her mouth to keep in the cries that threatened to escape.

Her sweet boy slept peacefully on his back, swaddled in a cotton blanket her grandmother had sent after his birth. He looked like a baby burrito, and Esme sank onto the carpet next to the crib, content to watch his chest rise and fall. Chase was her son, she reminded herself.

No test results or mix-up in a lab would change that. Tomorrow, she'd go to the hospital and demand an explanation. Standing up for herself didn't come easily to Esme, but she'd do anything for her baby boy.

After a while, exhaustion got the best of her, but she couldn't bring herself to leave the nursery. She grabbed a blanket and a pillow from the glider in the corner to arrange a makeshift bed on the floor. Then she closed her eyes and commanded her heart to remember that Chase belonged to her—forever.

CHAPTER TWO

RYDER HAYES WAS determined to be a calm, organized, totally together single dad to his three-month-old son, Noah.

Just not this particular morning.

After staying up past his embarrassingly early bedtime last night to wash and dry dirty bottles, fold laundry and pack his son's extra clothes for the babysitter, he'd almost made it out the door on time.

Then Noah had a diaper blowout—all over Ryder's crisp white button-down. Weren't diapers supposed to hold *in* the poop? Ryder's baby seemed to be a master at pooping sideways, diagonally and with the force of Old Faithful erupting.

Thirty minutes after his planned departure, Ryder clicked Noah's infant seat into the base in the back of his car and headed toward the house of the older woman who watched him daily.

Anna Mitchell was an absolute angel, and he honestly didn't know how he'd manage without her. Although he'd offered to marry his late ex-girlfriend, Stephanie, after discovering she was pregnant, she had wanted nothing to do with marriage—or motherhood, as it turned out.

He shook his head, committed to believing that if a car accident hadn't taken her life a few weeks after Noah's birth, she would have eventually warmed to the idea of being a mom.

From the moment Noah's tiny hand curled around Ryder's finger in the hospital, he'd been a goner—completely smitten with his son. Too bad that loving a baby didn't intrinsically equate to knowing how to care for one. Ryder was doing his best, but most days, it felt like his life was on the brink of collapse in almost all areas.

Speaking of collapse...

He grabbed his phone from where he'd tossed it on the passenger seat, ready to call his father and offer a better excuse than a diaper blowout for why he would be late to the meeting with Hayes Enterprises' senior management team along with several key investors. After deciding to retire in this small town, his dad had made plans to move the headquarters for their family's portfolio of private social clubs and resorts to Chatelaine. Chandler Hayes was ready to give up running the mini empire he'd built but refused to relinquish complete control.

The question was whether Dad would be handing over the reins to Ryder or his brother, Brandon, who was a chip off the old womanizing block and seemed to relish Ryder's struggle to balance his work duties with fatherhood.

Noah's uncle Brandon would have laughed his butt off at the diaper emergency, only Ryder would keep that debacle to himself. Because anything that revealed a perceived weakness could and would be used against him, and he had a son to care for now, entirely on his own. He *needed* this promotion.

Before he could place the call, his phone began to ring. He answered, his heart pounding as he listened to the hospital administrator's cryptic request that he bring Noah to the facility immediately for an urgent meeting with the hospital's attorney.

An attorney—what the hell was that about?

The woman, who identified herself as County Hospital's chief executive, refused to answer the questions

Ryder fired off and insisted everything would be explained in person.

His mind raced as he turned the car around and quickly called his father's assistant to explain that an emergency would prevent him from attending the board meeting. Cynthia's voice was tight as she promised to relay the message, and he knew it was cowardly not to call his dad or Brandon directly, but he had more important things to worry about.

Nothing took precedence over Noah, and the fear pounding through Ryder refused to abate no matter how many times he reminded himself that though he might not have a handle on parenthood, Noah was his son. No one could take that away from him.

But what if Steph's family wanted to try? He assured himself they wouldn't have contacted the hospital. That didn't make sense. None of it made sense, but Ryder would figure it out. He glanced into the rearview mirror and took a deep breath.

Noah had drifted off to sleep, which he often did in the car, blissfully unaware that his daddy was having a slight panic attack in the front seat.

Ryder stiffened his jaw. He would protect his son no matter what this impromptu meeting threw his way. He might not be confident in his skills as a parent, but he would do anything for his child.

Esme stared out the window in the empty conference room next to the administrator's office at County Hospital, hoping the view of the outside world would calm her nerves.

As a kid, she'd been a shy bookworm and often escaped to the woods behind her family's two-story house to sit under her favorite tree and read for hours. Making real-life friends hadn't come easily to her as it had for her effervescent sister, so Anne Shirley, Hermione Granger and a host of other fictional characters became her beloved companions.

Today, the winter sky was a vivid blue, and a light breeze made the few leaves clinging to the branches of the trees along the edge of the parking lot flutter like a moth's wings. Sunlight shone brightly, a beacon from above that was in direct contrast to Esme's gray and turbulent mood.

After this meeting, she'd take Chase for a walk on the path bordering Lake Chatelaine to the west of downtown. Although she wasn't much for water sports, she loved being near the lake and watching birds dive toward the tiny bubbles that floated on the surface when the resident fish popped up.

"What is taking so long?" she asked her son, who sat in his infant carrier next to the table. Chase gurgled an answer before shoving one fist back in his mouth.

Maybe she should have called first, the way she'd planned, but after waking on the floor of the nursery with a kinked neck and aching back, Esme had decided the best way to gauge the response to her unthinkable suggestion would be to ask the question about the night Chase was born in person.

When Esme first arrived, the hospital's chief executive, Mary Dill, a woman who had to be nearing retirement age with a short pixie cut and round glasses that made her look like a blinking owl behind them, had appeared as shocked as Esme felt explaining the situation.

But Mary quickly converted to cover-your-assets mode, ushering Esme into the conference room to wait while she looked into the matter.

The matter, Esme had reminded the woman, was a human life—her baby. Chase was not simply a potential PR nightmare for the hospital to brush under a rug. The administrator had agreed and promised to handle her inquiries with the delicacy the situation warranted.

That was nearly forty minutes ago, Esme realized as she glanced at her watch. She stood, ready to track down some answers, but took her seat again when the door opened.

Mary entered, her skin noticeably paler than when Esme had interrupted her mid-bite of a breakfast sandwich. She was followed by a stuffy-looking man with shifty eyes and a paunch that seemed out of place on his wiry frame.

"Mrs. Fortune, this is Greg Oachs, hospital counsel."

"It's Miss, not Mrs.," Esme corrected as she shook the lawyer's outstretched hand. His grasp had all the enthusiasm of a stunned fish. "You can call me Esme."

"Then please call me Greg," he answered in a booming voice that seemed forcibly cheerful. "I understand we have a bit of a conundrum, Esme, but I assure you we'll get to the bottom of it. You can trust me on that."

She didn't trust anyone who made that claim but couldn't meet her gaze. Instead, the fine hairs on the back of her neck stood on end. Something was very wrong.

"Have you determined why my baby's DNA report came back the way it did?"

"We have an idea," Mary began before the lawyer cut her off with a sharp flick of the wrist.

"Let's wait until the other party arrives," he said in a commanding tone.

Normally, Esme would defer to someone in a position of authority, but Chase yawned at that moment, melting her heart and reminding her that there was someone more important than the attorney in this room. Her son mattered more than anyone or anything.

"I'm through waiting," she huffed, rising from her seat. "I expect answers to the questions I raised."

"She's not the only one," a deep voice said.

All three turned as a man in a well-cut suit entered the room. Esme would have pegged him for another attorney, except he had one arm looped around the handle of an infant carrier and sported a somewhat desperate glint in his piercing green eyes that convinced her he was the father of the baby he carried.

He looked to be around Esme's age, tall with sandy blond hair, broad shoulders and a chiseled jaw. The man possessed a kind of movie-star attractiveness that seemed out of place in this nondescript conference room.

As the stranger stepped closer, and his green eyes met hers, a memory tugged at the corner of Esme's mind. The realization dawned that she was staring at the big oaf from the night of her labor and delivery.

"You must be Ryder," Mary Dill said, thrusting out her hand with more enthusiasm than she'd displayed when Esme had appeared asking questions. "Thank you so much for coming in on such short notice."

"I didn't feel like I had a choice, given the ambiguity of your phone call." He briefly shook her hand and then glanced toward the other man in attendance. "You must be the lawyer."

"Greg Oachs of Oachs, Hart and Meinig. I'm general counsel for County Hospital."

"General counsel." Ryder frowned and placed the infant carrier on the conference table like it was the most natural thing in the world. "That sounds serious." His gaze tracked to Esme. "Do you know what this is about?" he asked as if somehow understanding they were on the same side, although he clearly didn't remember their brief eye-contact connection three months earlier.

"Not a clue," she said quietly.

"I can explain," Mary told them, although she looked like she might rather stick a fork in her eye.

"*I'll* explain." Greg placed his hands on the table and leaned forward before glancing at Ryder. "Would you like to put that thing on the floor?" He gestured toward the infant carrier.

"My *son*?" Ryder shook his head and placed a protective hand on the baby, making Esme's heart flutter. "No. He's fine right where he is."

Chase wasn't fine. He'd started to fuss a bit. She undid the harness and picked him up from the carrier, cradling the boy in her arms.

"About three months?" Ryder asked, his tone gentler than when he'd spoken to the attorney.

"Yes."

"Mine, too."

Should she tell him they'd been in the hospital on the same fateful night? Esme wondered where his baby's mother was, hoping the woman had managed to overcome her insistence that she wasn't meant to be a mom.

Before she could say anything, Greg Oachs cleared his throat. "These two babies were born on the same night."

"You both remember?" Mary asked hopefully.

Greg sent the administrator a quelling glance, and Esme nearly scoffed. Of course, she remembered the night her son was born.

"Why are we here?" Ryder demanded, clearly not in the mood to walk down memory lane with a trio of strangers. "Is someone threatening to sue the hospital over the conditions we dealt with the night of the storm?"

"We did our best," the hospital administrator insisted.

"No one is filing suit." Greg straightened and tugged at his tie, leaving it crooked against his white oxford-cloth shirt. "There was a misunderstanding back in October." His throat bobbed as he swallowed and looked at a place past Esme's shoulder. "We have reason to believe your babies were accidentally switched shortly after they were born."

Esme had been expecting the words, but they still hit with the force of a mallet cracking the side of her skull. She drew Chase closer to her chest, sending a silent prayer that this was a nightmare she'd soon wake from.

Ryder stood in stunned silence for several seconds, then dropped into a chair like his legs wouldn't hold him.

She understood the feeling. Her entire body had gone numb, except her heart, which burned as if the words were a hot poker stabbing into it.

"What makes you think that?" Ryder demanded finally.

"Chase and I had testing done," she told him before the attorney or administrator could spin the story. "My ex-husband was in an accident and died suddenly. I wanted to know more about his side of the family." In truth, she hadn't considered learning more about Seth's family history until Freya gifted her the two test kits.

Ryder inclined his head. "I'm sorry for your loss."

"My *son*'s loss," she clarified, unsure why she needed to make that distinction. "His results came back with no one from either side of the family listed, as if we don't share DNA."

"Could it have been a mistake at the testing facility?"

The attorney cleared his throat again. "I think—"

"I didn't ask what you thought," Ryder snapped. "We'll get to you in a minute."

Greg Oachs crossed his arms over his chest with an audible harrumph but said nothing more.

"I apologize." Ryder returned his gaze to Esme. "I also didn't catch your name."

"Esme Fortune," she told him. "I spoke with someone at 411 Me last night. They assured me Chase's results are valid."

"We'd like you and your son to take a DNA test," Mary

said to Ryder, then transferred her gaze to Esme. "You and your baby as well."

"I've already done that," she answered.

"For our purposes," the woman explained. "We'd like to have both of your test results on file here at the hospital."

"Okay," Esme murmured.

"You don't have to agree to anything," Ryder said, his deep gaze intense on hers.

"I have to know." She dropped a kiss on the top of Chase's downy head. "Don't you want to know?"

"I want to go back to bed, wake up and pretend this day never happened."

She smiled slightly. "If only that were an option."

"It is," Greg offered with more of that fake cheer. "Or you can take the tests, and if the results come back the way we think they might, it's an easy swap. No harm, no foul."

Even Mary Dill gasped at that suggestion.

Esme felt like she'd taken another blow, this one directly to her heart. Chase was her child, the baby she'd brought home from the hospital. Her son. How could she conceive of any other possibility?

"You're going to want to stop talking," Ryder told the attorney. "Because everything coming out of your mouth makes me want to slam my fist into it."

"Th-there's no need to get violent," Greg stammered, taking a step away from the table.

"You have no idea what I need," Ryder muttered.

"I need to get out of here," Esme blurted, then looked at Mary. "Can we do the tests right now? I want to go home."

"Of course," she answered without hesitation.

Esme kept Chase cradled close in one arm and picked up the infant carrier with her free hand.

"We'll put a rush on the tests," Mary said as Esme moved around the conference table. Sunlight streamed through the windows she'd been staring out earlier, and the brightness of the day felt like it was mocking her. "But it will be later today until we have the results."

The attorney reached for his briefcase. "I have some papers for you both to sign granting the hospital indemnity in this matter."

"Neither of us is signing a damn thing," Ryder answered for them both, which was fine. Esme didn't have any fight left in her at the moment. This new version of her reality was too much to manage.

She was surprised when Ryder followed her and Mary out of the room, gripping his son's infant carrier with the same tight hold she had on Chase's.

"Are you willing to have the tests?" she asked, then glanced at the sweet baby sleeping in the carrier. "What's his name?"

"Noah," Ryder whispered, then touched her arm. "I understand we're strangers, Esme Fortune, but as far as I'm concerned, we're in this together."

She nodded, his unexpected words comforting her, much like his gaze had the night their babies were born. Once again, she needed all the reassurance she could get.

CHAPTER THREE

A HALF HOUR LATER, Esme stood outside the hospital's entrance and dialed her sister's number with shaking fingers. Bea answered on the first ring, and she quickly explained the situation, even the awful part where the attorney suggested they swap babies.

Bea was outraged but also shocked at how calm Esme sounded. It wasn't calm—she couldn't feel anything. Her body—her entire being—had gone numb because the alternative of feeling fear, panic and dread about the potential outcome of this situation was too much to cope with at the moment.

"Who are the parents of the other baby?" Her sister's voice was low like she hated even asking about them.

"I only met the father." Esme realized she hadn't thought to ask about the absence of Noah's mother from the meeting. Chalk it up to one more unanswered question. "His name is Ryder Hayes, and he—"

"Oh, no," her sister murmured. "Stay away from anyone in Chatelaine with the last name Hayes. I'm serious, Esme."

"How can I do that, Bea? What's wrong with Ryder Hayes?" Esme glanced down at the infant carrier that held her son, which she'd placed on a bench in the shade while she called her sister and regrouped. Chase was sleeping peacefully, his rosebud mouth working like he was having a delightful dream. If only Ryder's wish for a do-over on this nightmare of a morning could come true.

"There are two brothers, but I don't know which is Ryder. One seems more reserved, but the other is a total player. They work for their dad, who bought the LC Club with plans to make it even fancier than it is already. The father acts like he owns the whole world, and the rest of us are lucky to breathe the same air as him."

Esme's least favorite type of person. She was familiar with the exclusive gated community and private club situated on the banks of Lake Chatelaine, although she'd never stepped foot in the place. Swanky social clubs weren't exactly her style, but she could see the handsome man with the expensive suit and vibrant eyes fitting in there.

"I don't have the choice to ignore him," she told her sister. "We're in this together." Repeating the words Ryder had spoken made her heart catch. Had he meant that, or had he been feeding her a line to soften her defenses so he could manipulate her?

Before she'd been caught in the spell of her late husband's magnetic personality and the lies he'd told, Esme had believed she possessed a strong sense for reading people. But she'd been so wrong about Seth. His subtle digs at her confidence and discovering after his death that he'd been cheating on her almost from the time of their first date caused her to doubt everything—especially herself.

"Okay, but I'm warning you to be careful. You can't trust Ryder Hayes."

A slight shiver passed through Esme, and she turned to see the man in question exiting the hospital. Her and Chase's tests had been completed first, and she'd slipped out of the hospital lab after they were finished. She'd heard Ryder in the next room demanding that Mary Dill give him a list of everyone on staff during the shift when Chase and Noah were born.

All she'd wanted was to get out of the building. What she longed to do was run and ignore everything, but something had stopped her from driving away.

Ryder stood outside the sliding doors, unaware of her presence. He held the handle of the infant carrier in both hands, and his head dropped forward, shoulders slumping like they carried an unbearable weight.

"I've got to go, Bea," she said into the phone. "I'll call you later."

"I'm here for whatever you need. We'll get you and Chase through this, Es."

She said goodbye, disconnected and placed her phone in one of the pockets of the diaper bag she always carried. As much as Esme appreciated her sister's support, Bea couldn't possibly understand the impact those routine test results were having on Esme's future.

No one did, except perhaps Ryder Hayes. But still, she couldn't afford to be naive about the situation. Maybe Bea was right, and he couldn't be trusted and was a womanizer like Seth. Was that why his wife or girlfriend hadn't come with him today? She hated to think about her son being exposed to that kind of a role model.

But it wasn't only Chase she needed to worry about. Noah was a part of the equation that couldn't be ignored.

As the numbness wore off, a tumble of tumultuous emotions threatened to drown her. Of all the things Esme wanted right now, first and foremost, she did *not* want to be alone.

She picked up Chase's car seat and walked in Ryder's direction. He continued to stand like a statue, seemingly unaware of anything around him.

"Hello?" She stopped a few feet away, and the panic

in his gaze when he glanced up at her felt like a direct hit to her heart.

Then his eyes cleared, and he offered her a weak smile. "I'm trying not to freak out."

"How's that going?"

He chuckled weakly. "Not well."

Ryder's phone vibrated from inside his suit coat pocket, and he absently patted the device but didn't answer the call.

"I heard that thing go off several times during the meeting." She tucked a lock of hair behind her ear, noticing that his gaze tracked her movement. "It sounds like someone is desperate to get a hold of you." Was it Noah's mother? She wanted to ask.

"I missed an important work meeting this morning." His throat bobbed as he swallowed. "Quite possibly wrecked my career because of it. Somehow that doesn't seem to matter."

Those weren't the words of a manipulative, power-hungry man as far as Esme was concerned. Seth's smarmy behavior might have shaken her faith in her instincts, but she believed Ryder was as disturbed by all of this as her. Either that, or he'd missed his calling as an actor.

For the first time since discovering how badly her late husband had betrayed her, she wanted to trust someone again, even though the man in question was almost a stranger. A stranger with whom she shared an unimaginable connection.

"What are we going to do?" He searched her face as if he believed she'd have an answer.

Apparently, Ryder Hayes trusted Esme with a confidence she hadn't granted herself in a long time, and she wanted to live up to his expectations. She needed to prove—mostly to herself—that she was strong and capable. Her son was going to need her to be just that.

"I'm not sure," she answered because there was no denying that truth. "But I know we'll figure it out. We both want what's best for our babies." She cleared her throat and then offered the most genuine smile she could muster under the circumstances. "Would you like to come back to my house while we wait for the results? We could talk and…"

He offered a small smile. "Yes, we could talk."

She shrugged. "I guess we should get to know each other, given how our lives are about to be intertwined."

"Intertwined," Ryder repeated like he was testing the word to see how it felt on his tongue. "Yes, I'd like to get to know you." He flashed a grin before glancing at Noah's infant carrier and then Chase's. "I'd like to get to know you both."

Awareness skittered along her nerve endings, which was silly because the only connection she and Ryder had was the unfathomable situation they were facing together. This was not the time for her lady parts to wake up from their long slumber.

"I'm parked in the second row." She gestured to the half-full lot. "My address is 432 Maple. Easy enough if we get separated."

Ryder nodded and placed a hand on his jacket as the phone continued to vibrate. "We won't. I'll see you in a few minutes, Esme."

She liked the way her name sounded when he said it. That was *not* good. As Esme secured Chase's car seat in the base, she reminded herself that she had approximately ten minutes to kill the fluttery feelings that flitted through her stomach unbidden each time Ryder's green eyes caught on hers.

This was business—the business of taking care of her baby. It would never be anything more.

BEFORE CLIMBING OUT of his BMW sedan in front of Esme's house with Noah's baby carrier in tow, Ryder switched his phone from vibrate to full-on "do not disturb" mode. He'd made the mistake of glancing at it on the way over. The multiple voice mails he'd received from his brother and the half dozen texts his father had sent demanding that Ryder get his ass to the office sooner than later were a reality check he did not want or need. This latest development in his complicated life would make things even more challenging.

He wasn't sure when it had become an unquestionable fact within their family that he and Brandon, thirteen months younger than Ryder, would be expected to compete in every aspect of their lives.

Dear old Dad loved a good challenge, never shying away from a chance to battle for a top spot, and Brandon was happy to emulate him. Although he did his best to hide it, Ryder took after their mother in ways that would send his father into an apoplectic fit if he realized the extent of it. He had learned early on to tamp down his sensitive nature, and by the time he was ten, the fleshy part of his palms had deeply worn grooves from where he dug his nails whenever he'd had the urge to cry or show weakness in front of his dad and brother.

Chandler Hayes pitted his sons against one another in everything from backyard games of tag and shooting hoops to grades, girls and football. Ryder had done his best to deflect the expectations without making his father think he was a wimp, which, according to Chandler, was the worst thing a boy could be.

He'd tried just enough in school not to draw attention, avoided dating altogether and opted to play tight end instead of quarterback so he wouldn't have to compete with Brandon for the marquee spot on their high-school team at the private school they'd attended in one of Houston's poshest neighborhoods.

It wasn't that Ryder didn't believe he deserved a chance to shine or that he couldn't beat his brother when push came to shove, which it often had in the backyard. He just hadn't wanted to put his energy into fighting and instead liked to lead a team by example and earn a grade or an award on his own merit, not motivated by some false sense of resentment toward his brother.

But the CEO position his father was vacating at the end of the month was a different story. Ryder had the talent, commitment and vision to lead Hayes Enterprises into the future, and he wanted to create a legacy to leave for his son, only not at the expense of being a father who was present in a meaningful way.

Ryder had dealt with that reality his entire life, and it wasn't worth the price he or Noah would pay.

He drew in a deep breath as he approached the front porch of the compact brick house painted a cheery yellow. Black shutters framed the front window, and the rocking chair on the porch sported a pillow with a heart embroidered on it that matched the heart-shaped wreath hanging on the door.

Valentine's Day. The holiday for people who believed in love was fast approaching, not that it would make a difference in Ryder's solitary life. Maybe he'd order Noah one of those "heartbreaker" onesies he'd seen online.

Esme had mentioned her husband dying in an unexpected accident, which was another thing they had in common. Unlike Ryder and Stephanie, had she and her late husband been blissfully in love?

Although their relationship had been fraught with drama, Ryder's chest still tightened each time he thought about the fact that his son would grow up without a mother.

When the door opened and Esme stood smiling at him from the other side, the vise that held his chest in its grip loosened considerably. He wished he could explain what it was about his unexpected partner in this dramatic turn of events that had such a calming effect on his nerves.

Esme was pretty in a girl-next-door kind of way. She had shiny dark-chocolate-colored hair that fell just below her shoulders and the clearest green eyes he'd ever seen. As he stared into them now, he noticed they'd taken on a gray hue, like the waves the wind whipped up across Lake Chatelaine, which he could see from the apartment he'd rented near the LC Club on the other side of town.

As far as Ryder could tell, she wasn't wearing makeup, and other than tiny gold hoops in her ears, she sported no jewelry. He dated women with more outward flash and pizzazz because they seemed to be the type who didn't expect more from him than an expensive dinner and a mutually pleasurable roll in the sheets.

Esme was the type of woman a man would bring home to meet his family, although he didn't consider that an option with his dad and brother. The last girl he'd introduced to his family had been someone he'd brought home over fall break during his sophomore year of college.

He'd liked her quite a bit, but the very next weekend, his brother had taken that same girl to a fraternity formal. Always a competition between the two of them, at least from Brandon's viewpoint.

Ryder couldn't put his finger on what had made him suddenly so consumed with ruminating on the past. He typically kept his gaze forward because looking back didn't do a damn bit of good.

He blinked when he realized Esme was snapping her fingers in front of his face.

"I asked whether you wanted to come in or if you

planned to stand on the porch all day?" She scrunched up her nose in a rather adorable way. "I can bring you a glass of water if you'd like."

He scrubbed a hand over his jaw. "Sorry. I'd love to come in. It feels like my head is spinning in a million different directions."

"Mine, too," she admitted as he walked past her into the cozy living room.

There was an overstuffed couch on one wall with a leather chair and ottoman and a coffee table that looked like it might have been up-cycled from wood pallets. A basic TV sat on an entertainment center with framed photos on either side, including several of Esme's baby, Chase.

Glancing down at his son, it made him realize that although he'd taken loads of photos of Noah and texted them regularly to his mother back in Houston, he hadn't thought to have any printed and framed for display. His apartment held none of the homey touches like the colorful throw pillows and the fuzzy blanket draped across the back of the chair that made Esme's small house feel so warm and inviting.

"Do you sing lullabies to Chase?"

She looked surprised by the random question but nodded. "At some point, he's going to realize his mother can't carry a tune, but so far, I haven't made him cry outright with my singing."

"I don't know the words to any kids' songs." He placed the infant carrier on the sofa, Noah snuggled inside it and dozing peacefully. Ryder wished he felt any sense of that peace. "It probably seems like a minor detail, but I feel like somebody gave out parenting manuals, and I missed that day of class. I sing Bruce Springsteen songs just like my dad did when I was a baby."

As if he'd heard his father's words and wanted to make a request, Noah began to fuss.

"There aren't any manuals, and I don't think you can go wrong with The Boss." Esme bent down to trace a finger over Noah's soft cheek. "Would it be okay with you if I held him?"

"I'm sure he'd love someone more capable than me giving him a cuddle," Ryder said with a laugh, immediately realizing his lame attempt at humor had fallen flat based on the incredulous look she gave him.

"I'm sure he loves his daddy," she assured him, then turned her attention to Noah. "Is your daddy the best?" she asked in a tone so gentle it made Ryder's knees turn to mush. Noah responded with a few plaintive cries but quickly settled into Esme's arms.

She kept her gaze on the baby for a few seconds, but when she looked up at Ryder again, her eyes were filled with tears.

"What's wrong?" His heart began to hammer in his chest. He might not know Esme well, but the last thing he wanted was to see her cry.

She shook her head. "He looks like my brother and I did in baby photos," she whispered. "I'm sure that sounds—"

The sound of crying crackling through the monitor on the coffee table drowned out her words.

"I put Chase down in his crib when we got home, but I didn't swaddle him. He doesn't go down as well on his own." She started for the stairs and then seemed to realize she was already holding a baby.

"I'll get him if that's okay," Ryder offered.

"First door on your left at the top of the stairs."

Mind reeling all over again in response to Esme's claim that Noah resembled her as a baby, he sprinted up the steps and let himself into the lavender-scented nursery.

Chase, who seemed to be a bit further along with his ability to self-soothe than Noah, was happily sucking on his fist when Ryder peered over the side of the crib.

The baby's arms and legs began flailing in excitement as he spotted Ryder, who smiled as he scooped up the boy. His smile faded as a realization pounded through him.

Chase Fortune looked like a Hayes, right down to the cleft in his chin. Ryder locked his legs and closed his eyes as emotion pushed him to the edge of his control. Then he leaned down and kissed the head of the child he knew without a doubt to be his biological son.

CHAPTER FOUR

"IF MY GREAT-AUNT hadn't gifted me the 411 Me testing, I don't know when or if I would have realized the switch occurred." Esme stared at the paperwork on the empty sofa cushion between her and Ryder. If only her house had a fireplace, she could burn the report that had changed her life.

Not that destroying it would do any good now. They knew the truth, and there was no going back. In a way, she owed even more of a debt to Freya Fortune. It would have been horrible to discover what had happened that night at the hospital years from now. She and Ryder would have missed so many milestones with their sons.

"I can accept the facts," she said, placing a gentle kiss on Chase's forehead. "But I don't know how I'm supposed to stop loving one baby because I now have room in my heart for both of them."

"Noah's test results haven't come back yet," Ryder reminded her, then shook his head. "Sorry. That's a stupid thing to say. We don't need tests to confirm what we know in our hearts."

He looked down at Noah, who was sleeping in his strong arms. "I'm still having trouble accepting any of this, especially when the hospital doesn't seem to have answers."

As soon as Ryder came down the stairs holding Chase, he'd insisted on calling Mary Dill at the hospital with another request for a list of the staff working the night

Chase and Noah were born. It was obvious the lawyer had coached the hospital administrator on what to say because she'd been unwilling to divulge any information, citing privacy laws and making excuses about bureaucratic red tape.

Ryder's frustration had been palpable, and both babies fussed in response to the tension filling Esme's living room. She shared his exasperation but knew they had to stay calm and work together for the best interest of both of their sons.

She'd pulled out a notepad and the 411 Me report so they could regroup and make a plan of action while they waited for the official results from the lab.

"You're amazing," Ryder said out of the blue, and Esme did a double take, finding it hard to believe he was directing the compliment toward her.

She squirmed under the weight of his impassioned stare. "I haven't done anything."

"Yes, you have. You're keeping me from losing it," he answered with a laugh. "I can tell Noah is also responding to your steady presence." Ryder checked his watch. "He typically has a meltdown around this time of day. Even his babysitter has commented on how she can set a watch by his crying."

"I'm happy to help, although I'm not sure I deserve much credit." Esme shrugged. "Chase has his days and nights mixed up, so it's party time here in the wee hours."

He grinned. "I never realized how much I took a full night's sleep for granted."

"Can I ask you a question? It might be too personal, but—"

"Anything," he interrupted. "You can ask me anything."

"It's about Noah's…" She paused and swallowed around the emotion that bubbled up in her throat. Esme *was* Noah's biological mother. They were waiting for confirmation from the hospital, yet the truth of her connection to Ryder's baby was written on her heart. "Where is your wife or girlfriend in all of this? Doesn't she—"

"Stephanie died in a car wreck when Noah was a month old." Ryder closed his eyes for a moment and drew in a shuddery breath.

"I'm so sorry."

He nodded and focused on her again, his green eyes now the color of a dark evergreen tree. "Can I tell you something I haven't shared with anyone?"

"Yes," she whispered.

"Steph was on her way from Chatelaine to San Antonio when the accident happened. Things had not been going well between us. She'd gotten pregnant less than a month after we started dating and was nearly six months along before she realized it." He shook his head. "She thought she had a chronic case of indigestion."

Esme had heard of circumstances where a woman remained unaware of the baby growing inside her but found it difficult to fathom. She'd felt the difference in her body almost immediately.

"We were no longer together when she found out she was pregnant," Ryder continued, "but she wanted to have the baby so we decided to try again for the child's sake. I proposed marriage, but Steph refused. That should have been a sign. There were so many signs, but I figured they could be chalked up to nerves. Things got worse after Noah was born."

"Worse, how?" Esme asked, almost dreading the answer.

"She didn't like being a mother. We talked to the doctor, and I suggested she see a therapist. I thought maybe she was dealing with postpartum depression and tried to support her. But I couldn't do it in the way she needed. My job is demanding…"

"Yeah, I got that impression based on how your phone vibrated nonstop," she murmured.

He sighed. "I should have taken more time off, but my dad had just moved the company headquarters to Chatelaine and announced his impending retirement. I travel a lot in my current role, so earning a promotion that would allow me to stay close to home felt essential for Noah."

Ryder tightened his hold on the baby, and it was obvious that he felt the strain of balancing work with fatherhood. "Steph didn't like being a full-time caregiver. We had a fight the night she left, and she packed a bag and headed out the door, telling me she wouldn't be back."

Esme gasped, then reached for his free hand at the look of guilt that flashed in his gaze. "You couldn't have known what would happen."

"No," he agreed hoarsely. "But that doesn't stop me from blaming myself. My son doesn't have a mother, and maybe if I'd taken a true leave of absence or changed more diapers—"

"You can't do that." Esme squeezed his large hand, noting the calluses inside his palm. She wouldn't have expected work-roughened skin from a man who appeared so polished and professional. "Neither of us can be blamed for the circumstances that brought us here."

He didn't look convinced.

"Ryder, I carried a baby inside me for nine months, and I loved my son from the moment I learned about him. I'm sorry it wasn't the same for your Stephanie."

"You're nothing like her," Ryder said quietly. The conviction in his voice assured Esme he was offering her a compliment, but she didn't take a chance on asking.

Based on the tidbits of information her sister had shared

about the Hayes men and their family's reputation, she wasn't anywhere near the type of woman Ryder would consider a romantic partner. But that wasn't what was important at this moment.

"I gave birth to a baby I thought I knew. As a mother, I would have told you I'd recognize my child anywhere and under any circumstance. Now it's just as clear that you are holding the baby I gave birth to. How do you think it makes me feel?" It was his turn to squeeze her hand; the warmth of his skin seeped into her body, grounding her with his solid touch.

"I imagine it makes you angry, confused and like you want to understand how this could have happened as much as I do."

If only it were that simple. "It makes me feel like I failed as a mother from the very start. Not only my son but yours as well."

She tugged her hand out of his and dashed it across her cheeks. Tears would do no good, but she couldn't stop them. She looked down at the boy in her arms, unwilling to meet Ryder's gaze and the censure she expected to see there. Of course, he hadn't recognized her negligence as a mother at the start of all this. The shock had precluded every other rational thought. But now that she'd pointed it out, how could he help but agree?

If she'd noticed the mistake—whether done unintentionally or…well…she couldn't imagine someone would have caused this chaos on purpose. But she should have seen it. She was a *mother*. She should have known.

She didn't look up as she heard Ryder rise from the couch. Was he going to walk out on her the way Seth had? Could she blame him? A moment later, his weight settled next to her, and his arm came around her shoulder in a tender embrace.

"You can't be kind to me right now," she said, her voice shaking. "That's really going to start the waterworks, and I know from experience that men don't like waterworks."

She felt more than heard the laugh reverberate in his chest. "I never want to make a woman cry, but I'm not afraid of your tears, Esme. There are plenty of things that scare the hell out of me, and being a good father tops that list. But you can cry all you need to, sweetheart. It's fine by me, and I can guaran-damn-tee you that we're not going to raise our boys to be put off by emotions. I've been there—done that. I don't recommend it."

Esme wiped a tear off of Chase's forehead, then transferred her gaze to Noah, who was still sleeping soundly in the crook of Ryder's arm. Finally, she looked up at the man who'd become her closest—if unlikely—ally in this mess of a situation.

A sudden idea flashed across her mind like a lightning bolt from that October storm. Goose bumps erupted along her skin and then disappeared just as quickly as the notion settled with the weight of a boulder in the middle of the road that would not be ignored.

"What is it?" Ryder asked softly. His green eyes darkened as he leaned in closer. For a brief moment, she thought he might be about to kiss her.

"I think we should raise our sons together."

His head snapped back, and whatever potential moment had been about to occur was forgotten. Maybe it had only been a figment of Esme's too vivid imagination.

"How would that work?" His thick brows drew together. "Are you proposing—"

"A partnership. Platonic, of course," she amended quickly, knowing he'd never agree to anything more. Not that she wanted more. Her focus was doing what was best for Chase and Noah.

Liar, her body whispered, and Esme patently ignored it.

"A partnership," Ryder echoed. "We'd raise the boys like we were both their parents?"

Color rose to her cheeks. "It probably sounds outlandish, but that's how my dad was raised."

"Your dad was switched at birth?"

She shook her head, trying to make sense of her muddled thoughts, which was difficult with Ryder so close. "No, it was a different circumstance. My grandfather, Edgar Fortune, and his brother, Elias, were not the most upstanding men or fathers. The family rumor is that they were on the run after an accident here in Chatelaine at the mine they owned with their brothers."

"I heard about that tragedy," Ryder said with a nod. "There's a plaque hanging in the foyer of the LC Club commemorating the fifty men who died when the silver mine collapsed. However, there's no mention of a connection to the Fortunes."

"They were chased out of town—or took off on their own, depending on who you ask—pretty quickly after pinning responsibility on the mining foreman. Edgar and Elias spent some time in Cave Creek and met my grandma and great-aunt. But they didn't stick around there either, even after learning they were going to be fathers. So the jilted girlfriends decided to raise their babies together. My dad and his cousin grew up as close as brothers. Neither of them knew their fathers, but the family my grandma and great-aunt created was something for them."

He continued to stare at her, so she went on, "My sister and brother and I weren't close with our cousins growing up, but that could change now that we're all here. I moved to town because my great-uncle's widow—her name is Freya Fortune—is using part of the inheritance Uncle Elias left her to help out his three grandchildren and my brother, sister and me. She wants to transform the reputation of our branch of the Fortunes in Chatelaine. She's helping each of us fulfill our dearest wish."

"That's amazing," Ryder murmured. "It must have come as quite a surprise."

"It did. My older sister, Bea, has been a waitress forever, but now she's going to open her own restaurant. And Asa, my big brother, came to town last summer and fell in love with a dude ranch he hopes to buy. They're going to make a difference in this community."

"What's your wish, Esme?" Ryder's voice felt like a caress against her skin, and she had a hard time remembering her own name, let alone how Freya was helping her.

She winced as the answer came to her. "This is going to sound silly compared to what my siblings plan to do, but I was already pregnant when Freya contacted us. Ever since the first test came back positive, my wish has been to be a good mother to my baby."

Gesturing to the room around them, she continued, "I was able to buy this house with my late husband's life insurance policy payout, and Freya has given me an amount that matches what I'd make as a teacher for the school year. She also gave me an open account at GreatStore to buy whatever I need for Chase."

"You're a teacher?" he asked, his mouth curving at one end. "That suits you."

"Thanks, I think." She bit down on her lower lip. "I'll go back to work next year, but I adore being with Chase for now." She smiled down at her baby, certain this was the right thing to do. "I'd love to be able to take care of Noah as well. I'm sure your babysitter is great, but I can give them a mother's love. I want to be a mother to *both* of our sons."

When Ryder's eyes widened, Esme wondered if she'd

said too much. This wasn't one of her beloved stories with a guaranteed happy ending. If Ryder decided he didn't want her in his son's life…where would that leave her? Chase might not be her biological child, but her heart didn't care, and it immediately expanded to include Noah.

She didn't have the charm that Asa did or the drive Bea possessed in wanting to make her dreams come true. All Esme had ever wanted was a happy life with a family who belonged to her.

Before the plane crash took their lives, her parents had lived more like bickering roommates than a couple who treasured growing old together. She knew they'd started as high school sweethearts, but by the time Esme had any concrete memories of their marriage, that bloom of first love had all but disappeared.

Her aunt and uncle hadn't been happy either, and with her grandfather's history, she wondered if it were possible that there could be some kind of missing piece in her branch of the Fortune family tree that would prevent her from being happy.

Esme had hoped to find true love, but after Seth's betrayal, she couldn't imagine opening her heart again and being hurt by a man. Maybe she simply wasn't worthy of being loved and carried the black mark of the unhappy couples who came before her. But she liked Ryder, and her gut told her he was a good man. He would be a great father, and really, what more could she ask for?

"My son," Ryder said slowly, then cleared his throat. "Both of our sons would be lucky to have you as a mother. I might not know what I'm doing as a parent, but I'm not a fool." He nodded. "Raising them together is the right decision. We're a team, Esme."

She released the breath lodged in her lungs and smiled. "We're going to make this work," she assured him. "It will be okay because Chase and Noah will remain our top priorities." She waved a hand. "Not that I'm going to place expectations on you like that you can't date or whatever. I'm sure you—"

"The last thing on my mind is dating," Ryder said, then seemed uncomfortable at what his comment might insinuate about Esme and glanced at his watch. "I should check in at the office. It's nearly the end of the business day, and I'm guessing we won't hear from the hospital until tomorrow."

She tried not to be disappointed. She hadn't been referring to the two of them dating, anyway, so had no reason for the pang in her chest. Besides, if Ryder was the player her sister seemed to believe, he'd show his true colors soon enough. Nothing else mattered as long as he followed the rules they established and was a kind and loving father to the two boys.

"We'll need rules," she announced.

One of his thick brows raised in response. "For the record, I'm better at making rules than following them."

"We'll make them together after we get confirmation from the hospital," she clarified. "I know what the tests are going to reveal, but we should hear it from them just the same."

"Fine," Ryder agreed. "And if they don't give us information on the nurses and doctors who staffed the labor and delivery unit that night, then we'll track down those individuals on our own."

There was a confidence in his tone she hadn't heard before, and for the first time, Esme understood that Ryder Hayes was not a man used to compromise or making concessions.

"Do you want me to keep Noah here while you go to your office? I'm happy to watch both of them during the

week while you're at work. I don't have much of a life outside of being a mom."

Ugh. Why had she shared that with him? It only made
her sound even more pathetic. Like she had no aspirations beyond being a mother and nothing to occupy her
time but babies.

She had to be the most boring woman Ryder had ever
met.

"I'd appreciate that." He stood, then frowned as a loud
gurgle followed by a foul stench came from the vicinity
of Noah's diaper. "I can change him first."

"Leave him to me," she said and shifted Chase's weight
to one arm so she could cradle Noah with the other. "Go
be corporate and important and all that," she told Ryder,
who looked both grateful and incredulous. "We'll be here
when you get home."

Home. What an odd concept to share with a virtual
stranger, but the word felt appropriate. She believed in her
heart this was right.

CHAPTER FIVE

As RYDER WALKED through the Hayes Enterprises offices on the LC Club's first floor, a hush fell over the open-concept office space. No one, from the receptionist in the lobby to the sales team to the accounting and HR staff, would make eye contact with him.

The silence felt like a judgment, and he began singing what he considered Noah's favorite Bruce Springsteen song in his head to distract himself from the dread he felt. Esme had told him he couldn't go wrong with The Boss, but the gaping pit in his stomach widened on the way toward his father's corner office.

As he passed the conference room, his brother walked out, briefcase in hand. Ryder wasn't sure if Brandon kept supplies besides gum and hair gel in that leather satchel. Because he didn't use it for anything other than holding it up to wave, as he did now.

"Bro, you missed a hell of a meeting," Brandon said. "I'm heading out to catch up with a few team members at the LC Club bar. Do you want to join us and congratulate me on how impressive I was?" His brother chucked him on the arm. "By *impressive*, I mean at least I had the good sense to attend a meeting with half the upper management staff and several key investors. I hope you had a good excuse this time, Ryder. Not like those bogus doctor's appointments."

Brandon emphasized the phrase *doctor's appointments*

with air quotes, and Ryder silently counted to ten. "No-ah's well visits aren't bogus." He forced a smile. "I'm glad things went smoothly. We all play for the same team. Remember, this isn't horse under the basketball hoop in the backyard. You're not trying to outshoot me. I want you to do well."

Brandon's mouth opened and closed a couple of times like he didn't know how to respond to Ryder not engaging in an argument. Arguing was typically the bulk of his relationship with his brother, but no matter how much he wanted the CEO position, Ryder was sick and tired of fighting.

The events of this day had put his priorities into sharp focus. The truth was that even though he hustled to be the best parent he could, he hadn't been doing enough, especially considering how effortless Esme made it look. Ryder would have ended up rocking in a corner if somebody had asked him to take care of two babies at once. Not that he could say any of that to his brother.

"Is Dad still in his office?"

"Don't tell me you're going to try to patch things up with him right now." Brandon narrowed his eyes. "It's not going to work. Give it a day or so. I doubt he's in the mood for your excuses, Ry."

Excuses. That was rich. "I need to talk to both of you," Ryder said. "It has to do with Noah. This is serious, Bran."

His brother's demeanor changed instantly. He shifted from smug victor to concerned uncle, and Ryder knew it was genuine. Even though Noah couldn't appreciate it yet, Brandon took his future role of a fun uncle, or "funcle" as he called himself, just as seriously as he took outdoing Ryder at every turn. "What's going on with Noah?"

Instead of answering, Ryder continued toward their dad's office, confident Brandon would follow. He waved off his father's assistant, opening the door after a cursory knock.

Chandler Hayes sat behind his massive mahogany desk, the same one Ryder and Brandon had played under as young boys. The custom piece had been ordered from Italy early in their father's career to commemorate Chandler's first million-dollar deal.

The ornate desk looked out of place in the LC Club building, which boasted a rustic vibe, but it represented something to Ryder's father, a reminder to everyone who walked in that Chandler Hayes was an important man.

Ryder recognized the look of dissatisfaction in his dad's hard brown eyes. He'd seen it often enough over the years.

"I'm busy at the moment, Ryder," his father said, glancing down at the papers before him. "Just like you apparently were this morning. You should have answered my calls. Make an appointment with—"

"Noah was switched at birth with another baby." Ryder heard the soft click of the door shutting behind Brandon as his announcement was greeted with stunned silence.

"What are you talking about?" his father asked finally, pushing back from the desk, his fingers tightly gripping the edge.

"That was what kept me from being here earlier."

"It has to be a mistake," Brandon said, coming to stand next to Ryder. "Noah looks like a Hayes. He *is* a Hayes."

Somehow, the shock his brother and father displayed was a comfort to Ryder. The relationship the three of them shared often felt dysfunctional at its core, so he'd been unsure how the two of them would greet his news.

"We're waiting for his DNA test to come back—"

"Then you don't know for certain," Chandler interrupted.

"I *know*," Ryder answered definitively. "He and the

other baby, born the same night, could be twins. But Chase has the Hayes cleft in his chin." Ryder rubbed a hand against his jaw. "And Noah looks like his biological mother."

"I don't understand…" his father muttered.

"Esme, the other baby's mother, had DNA testing done for her son—a gift from a family member. The results reported that she shared no DNA with her child, and members of our family showed up in his genetic profile. The hospital attorney called me this morning, and Noah and I went in for a meeting." He shook his head. "I don't need a test to confirm what I know in my heart to be true. I can't explain how the mistake happened, but we'll get to the bottom of it."

"We?" his father asked.

"Esme Fortune and me," Ryder clarified. Simply saying her name out loud calmed him. He wished he could bottle her soothing and sweet personality to call upon whenever he needed to talk to his dad or Brandon.

"Your new baby mama is a Fortune?" Brandon snorted. "Way to set a high bar."

"Don't call her that," Ryder snapped, his temper flaring. "Neither Esme nor I chose this, but we're going to work together to do what's best for our boys."

"I was joking," Brandon insisted, lifting his hands like he was ready to ward off a physical blow. "You're a good father, Ry. You'll do the right thing."

"Do we need to get the lawyers involved?" his father asked, already picking up the phone. Chandler Hayes was the only person Ryder knew who still preferred talking on a landline.

"No, Dad. It's fine for now." Ryder stepped toward the desk and then sat in one of the tufted leather chairs in front of it. "Though I appreciate the support."

He was both grateful and slightly shell-shocked. Offering to sic the company attorneys on someone was akin to a warm hug from his dad.

Chandler placed the receiver back on the cradle and frowned. "What do you know about this Fortune woman?"

"Not a lot yet, but my gut tells me to trust her. She's a good mother and wants to do the right thing." He drew a deep breath and continued, "So do I, which is why I'd like to take personal leave for the next two weeks."

Brandon let out a low whistle behind him and whispered, "Bro."

The one syllable was thick with meaning, but Ryder couldn't worry about that now.

"Why?" his father demanded.

"Because Noah and Chase need me to step up. That means being fully present during this transition. Esme and I are going to raise our sons together." His heart clenched at the thought of those two innocent babies thrust into this inconceivable situation. "Just because Noah isn't my biological child doesn't change the fact that I love him. I love Chase, too."

"The Fortune woman shares this sentiment?" Chandler raised a brow. "What about her husband?"

"Late husband," Ryder clarified. "And she's not after my money, Dad. Neither of us asked for this, but we're going to make it work." Saying the words solidified his conviction that they were doing the right thing. "I don't have a lot of answers, but you can bet I'm going to find them. I need time to work out our arrangement and do some digging at the hospital. Someone has information on what happened the night the babies were born, and I'm going to figure out who made this mistake."

"If you need help, I'll be your wingman," Brandon announced. "I'm tougher and smarter than you."

Ryder laughed at his brother's ego shining through even in the middle of an offer of assistance.

His smile faded as his father continued to frown. "I'm sorry, Dad," he said automatically. "I know this is a critical time for the company's future, and I'm letting you down."

"You're not," Chandler answered without hesitation, but Ryder didn't believe him. His dad had expressed disappointment for far less.

"As soon as Esme and I settle into a routine, I'll be back."

"Probably not as CEO," Brandon couldn't help but mutter.

"Stop." Chandler held up a hand to his younger son. "This isn't the time for petty posturing."

"It was a joke," Brandon insisted.

"Not a funny one." Their father turned his attention back to Ryder. "You're doing the right thing. Taking care of your son—both of your boys—takes precedence above everything else."

"It does?" Brandon asked.

At the same time, Ryder agreed, "It does."

"Yes." Chandler gave a decisive nod. "I'm proud of you for having your priorities straight," he continued. "The company will be here when you get back, and nothing will be decided about my position until that time." He glanced at Brandon. "Don't be in too much of a hurry to kick me to the curb, son."

"I'm not," Brandon mumbled, obviously chastised.

"Thank you, Dad." Ryder stood and tried not to gape as the older man came around the side of the desk and offered a fierce—if formal—hug. This wasn't how he'd expected the meeting to go, but he'd take a win wherever he could get it at the moment. He wanted to believe his father's support indicated a positive outcome overall. He needed to believe in something.

"THAT WAS FAST," Esme said as she opened the door a half hour later. "How was the meeting?"

Bea stood glaring at her from the other side, hands on hips as she tapped an impatient booted toe against the concrete porch. "I sure hope you don't think my interview with a potential chef for the Cowgirl Café went well. All I could think about was whether my sister had been chopped into a million pieces and shoved into her freezer by her baby's biological father."

"Wow," Esme murmured as she stepped back to allow her sister into the house. "Somebody has been listening to too many true crime podcasts."

"Well, what am I supposed to think?" Bea demanded, her voice rising in obvious frustration.

Esme made a hushing sound. "I just got the boys down for a nap. They need some rest."

"The *boys* plural?" Bea spun on her heel. "Are you telling me you have both babies here? Esme, what in the world happened today?"

"My life changed," Esme answered, then sighed, feeling suddenly exhausted. She'd been running on nothing but emotions and adrenaline since reading the 411 Me report yesterday. Now the reality of what she'd agreed to slammed into her like a bassinet full of concrete blocks.

"So Ryder Hayes just gave you his baby?" Bea looked flabbergasted. "I knew the guy was a player, but I didn't realize he was a heartless cad. What about his wife or girlfriend?"

"He didn't *give* Noah to me," Esme answered in a stage whisper. How could her sister suggest such a thing? "His girlfriend died in a car accident shortly after giving birth."

Bea's big eyes widened even more. "That's awful."

"I know." Esme swallowed, then said, "We're going to raise the boys together."

"Okay, that's preposterous."

"It's *unconventional*, but I love Chase even though we don't share DNA. As soon as I held Noah, I knew he belonged with me. Ryder feels the same way."

"Oh, yeah?" Bea made a point of glancing around the empty living room. "Then where is this paragon of fatherhood?"

"He had some things to take care of at his company."

"Right," her sister said slowly. "How convenient for him to just dump his baby with you. Is he going out for drinks with his womanizing brother? I've seen one of them around town with a different lady on his arm every time."

"Ryder isn't like that."

"How do you know?"

Esme didn't know, but she wanted to trust him. After everything she'd been through, she *needed* to believe she wasn't alone in all of this.

"Come on," Bea coaxed. "Use your head, Es. I know how big your heart is, and you've always put too much stock in fairy tales. I don't want to see you get hurt the way you did with Seth. You need to be real."

Biting down on the inside of her cheek to keep from screaming, Esme gathered the shreds of her tattered composure and nodded. "Trust me. This situation is as real as it gets, and I still have trouble believing it's happening to me. I'm not giving up a chance to raise the two children I love. Raising them with Ryder—who wants to be a good dad—is the best thing I can do."

The doorbell rang, interrupting her tirade, and she stalked toward the door, flinging it open to find Ryder on the other side, holding a large brown takeout bag in his hand. "Sorry it took me so long. I stopped to pick up dinner from Herv's BBQ. I realized I haven't eaten a thing all day, and I'm guessing you might be in the same situation with two babies to look after."

He looked past her to where Bea was staring at the two of them. "Hi." He held up his free hand to wave.

"Come in," Esme told him. "This is my sister, Bea."

"Her *older* sister," Bea clarified. "And very protective."

"It's a pleasure to meet you." He placed the takeout bag on the narrow table next to the door and held out his hand. "Although the circumstances aren't ideal, I guess we'll see quite a lot of each other in the upcoming years."

Bea ignored his outstretched hand as her gaze darted between Ryder and Esme. "You can't be serious. Two strangers don't raise children together."

"Grandma did with Aunt Vanna," Esme pointed out.

"This isn't the same thing," her sister insisted as Ryder shoved his hand into his pocket. He'd changed out of his suit into dark jeans and a gray Henley that hugged his broad shoulders and an incredibly toned chest and arms.

Now was not the time to get distracted by her too hot parenting partner, Esme chastised herself as she focused on her sister. "Dad wouldn't have grown up feeling like he had Peter as a brother if their moms had tried to manage on their own. Ryder and I can be better parents together, Bea. You have to believe me."

When Bea looked like she would continue arguing, Esme held up a hand. "Or don't. That's your choice. But this is mine. Ryder and I are in this together."

She hadn't realized her hands were clenched at her sides until he reached out to hold one of them. The small gesture of solidarity made her heartbeat accelerate.

"I'm going to take care of your sister," he said, speaking directly to Bea. "And our sons. You have no reason to trust me." He squeezed Esme's fingers. "Neither of you do, but I'm going to work to earn it every day. That much you can take to the bank."

"Speaking of the bank," Bea said to her sister, "or our fairy godbanker, as I like to call her. Have you talked to Freya about this?"

Esme shook her head. She thought about pulling away from Ryder, but her hand felt too right cradled in his grasp. "You're the only one who knows. I need a couple of days to process everything, okay? Then I promise I'll talk to Freya and Asa. Please support me, Bea."

Bea groaned and threw up her hands. "I always support you, little sis." She ran a hand through her long red hair and stepped forward, hugging both Esme and Ryder at the same time. "I'm here for both of you. So when do I get to meet my new nephew?"

"I'll call you tomorrow," Esme promised. "I think the babies need time to adjust to their expanded family, as well."

"Call or text any time." Bea drew back. "You, too, Ryder Hayes. Let me know if you need anything."

Esme nearly smiled at the look of consternation on his face at Bea's words. He didn't seem bothered when her hackles were raised but was clearly disconcerted by her kindness.

"Okay," he agreed slowly.

Bea gave Esme another hug. "Call me," she whispered, then let herself out the front door, leaving Ryder and Esme standing in the living room still holding hands.

The air between them sparked with something she couldn't name, but she yanked her hand back and stepped away. This arrangement would only work if they stayed focused on the boys, which should be simple enough.

One baby was a lot of work, so two should keep her busy enough not to fixate on her attraction to Ryder.

Good luck with that, her body and heart whispered at the same time. Esme chose to ignore them both.

CHAPTER SIX

BESIDES THE CONTINUED runaround they were receiving from the hospital administrator and attorney after Noah's test confirmed what they already knew, the next three days were the best Ryder could remember in a long time. Sharing parenting responsibilities with Esme, who was calm and competent in the face of blowouts, crying jags and even an unexplained rash on Noah's back, gave him the ability to breathe easy for the first time since he'd held his son in his arms.

He knew he wasn't the most capable parent but hadn't realized how much his obvious lack of skill added to the normal stress of being a new dad. Esme's presence relieved his anxiety as easily as if she were yanking a sheet from the bed.

He couldn't hope to compete with her soothing presence and natural aptitude for mothering babies, so Ryder became more determined to discover how the mix-up had occurred at the hospital the night his sons were born.

Greg Oachs called or emailed at least once daily, asking the two of them to sign paperwork that would absolve the hospital from responsibility for the mistake. Although neither he nor Esme had any desire to pursue legal action, he wouldn't let the smarmy lawyer off that easily.

In contrast, the hospital administrator, Mary Dill, sounded genuinely apologetic and willing to help, contritely explaining she'd been given strict instructions not to share any information about the on-duty staff back in October.

However, Ryder wasn't giving up, especially since, earlier in the day, Esme had suddenly remembered overhearing that one of the nurses was called Nancy. It hadn't taken long to narrow down the employees with that name working at County Hospital.

Despite knowing it would anger the attorney and administrator, he'd called all three Nancys and discovered that one of them was a labor and delivery nurse who'd remembered the night of the terrible storm and the chaos on the floor after the patients had been moved into their temporary rooms.

He had a meeting scheduled with her tomorrow for breakfast at the diner in town and hoped she could shed some light on the situation or point him in the right direction to get to the bottom of how something with such long-term consequences could have happened.

"Is everything okay?" Esme asked as she came down the steps. "That's a pretty serious frown you're sporting."

Ryder sighed and made a concerted effort to fix his face. "It's been a long day." He hated to admit how familiar a scowl felt for him. But he'd smiled and laughed more since meeting Esme than he had in ages.

He'd always been serious and intense but now wondered whether that was indeed his nature or a result of the constant pressure to succeed he felt from his father, plus the additional challenge of being a single dad.

A few days into his leave of absence, a weight had been stripped from him, replaced by the sweetness of genuinely enjoying the comforting routine of full-time fatherhood. He and Noah came to Esme's each morning and spent the entire day with her and Chase. He loved every minute of it.

But who was he if he wasn't achieving something?

Ryder didn't know the answer and was afraid he could never offer the boys what Esme was able to just by being her true self.

"I was just thinking about how to make this situation better. I want answers for us as well as for the boys."

She padded closer and took a seat on the other end of the sofa. Too far, his body silently complained, although Esme had no idea the effect she had on him.

They were always together, making food in the galley kitchen or walking next to each other when they took the boys out in the double stroller he'd purchased at Great-Store. She seemed to think nothing of their arms brushing, or not to notice the way Ryder's libido went on high alert every time he caught her sweet scent in the air.

"I have an idea about how to make our arrangement better—easier for you," she said with a shy smile.

He stared at her and tried to hide his shock. How could she not see how much she tempted him?

"What do you think about the two of you moving in with Chase and me?"

His body went wild, every cell cheering like the Texans had just won the Super Bowl. Was she suggesting what he hoped?

"I don't mean anything romantic, of course," she said on a rush of breath. "We've established the rules for this arrangement, and I plan to honor them. You don't have to worry in that regard."

"You want to follow the rules," he echoed, and his shoulders sagged in disappointment. He masked the reaction with a wide smile. "That's a smart idea." It was the *worst* idea he'd ever heard. "Just so I'm clear, you want us to live together?"

She nodded. "I hope you don't mind me suggesting it. You and Noah are here every day, and even though your apartment isn't far, it would be better—more efficient—if you moved in instead of going back and forth all the time. You can take the guest room, and Noah will stay in the nursery with Chase."

She stifled a yawn. "This will help, especially at night. We can take turns getting up with them overnight. Maybe that way neither of us will be quite so tired."

It made sense from a practical standpoint, and if Ryder were being honest, he liked being at her cozy home more than his sterile apartment.

"I'm sure you have a lease," she continued, "and probably would want to keep your place anyway. You know… in case you're going on a date or whatever."

A blush rose to her cheeks. It wasn't the first or second time Esme had suggested Ryder was missing out on the dating scene in Chatelaine, even though he'd assured her that wasn't the case. He was too consumed with being a dad to think about anything else. Except that wasn't exactly true because lately Esme was also consuming his thoughts.

But if he admitted that, she'd probably rescind her invitation, which could ruin the entire arrangement. She'd been clear about agreeing to parameters regarding who paid for what and how they would make decisions about the boys.

It was smart and practical, and he appreciated her forethought. It was also another reminder of how much better equipped she was for this role than him.

"I like your idea," he said. "Noah and I would love to move in with you and Chase. I promise not to use all the hot water or leave the toilet seat up."

She giggled and then yawned again.

"In fact," he added, "how about if we stay tonight? I can pick up my things tomorrow, but you've been doing the lion's share of caring for the babies—"

"Only because you've been working hard to track down the hospital staff."

He nodded. "I wish I had more to go on. I'm going to ask the nurse, Nancy, about the volunteer no one can remember seeing before or since. Maybe talking about it will jog her memory. She mentioned seeing the older woman with the babies that night."

"One of the two grandma volunteers," Esme murmured, leaning back on the sofa cushion.

Ryder wanted to cradle her head in his arms and tell her she could use him for support, but that might come across a little *too* enthusiastic.

"On the phone, Nancy said that the woman had made an impression on her because she seemed so light on her feet even though she used a cane. But Mary has no record of a second hospital volunteer signing in for a shift that night."

"Do you think this mystery volunteer is involved?" she asked.

He sighed and ran a hand through his hair. "It seems doubtful, but we don't have any better leads."

"Why would someone switch our boys' ID tags on purpose?" Esme asked. The question had plagued Ryder in the same way. "What did you or I ever do to the people in this town?" She suddenly sat up straighter. "But what if it's not about us? We haven't done anything, but could it have something to do with my family? People remember Edgar and Elias—if not, they've heard the story. According to Freya, many of the miners who were killed still have relatives and descendants in town."

"Why would anyone want to take revenge on you for your grandfather's sins?"

Esme's chin dipped, her long hair falling forward to hide her face from view. "I don't know. But Freya invited us here to make amends for Edgar and Elias's behavior.

There could be people who think my siblings, cousins and I don't deserve the help we're getting. We have a direct connection to a tragedy that in so many ways defined this town." Her chest rose and fell with a shaky breath.

"This is not your fault," he said, shifting closer on the sofa and wrapping his arms around her. If there was anything he knew for certain, it was that Esme had nothing to do with the situation they found themselves in now.

She sagged against him like she needed his strength to bolster her own. He would gladly offer that to her. He wanted to provide more, which made no sense. After all, this arrangement wasn't about him. It was for the benefit of the two innocent boys sleeping upstairs.

"Thank you for everything you're doing, Ryder." She pulled away slightly, and her pale green gaze crashed into his. "I'm not sure what I'd do without you."

Her body was soft and warm against him, and once again, the smell of vanilla wafted through his senses, making him feel like they were in a world all by themselves. Awareness clutched at his chest, and her eyes darkened.

He wanted to kiss her so damn badly and would have given in to the desire, except at that moment, Esme's beautiful mouth widened into another yawn, breaking the spell that had him tangled in its grasp. It must have had the same jarring effect on her because she popped up from the couch like she'd just been stung by a bee.

"There's only one bathroom upstairs," she announced, folding her arms over her chest. "I'll leave clean towels on the sink, and there are fresh sheets on the bed in the spare bedroom. If you need anything before tomorrow…"

"I won't," he said definitively because he couldn't very well tell her that the one thing he needed was her in his arms. He motioned to the baby monitor sitting on the coffee table. "I'll take tonight's shift," he offered. "You don't have to worry about a thing."

Esme looked like she wanted to argue but then nodded. "Good night," she whispered and hurried up the stairs.

He stayed on the sofa for a long time after she'd gone to bed, reminding himself over and over that he couldn't give in to the unexpected yet overwhelming attraction he felt for Esme. She was important to him and his son— both of his sons—and he wasn't going to do anything to jeopardize that.

He climbed the stairs slowly, and after checking on the boys, got ready for bed, although sleep didn't come quickly. His thoughts were far too consumed by the beautiful woman sleeping across the hall.

"THEY'RE CLAIMING SOMEONE switched your baby for another child?" Freya Fortune asked the question with no small sense of incredulity.

"And now, instead of raising one kid," Esme's brother, Asa, added, "you're going to play mom to two of them?"

Esme gripped her coffee cup more tightly and frowned at her older brother. She'd invited Freya and Asa to breakfast at the diner in the heart of downtown so she could explain the situation with Chase and Noah before they heard it from someone else.

It had been a week since her world had been turned upside down, and although she was content to remain in the tiny bubble she and Ryder had created to get to know each other and the boys, who held both of their hearts, it couldn't last. Chatelaine was a tiny town, and word traveled fast in the tight-knit community.

They'd fallen into a routine like it was the most natural thing in the world. He seemed to want a real partnership and pitched in with everything from diaper changing to laundry to housework and meals.

He'd also started ticking off small projects around the house, like her squeaking back door and the bathroom faucet that dripped. But as helpful as the practical side of their arrangement was turning out to be, getting to know Ryder was pure magic.

She'd finally gotten to a point where her breath didn't catch every time he walked into a room, but the butterflies in her stomach were becoming a real issue. Despite repeatedly reminding herself that they were doing this for the benefit of the boys, she wasn't sure how to stop herself from falling for him.

"I'm not playing at anything," she told Asa. "Ryder and I both love Chase and Noah. I'm honored to be their mother."

Her brother shared a look with Freya, setting Esme's teeth on edge. She understood the situation was unique, but she wanted her family to trust that she was doing the right thing.

"What do you know about Ryder Hayes?" Asa demanded, pointing a slice of bacon in Esme's direction before taking a bite. "Did you do a background check on this stranger before inviting him to live with you?"

"Your brother is right," Freya said gently. "We wouldn't want anyone to take advantage of you or your situation as a single mom."

"Maybe he's after your money," Asa suggested, running a hand through his dark hair. At thirty, he was four years older than Esme and four years younger than Bea. A classic middle child, he was charming and confident in his ability to make friends and go after his dreams.

At the moment, Asa's dream involved buying a dude ranch, although the current owner, the widow Val Hensen, wasn't making it easy for him. Unlike Esme, Asa seemed to have no doubt things would work out the way he wanted in the end.

"I'm not rich," Esme reminded him. "Do you think he's interested in stealing my extra diapers?"

"You *are* a Fortune," Freya insisted. "There are a lot of people who have strong thoughts about our family, especially in this part of Texas."

The older woman's tone held an unexpected edge, and not for the first time, Esme wondered about her great-uncle's widow and what she'd been through. Freya didn't like to talk about herself, instead focusing on how she could help Edgar's and Elias's grandchildren.

She was in her eighties but appeared decades younger with smooth skin, an ash-blond bob and bright green eyes. While she'd been extremely generous with her time and financial support, there was still a bit of distance there, as if Freya wanted to be part of their lives but wasn't exactly sure how to truly open up.

"Ryder is successful in his own right," Esme said, wondering at her fierce sense of protectiveness toward him. "He's vying for the CEO position of his family's company."

Asa snorted. "And probably using you as free childcare for his kid." He paused as he lifted the coffee cup to his lips and added, "For both of his kids, if that's how you want to look at it."

Tears sprang to Esme's eyes, and she bit down on the inside of her cheek to keep them from spilling over. She understood the concerns Asa and Freya were expressing. Those same niggling doubts kept her up at night, adding to her exhaustion as much as caring for two three-month-olds did. Seth had done a number on her ability to trust people and learning more about her paternal grandfather and great-uncle didn't bolster her overall belief in men.

She loved Asa dearly, but he wasn't exactly a poster

child for commitment or how to maintain a mature relationship. Her brother was a ladies' man, although he always seemed to remain friends with his exes—everyone loved Asa.

"There's only one way to look at it," she said, gathering her resolve. Doubts could swirl all they wanted when it came to her and Ryder, but she was sure about her commitment to their sons. "Do you consider Chase any less your nephew given what I've just told you?" she asked her brother.

"Hell, no." Asa looked affronted by the suggestion. "I love that kid."

"I know you do." Esme murmured. "So, is there room in your heart for Noah as well?" She picked up her phone from the table. "He looks like you and me when we were babies, Asa."

"I wouldn't care if he had Bea's carrot top or was a dead ringer for the man in the moon." Asa took the phone from her, smiling as he scrolled through her camera roll. "He's family, too. I'm going to teach both those boys to ride a horse and throw a ball and—"

"If Ryder Hayes will allow it," Freya said softly. "Esme isn't in this alone anymore."

"She was *never* alone." Asa shifted the phone so Freya could look at the photos with him.

"I felt alone," Esme admitted. Although her brother looked shocked, it was apparent Freya already had an inkling as to the way Esme had been struggling despite doing her best to appear like she had it all together.

"I understand what Ryder and I are doing seems unorthodox, but it also means that I have someone to share the responsibility of parenthood with. And I needed that more than I let myself acknowledge."

Asa leaned forward, his familiar dark brown eyes shimmering with brotherly affection. "You're my little sister.

I'm here for you…whatever you need, Es. I'd like to meet my new nephew and Ryder Hayes, too. This guy needs to know that you are something special and not just because you're available to watch his children."

She shook her head. "That's not how he treats me, Asa. I promise. Ryder has an important job, but he's taking a leave of absence from his company while we transition to this co-parenting thing. Neither of us has all the answers, but he values me. He makes me feel like I'm important to him, and that's a big change from my late husband."

"Rest his soul," Freya murmured.

"Not to speak ill of the dead." Asa rolled his eyes. "But your late husband was an undisputed jerk."

Freya and Esme both chuckled at Asa's plainspoken assessment.

"You have to say that because you're my brother, but I appreciate it anyway. That's the kind of I've-got-your-back loyalty I want Chase to have with Noah. We both know that growing up without a father was hard on Dad and Uncle Peter, but they were in it together, and that made a difference." She sighed. "My sons are going to have both a mother and a father. They'll never have any reason to doubt how much we love them. We might not be a typi-cal family, but Ryder and I are dedicated to the boys and making this work."

They all had a few moments to digest the conversation as the waitress came to clear the plates, blatantly flirting with Asa as she did. He had an easy way with women, al-though he didn't seem interested in being tied down.

Bea's initial comments about Ryder, his brother and dad still lurked in the corners of Esme's mind and heart. It was simple enough to tell herself not to get overly attached to him. Theirs was an arrangement of convenience—just last night over dinner, he'd tentatively suggested they begin the search for a new house, one where they could raise the boys together but each have more privacy. He seemed to think there were options around Chatelaine for properties with multiple dwellings.

The suggestion was a reminder that the situation wasn't merely temporary, but forever. She'd immediately wondered if her worries about him needing space for entertaining potential lady friends might be justified in spite of his denial about wanting to date.

So far, the two of them had been together every night, making dinner in her galley kitchen or ordering carryout. They took the boys on daily walks and had paid a visit to the local bookstore, Remi's Reads, because it turned out that Ryder was as avid of a book nerd as Esme. He was handsome, sweet, successful *and* a reader. Was it any wonder she was drawn to him?

She could also imagine him attracting the attention of eligible women around town the same way her brother did, and she didn't know how she would eventually deal with that and not let him see that it hurt her.

"Do you have an idea of how the switch occurred when no one at the hospital realized it?" Freya asked as she handed her credit card to the waitress. Their great-aunt always insisted on paying, which bothered Esme.

She knew Freya had loads of money, although the older woman chose to live at the Chatelaine Motel, an aged and somewhat shabby motor lodge at the end of town, because she claimed to enjoy the charm of it.

But Esme didn't want her to feel like they only spent time with her because of her financial support and hoped eventually Freya would feel close enough with the Fortunes to open up about her life. Esme's grandma still lived in Cave Creek and remained uninterested in visiting Chatelaine. Ryder was close with his mom, but she lived hours away in Houston. They didn't see each other often based on what he'd shared, particularly given that his father's serial cheating and his parents' eventual divorce had been difficult on his mother. So, as far as Esme was concerned, Freya was the closest thing her boys would have to a grandma figure living nearby, and she wanted to find a way to forge a meaningful connection in a way that made her great-aunt comfortable.

"Ryder is determined to get to the bottom of who's responsible for what happened that night," Esme said. "Although, I'm not sure it matters. What's done is done, and I don't see the point of dwelling on the past."

Freya's mouth pressed into a thin line. "People need to be held accountable."

"I suppose," she agreed. "But the only lead we have so far is a nurse who remembers an older woman with a volunteer badge hanging around that night."

"Well, no matter what you find out, there's no doubt in my mind that you'll be an excellent mother to Chase and Noah," Asa said, pushing back from the table. He gave Esme a hug that turned into a gentle headlock, one of his signature older brother moves. "I remember when you were a pipsqueak and you played dolls for hours on end."

"You were extremely rude about wrecking my teddy-bear tea parties," Esme retorted as she elbowed him in the ribs.

Freya gave them each an awkward pat on the back. "We should get out of here before the two of you knock into a waitress carrying a tray of dishes."

Esme grinned and blew out a satisfied breath as she led the way out of the diner. This morning was the reminder she'd needed that even if there were questions about her arrangement with Ryder, the people who loved her would support her in the end.

CHAPTER SEVEN

RYDER WASN'T SURE how long someone had been knocking at the door before he finally heard it over the persistent wailing of two babies mid-meltdown. He couldn't believe how badly he was struggling to handle Chase and Noah by himself while Esme had breakfast with her brother and great-aunt and then ran errands.

Initially, he'd encouraged her to take the entire day for herself, insisting that he would love the time with their boys. He'd even bristled a bit when she'd seemed unwilling to leave them solely in his care for that long.

The first fifteen minutes of her time away had been without incident. Both babies were down for their morning nap, so Ryder had spent his time researching the history of the Fortune family in Chatelaine on the internet. He didn't believe the tragedy of the silver miners could have anything to do with his baby being switched for Esme's at the hospital, but her concern was enough to prompt him to learn more about it.

Through the course of his research, he'd discovered her grandfather's older brother, Wendell, had returned to town and reconnected with his grandchildren during the past year.

Although he and the fourth Fortune brother of their generation, Walter, had no involvement with the accident at Elias and Edgar's silver mine, the death of those innocent miners had weighed heavily on Wendell. So much so that he'd assumed a new identity for many years as a way to distance himself from the painful past.

Ryder had just started perusing a story on the life of the mine's foreman, who'd been blamed for the accident by Edgar and Elias, when he heard the sound of a baby crying through the monitor. By the time he got to the nursery, both boys were fully awake and not happy about it, even though Esme had been confident they'd nap for most of the time she was gone.

Ryder had learned quickly that if he could count on one thing with babies, it was that as soon as he understood their schedule, the routine would be upended.

He tried not to take it personally that Chase and Noah cried more with him than they did when Esme was taking care of them. She repeatedly told him that crying was a regular part of this stage of their lives, but he suspected it had something to do with him. They would typically settle after mere moments in Esme's soft, soothing hold, but neither seemed to have any more faith in Ryder than he had in himself.

He opened the door with a screaming baby in each arm and found himself staring at Esme's sister, the one who didn't seem to like him very much.

"Hello!" He shouted to be heard over the crying babies. "Nice to see you again, Bea. Your sister's not at home right now, so you might want to come back when—"

"I know she's not here," Bea interrupted, reaching out to take Noah from him as she stepped into the house. "I'm here to talk to you, Ryder. Apparently, I got here in the nick of time to offer respite childcare. You look like you're about to start sobbing along with these two cuties."

"That's my usual emotional state," he muttered under his breath as he closed the front door, unable to muster embarrassment that a woman he would like to impress, given his relationship with her sister, was seeing him so at a loss.

He might feel confident in his ability to run Hayes Enterprises, although whether he would get a chance to do that remained to be seen, but he had no such certainty in his parenting skills. Esme was the expert, and he'd quickly come to rely on her to take the lead in every aspect of caring for the boys.

Bea couldn't compare with her sister in the baby whisperer department, but between the two of them, the boys eventually quieted. Ryder placed Chase in the motorized swing that sat in the middle of the kitchen, and the baby yawned and then stuck his fist in his mouth.

"I can take Noah if you'd like," Ryder offered, but Bea shook her head.

"Have you seen pictures of Esme or our brother, Asa, when they were this age?"

"I haven't yet."

"He looks just like the two of them. The resemblance is striking." She stared at Noah in amazement.

"He's lucky to look like his mother. She told me everything left from your parents' house has been put into a storage unit. Once we're more settled, I'll take her to Cave Creek to move what she wants to Chatelaine. I think it's important to Esme to have some of those family things here."

"You're right," Bea said slowly, then glanced over at Chase, who was losing the fight to keep his eyes open. "Now I know where he got the cleft in his chin. I had assumed it was from his father's side of the family."

"It was," Ryder confirmed, wanting to clarify that no other man would play that role in either of the children's lives.

"My sister has a big heart." Bea gazed at Noah as she

spoke, although the words were clearly meant for Ryder. "Her husband took advantage of that. He took advantage of her under the mistaken assumption that she had access to…well, a fortune, given our last name."

"I'm not interested in Esme's money," Ryder answered, affronted at the suggestion. "I have plenty of my own."

"So, in what way are you interested in her exactly?" Bea demanded, dropping a kiss on Noah's forehead.

He resisted the urge to fidget. There was no way anyone could have guessed that he was often nearly done in by his attraction to Esme. "Has she explained our arrangement to you?"

"Right down to the rules. I was surprised the two of you have already agreed you're free to date other people."

"Did we agree to date other people?" he murmured. "I don't remember that."

Bea looked amused. "Esme read your rules to me."

"*Her* rules," Ryder clarified. "You saw the state I was in here. Do I look like somebody who would be a big draw as a date?"

"Either that's a rhetorical question, or you don't own a mirror."

Ryder felt color race to his cheeks. "I wasn't fishing for a compliment, and I'm not interested in dating." At least, not other women if Esme was a possibility.

"And what exactly is your interest in my baby sister?" Bea Fortune asked the question lightly, but Ryder got the impression she expected a serious answer. Was he so transparent in his interest?

"Obviously, I don't know Esme well yet, but I like her, and more importantly, I respect her. She's a great mother and has handled this situation with a huge amount of care and maturity. She's someone I'd like to emulate as far as how a parent should act in the face of a crisis."

He cleared his throat. "I'm never going to do anything to hurt her if that's what you're worried about."

"You're right. She's an amazing mother and has a heart the size of this great state we live in. She considers both of these boys her sons, and it doesn't matter which one she brought home after giving birth or which one shares her DNA. Noah and Chase are hers as far as Esme is concerned."

"I feel the same way." Ryder inclined his head and studied Bea. "Is there something I've done or Esme has told you I've done that gives you a different impression? I feel like we're dancing around a topic, and I'm a couple of steps behind."

The pretty redhead shifted but didn't drop her gaze from Ryder's. He respected her for that. "You're relatively new to Chatelaine. So are we. I'm not sure if Esme mentioned that I'm opening a restaurant in town?"

"She did. She's very proud of you and your brother."

Bea smiled. "The feeling is mutual. I've met a lot more people than she has at this point. The men in your family have a reputation around town already. I'm not sure if it's gossip or has been earned, but it doesn't mesh with the kind of person I want my sister to have in her life."

Ryder's stomach churned. He knew what that reputation would be, and although he'd guessed and expected this news, he still hated to think that Esme might believe him to be a player. No wonder she went out of her way to clarify that she was willing to give him space to date.

"She doesn't know I'm here if you were wondering," Bea offered. "I just wanted to—"

"Vet me?"

"Speak to you," she countered.

He nodded, and although he didn't appreciate people making assumptions about him, he understood the concern. He also liked that Esme had people looking out for her because, with her gentle soul, he imagined she had the self-preservation instincts of a kitten.

"Your sister can make her own decisions, but I meant it when I said I respect her and I'm not going to hurt her." He should leave it at that. Because while he understood Bea's protectiveness, he didn't owe her anything. Still, he added, "I'm not like my father or brother. Not in the ways that would impact my ability to live up to my end of the bargain or be the kind of father these two deserve."

Bea was silent for a moment, then smiled and visibly relaxed. "I like you, Ryder Hayes, and I didn't expect to. Thank you for being so honest, and if it's not too much trouble—"

"I won't mention this visit to Esme," he promised.

She snuggled Noah for another minute, then transferred him to his father's arms. Ryder half expected the boy to wake immediately and cry again, but Noah remained blissfully asleep. Chase had also fallen asleep in the swing. He should move both boys upstairs to their shared crib, but he was too worried about waking them again.

After locking the door behind Esme's sister, he returned to the couch and made himself comfortable while he watched his two sons.

For the first time in his life, striving for success or his father's love wasn't first on his list of priorities. Instead, he enjoyed this moment and the opportunity to appreciate how special it was to have not one but two sons in addition to the woman at his side helping to raise them. The time had come to finally allow himself to become the man he wanted to be.

ESME BLINKED AWAKE in the darkness, heart pounding like she'd just run a fifty-yard dash. She was confused and disoriented for a few terrifying moments, the nightmare holding her in its grip.

In her dream, she'd returned to the night she gave birth, and the storm had raged even more violently. There'd been two bassinets at the end of her bed, but instead of a nurse checking on her babies, the older volunteer Ryder was intent on tracking down had slowly entered the room, cane in hand and her vivid blue eyes glittering with an emotion Esme couldn't name.

The woman had shaken her head at Esme as if admonishing her. Then she hooked the crook of her cane over the edge of one of the bassinets and wheeled it out of the room. The relentless crack of thunder drowned Esme's scream as she watched one of her precious children being taken from her.

Her body quivering with residual fear, she climbed out of bed and silently made her way across the dark hall. Although she knew the dream wasn't real, she had to check on Chase and Noah and see for herself that both boys were safe.

The nursery door was slightly ajar, causing panic to flare inside her, but the band around her chest loosened as she pushed it open to reveal Ryder standing in the middle of the room, a swaddled baby tucked under each arm.

He swayed back and forth, singing what sounded to Esme like a quiet rendition of "Born in the USA." He wore a white T-shirt and gray athletic shorts, his hair tousled from sleep. Maybe it was her own exhaustion or the leftover adrenaline her dream had produced, but she'd never seen a sexier sight.

She must have made a sound, or he sensed her presence because his gaze collided with hers, green eyes sparking with awareness.

"What are you doing up?" he asked, his voice soft. "I'm on duty tonight."

"Bad dream," she answered and stepped into the room. "The mystery volunteer from the hospital was trying to take one of the boys."

The description didn't convey the panic the nightmare manufactured inside her, but Ryder must have understood how bad it had been. He moved toward her and wordlessly transferred Noah to her arms.

Esme sighed as she drew the baby closer and leaned down to breathe in his sweet scent.

"No one's going to take either of them." Ryder was so close she could feel the warmth of his body and took comfort in his vow. It was easy to believe everything would be fine with this man to protect her.

Undoubtedly, he'd use his strength and power to keep Noah and Chase safe, but who was going to protect Esme's heart when she was so vulnerable to losing it?

They stood together for a minute, their arms brushing as they rocked back and forth. Then she began to sing a lullaby her mother had favored when Esme was a girl. "'Hush, little baby, don't say a word,'" she crooned. The classic song might not have the same resonance as a selection from the Springsteen catalog, but each of the boys smiled in their sleep as she continued with the verses, whether in response to her voice or their private dreams, she couldn't say.

When the last note ended, they placed the babies in their shared crib. Ryder had moved Noah's crib from his apartment to the nursery, but the boys slept better when they were close together, so until that changed, Chase and Noah slept side by side in their swaddles.

Ryder placed a hand on Esme's back as they left the room, and his touch pulsated through her, making her knees weak. As the door clicked shut, she turned, ready to apologize for her silly overreaction to a dream.

However, the heat in his eyes had the words catching in her throat.

"You're so damn beautiful," he said, shaking his head like the words pained him to say. "I don't know what to do next, Esme."

She had a few ideas, but it wasn't easy to fathom he felt the same about her.

Then he reached up and threaded his fingers through her long hair. His chest rose and fell in shallow breaths as if touching her undid something in him. It certainly had that effect on Esme.

Longing coursed through her like a rushing stream, and she wasn't sure how to dam up her desire. Her mouth had gone dry, and she licked her lips, causing Ryder to let out a soft groan in response.

She lifted onto her toes and kissed him, unable to resist and unwilling to worry about the consequences. This moment felt precious, and she had to believe the quiet night and the bond they already shared would keep her safe.

Either that or she'd deal with the eventual consequences, but not now. All she wanted was to savor the taste of him and how perfectly they fit together. He cupped her face and angled her head to deepen the kiss as Esme spread her palms over the hard planes of his chest.

She could feel his heart beating a frantic rhythm under the thin fabric of his shirt, but it wasn't enough. Her body seemed to have a mind of its own, and her yearning surged to become a full-blown torrent of need.

Their tongues melded, and she lost herself in the moment even as her hands slipped under his shirt to move up and over his back. He trailed kisses along her jaw and neck, one finger tracing the sensitive dip of her collarbone.

Her pajama top was blessedly a scoop neck, and it felt like heaven when Ryder tugged on it and gently kissed the top of her breast.

Esme was ready to shuck the cotton fabric over her head, but the sound of a baby's sudden cry split the air. Both she and Ryder jumped back like two teenagers discovered in the basement by angry parents.

They stood silently for several seconds, but whichever boy cried out had also settled himself. It didn't matter. The interruption reminded Esme that there were more important things to consider than her red-hot desire for Ryder Hayes.

"That can't happen again," she said, unsure whether she was hoping to convince him or herself.

She could see Ryder's thick brows draw together in the pale light from the moon shining in the window at the end of the short hallway. He looked like he wanted to argue, but after a few more charged moments of tense silence, he nodded.

"Whatever you want," he answered, which was not the response she'd expected.

Esme figured he'd understand that nothing could happen between them but quickly realized that physical intimacy probably didn't mean the same thing to Ryder as it did to her.

He meant something to her that went beyond kissing or even sex. The way he listened to her, laughed at her silly jokes and truly seemed to respect her as a person was more of a gift than Esme could have expected to receive.

Ryder had made it clear they were together because it was the right thing for raising the boys. But she was a woman built for love and commitment and could not risk letting him capture any more of her heart. Not with the future they'd committed to sharing.

"Good night," she said and retreated to her bedroom, pressing her back to the door as she listened to the door across the hall close a few seconds later.

At least Esme wouldn't have to worry about any more nightmares tonight. Sleep would be a long time coming with the memory of Ryder's mouth on hers branded into her heart and mind.

CHAPTER EIGHT

"ARE YOU SURE about this?" Esme asked the following Monday afternoon as she stared up at the rustic yet elegant exterior of the LC Club.

The weekend's unseasonably warm temperatures and sunny days had morphed into an overcast start to the week, one Ryder refused to take as an omen.

"I'd like you to meet my father and brother," he told her. "Although today you're just going to be getting Brandon because Dad missed his flight home from Miami last night."

Whether Chandler had accidentally gotten the time wrong or chosen to take an extra day in the warm and sunny weather of South Florida, Ryder didn't care to hazard a guess. It wouldn't have been the first time his dad had extended a work trip to include a three-day weekend, especially when in a location filled with an ever-present bevy of beautiful women.

It shouldn't come as a surprise. His father claimed that welcoming Chase and Esme to the Hayes family in whatever way their arrangement allowed was a priority, but Ryder knew the man too well to believe that.

"I appreciate that," Esme said as she took Noah's infant carrier from Ryder, leaving him with Chase's. "I want to meet them as well, but we could have planned a dinner at the house like we did with Bea and Asa."

Ryder swallowed against the uncomfortable emotions

that burned his throat. "The difference is you enjoy your siblings. I did, too. Asa and Bea are great. I'm just sorry your great-aunt had to cancel."

"Me, too," Esme agreed. "Freya texted this morning and said her headache is much better, and she wants to meet you and Noah soon."

Maybe that was true, or maybe Freya Fortune was working from the same playbook as Chandler Hayes.

"Very soon. But it's better to spend time with my brother somewhere public." He hadn't shared with Brandon or his dad that he and Noah had moved into Esme's house or anything about his hunt for a property they could buy together that would give them each more privacy.

He also had yet to convince Esme that a move would benefit her as much as him. If the kiss they'd shared the other night hadn't proved that he had no interest in dating anyone else, he wasn't sure what would.

Esme nodded but still appeared hesitant. "This place seems even fancier up close than it does from where I can see it on my walks around the lake."

"My dad decided to make it the jewel in the Hayes Enterprises' crown because of the location and the potential he sees in Chatelaine. I'd like to focus on improving the club's already impeccable customer service and the attention to detail the staff offers. That's what makes a property special, and if we have everyone in the company from the top down committed to that vision, it will benefit all of us as well as the bottom line."

Ryder had walked several paces before he realized Esme was no longer in step beside him. He glanced over his shoulder to find her staring at him, a smile playing around the edges of her lips.

"What's wrong?"

"You need to go back to work."

"I told you I'm going to take some extra time off. I don't want you to feel like I'm leaving you in the lurch. These boys are both of our responsibilities, and I'm going to prove to you that I take it seriously."

Ryder also needed to prove that he wasn't as incompetent a parent as he felt each time he compared himself to Esme. Just last night, he'd accidentally pinched Noah's chubby thigh while buttoning the boy's pajamas.

Esme had assured him that the angry half circle of tender pink flesh was something either of them could have caused. Even so, Ryder had been gutted by his son's cries, especially when the baby seemed to struggle to gulp in air, which Esme also claimed was a normal thing babies did when they were crying too hard. He'd never heard Noah, who was typically calm and content, cry like that.

She was kind enough to refrain from mentioning that Noah was wailing so hard because of Ryder's ineptitude. Sometimes, he wasn't sure why Esme would bother to keep him around. How had he managed to handle fatherhood before her?

Between his family's reputation and his deficiencies, plus the fact that he'd clearly shocked her with the level of his desire in the hallway, she had to know she could manage parenthood on her own just as easily as having to coach him through it. He wondered if encouraging him to return to work was a shrewd attempt to get him out of her hair.

"Your dad hasn't decided on the CEO position," she reminded him. "I can't comment on your brother yet, but I know you'd be a fantastic choice to run the company. Don't give up your dreams or aspirations, Ryder. They're important."

"Not as important as being a father," he countered, willing her to believe him.

"Just consider it," she pleaded and reached out to squeeze his arm. "It's okay to want both."

He nodded tightly but didn't answer. Was it okay to want her most of all?

They entered the club and took the stairs to the second-floor restaurant overlooking the banks of Lake Chatelaine that served lunch on weekdays. He introduced her to a few of his coworkers, proud to have Esme at his side. She wore a navy-colored dress with pleats around the skirt. It flowed over her luscious curves and stopped just below her knees, and she'd paired it with tan ballet flats and pulled her hair into a low ponytail.

Despite the demure look, he found himself riveted by her shapely ankles and the delicate heart pendant she wore around her neck.

He might have it bad when it came to Esme, but at least she wasn't the type of woman his brother would typically notice. Ryder held out hope that Brandon would behave himself and treat her with the level of respect she deserved.

As it turned out, Ryder had been worried about the wrong thing. Brandon was not only kind to Esme, but the jerk also blatantly flirted with her. Granted, Ryder had no claim to her other than in his secret fantasies, but she was clearly important to him.

Brandon knew that, so his flirtation made him feel like diving over the glasses of sparkling water and sweet iced tea and tackling his brother to the polished wood floor of the club's dining room.

He should have expected this. Brandon was like an annoying truffle pig who could snuffle out anything meaningful to Ryder so he could take it for himself.

Esme appeared flustered and amused by the younger Hayes brother's charm. She laughed at his jokes and beamed when Brandon played peek-a-boo with the two babies, whose carriers had been fastened in infant seat cradles next to each other at the table.

"How are you adjusting to life in Chatelaine?" Esme asked Brandon after the food was brought to the table—cheeseburgers for Ryder and Brandon and a club sandwich for her. "The pace of life here must feel slow compared to what you're used to in Houston."

"I like that there's no traffic," Brandon said, popping a fry into his mouth. "The local highways feel like they're made for hitting the gas pedal. Have you ever driven a Porsche, Esme?"

She giggled. "I can't say I've ever had the opportunity."

"We're going to have to remedy that," Ryder's irritating brother said with a wink. "Daddy Daycare over there—" he pointed toward Ryder but didn't take his eyes off Esme. "—can babysit while we go for a drive."

"It's not babysitting," Ryder said through clenched teeth, "when I'm their father."

"Sure, sure," Brandon agreed. "Everyone in town is so nice, and it's obvious you're no different, Esme. Do you like picnics? I could take you on a picnic."

Ryder sniffed. "I can take her on a picnic."

"I asked first," Brandon countered.

"So what?"

Esme held up her hands, palms out. "Hold on. There's no need to argue about a hypothetical picnic." She grimaced. "Is this what we have to look forward to with Chase and Noah?"

"No," Ryder answered at once. "Our boys are going to be friends."

"What the...?" Brandon looked legitimately hurt, which made Ryder's gut clench. "We're friends, bro."

Ryder shook his head to clear it, unable to believe what he was hearing. He loved Brandon but had never considered them friends. "Then why do you always try to best me in every way?"

Ryder placed his napkin over his plate, stomach suddenly churning too much to think about eating. "I understand Dad set us up for that when we were kids, but we're grown men, Bran."

"You're my big brother. I don't want to best you." Brandon laughed and loosened his tie like it was choking him. "I want to *be* you. I always have. Clearly, Dad wanted that, too, so he pushed me to do everything you did. I could never be you, so I had to be better."

If Brandon had revealed he was heading off to join a monastery, Ryder couldn't have been more shocked.

Had he made a terrible mistake in keeping his distance? Had he let their father's behavior influence his feelings to the point that he'd missed out on being closer with his brother? Could he make it better now? What would he risk if he tried?

"I love knowing this about the both of you," Esme told them with a wide smile. "I could tell you shared a bond, even if it was messed up for a while. It's how I want Chase and Noah to grow up, only..." she grabbed Ryder's hand "...how about we skip all that business about competition and pitting them against one another?"

He nodded numbly while Brandon roared with laughter.

"Oh, you're a keeper," his brother told Esme. "You're going to be good for too-serious-never-cracks-a-smile Ryder. I can tell."

"I smile," Ryder proclaimed with a frown.

"Maybe when you pass gas like a baby. Otherwise, it's all business." Brandon leaned toward Esme like he was revealing a secret. "The crazy part is people love him for it. Almost every day, I bring in a treat for the staff. This week was doughnuts on Monday and cookies on Wednesday. I even rented a karaoke machine for an office happy hour last Friday night."

Esme focused on Brandon but didn't let go of Ryder's hand. He was grateful for her steadying touch.

"That must have been so much fun," she said.

"Not one of them can carry a tune, although that didn't stop the sales staff from belting out the worst songs imaginable. But as much effort as I put into being the fun boss, apparently, I need to bulk order rubber bracelets that say WWRD. That's the theme of the office—'What would Ryder do?'"

"I told him he should return to work," Esme confided, her head close to Brandon's so that it also appeared as if she were sharing something private.

Ryder tapped his own chest like he needed to make sure he wasn't invisible. "You both know I'm sitting right here."

"Yeah. You're hard to miss." Brandon waved a hand in Ryder's direction. "But I'd much rather focus on your better half."

He liked the sound of Esme being his better half, as if they shared a true partnership. To Brandon's credit, he cut back on the flirting, and the remainder of the lunch was actually enjoyable.

How could she make everything better—even the relationship with his brother that had been antagonistic as long as he could remember?

He hadn't given much thought to how he'd contributed to the animosity between them, but as he watched Esme laugh at Brandon's wild stories and running litany of jokes, Ryder saw his sibling in a new light.

Maybe there was more to Brandon than the shallow, slick, skirt-chasing role he seemed to embody like a second skin. He was fun and funny, and he had a way of making people feel comfortable that didn't come naturally to Ryder.

Although they were barely old enough to have personalities, he could already see differences between Chase and Noah. Noah might share DNA with Esme, but he was an observer like Ryder, often studying the world around him with his brows furrowed like he needed to make sense of every aspect.

On the other hand, Chase liked to pump his arms and legs as if he couldn't wait to start moving and shaking.

Ryder would do his best to encourage both boys to be their best selves and each other's staunchest ally. Maybe he would have learned to laugh more if his dad had given him and Brandon that gift.

"It was great to meet you," Brandon told Esme as they rose from the table after the dishes had been cleared and the check paid. He thwacked Ryder on the shoulder. "Always a pleasure, bro. Take all the time you need away from the office." He winked. "That'll give me the time I need to ensure I'm chosen as Dad's successor. Don't worry though... I'm going to be a great boss. You'll love working for me."

Brandon grinned as he made the pledge, but Ryder didn't see the humor in it. He was about to offer a stinging retort when he felt Esme place a gentle hand on his back.

"I imagine the two of you will do great things working *together*," she said with a pointed look at his brother.

"Right," Brandon agreed, winking again. Did he have something in his damn eye? "That's what I meant to say. I'll talk to you soon, Ry. Esme, that offer for a ride is always open."

Ryder narrowed his eyes and resisted the urge to growl low in his throat as his brother sauntered away. He followed Esme out of the restaurant and down the stairs, unsure whether he wanted to throttle Brandon or try to repair their relationship. Both felt like viable options.

"Here's the plaque you mentioned." Esme stopped in front of the small memorial to the fifty miners who'd died in the tragic accident years earlier. "It bothers me that my grandfather's greed caused something like this. Growing up, we didn't hear much about him or Uncle Elias. I never gave either of them much thought. When Freya talks about my great-uncle, it's obvious how much she loved him. I don't know that anything my generation can do to contribute to the Chatelaine community will right the wrongs of the past."

He took her hand. "That isn't your responsibility, and I believe everything you do makes the world a better place."

The golden flecks in her green eyes shimmered as she smiled at him. "You're too nice, Ryder."

He barked out a laugh. "No one has ever accused me of that before."

They continued toward the parking lot, and Chase began to fuss as they latched the car seats to their bases in the back seat, while Noah had fallen asleep in his.

Esme smoothed a hand over Chase's cheek and then offered him a pacifier, which quieted him. "I think Chase is going to be our social butterfly." She settled herself in the passenger seat and fastened her seat belt. "It's funny how those two can be so much alike yet have their own distinct personalities. It was nice to meet your brother today."

"Do you want to go out with him?" The question popped out before Ryder could stop it.

Esme laughed like he was making a joke. "Oh, sure. That's a good one."

"I'm serious," he said, focusing on the road before him as he pulled out of the LC Club parking lot. "I guess I am too serious. You laughed a lot with Brandon. I liked hearing it."

"Your brother is entertaining."

"He's fun," Ryder admitted gruffly. "I should be more fun." He glanced over when she didn't immediately answer. "It's fine if you want to take a ride with him. Driving his Porsche roadster is the definition of fun."

"Not my definition," she said softly. "I don't want to go out with your brother."

Her tone sounded like he'd hurt her feelings, which was the last thing he wanted.

He gripped the steering wheel more tightly. "I just meant—"

"Do you know what fun is to me?" she asked, adjusting the seat belt so she could turn toward him. "Having an extra ten minutes to finish a chapter in the amazing book I'm reading because you offered to put the boys down for their nap. Or when one of them hits a milestone, and we're both there to see it."

"How about when Noah realized he could get his toe into his mouth for the first time like it was the greatest discovery in the history of man or baby?"

Her grin warmed his heart.

"Yes, *that*'s what I find fun, Ryder. I liked getting to know your brother, and I'm excited, although a bit nervous, to meet your dad. But please don't make me part of whatever ongoing competition the two of you have. From this outsider's perspective, it's clear that you each have something different to bring to the CEO position. I'm sure it's going to be a difficult decision for your father, but no matter who he chooses, you and Brandon will still need to work together."

"You heard what he said about being my boss," Ryder insisted, hating that he sounded like a petulant schoolboy or maybe a big brother short on patience. Old habits were hard to break.

"I'm not sure he knows how to relate to you differently." She tapped a finger on her chin. "Is it possible you're dealing with a similar issue?"

Yes, and Esme Fortune was smart to realize it. It was also distinctly probable he was falling for her. Ryder knew he could figure out how to deal with his brother. However, his feelings for Esme were a different story.

CHAPTER NINE

"Are you sure you don't want to hold one of them?" Esme asked Freya, who looked as shocked as if she'd been asked to hold a venomous snake.

Esme had finally convinced Ryder to end the workweek with a day at the office and made plans to meet Freya and Wendell Fortune at the small café situated inside Great-Store after she and great-uncle's widow finished their latest shopping trip.

Freya might not feel comfortable with either of Esme's babies, but she certainly liked spending money on them. She'd bought several new toys and some clothes for Noah and Chase, reasoning that it would be cute to dress them in matching outfits for Valentine's Day, which was fast approaching.

The whole town was decked out in pink and red decorations. Many of the displays in GreatStore featured Valentine-themed merchandise, and a pop-up flower shop took center stage near the big-box store's front entrance.

Pushing the double stroller through the automatic doors, Esme remembered that it was around this time last year that she'd found out she was pregnant. When she'd first shared the news with Seth, he'd seemed overwhelmed but excited and committed to her and their unborn child. She refused to compare his behavior with Ryder's, reminding herself that Ryder hadn't done anything to warrant her mistrust. But she'd been betrayed, and it was difficult not to worry that she might be taken advantage of again if she let down her guard.

It had been Seth's idea to get married quickly. The Dallas courthouse where they'd exchanged vows had been filled with leftover Valentine's decorations, even though the holiday had fallen a couple of weeks before their official ceremony.

Was it any wonder the displays of love and romance made her feel a little queasy? She hadn't even been able to muster any eagerness for the new shipment of romance novels that had arrived on her doorstep a few days prior, instead borrowing one of Ryder's thrillers for their evenings on the couch.

She'd been satisfied living in the make-believe world of books for so long. But being deserted by her husband, then finding out he hadn't been faithful for even a brief time, had soured her on the belief in happily-ever-afters.

She had been dealing just fine with the lack of romance in her life until Ryder Hayes came along, embodying everything she wanted in a hero.

The kiss they'd shared had rocked her to her core, but it had been a mistake. Her body didn't agree, but her heart was already so lost to Ryder—how could she take the risk of complicating their partnership even more?

Besides, he didn't seem the least bit interested in repeating the kiss. Although she couldn't seem to help finding excuses to take his hand or brush up against him, she noticed that he pulled away as soon as possible.

Forcing her attention back to the present, she smiled as Wendell Fortune cooed at Noah, who sat contentedly in the older man's arms.

"I'm gonna leave the baby holding to this guy." Freya murmured, hitching a polished nail in Wendell's direction. "I'm not a baby person."

"Turns out I've got a way with the little ones." Wendell scrunched up his face and then stuck out his tongue at Noah, whose blue eyes widened as he flashed a gummy grin. "I'm glad to have a chance to know the offspring of my brothers. It gives an old man a heap of pleasure to know that, despite everything, you and your siblings and cousins turned out good. Your grandfather and great-uncle would have been proud."

It was silly to be grateful for the approval of a relative she'd only recently met, but Wendell's words delighted Esme. She wasn't sure of his actual age, but he seemed quite a bit older than Freya, and Esme knew he was dealing with some heart health issues. In contrast, her great-aunt was trim and spry, her hair curled in a becoming shorter style that framed her face.

She wore jeans and a soft sweater that looked more on trend with current fashion than most of the clothes Esme owned. On the other hand, Wendell appeared weathered and walked slowly, his shoulders slightly stooped.

Esme knew he was worth millions even after bequeathing much of his fortune to his grandchildren, but he didn't look wealthy or act snobbish like some of the people she'd seen during her lunch with Ryder and Brandon at the LC Club.

"Wendell is right," Freya confirmed. "Your generation of the Fortunes is more deserving of the family's legacy in this state and this town than your great-uncle or grandfather were." She fiddled with one of her delicate hoop earrings and spoke in a hushed tone as she added, "You're good kids."

Her voice broke on the last word, like the fact that she might be coming to care for her late husband's family truly surprised her. "I wish things would have turned out differently, especially for those fifty families who lost loved ones in the mining tragedy."

"Or perhaps fifty-one families," Esme said as Chase finished off the bottle she was feeding him. She lifted the boy onto her shoulder and patted his back. "Asa told me that last summer, they found a note near the castle where the number fifty is etched into the concrete to honor the miners."

"There were fifty-one," Freya said tightly, repeating the phrasing of the note. "I heard about that, but it's ridiculous."

"I'm not sure the rumors have merit," Wendell acknowledged. "But I'm checking it out. In fact, Devin Street called me the other day to ask for an on-record comment about this new development to an old story."

"The owner of the *Chatelaine Daily News* is interested in the note?" Esme let out a low whistle. "Does that mean there's an official investigation?"

"I hope not," Freya snapped, then offered an apologetic smile when Esme and Wendell looked at her in surprise. "It feels like a waste of time. Why would an additional death be brought up after all this time?"

Wendell pointed a finger at her like she'd hit the nail on the head. "Devin told me it got his attention. I think he believes where there's smoke, there must be fire."

"But who would the mystery missing person be?" Freya asked. "It doesn't make sense. Everyone in the mine shaft was accounted for that day. I knew those men and—" She cleared her throat. "Not personally, of course, and Elias didn't like to speak of the tragedy. But I read up on it, so I felt like I knew the men."

"Walter and I did, too," Wendell agreed. "Although we were busy with our business ventures at the time, I wish I'd paid more attention to what my brothers were doing.

I knew they'd overheard our conversation about finding gold around Chatelaine but never dreamed they'd take the risks they did to make more money."

"I wish you'd known him the way I do," Freya said softly, then amended, "The way I did."

"I get it." Esme reached across the table, but at the last moment, Freya pulled her hand into her lap. She was generous but a hard nut to crack sometimes.

"Sometimes, it feels like my parents are still with us," Esme said, drumming her fingers on the cool Formica, "even though they've been gone over five years now. Things weren't the happiest growing up, but I loved them."

"The ones we love stay close in our hearts," Wendell agreed, then touched a fingertip to Noah's nose. "Along with the new loves we discover."

Esme knew Wendell was talking about babies, but an image of Ryder filled her mind. Her phone pinged with an incoming text, and she welcomed the distraction.

"Speaking of new love, Bea apologizes for being unable to join us this morning. She's finishing up a meeting about the new restaurant." Esme grinned at Freya. "I think you've introduced my sister to her one true love, the Cowgirl Café. I don't know if she's told you, but our mom once dreamed of opening a restaurant. You're helping Bea honor our family in multiple ways, Freya."

"I'm happy to do it," the older woman answered, although she looked anything but happy at the moment. Esme figured that could be blamed on the way her heart still grieved for Elias, and decided to change the subject.

"My sister's food is sure to be a hit around here. She has such a clear vision for the restaurant."

Wendell chuckled. "And she promised to put meatloaf on the menu in my honor. It's my favorite."

"It's Elias's favorite, too," Freya shared. "It *was* his favorite," she corrected.

Esme's heart ached for the older woman. Despite her great-uncle's unsavory past, it was apparent Freya had loved him dearly. Sometimes it felt as if the older woman couldn't truly accept that her husband was gone.

"Like you said, I wish we'd gotten to know him." Esme returned a drowsy Chase to his infant carrier. "But at least we have you. You're a blessing in our lives, Freya."

Her great-aunt looked uncomfortable at the compliment. "I haven't done much."

"But you've done *something*," Wendell said as he handed Noah to Esme. "Which is more than my brothers ever did."

Esme glanced at Freya, whose face had gone white as a sheet.

"What's wrong?"

"Nothing," she insisted, but Esme didn't believe her.

"You really have helped us so much. Without you, I never would have thought to get Chase's DNA tested. You helped me discover what I might not have otherwise known. In the process, I found a father for both of them."

Freya's smile was grim. "I don't think you should give me credit."

"Any news on figuring out what happened that night?" Wendell interjected, scrubbing a craggy hand over his jaw.

Esme adjusted Noah's bib and shook her head. "Unfortunately, no. One of the nurses Ryder talked to said two volunteers were working on the labor and delivery floor when the boys were born. We're meeting with the second woman early next week. She's in Florida right now visiting her daughter."

Wendell nodded. "That seems promising."

"Of course, we also received a terse email from the hospital's attorney telling us to cease and desist from contacting their staff members because it's a form of harassment."

"You wouldn't have to take matters into your own hands," Wendell scoffed, "if they were doing anything to handle it."

Freya stood and helped Wendell up from his chair. "Perhaps you should let it go," she suggested with a shrug. "Does it really matter what happened in the grand scheme of things?"

"Hell, yes, it matters." Wendell got to his feet, his movements stiff. "If I know one thing for certain, it's that secrets and lies don't do a damn bit of good. This family has had too many of those, and they've come close to tearing us apart."

Esme nodded, although in some ways, she agreed with Freya. Ryder seemed almost consumed with finding out the details of the switch and who was responsible. She couldn't help but wonder if his anger and irritation over the situation they'd been thrust into drove his determination.

She was trying her hardest not to get caught up in fairytale fantasies when it came to their practical and far-too-platonic partnership. Yet he couldn't seem to release the need to find someone to blame. What would happen if he never got to the bottom of it? Would his frustration transfer to Esme?

She hoped that wouldn't be the case. Wendell hugged her, and Freya offered an awkward pat on the arm as they said goodbye.

Esme stopped to catch up with her friend Lily Perry, who worked at the café in GreatStore and had helped Esme choose some items for Chase's nursery.

Lily cooed over both babies and commented on how refreshed Esme looked as the mother of two infants. It was easy to give credit to Ryder. He was a good dad, though he didn't seem to believe that about himself.

Halfway through Esme's recitation of Ryder's best qualities, Lily grabbed her hand. "You like this guy!" the slender brunette with the adorable freckles dotted across her nose exclaimed.

"I hope so." Esme gave what she prayed was a lighthearted laugh. "We're raising two kids together."

"That's not what I mean. You *really* like him, the way a woman likes a man."

"That would be foolish of me," Esme said, which wasn't exactly a denial. "Ryder doesn't see me that way. Besides, the boys are my priority, and I won't do anything to jeopardize the arrangement we've made."

"Foolish or not…"

"Don't say anything," Esme begged. "Not to anyone. It's so silly. I blame hormones."

Lily squeezed her fingers. "Hormones can be blamed for a lot of things, but it's not silly. The two of you are spending almost all your time together. He sounds great, and you're amazing. Why wouldn't it work?"

"I'm not his type," Esme whispered, hating how the words felt like sandpaper on her tongue. "I doubt you could understand falling for someone who doesn't see you like that but—"

"Don't be too sure," Lily interrupted and gave Esme a quick hug. "But the man you describe doesn't sound like a fool, and he'd be one if he weren't already half in love with you."

Esme rolled her eyes. "I wish, or maybe I don't. I've tried love before, and I prefer the kind I read about in romance novels. Less heartache that way."

Lily grinned. "Book boyfriends are usually better, but I'd still give Ryder a chance."

If only Esme could believe he wanted one. As much as she appreciated Lily's confidence that Ryder wouldn't be able to help falling in love with her, she didn't hold that same faith. That made it even more imperative to guard her heart.

ESME HAD JUST gotten both boys fastened into their car seat bases when Ryder texted to ask if she would bring the babies to meet him at the park that bordered Lake Chatelaine near the LC Club.

Her heart fluttered in response. Maybe it was the fact that she'd admitted her feelings for him out loud to Lily— hinted at them, at least—but there was no more denying to herself that she was definitely at risk of being hurt by Ryder Hayes. She tried to tell herself that it was new enough to be only a simple crush. Hormones would be an easy answer, but she suspected it was more than that.

He was attractive and being near him did wild things to her body, yet she enjoyed his company on a much deeper level than physical attraction. Despite how different their backgrounds were, they shared a connection beyond raising kids together.

"No", she said aloud, shaking her head. This was nothing more than a combination of circumstances, his kindness and the gratitude she felt at not being alone any longer.

She thumbed in a reply, agreeing to meet him and offering to pick up carryout from one of the restaurants in town, but he said no, it wasn't necessary. She'd skipped breakfast other than the coffee she'd shared with Freya and Wendell and wanted to believe that the caffeine rush was what made her so tingly as she drove toward the park.

Maybe if she could get the physical need for Ryder out of her system, it would be easier to focus solely on their co-parenting arrangement. That notion of exploring something more with the handsome businessman appealed to her body, although her heart was still skeptical.

Sunshine sparkled off the surface of the lake, and she pulled in next to Ryder's BMW. There was only one other vehicle parked in the lot, although she knew the popular spot would be crowded if the unseasonably warm weather continued through the weekend.

This was her home now, and she felt grateful to be raising her boys in a community that already meant so much to her.

He is your home, a little voice inside her declared as Ryder walked toward her from the edge of the parking lot.

Hayes Enterprises adhered to a casual Friday dress code, so he wore a fine wool sweater in a deep rust color along with dark jeans and Western boots. As per usual, when he smiled, it took her breath away. Esme had a feeling if she polled the women in his office, she'd discover that she wasn't alone in her reaction.

The thought actually made her feel better about her crush, as she was determined to refer to it. Ryder's movie-star features and thick blond hair were universally appealing, so there was no reason to read more into it than necessary.

"How was shopping?" he asked.

"Freya outdid herself once again." Esme put a hand on the car's back door to open it but was suddenly enveloped in a tight embrace.

"Thank you," Ryder said, kissing the top of her head.

She glanced up, confused by the force of his tone. "For meeting you here?"

He bent down and gently kissed her lips. The touch was fleeting, but it ignited tiny fires of need all through her body. "For encouraging me to go back to work. I didn't realize how much I missed having a sense of purpose until

I returned to the office." He kissed her again. "But you knew, Esme. You knew I needed it, and I can't thank you enough."

It felt as if he'd tossed a bucket of cold water onto those fires. She appreciated his gratitude but hearing him talk about his purpose and feeling the energy palpably pulsing through him made her understand that being with her and the boys wasn't enough for Ryder.

The knowledge didn't come as a surprise, and she couldn't fault him for it. She was glad to support his happiness, but somehow seeing him so charged after a morning away from her and their sons created a wide gap in their connection.

Taking care of Noah and Chase fulfilled her soul because she was uncomplicated at her core. She'd already been researching recipes for homemade baby food and took so much pleasure in planning her days with the babies, simple as their schedule might be.

What could she offer Ryder that would keep him interested in lackluster, stay-at-home Esme when he probably interacted with so many interesting people doing big things at Hayes Enterprises?

And if his brother was given the CEO position the way Ryder suspected he would be, that would leave him in a position where he was still expected to travel each week for work, wining and dining clients plus hobnobbing with guests at the properties the company managed around the state and beyond, if they expanded the way he'd told her his father planned.

"I'm glad it was a good morning." She kept her tone purposefully light. "I hope the rest of the day goes just as well." There was no doubt the highlight of hers would be the moment when he'd take her in his arms like it was the most natural thing in the world.

"Are you hungry? Because as great as the morning was, I missed…" He gave her an almost bashful smile, which looked out of place on his confident face. "I missed the boys. It's strange not being with them every moment."

"I can't imagine, although I guess I will next year when I go back to work. Freya really did give me the greatest gift making my wish to focus on being a mother come true."

Ryder drew back. "You're amazing, Es. Most women I know would wish for a shopping spree in New York City, not the baby department at GreatStore."

Did that make her amazing or boring? Before Ryder, Esme hadn't given her dream a second thought. In the wake of Seth's cheating, the choice to devote herself completely to being a mother had been an obvious one. But would her late husband have strayed if she'd been enough to keep his attention?

Ryder was more successful and worldly than Seth had ever been. It was ridiculous to think she stood a chance of capturing his attention or affection in any long-term way.

She grabbed the diaper bag and Chase, who was sleeping in his infant carrier, while Ryder hooked Noah's car seat under his arm. He led her toward the grassy area under a cedar pergola that offered a picture-perfect view of the lake.

"I had the restaurant at the club pack a picnic for us. I know my brother came up with the idea, but he's stolen enough of mine over the years that I'm not too concerned. You and I are having lunch al fresco."

"That's sweet of you to plan." Esme tried not to read too much into the gesture. He'd just told her the boys were who he'd missed, which she should appreciate without the ache in her heart. Their arrangement was about parenting together, and this impromptu picnic, plus the fact that he

wanted to see Noah and Chase, was proof he took fatherhood seriously.

There was a blanket spread over the grass and an adorable wicker basket that Ryder opened after getting the boys
settled. "They don't normally make tater tots on Fridays,
but I talked the chef into whipping up an order for us. I
know how much you like them."

Esme's stomach growled in response, and Ryder looked
quite satisfied with himself as he continued to pull many
of her favorite foods out of the basket. There was a turkey sandwich on fluffy brioche bread, a Caesar salad with
fresh Parmesan shavings and gorgeous, red, juicy straw-
berries, which were not easy to come by in the middle of
winter.

She was touched by his thoughtfulness and how he'd
obviously paid attention during one of their late night con-
versations, getting to know each other, when he'd quizzed
her on the food she liked best.

"The chef kept trying to box up the leftovers from
some of the fancy specials on the menu this week." Ryder
grinned at her. "But I told him you've got simple taste, so
we're going to stick with the basics."

Right. She was basic while he was used to running in
circles with women who liked big-city shopping and probably gobbled spoonfuls of foie gras for lunch.

But despite her niggling insecurities, he seemed to enjoy
their lunch as much as she did and animatedly shared the
plans and ideas he had for the company's future.

They continued to talk, Esme mostly directing the conversation back to Ryder when he asked about her day. No
point in highlighting how dull she was by detailing shopping for baby clothes and coffee with two old people.

He placed a hand on her knee, one finger tracing small
circles that she felt through the soft fabric of her jeans like

he was directly touching her skin. "I'm grateful we're in this together," he said huskily. "There's no way I would have had the mental bandwidth to come back to work with the renewed energy I feel otherwise. When it was just Noah and me, I constantly worried about how to handle my workload and the expectations, particularly if I needed to keep traveling. Being with you changes everything."

Esme took a small bite of turkey sandwich and nodded. Both Bea and Freya had expressed concern about Ryder coming to view her as a glorified babysitter, and she hated to admit that his words gave her trepidation.

Surely that wouldn't be the case when she returned to work. Even though her career as a first-grade teacher wasn't as important or anywhere near as lucrative as his job, she loved teaching and was committed to finding a position at the local school this coming fall.

They'd established ground rules for the babies at their current age and would need to ensure those rules continued to work for both of them as the boys got older. Yet Ryder's hand on her leg felt so good—shockwaves of awareness skittering along her spine—that she longed for more. If she could change the rules to her liking as the boys got older, could she also modify them to accommodate her growing physical attraction to Ryder?

After all, if they were going to be living in such close proximity, with neither of them dating at the moment—and Esme not planning to start anytime soon—what would be the harm in upping their physical connection? She'd just need to keep her heart out of it, which should be manageable. Or would it…?

"What's wrong?" Ryder asked suddenly. "You have a funny look on your face, and you're blushing."

"I think I'm having a reaction to something I ate," she lied, pressing her lips together.

He straightened and gripped her shoulders with his strong hands. "Can you breathe? Is it anaphylactic? Do we need to get you to the hospital?"

Okay, his worry was adorable if unnecessary.

"I'm fine," she said. Then before she lost her nerve she added, "It's really nothing. But I'd feel better if you'd kiss me again."

"Kiss away your allergy?" He stared at her for several seconds and then his mouth curved into a grin.

"Or give me another reason to feel flushed," she suggested with uncharacteristic boldness.

"Why, Miss Fortune, are you asking me to play doctor?"

A nervous giggle bubbled up inside her. "Well, we talked about each other's favorite foods, music and colors, but I guess we never covered our favorite fantasies…"

Ryder sucked in a breath, then leaned in and nipped at her bottom lip. "That's a no-brainer for me. My number one fantasy is anything that involves you." Their mouths melded, and she felt as overwhelmed by the intensity of his words as she did by the kiss. There was no point in pretending she could resist this man. Maybe this was how she'd get him out of her system.

And if nothing else, she'd be left with sweet memories of real-life passion and not just the kind she read about in the pages of her beloved novels. Ryder pulled her closer, lifting her into his lap and then lowering himself to the blanket, taking her with him. She could feel that he wanted her, and that knowledge solidified her decision.

Esme was a grown woman, not a naive schoolgirl unable to discern the difference between physical passion and romantic affection. Why couldn't they be friends with benefits?

It was more than she thought she'd get as a single mother and might be as much as she could handle. She'd given love—or at least commitment—a chance with Seth, and that had been a disaster. As much of a train wreck as her parents' marriage.

Esme had tried to convince herself that in real life she could have the kind of fairy-tale relationship she read about in so many books. But what was the old saying? Fool me once, shame on you. Fool me twice, shame on me.

She'd been fooled by the promise of love both in watching the painful, tension-filled demise of her mom and dad's love story and through her own experience at letting herself fall. Now with their sons to consider, she had to keep her heart guarded. Friends with benefits she could handle. Anything more was too big a risk.

Before things got too out of hand, Noah began fussing, and Esme scrambled off of Ryder.

"Who knew babies made the best chaperones?" Ryder grumbled good-naturedly as he began putting away the leftover food.

"I'm sure you need to get back to the office." Esme wanted to get physical with this hot, sexy man, but she did *not* want to talk about getting physical. She lifted Noah out of his carrier and moved off the blanket so Ryder could fold it. Chase, bless his heart, had slept through the entire lunch.

"Speaking of that, another reason I wanted to see you all today is because I'm going to be home late tonight. There's a dinner in town with some of the regional management team who have been staying here. Most of them are heading home this weekend, so it's important that I attend."

"Of course," Esme agreed. She turned toward the lake with Noah, hoping her disappointment wasn't written on her face.

"Esme?"

"It's all good."

"Okay," Ryder agreed, taking her free hand in his.

"I was just wondering if you'd wait up for me. I'd like a chance to…" He brushed his mouth over her knuckles. "To explore my favorite fantasy when we have more time."

"Oh." She nodded, heat sweeping through her once more. "I can wait up."

"I'm looking forward to it."

"Me, too," she whispered. He'd just never know how much.

CHAPTER TEN

HE WAS GOING to murder his brother. Brandon had insisted that after the dinner, the group head over to The Corral, a local bar known for its wings and being the best place in Chatelaine for a game of pool.

It was nearly midnight before Ryder, the evening's designated driver, dropped off the last group of out-of-town Hayes Enterprises' employees at the LC Club, where they were staying. As far as he knew, Brandon was closing down the bar with a couple of cowgirls he'd been flirting with most of the night.

He had finally given up on getting home at a reasonable hour and had texted Esme not to wait for him and that he'd see her in the morning.

A part of him had hoped she'd still be awake, although he knew that wasn't fair.

Taking care of two babies would exhaust even the most devoted parent, and he had no idea how she managed it each day with a smile on her face. If anyone deserved a few hours of peaceful sleep, it was Esme.

Walking through the dark, quiet house, he reminded himself there was no rush in taking their relationship to the next level. The fact that she wanted to had been a surprise, albeit a pleasant one. He suspected she was still worried about his intentions and whether he was the type of guy to hurt her as her late husband had.

Ryder would never disrespect Esme that way, but he

wasn't ready to share how much he cared about her. It made him feel vulnerable, and he hadn't let himself open up like that other than with Steph, which had turned out horribly.

There was too much at risk with Esme. He couldn't imagine his life without her, and not only because she was a better parent than he could ever dream of being. She made him *want* to be better but seemed happy with him just as he was.

With Esme, he didn't have to worry about needless complications or striving to hit some arbitrary expectation. He could completely relax, maybe for the first time in his life. Whether he was happy, sad or in between, she accepted his emotions with the gentle patience she showed their babies. As far as he could tell, nothing rattled Esme Fortune.

She was a gift, a true treasure, which made him wonder at the wisdom of giving in to his desire for her. What if he ended up wanting more than she was willing to give or vice versa? Ryder didn't think he could handle being a parent alone now that he knew how good it felt to share the responsibility with her.

He paused in the upstairs hall and thought about knocking on the closed door to her bedroom. The worry that connecting with her on a deeper, intimate level would come with strings attached, no matter what either of them claimed, might plague him, but deep down he knew that continuing to resist would be a losing battle. He wanted Esme, and when Ryder's mind became set on something, there was no stopping it.

But tonight, he didn't knock. She deserved better than to be roused out of her peaceful sleep. A woman like her was worthy of sonnets and rose petals and…no. He shook his head at his idealistic thoughts, which could only lead to trouble, as he walked into the spare bedroom.

She didn't want those things, not from him anyway.

He'd be grateful for whatever scraps of affection she offered and adhere to any guidelines she set for their relationship. He would do whatever it took.

Ryder paused inside the doorway. Something was different. A lamp on the nightstand had been left on, and the sweet scent of vanilla lingered in the air. His heart began to hammer in his chest as he glanced over at the queen bed and saw Esme curled on her side, the sheet and quilt that covered her rising and falling as she breathed.

Was this his imagination playing tricks on him?

As if sensing him, Esme rolled over to face his direction, her eyes soft and sleepy. "Late night," she murmured.

"Yes," he managed to respond, although speaking around the desire surging through him was difficult.

"I tried to stay awake." She sat up and patted the book on his pillow. "Didn't quite make it."

"But you're here," he observed, like she didn't realize it. "In my room." In his bed.

She inclined her head. "I hope that's okay."

"Yes," he breathed like a prayer.

Her mouth curved into a sensual smile. "Do you want to come to bed?"

He toed off his boots and then started on the buttons of his shirt, his fingers shaking with need. Don't read more into this moment, he counseled himself as he shrugged out of the crisp fabric. It was physical, convenient. They were friends with benefits.

None of it mattered because he wanted her so badly.

"How was your night on the town?" she asked, tucking a dark lock of hair behind one ear.

"Awful." He took the wallet from his back pocket and pulled out a condom, approaching the bed to set them both on the nightstand.

"Really?" Her eyes widened as she tracked his movement. "I've heard The Corral is a lot of fun."

"Nothing is fun without you."

Her smile widened. "That's not true."

"It is for me," he said, then shucked out of his jeans. Wearing only his boxers, he joined her on the bed, the mattress sagging slightly under his weight.

"Then I'm glad you're home."

Home. The word had never sounded so good.

"Are you staying in my bed tonight?" he asked, trying not to growl the question at her.

She seemed to think about her answer—for far too long, in Ryder's opinion. "I was planning on it," she answered and kissed him gently. "If that's okay with you."

He nearly groaned in response but, instead, pulled the sheet off her and then crawled up and over her, placing his knees on either side of her hips. "I'd keep you here forever if I could."

Her green eyes darkened to the color of moss in a shady forest, and he trailed one finger along her jaw and lowered his head.

The kiss was practiced and controlled—that's how it started, anyway. But Esme was so soft and pliant against him, her mouth perfectly fit to his. Soon, he lost himself in the taste of her, feeling reckless and wild. When she grazed her nails over the ridges of his shoulders, it nearly undid him.

He ached for her even though she was right there with him. He yearned for this feeling Esme gave him—not just the physical pleasure of kissing and touching her but the sense that in her arms, he was truly home.

She wore an oversize T-shirt that he efficiently lifted over her head in one movement. Then he was dizzy with the vision of her glorious breasts, which he cupped in his hands as she let out a soft moan. He sucked one pink tip into his mouth, the taste of her like honey, as he caressed the other with his thumb.

"Ryder, I need…" she whispered, her voice strained.

"Me, too, sweetheart," he assured her as he came up for air. "You're beautiful, Esme."

"You're beautiful, too," she answered, and he felt his cheeks heat.

She could make him blush with one simple compliment, but he knew that when Esme said the words, she meant them from the bottom of her heart.

He kissed her again, shifting his weight off her. Then he took his time as his hand moved down her rib cage, her waist and her hips. He hooked one finger in the waistband of her panties and tugged them down. Her vanilla scent mixed with the earthy aroma of a woman, and it once again drove him toward the edge of his control.

She was slick when he touched her, opening for him like she'd been waiting for this moment as much as him. He could have stayed like that all night, kissing and touching her, and been satisfied.

But Esme had other ideas. "Not like this," she said against his mouth. "Together, Ryder. I want to be with you fully. Now."

Her eyes were filled with a mix of passion and determination, and who was he to deny her?

He climbed off the bed, pushed down his boxers, then plucked the condom from the nightstand and sheathed himself.

She lay back on the pillow and stretched her arms above her head, her breasts high and proud and making every last brain cell in his head take a fast train south.

He settled himself over her, then hissed out a breath

when her soft hand enveloped his length, guiding him to her center. She surprised him with her assuredness and lack of reserve—a pleasant surprise that made him wish they'd done this sooner.

Then he pushed into her and lost all ability for coherent thought. He filled her completely, and she dug her nails into his back as if she couldn't get enough of him. Which was funny because, at this moment, he intended to give her all that he could.

He thrust in and out, and Esme matched his movements until it was impossible to know where he left off and she began. She moaned—or maybe that was him—and their tongues melded as he drove into her.

"So close," she whimpered after a time, and he could hear the need for release in her voice. Murmuring words of encouragement, he lifted slightly to place his hand between them. Two fingers found that tender spot that sent her over the edge with a strangled cry.

She lifted to bury her face in his neck, then sucked at the base of his throat. It was unexpected enough to make him lose control, and he followed her over, whispering her name as his body trembled in her arms.

"We should have done that sooner," she said, her voice raspy.

"Like the day we met," he agreed, making her laugh. When was the last time he'd laughed with a woman in his bed? He couldn't remember, and the intimacy of it made his chest ache.

When they'd both regained their breath, he rolled off her, took care of the condom in the hall bathroom, then returned to the bed. Esme had the cover tucked up to her chin, and he snuggled behind her, wrapping an arm around her waist.

This felt almost as right as being inside her; only it was a hell of a lot scarier for Ryder since his heart was filled with longing.

"What happened to you?" Bea asked Esme Sunday morning as they perused the shelves inside Remi's Reads. The sisters had met at the bookstore before they were scheduled to join Asa for breakfast.

The three of them did their best to get together for a meal or visit every week, often with Freya or their cousin Camden joining them.

Esme returned the book she held to the shelf and shook her head. "I don't know what you're talking about."

Except she knew exactly what Bea meant. One night— now two—spent in Ryder's arms had changed something inside her. It was as if she'd locked away a part of herself in the wake of Seth's death and learning about his unfaithfulness.

She'd embraced her identity as a mother like that was the only thing that mattered. While she'd rebuilt her life, starting over in Chatelaine, the single-minded focus had centered her and kept her from sinking into sadness and regret.

However, so much had changed since meeting Ryder and Noah. *She*'d changed, but it was too soon to discuss the details with her sister if she could help it.

"Seriously, there's something different about you. You're glowing."

Esme shrugged and waved off the comment. "I picked up a new face scrub at GreatStore last week. I'll text you a picture."

"It's not a new cleanser." Bea sounded suspicious.

"I can't decide what subgenre to choose for my next read. Historical or romantic suspense?" She made a show of glancing at her watch. "I'll think about it and come back later. Asa's going to be waiting for us, and you know how annoyed he gets when he's hungry."

She headed for the front of the store, assuming her sister would follow, then waved to Remi, the bookstore's owner, on her way out.

The door hadn't quite clicked shut when Bea yanked on Esme's arm. "You had sex with him."

She sounded as shocked as an on-the-shelf maiden sister in a historical romance.

Esme tried to look affronted. "You don't know what you're talking about. Who's the one living in fantasyland now?"

She picked up her pace as they approached the diner. If she could get inside, maybe the restaurant would act as a home base. Surely Bea wouldn't discuss something as sensitive as this topic in front of their brother.

Both her siblings had mile-wide protective streaks when it came to Esme, but Asa tended to tease her mercilessly on anything involving real-life romance.

"You slept with Ryder Hayes," Bea insisted.

Esme rarely came close to losing her temper, and she understood the origin of the concern she heard in her sister's voice. But she had no regrets, none that she was willing to hold up to the light of day and truly examine.

She was a grown woman despite being the youngest in her immediate family. Bea and Asa sometimes treated her like the shy, introverted girl she'd once been, but Esme was more than that now. She'd thought she found love with Seth—or at least the family she'd always wanted.

She'd endured heartbreak, betrayal and the terror of wondering how she would support herself and her son as a single mother. On top of that, she'd moved to a new town and made friends, connected with the great-aunt and

-uncle she'd never known and then managed to find a way through the unthinkable situation of discovering the child she'd given birth to had been switched for another without her knowledge.

Guilt that she hadn't realized the mistake still knocked around her heart like an unwanted houseguest who had overstayed their welcome.

But despite everything, she kept going, and if this new development in her relationship with Ryder made her happy, she didn't see that it was anyone's business other than theirs.

"For the record, there was very little sleeping involved." She entered the diner and didn't bother to hold open the door for Bea. "And that's all I'm going to say on the matter."

Asa waved from the booth he always chose in the back of the restaurant. The establishment was already standing-room only, and she knew it would get even more crowded once the late sleepers wandered in. The scent of coffee, bacon and thick maple syrup made her stomach growl. Several people she'd met around town—either during her frequent trips to GreatStore or at one of the local parks or trails—said hello.

She liked that Chatelaine was coming to feel like home and didn't want to think about how she'd manage if and when she and Ryder returned to their platonic partnership. She told herself he'd be out of her system by then, but who was she kidding?

"Where are my two favorite babies this morning?" Asa gestured to the high chairs he'd pulled up to the table. "I thought Ryder and the double pack of trouble were joining us."

Esme slid into a chair across from her brother. "That

was the plan, but Noah was fussy this morning, so Ryder decided to stay home with them."

Bea took the seat next to Asa and grabbed the carafe of coffee the waitress had left on the table. Although Esme wouldn't have thought it possible to pour coffee aggressively, that was exactly how she would have described her sister's actions.

"I think it's more probable to assume Ryder didn't want us to read his body language the way I so easily could with our baby sister."

Asa put down the menu and studied Esme. "What body language?"

"She slept with him," Bea whispered through clenched teeth.

A throat cleared, and Esme turned, her face on fire, to see a waitress standing beside the table, order pad in hand.

"Sorry," Bea muttered, and then each of them gave their order, although Esme seriously considered storming out of the diner and having a bowl of cereal back at home.

But the proverbial cat was out of the bag, and if she didn't have this conversation with her siblings now, she'd be stuck having it later.

The waitress placed a hand on her shoulder before walking away. "Don't let anyone slut shame you, girl," she advised.

Esme nodded, then covered her mouth when a laugh threatened to escape. Asa looked just as amused, while Bea's cheeks were nearly as red as her hair.

"You heard the woman." Asa nudged their older sister with his elbow. "Don't shame her."

"I wasn't," Bea insisted. She leaned forward, palms flat on the table. "I just don't want to see you hurt, Es. It's clear you like Ryder, but with his family's reputation, you need to be careful."

"What makes you think I'm not?"

Bea frowned. "Well, if he convinced you to—"

"It was *my* idea," Esme interrupted.

"Go, Es," Asa said with a wink.

"I thought you and Ryder were together for the purpose of raising the boys."

"We are." Esme poured herself a cup of coffee and then added two packets of sugar, needing both the caffeine and a small sugar rush. "We're friends."

"That's my kind of friendship." Asa lifted his hand to high-five her, making Esme laugh again.

"I don't want you to get your heart broken," Bea repeated.

Esme knew her sister was telling the truth, and she had a hard time holding on to her anger.

Bea had been the first person Esme called, both when she got the news about Seth's accident and a few days later when she'd been closing out some of his social media profiles and had come across subscriptions to three different dating sites, all very active.

Bea had also been Esme's biggest cheerleader throughout her pregnancy. Despite the waitress's comment, her sister would never shame her. But she needed Bea to respect her decision, even though Esme harbored some of the same concerns deep inside.

"I know, and I appreciate it. I'm not going to jeopardize our partnership for a casual roll in the sheets."

The waitress returned with their meals, darting Esme a pointed look. "Is everything okay here?"

"All good," she assured the stranger, again marveling at life in a small town. While Cave Creek, where they'd grown up, had also been a faded spot on the map, she had never felt like she belonged there the way she did in Chatelaine.

When the woman walked away again, Bea reached across the table and placed her hand on Esme's. "I don't think your feelings for Ryder are casual. That's what worries me."

It worried Esme, too, but before she could answer, Asa chimed in. "Have a little faith in our girl," he counseled Bea. "She might read a lot of romance, but she knows the difference between real life and make-believe."

He forked up a big bite of hash browns, frowning as he chewed. "You do know the difference, right?"

Esme nodded but didn't answer him directly because her throat had gone tight. Knowing and accepting were two different things as far as her heart was concerned.

As usual, Bea seemed to be able to read what Esme was thinking without her saying a word.

"Let's change the subject," her sister suggested. "How are things going with the dude ranch owner?" she asked Asa.

He shrugged. "One step forward and two steps back. We have a meeting at the end of next week, although I heard there's somebody else ready to make an offer on the place. Given all the hoops I've already jumped through, it's hard to believe I have competition. Did you ever want something so badly you knew you'd do whatever it took to have it?"

There was a beat of silence, then Esme and Bea both nodded.

He placed his fork on the plate and leaned back, stretching his arms behind his head. "That's how I feel about this property. I know I'm meant to buy it."

That was how Esme felt about Ryder, unfortunately— like they were meant to be. They were meeting with one of the hospital volunteers later in the week and also had a call scheduled with the doctor who'd delivered both Chase and Noah.

Ryder continued to push for more information about the mysterious volunteer. At the same time, Esme wanted to let the matter go and get on with their lives, although she felt like she'd be doing her boys a disservice by giving up.

She explained her dilemma to Asa and Bea, who also seemed conflicted as to the right course of action.

"Speaking of mysteries," Bea said. "Has anyone heard from Bear yet? The last time I saw Freya, she said he still hasn't responded to her emails or voice messages."

Asa lifted a toast triangle into the air and swooped it around like he was flying a plane. "Our renegade cousin is probably off on some amazing adventure with zero service or cares in the world."

Esme, Bea and Asa hadn't grown up feeling close to Elias Fortune's three grandchildren. Bear, who'd been adopted by their aunt and uncle as a toddler, was the oldest and had always been a free spirit. He'd also made a killing in the oil business.

The middle brother, West, had died a couple of years ago in a shocking accident, but Camden, who at twenty-nine was closest to Esme's age, was more down-to-earth than Bear and had arrived in Chatelaine for the new year. He was as busy as the rest of them, so they hadn't been able to get together as often as Esme would have liked, but they kept tabs on one another.

"I hope Bear's okay," she mused. "It's not like him to go radio silent for so long."

"I'm sure he's fine," Asa said, sounding confident. "He'll no doubt have some incredible stories to share when he finally resurfaces." He polished off the last bite of toast. "And I bet Bear and Ryder will get along. Your guy was telling me about the semester he spent studying abroad in Italy and a few of the other epic trips he's taken."

"What kind of epic trips?" Bea asked as she sipped her coffee.

"Hiking Mount Kilimanjaro and fly fishing in Patagonia were the two that made me the most jealous." Asa's eyes lit with excitement. "Oh, and he visited a dude ranch in Uruguay run by authentic gauchos." He looked at Esme expectantly. "You've probably heard the stories."

"I have." Esme smiled, but it felt strained. Yes, Ryder had shared his travel adventures with her, but hearing her brother talk about them and how Ryder and Bear might connect over their mutual love of adventure brought into sharp focus another difference between her and Ryder.

The farthest she'd ever traveled had been a family vacation to the Grand Canyon, and she'd been carsick half the way from Cave Creek to Arizona.

Ryder was already talking about how to work out a parenting schedule if he had to start traveling again for work. The bulk of his plan involved him taking most of the responsibility for childcare on the weekends, holidays and his vacation time. But what would happen if he developed a case of wanderlust? Or general lust for someone besides her? Esme didn't care to consider either of those options.

They paid the check and then headed out. Esme hadn't wanted to discuss her relationship with Ryder but had to admit she felt a sense of relief that her siblings knew and supported her to the best of their ability.

"If I don't talk to you before you meet with the dude ranch owner, good luck," she told Asa as they said goodbye on the sidewalk. "I'll be sending all my best close-the-deal thoughts your way."

He chucked her on the shoulder. "Thanks, sis. Let's face it, she can't resist my charm forever."

Esme didn't doubt her brother for an instant.

"I do love and support you," Bea said, wrapping her arms around Esme's shoulders for a tight hug.

"She can't help but boss both of us around." Asa enveloped both of them in his embrace. "It's the oldest-child syndrome. She thinks she knows best."

Bea opened her arms to include him in a three-way hug. "I *do* know best. But what I know for sure is that Esme can be trusted to make her own decisions regarding her life."

Esme wasn't confident she deserved her sister's faith, but it made her heart happy. That was a start.

CHAPTER ELEVEN

"I WISH I had more information to give you," Jackie Ashwood, the second volunteer who'd been in the hospital on the labor and delivery floor the night Chase and Noah were born, told Ryder and Esme when they met later that week.

Ryder had suggested they speak with the woman in the Hayes Enterprises' conference room, which offered privacy. Jackie had been accompanied by her granddaughter, who happened to be a labor and delivery nursing assistant who'd also been working that night.

"Is it typical that you wouldn't recognize or already know another volunteer?" Ryder asked. County Hospital wasn't big, and most of the staff he'd talked to before today had known everyone on the floor that night. However, several people had mentioned that Jackie's granddaughter, Ruby, had been a new hire in October.

"That night was chaotic with the storm and flood," Jackie said, sending a sympathetic glance toward Esme. "I'm sure it made giving birth more of an adventure."

"An *adventure* is one way to describe it." Esme's tone was light, but she barely cracked a smile and immediately turned toward the window. She was holding Noah, who'd been particularly fussy for the past couple of days—teething, they both assumed.

Ryder wasn't sure if he'd said or done something wrong, but she'd been distant all morning, her mood directly contrasting with the warm and welcoming woman he shared a bed with at night. They'd been together the past five nights, although it felt like he'd known her forever.

Their bodies fit together like destiny had joined them, and he couldn't imagine anything that would change the way he wanted her.

By unspoken agreement, they didn't talk about this shift in their relationship. It was as if it were too precious for words, which could be misconstrued and dull the power of their connection.

Ruby, the young nursing assistant, stepped closer to Ryder, who was holding Chase in his arms. "What a sweet boy. I bet you love your daddy, don't you?" She cleared her throat and then looked over her shoulder. "You really didn't realize they gave you the wrong baby?" The question was directed at Esme, whose shoulders visibly tensed.

"It was a stressful night," Ryder answered before Esme could. She wasn't the only one who hadn't realized the mistake. "They whisked off the babies as soon as they were born to get their Apgar scores and the initial measurements. We didn't get to hold our sons until the staff brought them back to us. That was nearly a half hour later."

"Yes," the young woman agreed. "I was in charge of weighing the newborns and getting their footprints and measurements."

"Did you put on the ID bracelets?"

"I don't remember that," Ruby said offhandedly, and Ryder felt bad pushing her. She seemed nice enough.

"As Nana said, it was a chaotic night." She held out her hands. "Do you mind if I hold this little sweetie for a minute? I love babies. That's why I chose to work on the labor and delivery floor."

Ryder was slightly surprised at the request and how close the woman stood to him. There was something in the air, a tension he couldn't explain. He wanted to end this meeting prematurely and take Esme in his arms to comfort her however he could, but they might not have another chance to talk to Jackie and her granddaughter. The emails and voice messages he was receiving from the hospital's attorney were becoming more threatening in tone. The powers that be at County Hospital wanted Ryder to drop his unofficial investigation, and he worried they were going to forbid their employees from speaking with him going forward.

Jackie smiled as she watched her granddaughter bounce the baby in her arms. "It's funny," the older woman said. Jackie was heavier set with white-gray hair and the air of a woman who doled out hugs and advice in equal measure. "According to your mama, you never showed much interest in children. She thought you took the job working with babies because of your crush on that single obstetrician."

Ruby made a face. "Mama doesn't know what she's talking about. Sometimes mothers don't have the sense God gave them," she told Chase, like she was imparting great wisdom. "But I'll bet you can always trust your daddy. He's one of the good guys."

Ruby winked at Ryder, and he didn't know how to respond to the compliment, but she didn't seem to need or expect a reply. "I can tell," she cooed to the baby.

If this had been a cartoon, Ryder was reasonably certain he would have seen smoke billowing out of Esme's ears, although he wasn't sure why. The nursing assistant certainly wasn't insinuating Esme was anything less than sensible.

He figured it was a subtle dig at him for how Stephanie had behaved the night of her labor and delivery. Not that he blamed his late girlfriend for her screaming and crying. He'd never given birth, so he didn't have room to talk. But every staff member he'd met with remembered Steph and how vocal she'd been about not wanting to be a mother.

He wondered, as he had several times before now, if she'd changed her mind about sticking around whether the accident would have claimed her life. He highly doubted it, making him sad for Noah and particularly grateful that they both had Esme in their lives.

"If you need anything…" the young nursing assistant told him, leaning forward with Chase in her arms. He hadn't noticed the deep V of her pale pink sweater before that moment but quickly looked away. His gaze crashed into Esme's, and she gave a small shake of her head.

"I think Noah needs his diaper changed," she said tightly. "I'm sure you three can finish up here. Jackie, thank you so much for your time and the ice chips that night."

The older woman beamed. "You remember? I felt bad for you, darlin', because you were alone. Things were such a jumble, and I didn't want you to feel like no one cared."

"Thank you," Esme whispered again, and her voice sounded hoarse with emotion.

Ryder hoped it wasn't sadness. He wanted her to know she would never be alone again. That he would be at her side.

"I have the boys now," she said to Jackie, and Ryder suspected he was not included in that group, which stung. "It was nice to meet you, Ruby. I have a feeling I'll be seeing you again sometime." She darted a pointed look toward Ryder before grabbing the diaper bag from the table and walking out of the room. Trying not to read too much into Esme's parting remark, he asked the women a few more questions before taking Chase back from the nursing assistant. The boy smelled like a bouquet of expensive flowers, which must have been from Ruby's perfume.

Ryder would be bathing his son tonight. Lavender and vanilla were the only scents he wanted to be associated with either of his babies. Like most other staff members he'd talked to, Jackie promised to call if she remembered anything about the other volunteer or additional details that could shed light on who was responsible for the mix-up.

He walked them to the building's entrance, and as he headed back to the conference room, he heard Esme laughing, which did funny things to his heart. He followed the sound to Brandon's office.

Their father was off on another trip, and it was hard to tell whether he was traveling so much in recent weeks in preparation for his retirement or because he was avoiding meeting Esme and Chase.

Brandon had no such qualms and had stopped by her house several times with toys for his nephews.

His younger brother also seemed interested in discussing the goings-on at the company and plans for the future with Ryder. It wasn't pleasant to admit that he couldn't tell whether Brandon was interested in working together or if he would use the information Ryder gave him to get ahead on his own.

Maybe it didn't matter. Ryder wanted the CEO position, but it was nowhere near as important as being a father. He'd deal with whatever his father decided.

"Hey, bro. I changed a diaper." Brandon pumped his fist in the air. "A stinker, too. It turns out I'm a natural. I didn't even mistakenly put it on backward like somebody we know."

"I only did that at the beginning," Ryder said, trying not to feel annoyed. Esme was grinning and looked a hundred times more relaxed and happy sitting in his brother's office than she had with him in the conference room.

"You better be careful," she teased Brandon. "If you get too good at it, I'll put you to work as a babysitter."

"You can call me anytime." Brandon glanced from Esme to Ryder, a startled look flashing over his boyishly handsome features as he took in Ryder's scowl. His brother had the reputation of being irresistible to most women. But after that first lunch where they'd seemed to clear the air, he'd never considered that Brandon would continue to turn his considerable charm on Esme.

Funny how his mood seemed to match hers from earlier, while Brandon had managed to put her in better spirits. They were quite a pair.

"We should go." The words must have come out harsher than he'd intended because her smile faded. She nodded and stood, then picked up a vase of flowers Ryder hadn't noticed sitting on Brandon's desk. "What are those?"

"Your brother got them for me, which was unnecessary but very sweet. Thank you, again."

"Why did you get her flowers?" Ryder knew he sounded like a jerk but couldn't quite stop it.

Brandon shrugged. "It's Valentine's Day. I was buying flowers for all the women in the office. I knew the two of you were going to be here today, so I included Esme in the order. Didn't you give her anything?"

Ryder's face burned. Not only was he a jerk, but he was also an inconsiderate one.

Esme smiled again, but he knew her well enough to recognize that it was forced. "I didn't expect anything," she assured Ryder, then turned to Brandon. "It's not a big deal. He isn't…we aren't…it's complicated."

Brandon guffawed. "Giving flowers to a woman on Valentine's Day is about the least complicated gesture imaginable." He gave Ryder a clear "what the hell, man" look, which Ryder had to admit he deserved.

"How about you babysit for us tonight?" he asked Brandon.

"Ryder, that isn't necessary," Esme protested. "I'm sure your brother has plans."

"Actually, my calendar is completely open for tonight." Brandon placed his palms on the desk and leaned forward, much like their father did when making a point. "I have a rule against dating on Valentine's Day. It gives the wrong impression if you know what I mean."

Ryder knew exactly what his brother meant, which was also why he wouldn't miss the chance to take out Esme.

"Be at the house at seven. We'll get the boys down for bed, so you won't have much to do."

"I can handle whatever you need," Brandon promised.

Esme looked slightly alarmed, and it was a toss-up whether that was in response to the thought of leaving her babies in Brandon's care or the fact that Ryder had asked—well, not exactly asked, but made plans for them to go on a real date.

"But, Ry, even in a one-horse town like Chatelaine, you'll be hard-pressed to get a dinner reservation on Valentine's Day at this late date," Brandon told him. "Unless you're taking her out for popcorn and wings."

"For the record, two horses are often hitched outside The Corral. And I've got a plan."

Esme appeared as surprised by that news as Brandon. "You do?"

He nodded. Not quite yet, but he'd come up with one quickly.

"Then I'll see you at seven," Brandon confirmed.

Esme picked up the flowers Ryder still wished he would have bought her, and they headed for his car.

"I'm sorry I messed up this day," he told her quietly. "I'm going to make it up to you."

"You don't have to do anything. You're not even obligated to go out with me tonight. Ruby seemed nice. I saw her slip you her number during the meeting."

"She did not."

Esme reached forward and pulled a scrap of paper out of the front pocket of his button-down shirt. "She absolutely did when she took Chase from you."

"I swear to God, I didn't notice. I would have given it back to her if I had. I'm not interested in dating Ruby or anyone."

They'd made it to the car by this point and silently latched the babies into their car seat bases. "Then why did you ask your brother to babysit?"

"I'm not interested in dating anyone but *you*," he clarified.

She stared at him over the roof of the car. "Do you mean that?"

"Esme, do you think I'd sleep with you if I didn't?"

"I thought we were friends with benefits," she said, then ducked into the passenger seat like she didn't want to meet his gaze.

He climbed in and hit the button to start the car but didn't shift it into gear. "We could be more."

"What kind of more are you talking about?"

He pulled out of the LC Club parking lot and glanced at the horizon. The swirling white clouds rolling in from the east seemed to mimic his mood, covering the sky like a thin veil. Esme's question threw him for a loop. It should be simple enough to answer, but nothing felt straightforward to him when it came to matters of the heart.

Ryder didn't want to make promises he couldn't keep and wasn't sure he felt ready to make any vow, not after how Steph had trampled his emotions. Yet deep down he also knew it wasn't fair to compare that relationship with the one he and Esme shared. Falling for Stephanie had been a dive off a high cliff with nothing but rocks at the bottom to break his landing.

His feelings for Esme were different and more profound,

but he didn't know how to trust them or her. While Brandon was the one who took after their father in the obvious ways, Ryder still worried that he had enough Chandler Hayes in him to perpetually mess up his love life—and anyone who made the mistake of falling for him.

"Do we have to put labels on it?" he asked, trying to sound both confident and convincing. "We're already living together and raising our sons. I enjoy being with you, Es, and I'm unsure how I'd manage parenthood alone. Let me take you out on a real date—your rules are fine for co-parenting, but we've been dealing with some big changes in our new reality. Maybe it's time we loosen up and go with the flow."

"You think I need to loosen up?" Her hands were gripped together in her lap, knuckles white from the tight hold. "My late husband also thought I needed to 'loosen up.' Those were the exact words he said to me before he walked out the door that final time."

"It's not a criticism," Ryder assured her, reaching across the middle console to take her hand. "I mean it for both of us. Let's have a little fun. We'll start with one night. It doesn't have to mean anything."

Ryder wished he had a bottle of water in the car so he could wash down his foot, which seemed to be firmly lodged in his mouth.

When he'd proposed marriage to Steph for the sake of their unborn child, she'd accused him of having a heart made of stone. That wasn't true, but every time he let his heart lead, it took him down a dark and dead-end path.

He felt as incompetent at romance as he did at fatherhood and wondered when Esme would realize she could manage both without him. Before this moment, he hadn't given much thought to why he'd never been interested in a long-term commitment with a woman.

There was too much to risk, which went double and triple for a romantic relationship with Esme. If things went south, it could ruin the good thing they had going. Damn, Valentine's Day! He wouldn't be dealing with this dilemma if it weren't for the manufactured holiday.

Her house, which felt more like a home to him than anywhere he'd ever lived, was only a short drive away. As soon as he parked the car, Ryder jumped out and hurried around to the passenger-side door, opening it before she could.

"Esme Fortune, would you go on a date with me?" He placed his hand over his chest, surprised to find his heart beating at an irregular pace. Was he legitimately nervous about asking the woman he lived with, slept with and shared diaper duty with out on a date?

That would be a hell, yes.

She got out and looked at him like he'd lost his mind. "We've already made arrangements for your brother to babysit."

"But we can cancel if this isn't what you want. I want you to want this, Esme." To want *me*, he added silently.

She released a long breath, and it felt like some of the tension of the morning left her body as well. "I'd like to go on a date with you." She offered a shy smile. "Very much."

He leaned in and kissed her, his mind already whirling with ideas. If Ryder could handle anything, it was a plan. "I promise it will be the most memorable Valentine's Day of your life."

CHAPTER TWELVE

ESME TOOK HER time getting ready for their date that evening—as much time as the mother of two babies could manage. Chase had been fussy since they'd gotten home from the LC Club—unable to self-soothe and fitfully dozing off in either her or Ryder's arms.

They hadn't wanted to put him down in the crib, where he'd undoubtedly rouse Noah, who was napping like a champ, so they had taken turns trying to comfort him. Ryder thought he'd probably had too much stimulation, and it would take a bit of time before he could relax again, but Esme wondered if he was already protesting his parents leaving him with a sitter for the night.

She hoped it wasn't anything more severe or that the baby was picking up on her anxiety. Perhaps she should have said no to Ryder's offer of something more.

It seemed easy for him not to worry about how their actions today would affect tomorrow's future.

Seth had continually told Esme she needed to lighten up, although she thought she'd gotten over his little digs from their short marriage. Ryder was so kind and complimentary of her ability as a mother, but now she realized that didn't mean he saw her any differently than Seth in other areas.

Still, she wanted this night with him more than she'd wanted anything in a long time, even more than the passion they shared. What if a date could lead to something bigger? It was a risk, and Esme wasn't sure she trusted herself. But proposing the arrangement and that they move in together had also been a leap of faith—one that had paid off more than she could have dreamed.

What would be the harm in blowing off a little steam in the form of a romantic night out? She longed for real romance, particularly because, in the middle of the night, Ryder was everything she wanted in a partner—gentle, loving and attentive to her pleasure.

She couldn't imagine ever tiring of making love with him, but the time they spent managing daily life together was just as precious. It scared her, however, to want more with him. She was afraid of being hurt and then having to put on a brave face for the kids.

But that worry would hold, she reminded herself as she applied a pink gloss to her lips. She adjusted the flowing dress she'd chosen and stared at herself in the bathroom's full-length mirror.

There wasn't much in her closet that felt right for a romantic night on the town, but she loved the muted floral pattern and the way the silky fabric felt against her skin. She'd paired it with a fitted blazer and low-heeled ankle boots and hoped Ryder would notice that she'd made an effort. When she got to the bottom of the stairs, he and Brandon both did a double take, and admiration and desire shone in Ryder's green eyes.

"I can't say much about this guy." Brandon patted Ryder on the shoulder. "But you, Esme Fortune, clean up real nice."

"Thank you," she murmured, heat rising to her cheeks.

Ryder turned to stare at his brother. "How in the world did you get a reputation as a ladies' man when that's the kind of compliment you offer a woman?"

"And you can do better?" Brandon challenged. "You didn't even remember Valentine's Day."

Ryder walked forward until he was directly in front of Esme and then linked their fingers together. "You look so beautiful tonight, sweetheart. If I were a poet, I'd write a sonnet for you. I don't know what I've done to deserve you in my life, but I'm glad we have this evening together."

"If you tell her she completes you, I'm going to barf," Brandon complained.

Esme laughed.

"You look very handsome as well, Ryder. You always do."

He grinned. "Let's get out of here before my numbskull brother realizes exactly what he's signed up for."

Brandon held up the baby monitor. The only noise that came from it was the mobile playing "Rock-a-bye Baby." "Y'all did the hard part. I'm just going to watch a movie and enjoy my own delightful company."

Esme gripped Ryder's hand more tightly. "Are you sure Chase is down? If you think he's going to give Brandon trouble, we don't have to go out tonight."

"Go," Brandon insisted. "You two are giving me a complex like I can't even handle my nephews for a couple of hours."

"We won't be out late," Ryder assured his brother. "The keys to the BMW are on the counter, and their infant carriers are next to the kitchen table."

Brandon frowned. "Do you want me to take them for a ride if they wake up?"

"No, but you need to drive my car in an emergency. You can't just toss them in the back seat of your Porsche. But call us first, no matter what."

"Do all parents worry as much as the two of you?" Brandon looked skeptical.

Esme smiled. She didn't know how to answer that question, but it reminded her how grateful she was to be co-parenting with Ryder. He took the keys to her Subaru, and as they started out of the neighborhood, she tried to figure out their destination.

"I'm guessing you were probably able to get a reservation at the LC Club."

"Nope. Didn't even try."

"Then where?" Esme asked, although she had a feeling he wouldn't tell her quite yet. "I don't think we've covered this, but surprises make me nervous. Giving up control is weird and going with the flow doesn't come easily to me."

His mouth curved into a grin. "Is that so? I wouldn't have guessed that you like being in control." He reached over and squeezed her thigh. "Except when you do that one thing where—"

Esme slapped her hand over his. "You can't talk about that stuff...the stuff we do at night."

He laughed. "I know the *stuff* you're referring to, but why can't I talk about it? It's only the two of us here right now."

She bit her lower lip, embarrassed that she was not only a stick-in-the-mud when it came to surprises but a prudish one at that.

"Hey." Ryder wrapped his hand around hers before she could speak. "It's okay. You don't have to change who you are for me, Esme. Tell me what's going on."

She tried not to fidget as he studied her after parking the car along Main Street, which made her even more curious as to their destination. "Does this still have something to do with that nursing assistant? I had no idea she slipped her number into my pocket."

"I'm sorry," she said automatically. "I'm really trying to go with the flow, but it feels like tonight changes things."

"If you're worried about our co-parenting partnership, I promise nothing will change my commitment to raising our sons together."

"It's not that." Esme shook her head. "I know how to be a mother, Ryder. As silly as it sounds, I was born for that role. But being someone's girlfriend or a romantic partner is different, and I haven't been very successful at it."

She kept her gaze locked on their hands joined in her lap as embarrassment washed through her. "Heck, I don't even own any cute bras. I threw them all away after I learned about Seth's cheating. He wanted me to wear sexy lingerie, and it made me sick to look at the items I'd purchased to live up to some arbitrary standard he set."

"You never told me that." Ryder's tone was gentle.

"Because it's humiliating," she admitted. "You and I are on our first official date, and I'm wearing my boring cotton panties underneath this dress. I know it's easy enough to buy new ones, but even though we've been sleeping together, it hasn't crossed my mind. I buy diapers at GreatStore every week, and they sell nice matching sets of lingerie."

Ryder released her hand and got out of the car. She watched him walk around the front, and then he opened her car door and drew her out. A moment later, she was enveloped in his warm embrace.

"I don't care about fancy underwear. You could be dressed in a potato sack, and I'd still be over-the-moon attracted to you. You have no idea what you do to me."

He used one finger to tip up her chin and gently brushed his mouth across hers. "I don't think this is about lingerie, although once again, your late husband has proved himself to have been aggressively foolish when it came to valuing you. For the record, I'm scared, too."

Esme stared into his vibrant eyes, finding that statement difficult to believe.

"You're an amazing mother. I know I've said it before, but it becomes more apparent every day. We agreed on this arrangement, but you don't need me. Not like I need you."

He tightened his hold and rested his chin on the top of her head, and she wondered at the emotion he was clearly trying to hide from her notice. "Sometimes, I wonder why you keep me around at all," he told her. "That said, we didn't ask for this situation, but I'm not giving up on what we're creating. The men in my family aren't built for lasting relationships. I was determined to be different and change the story after Steph got pregnant. The consequences of that were worse than anything I could have imagined. There's no need for lingerie, Es. You're perfect the way you are. I'm not like you. I'm broken on the inside, and I don't know how to fix it."

Their love could fix it, Esme thought. It was time to admit, at least to herself, that she'd fallen in love with Ryder. She had a feeling he loved her, too, but the heartache of his past made him scared to acknowledge it.

She wanted to tell him what was written on her heart—to stop pretending. What if they skipped dinner and headed directly to the intimates department at GreatStore? That would be a promising way to spend Valentine's Day.

"Maybe together we can learn to trust again," she suggested softly. They could be the people they yearned to be—for their sons and each other.

She took a step back and looked around, suddenly aware of their surroundings.

"Why are we in front of the bookstore? Remi's Reads isn't open at night."

Ryder's flashed a satisfied smile. "I've become friends with Linc Fortune Maloney, Remi's husband."

"Another one of my cousins," she murmured. "He's Wendell's oldest grandson. Since moving to town last summer, Asa has been close to the Maloneys."

Ryder nodded. "As much as Freya is helping your branch of the family, Wendell outright gifted a large part of his fortune to each of his grandchildren. Linc joined the LC Club, which is how I met him."

"The inheritance is also how he and Remi opened the bookstore." Esme smiled at the cheery facade. "It was a gift to her."

"I can't gift you a bookstore," Ryder said with a soft laugh. "But I've arranged an evening in one. Remi and Linc left the keys under the flower pot next to the front door. We've got the whole place to ourselves."

She gasped, and he quickly added, "I know it's not a traditional Valentine's Day date, but I couldn't think of anything better than spending a quiet evening alone with you."

"Talk about fantasies coming true." She grinned. "As a kid, I dreamed of living in a bookstore."

"Hopefully, the next best thing is having dinner in one."

He led her forward and unlocked the door. Esme's breath caught in her throat as she took in the way the interior of the store had been transformed.

Remi had already put up several cute decorations for Valentine's Day, with paper hearts and red and pink garlands framing several of the tall shelves.

Now a narrow table with a red-and-white checked tablecloth had been positioned in the open area in front of the counter, where tea light candles flickered and the store's overhead lights had been dimmed, lending a truly romantic atmosphere to the space.

She looked at Ryder in wonder. "How did you arrange all this when you were home with me?"

"I had a little help from your sister," he admitted. "Bea

also provided the food for the night. I was going to order another picnic from the LC Club, but she offered to make us a lasagna to share."

"My favorite," Esme murmured. "Everything about this night is my favorite. Thank you, Ryder."

He kissed her again. "My pleasure. I don't know if I mentioned my long-standing library fantasy, but..."

She laughed. "I think we can work with that one."

As they sat down at the table, Esme offered him an apologetic smile. "Before we get started, would you mind texting Brandon? I know we've only been gone a short time, but it would put my mind at ease after Chase's fussy day."

Ryder pulled his cell phone from the pocket of his canvas jacket and frowned as he looked at the screen.

"What's wrong?" Esme's heart stuttered in her chest.

"Nothing. It's just strange that I only have one bar of service here, and my phone won't connect to the shop's Wi-Fi. Maybe Remi turns it off at night."

She watched as he typed in a message, then nodded as he glanced up at her. "Looks like it went through."

The phone dinged almost a second later.

"Relax, bro." Ryder read Brandon's incoming text out loud.

Esme blew out a breath. "Good advice from your brother," she agreed. "I'm going to do just that and enjoy this night with you."

The next two hours went by in a flash. They shared the delicious meal Bea had provided, and Esme made a mental note to text her sister *thank you* on the way home. Bea had thought of everything from disposable plates to a bottle of red wine that paired perfectly with the savory meal. There was also garlic bread and a chopped salad dressed with a tangy vinaigrette.

"I know your sister is going to be hiring someone to run

the kitchen at the Cowgirl Café," Ryder said as he pushed back from the table after they'd shared a heavenly piece of tiramisu. "But it's obvious that the restaurant business is a calling for her. This is far and away the best meal I've had in a long time, although your beautiful company might have something to do with it."

Esme smiled softly at the compliment. "Bea's very talented, and I appreciate you putting so much thought into this evening."

"Shall we do a little shopping? One other perk for tonight I forgot to mention is that we have an open tab, and Remi offered a fifty-percent discount on any selections we make. It's not flowers, but perhaps we can assemble a bouquet of books."

He looked so hopeful that Esme felt her heart melt even more. In between heated kisses, they took turns reading to each other from random works they drew from the shelves in various sections around the bookstore. They found books they were particularly interested in and settled onto the comfy couch on the far wall.

Ryder drew Esme's legs into his lap, and she lay back against the cushions while he took off her boots and proceeded to give her the most amazing foot rub. Truly, the people who had chosen fancy dinners in crowded restaurants were missing out because this intimate evening was extraordinary. She'd remember it always.

Ryder checked his phone several times, but with no incoming texts from Brandon, they lingered in the bookstore, enjoying the sweet intimacy of their night. Finally, Esme looked at her watch.

"We should probably go," she said reluctantly. "I'm sure one of the boys is going to wake soon enough. I want your brother to have an easy time tonight, so he'll want to babysit again."

She started to put on her boots as Ryder blew out the candles. "Are you saying you'd have a second date with me?"

His teasing tone made her feel giddy. "I think I could be convinced."

After finishing the cleanup, they walked out together, and Esme looked up at the night sky as Ryder relocked the door. The stars were putting on quite a show, but they couldn't compete with how her heart shimmered.

Ryder slipped his hand into hers, but they'd only taken two steps toward the car when his phone began dinging incessantly with incoming texts. A moment later, hers did the same.

"Oh, no," she whispered as she read the barrage of messages.

Ryder cursed. "We must not have had service inside the bookstore after all. I'll call my brother."

They hurried to the car as she tried to process the texts she'd received from both Brandon and Freya. Esme's great-aunt had stopped by the house to drop off a small Valentine's gift for each boy. At the same time, both babies had woken up crying, so Freya offered to stay and help Brandon.

But they'd discovered Chase was running a fever of nearly 103. After a call to the after-hours pediatric line, Brandon headed to County Hospital with the sick boy while Freya watched Noah at home.

"He's going to be fine." Ryder made the pronouncement with confidence, but Esme could hear the panic in his voice. He dialed his brother's number, but Brandon didn't pick up. After a terse message, Ryder disconnected.

"I'll call Freya," Esme said, already dialing the number. Her great-aunt sounded frazzled but insisted that Esme and Ryder go immediately to the hospital. Bea was already on her way to the house to relieve Freya, which comforted Esme, but she could hear Noah whimpering in the background.

"Are you sure he doesn't have a fever? Should he have gone with Chase?" As scared as she'd been the first time they put Chase in her arms, she'd never known terror akin to what she felt now.

"He's fine, and a hospital is no place for a healthy baby," Freya answered. "We'll manage until you bring that boy home."

Esme ended the call but continued to hold the phone with trembling fingers.

"He's going to be fine," Ryder repeated. She nodded and murmured her agreement, wishing the doubts weren't piling up in her mind like mounds of dirty laundry. The amount of fear she felt was nearly matched by guilt.

"If I'd been there, maybe I would have realized he was too warm. They are too young for us to leave them. What was I thinking?"

Ryder made a noise low in his throat. "Are you saying I was too intent on a child-free night that I put my son at risk? Is that what you believe?"

The intensity of his voice shocked her.

"I didn't say that, and I don't think it. He's not just your son—he's *our* son. We both chose to leave him with your brother during our date." She squeezed the phone so hard it was surprising the device didn't crack in her hand. "We made a terrible mistake."

CHAPTER THIRTEEN

TWO HOURS LATER, Ryder's stomach still churned as he watched one of his precious baby boys asleep in the hospital bassinet. It had been a chaotic arrival, mainly because the hospital staff had assumed Brandon was the father, so it took time for them to fix the paperwork and allow Esme and Ryder back to his room.

Was this hospital always so incompetent in identifying people?

Brandon had immediately transferred Chase into Esme's arms, and the three of them awaited the results of the blood tests. Finally, the doctor returned and explained that Chase was suffering from a bacterial infection he felt confident could be treated with rest and IV antibiotics.

Brandon had appeared stricken and apologized profusely, although Ryder knew it wasn't his brother's fault. Esme said the blame lay with the two of them, but she had to know he deserved the lion's share of the responsibility. He'd been the last person to hold Chase before his fever spiked, and he couldn't help but wonder if he'd missed something.

After answering a litany of questions from the attending nurse, Ryder had sent Brandon home with assurances that he'd done nothing wrong.

He and Esme had followed the nurse as she pushed the wheeled bassinet down the hall and then rode the elevator to the floor above where their baby would be spending the night.

Now they watched the boy, who appeared to be resting comfortably. Ryder had never hated something more than he did the thought of his sweet son hurting. Esme eventually got up from the chair she sat in to stand next to the crib.

"Hush, little baby," she began to sing, and tears sprang to Ryder's eyes. No one had told him about the pain he would feel when one of his children was sick. He would have done anything—made any promise—to take the child's suffering into his own body, but that wasn't an option.

He felt incapable of knowing what to do or how to comfort Chase or even Esme. She continued to sing, stroking the baby's soft cheek. Even under the weight of worry, she knew how to handle the situation. She was so much better than Ryder in every way.

Esme turned as a different nurse walked into the room. "Visiting hours are almost over," she said, her gaze traveling from Esme to Ryder.

Esme gripped the side of the bassinet. "I'm not leaving my son."

"Hospital policy only allows one parent to stay overnight with a minor."

"He's three months old," Ryder explained. "There has to be a special exception for babies."

"I'm sorry, but no there isn't." The woman looked sympathetic but resolute in sticking to the rules. "I'll give you a few minutes alone to decide."

A heavy silence filled the room, and although it killed Ryder to think about leaving his son, he knew the right decision.

"You'll stay," he said after a moment.

"Yes, I think that's best," Esme agreed, her gaze on Chase. "I'll text you any updates. Would you please let me know if Noah is okay when you get home? I can't stop worrying about him, too."

Was she so quick to dismiss Ryder because she didn't think he could handle the responsibility of keeping vigil with their sick child? Or because this awful night had shown her what he already knew—she didn't need him the way he did her.

Unwilling to consider either option, he rubbed his chest, which ached like it was splitting apart. Maybe she'd been right in her reluctance to take their relationship to the next level. Emotions complicated everything, as Ryder knew from past experience.

"I'll text you right away." He stepped toward her, but she backed up like she couldn't stand to be touched by him at this moment. Clearly, she blamed him for what happened as much as he blamed himself.

Another jab straight to his heart.

"I'll be here in the morning," he told her and then bent down to give Chase a kiss on the forehead. The baby slept soundly and didn't feel as hot to the touch, which Ryder hoped meant he'd taken a positive turn.

"Bring Noah," Esme said. "Please. If he's still well, and the doctor believes he's in the clear, I think it will help Chase to have his brother close by."

"You consider them brothers?" Ryder didn't know why the comment shocked him.

"Don't you?"

"I do, yes."

The whole point of their arrangement was to raise the babies together and not just for Ryder and Esme's benefit. He'd thought a thousand times about what he'd do differently from how his parents had treated him and Brandon.

Of course, Chase and Noah would grow up as brothers. If Ryder had learned one thing from this situation, it was that sharing DNA was not the only way a family could be created.

Esme, Chase and Noah were his family now.

"Noah and I will see the two of you as soon as visiting hours begin in the morning. Good night, Esme."

He didn't want to leave without holding her, but as if she could read his mind, she crossed her arms over her chest and gave a slight shake of her head.

"Good night, Ryder."

He walked out into the night, amazed at how a few hours could change everything. It felt like their date in the bookshop had been something he'd imagined instead of real life.

The stars twinkling above them hours earlier had been blotted out as thick clouds filled the sky. He did his best to ignore the tight worry that held him in its grip. There was no way he would risk losing Esme and their partnership now.

He couldn't bring himself to define the emotions swirling through him but refused to let this night pull them apart. As he drove through the quiet streets of Chatelaine, his mind searched for ideas of how to make sure he kept his family together—forever.

ESME'S NECK AND heart ached in equal measure the following morning after a night spent in an uncomfortable chair, although Chase was thankfully being discharged. After a course of IV antibiotics and fluids, the baby improved rapidly through the night.

He'd already had his first feeding that morning and offered a gummy smile to every nurse who came in to check his vitals. Ryder had also reported that Noah was com-

pletely healthy. Esme counted on him staying that way—
her heart couldn't take the stress of another night like the
one she'd just endured.

What made it worse was knowing that from now on,
she'd have to deal with these sorts of issues on her own.
Not completely, of course. She knew Ryder would be there
for whatever she or their sons needed, but Esme couldn't
keep pretending.

She'd fallen for him, even though she'd promised herself she was done with love after Seth. Knowing that one
of their babies had gotten sick on a night when Esme and
Ryder had left the boys with a sitter felt like a sign. She
could not be distracted or allow her focus on being a good
mother to be derailed.

Ryder clearly cared for her, but she was too afraid of
being truly hurt to let him in.

If Esme were going to take another chance on opening her heart, it would be to someone willing to risk that
fall in return. Maybe once she told Ryder how she felt, he
would open up, but she wasn't counting on it.

"Who am I kidding?" she asked Chase as she lifted him
into her arms. She couldn't help hoping and praying that
Ryder would love her in return. Esme had spent most of
her life immersing herself in fairy tales and love stories.
Was it so wrong to want one of her own? Sadly, yes if the
fairy tale turned into a nightmare, as it had in her family
growing up and with Seth.

The baby didn't appear to have an answer for her but
snuggled more closely into the crook of her neck. She
wanted both her sons to grow up in a happy home. There
were too many memories of her parents fighting and their
petty little wars of words, plus the affairs and backstab-
bing that had been so prevalent throughout her childhood.

Ryder had been nothing but kind, but she still didn't

know how to trust herself enough to trust him. It was safe enough to raise kids together, but she knew how being raised in a house filled with tension and animosity could impact a child.

Asa and Bea had done their best to protect Esme from the worst of it, and before becoming a mother, she would have claimed not to have been affected by the rancor that had filled her childhood home. But now, she wasn't only making choices for herself. Her decisions would have consequences for her children, and they deserved to see their parents content. She could be happy with Ryder if only she could trust him enough to give them a chance.

As the door to Chase's room opened, she expected to see Ryder enter. Instead, Freya walked in. Her great-aunt carried a giant stuffed bear with a blue bow tie around his neck.

Esme smiled and gestured her forward. "Good morning. I didn't expect to see you here."

Color stained Freya's cheeks. "I didn't expect to be here," the older woman admitted. "But I wanted to check on the baby and also see how you're doing after sleeping in a hospital room chair."

Esme wrapped her arms around the older woman. "I'm so glad you stopped by."

Freya was stiff for a few moments and then seemed to relax into the hug. It was clear that Elias's widow cared about Esme, her siblings and her cousins. Esme wanted to believe that as time passed, she'd continue to feel more comfortable about her role in each of their lives.

"My neck has seen better days." She rubbed the back of it with her free hand. "Would you like to hold him for a few minutes?"

"Oh, I'm sure he's happy in his mother's arms," Freya said.

"He'll be just as happy in yours," Esme promised. She

took the bear from the older woman and placed it in the bassinet, then gave Chase to Freya.

Freya's expression gentled as she glanced down at the baby. "It's still difficult to believe that the mix-up happened and nobody caught it." Her gaze sharpened on Esme. "Have you and Ryder discovered anything more?"

She shook her head. "No, but I'm not sure he's ready to give up the search. I wish I didn't feel like I should have been the one to realize it. How could I not recognize my own baby even with all the trauma and chaos surrounding that night?"

Freya traced a finger over the cleft in Chase's chin— the one he'd inherited from his father. "Love makes us see what we want to, even if it's not always the full breadth of the matter."

"That's true, and I trusted the staff at the hospital to get things right."

"Of course, you did," Freya agreed.

"Once again, I can't thank you enough. If you hadn't gifted me that DNA test, I'm not sure when or if we would have realized the switch happened. It's like I needed you to discover the truth. You truly are a gift in our lives, Freya."

Her great-aunt looked uncomfortable at the compliment. "I don't think you should give me all that much credit. I barely did a thing."

"But what you did changed my whole life," Esme assured her.

The woman's eyes widened in shock, but before she could answer, the door opened again.

"Hi." Ruby Ashwood, the young nursing assistant, popped her head into the room. "I heard one of your babies spent the night here."

Esme moved to stand behind the giant teddy bear propped up in the bassinet, feeling like she needed a shield between herself and the woman who'd so blatantly flirted with Ryder during their meeting.

"Ryder isn't here," she said, noticing that Freya gave her a funny look. "He's coming soon with Noah."

"Okay." Ruby nodded and stepped into the room. "How's that little guy?" She gestured toward Chase.

"On the mend, thankfully. You'll be relieved to know I spent the night with him because he's my priority."

"I know my comment came out badly." Ruby scrunched up her adorable button nose. "I don't have a great relationship with my mom, and I tend to project that on everyone else. I'm sorry." She blew out a breath. "My grandma raked me over the coals for making you feel bad, if that helps."

Esme thought about it and then offered Ruby a smile. "I suppose it does."

"The younger generation should listen to their elders," Freya murmured to Chase, although it was clear who the comment was meant for.

Ruby grinned at the older woman. "You must be Chase's grandma."

"No. I'm Freya Fortune. I'm…"

"His great-great-aunt," Esme explained. "Freya is the reason my siblings and I moved to Chatelaine."

Ruby whistled and grimaced slightly. "You must be really special. I don't know anyone who wants to come *to* this town, although I suppose things are getting better thanks to all the Fortunes moving here. But this place is still about as tiny as they come."

Esme laughed. "You haven't visited my hometown of Cave Creek."

"Can't say that I have," Ruby agreed.

"Chatelaine is a wonderful town," Freya insisted. "And

a great place to raise a family." She quickly glanced at Esme. "At least, that's what I've heard."

"I suppose." Ruby nodded. "My family has been here for generations. My great-uncle Joe died when that mine collapsed years ago. It took a toll on the whole town, almost like everyone was frozen in time, so it's nice to see new restaurants and shops opening."

"Like Remi's Reads," Esme supplied, still touched by the special evening Ryder had given her before everything had gone horribly awry.

"And your sister's restaurant," Freya added.

"The Cowgirl Café," Esme told Ruby. "You'll have to check it out when Bea has her grand opening in a couple of months."

"I will. Hey, Esme, no hard feelings about me giving my number to Ryder, right? It wasn't cool, I know, and not just because Nana lit me up. For the record, he never called."

Esme accepted the woman's apology without mentioning that she'd been the one to throw away the slip of paper.

"You look familiar," Ruby said to Freya, inclining her head as she studied the woman. "Have we met?"

"No," Freya answered definitively.

"She visited me in the hospital after Chase was born." Esme stepped out from behind the teddy bear and moved closer to her great-aunt, who seemed taken aback by Ruby's question. "You probably saw her then."

"Probably," the nursing assistant agreed. "Well, I've got to get back to the L and D unit. See you around, Esme. Nice to meet you, Freya Fortune."

"That girl was odd." Freya transferred Chase back to Esme's arms. "I don't think she's ever seen me before."

"Maybe you have a familiar face," Esme suggested.

Ryder walked in with Noah at that moment, and Freya made an excuse to leave almost immediately.

"Is she okay?" Ryder asked when it was just the two of them and the boys in the room.

"I think so." Esme's heart stuttered as Ryder studied her, then warmed as Noah wriggled in his carrier at the sound of her voice. She had about as much control over her heart as she did her tingling body where Ryder was concerned.

"Want to trade babies?" Ryder asked.

Esme gasped.

"I didn't mean it like that," he amended. "I'd like to hold Chase if that's okay?"

"Of course it is." She shook off the shock of his question. Something about the visit with Freya and Ruby had put her on edge even more than before.

"The nurse said she'd be in to finish his discharge papers within the next half hour."

"You had us worried, buddy." Ryder kissed Chase's forehead, then glanced up at Esme. "How are you doing?"

"I'm okay now that I know both of our boys are good. I'm also ready to go home and don't want anything like last night ever to happen again."

"We'll do our best to make sure it never does," he told her, even though she knew it was a promise he could not keep. "But no matter what, we'll get through it together."

"I'm sorry about last night. I was upset and had no right to take it out on you."

Esme had spent most of the night thinking about exactly that—her and Ryder together and what it meant for their future and that of their sons. There were no guarantees, but she also knew Chase and Noah had to be her number one priority, especially since she and Ryder had committed nothing to each other. It could impact the boys if she got too invested in their shared connection, and he lost interest.

She wished she had enough faith in herself to believe she was enough for him. They'd both been hurt by love and had a hard time trusting. That was undeniable, but Esme wanted more.

Even though she'd done her best not to have expectations or to put labels on their relationship, she loved Ryder Hayes with all of her heart. And if they kept on this path and her feelings weren't reciprocated, her heart could be shattered into a million pieces.

"I need to tell you something, Ryder." She looked around the sterile hospital room that had become so familiar to her in the last twelve hours. "Maybe I should wait, but I don't want to. I need to say it."

He nodded like he could read her mind. "I don't want to wait, either, Esme. I have something I need to tell you as well."

She couldn't decipher the mix of emotions in his green eyes, but was it too much to hope they had the same idea in mind? Should she wait and let him say it first?

No. She was ready to take this risk, and she didn't want him to think she was only doing it in response to his declaration. He needed to know it came from her soul.

"On the count of three, we say it together."

He looked slightly confused by her request but nodded.

"One, two, three," she counted, then drew in a breath and said, "I love you."

At the same time, he said, "We should get married."

It felt like a grenade went off inside her, shrapnel flying everywhere as she tried to make sense of his statement. While his words should've been a dream come true, something about his tone suggested he didn't feel the same way as her.

But before either of them could say anything more or respond to the other, the nurse walked into the room to discharge Chase.

CHAPTER FOURTEEN

RYDER WASN'T SURE he could have misread the situation with Esme more if he'd tried.

He sat on the sofa in their living room—her living room, technically—and stared straight ahead, unable to wrap his mind around the three little words she'd said to him.

I love you.

He'd honestly thought he had the perfect solution worked out for the two of them. Marriage would tie them together forever. Of course, he knew that plenty of marriages ended in divorce. His parents' bitter battle had been one for the ages.

But he was proposing they officially join their lives for entirely sensible reasons, taking out the complicated emotions that often sent couples spiraling. They wouldn't grow apart or fall out of love because, as he saw it, getting married was simply taking their practical arrangement to another level.

His idea would keep both of their hearts safe. He thought Esme understood that he couldn't let himself love again, but those three words and the look of hope in her eyes told a different story.

Neither of them had spoken on the way home about what they'd each said in the hospital room, and she'd immediately gone upstairs to put the boys down for a nap.

He thought they could just pretend none of this had happened, then cursed himself for being ten kinds of a fool.

There was no pretending, but Esme might understand if he could figure out a way to explain it.

He looked up as she descended the stairs, but instead of sitting next to him as was their custom, she chose the chair opposite the sofa. It wasn't as if they were that far apart, but to Ryder, it felt like an ocean between them.

Esme pulled her legs up, tucked them underneath her, then crossed her arms over her chest. "We need to talk about what we said at the hospital."

Rewind, a voice inside his head begged. *Do over. Forget any of it happened.* Ryder ignored that voice.

"I proposed marriage," he said, like she didn't remember.

"I told you I loved you," she countered, her voice strained.

"You can't. You shouldn't."

"I do." She uncrossed her arms and placed her hands on the arms of the chair, leaning forward. "And I think you love me, too."

For a moment, he couldn't breathe. "Marriage will solve our problems." It felt easier to ignore her statement, which couldn't be true. Not when he'd made the decision not to love again. Even his love for Chase and Noah terrified him, especially after Chase's health scare.

But kids were different. They were loyal to their parents, even when mistakes were made over and over. Ryder's family was proof positive of that.

Loving Esme would make him vulnerable in a way he couldn't comprehend.

"I don't think so," she said softly. "I spent most of my life dealing with my parents' unhappy marriage. By the end, they could barely tolerate each other, yet they refused to walk away. They certainly weren't in love anymore."

"Exactly." He nodded. "We're not going to bother with love."

She sniffed. "Is love such a bother?"

"You know it is. We both do. My parents hurt each other, too, and I swore I'd never do that to myself or someone else. But they did love each other at the start, which made it so much worse when things went bad. I heard my mom crying in her room when Dad didn't come home, and it broke my little-kid heart. If she hadn't loved him, maybe his betrayals wouldn't have hurt so much." He let out a deep breath. "And when I found out Steph was pregnant, I threw myself into loving her. Turned out it was more like falling on a bed of nails. Maybe she wouldn't have felt so trapped if I hadn't expected more from her. Without the pressure she felt, breaking free wouldn't have seemed so necessary."

Esme shook her head. "You can't blame yourself for Stephanie's death. We've talked about that, Ryder. You didn't force her into that car. I know you would have given her whatever space or support she needed."

He pressed his lips together and didn't respond. The rational side of his brain wanted to believe her, but it was hard to release the guilt that had lodged in his heart.

Esme studied him. "We can't pretend we have no feelings for each other."

"I don't want to pretend. I… I care about you, Esme. You're a great mom and a wonderful co-parenting partner. We get along great in everyday life and…" He glanced at the ceiling. "And at night. We've got a good thing going. There's no reason to mess it up with unnecessary labels."

Esme stared at him for several seconds, her greenish-gray eyes flashing like sparks danced inside them. "You don't think becoming husband and wife is a label? Because I've been in that kind of marriage, Ryder, and it almost broke me."

"This is different," he insisted. "We understand each other."

"Yes." She blinked as if to bank the fires burning in her gaze. "I think we do."

"This conversation is not going the way I wanted it to." Frustration pounded through him. "Can we go back to how things were last night, Esme? Before Chase—"

"We can't go back, and maybe we should have never started down this path in the first place."

The lack of emotion in her voice made his heart clench. Wasn't this what he'd feared in the first place—that she'd come to realize she never truly needed him?

"What are you saying?" he forced himself to ask. "Have you changed your mind about raising the boys together? Are you giving me some kind of ultimatum?"

It was a ridiculous accusation to lob at her. Still, memories flooded his brain of the times his father had complained about his mom and claimed that if she hadn't made so many demands, he wouldn't have been forced to repeatedly disappoint her.

Ryder didn't want to fail Esme, but clearly he already had.

"I would never jeopardize Chase's and Noah's happiness for my own benefit," she said with preternatural calm. "I hope you know that."

He nodded vigorously. "I do. I trust you." Ryder reminded himself they did not have the same toxic relationship as his parents. He and Esme would be able to work things out, provided they were both on the same page. "I just want—"

She held up a hand. "You've made it clear what you want, as well as the limits of what you can give. I'm willing to honor that for the sake of our sons."

The vise in his chest loosened slightly. "You won't regret marrying me," he assured her.

"I'm not talking about marriage. I married Seth believing I could make him love me if I tried hard enough. But that's not how love should work, Ryder. It needs to be freely given. I fell in love with you. It's not your fault. I didn't even mean it to happen, and like you said, I'm sure I'll get over it eventually, but not with how things are now. This house…"

She shook her head. "I think you need to move back to your apartment for the time being. You were right. We need to find a property that will allow us to live together but give each of us more privacy. The investigation into who was responsible for Chase and Noah being switched has taken priority, but I'm sure we can find something that will work for both of our needs."

Ryder wanted to tell her this house worked, even though buying a different one had been his idea. He needed Esme not to give up on him. "I don't understand. Everything was so good—"

"Was it?" She laughed without humor. "I suppose I thought so, too, but I believed the same thing when Seth and I got married. I guess that makes me the fool."

"You aren't a fool."

"Maybe I'm just a woman who isn't worth taking a risk to love." Her voice cracked on the last word, nearly gutting Ryder.

He didn't want to hurt Esme, yet he could see the tears shimmering in her beautiful eyes. He hadn't wanted things with Steph to go as badly as they did, yet he hadn't been able to stop that either.

Maybe he was cursed in a different way than his father and brother. Maybe his inability to love someone in the right way made him just as toxic as the other men in his family.

"Do you want me to go now?" As awful as this conversation was and the fallout from it would be, he still didn't want to leave her. She called herself a fool, but he was the bigger idiot.

"It's best for now. I think we both need a little time. But I don't want to keep you from either of the boys. We'll figure out how to successfully co-parent without having a romantic relationship. Come back around dinnertime," she told him. "Bea brought over a few meals for the freezer, so we can have dinner as a fam… We can have dinner together."

"If that's how you want it." He couldn't keep the disappointment from his gaze, so he didn't try.

"It isn't how I want it." She swiped a hand across her cheeks. "I told you I love you, Ryder. I want more than this. It's stupid and naive, but—"

"You want the fairy tale."

"No. I want real life, and I also want a true partnership. I want somebody brave enough to love me in return through the good times, laughter and moments like last night that frighten the heck out of us. I want passion and to butt heads and not to strive to meet some arbitrary standards I don't even understand."

She nodded as if willing him to be the man she needed. "But I don't want convenience. I won't settle for less than what I deserve. At the end of the day, my sons need to see their mother happy. Being with you has been wonderful for so many reasons, but a marriage of convenience isn't enough."

Unfortunately, it was all Ryder had to offer her.

He stood, his entire body itching to take her into his arms. Yet he didn't touch her. He had no right to anymore. "I'll see you later. Call or text if you need anything."

The smile she gave him broke his heart all over again. "I wish you were willing to give me what I need."

"I do, too," he agreed and walked away.

"I'M GOING TO *kill* him," Bea said the following morning as they walked along the path that circled Lake Chatelaine. "It's going to be slow and painful."

Esme adjusted her grip on the double stroller's handle and glanced over the top to make sure both boys were still content and cozy, bundled in blankets and protected from the wind by a plastic cover. "You can't kill him. He's the father of my babies."

"One of them." Anger darkened Bea's voice.

"Don't say that." Esme shook her head. "Would you want someone to suggest that I'm not Chase's real mom? Ryder is Noah's father, and no matter what happens between us, that won't change."

"I know." Bea let out a sigh. "I'm sorry. My comment was uncalled for. I know the babies belong to both of you, but seeing you hurt makes me so upset."

"It's my own fault." Esme hated to admit it, but she couldn't deny the truth. "Ryder and I made a deal. We were going to be friends and co-parents. I had rules, and I broke the unspoken one. The most important rule, as it turned out." The cold wind whipped up from the lake as if chastising her for her weakness.

"He broke the rules as much as you."

Esme appreciated her sister's loyalty but only had herself to blame for her broken heart. "I fell in love with him. I didn't mean to—it happened effortlessly, which I thought changed the rules."

"You were happy with him. He's a good father. Plus, you went through something traumatic together. Not many people can say they started a relationship because their babies were switched at birth."

"That's the whole point." Esme paused for a moment and looked up toward the pale blue sky. She needed to get a hold of her emotions. It wouldn't do her or the babies any good if she continued to be so undone by her feelings for Ryder.

"I was the one who suggested our arrangement. I came up with the rules. He didn't need them because he wasn't going to fall in love with me."

Bea placed a hand on Esme's arm. "You don't believe that. You told me you think he loves you. You said you told him that."

"Doesn't that make me an even bigger fool? Even if he feels something more, he's smart enough to focus on the boys."

"He proposed marriage to you. Marrying somebody you don't love is *not* smart. Our parents were proof of that. If he loves you, he needs to man up and admit it."

"It's too late," Esme said sadly and began walking again. Moving kept her from wallowing in her sadness. "Now I'd think he was just saying it to appease me. I don't want to be handled, Bea."

It would be difficult to be near Ryder and accept that their relationship would not be the same as it had been before. But if she focused on the practical aspects of caring for the babies, it made their long future together seem slightly more bearable.

"We're going to look at properties at the end of the week. There are a couple that have main houses plus a guest house. One is a ranch house in the gated community with two primary suites with private entrances." She took a steadying breath, then added, "So if he brings someone home…"

"If Ryder Hayes brings a woman home to spend the night in the house he's sharing with the woman raising his kids, then he is not the man I believe him to be."

Esme frowned. "You're the one who warned me about the Hayes men. Why would it come as a surprise to you?"

"Because I've seen the way that man looks at you. It is not the look of a guy who wants to date other women."

"I can't let myself think like that. You and Asa warned me for years about believing the stories I read in books. Maybe I should have paid more attention."

"You are the hopeful Fortune." Bea placed an arm around Esme's shoulder. "And there's no one more deserving of a happily-ever-after than you. I'm sorry that Ryder is too scared or chicken to give it to you, but I don't want you to stop believing."

How could Esme keep believing when each time she did, it left her with a broken heart? She'd been angry after discovering Seth's betrayal, but her sadness from ending things with Ryder was more profound. The loss of him felt woven into her DNA.

"Do you remember when I was eight years old and fell out of the tree, and the branch got lodged in my arm?"

"Yes, like it was yesterday." Bea sounded surprised at the sudden change in topic. "It's when we realized Dad was afraid of blood. You came in with that thing sticking out of the back of your body, and he nearly passed out."

"Mom and Dad were good at making things about them."

Bea smiled. "That's a nice way to put it."

"You bandaged me up," Esme reminded her. "I still have a scar. Because it's on the back of my arm, I don't often notice it. Sometimes out of habit, I run my finger along the ridge. I feel like that's what my heartache from Ryder will become—a scar that's always with me. I kind of hope so." She sighed wistfully. "I remember the pain of that fall, but I also remember your sweetness in that moment. I want to think about the sweet times I shared with Ryder. I don't want to hold on to the sorrow or bitterness at what could have been. That doesn't do Chase and Noah any good."

"You are one of the best people I know," Bea told her, admiration and deep affection glittering in her eyes.

"For years, you thought I was just a twerpy little kid," Esme said with a laugh. "We also have Chatelaine to thank for bringing us closer together."

"Do you think we owe any of that thanks to Edgar and Elias?" Bea asked.

"Not at all. Even I'm not *that* generous."

They both laughed. "Speaking of which, I saw Wendell in the diner the other day," Bea told her. "He and Freya were talking about mystery miner number fifty-one. He really thinks that note on the back of the castle was more than just someone stirring up trouble. Freya seemed pretty bothered by the possibility."

"The same thing happened when I talked to them about it. I don't like to think about anything upsetting her," Esme said, "but I understand. She knows her husband holds some responsibility for fifty deaths, and maybe the thought of one more being added to the count is too much."

"That's understandable," Bea agreed. "I wish she didn't feel responsible for making reparations. She was nowhere near Chatelaine when everything happened at the mine."

"I think as much as Freya is helping us, we're also helping her."

Bea looked skeptical. "By spending Uncle Elias's money so she doesn't have to?"

"No, silly." Esme rolled her eyes. "It's not about the money."

"Then what is it about?"

"We're helping her let go of the past and move forward. It's what I tried to do by taking the risk of telling Ryder I loved him. Too bad it didn't work out for me."

"I think it's working out for Freya," Bea said. "If that makes you feel any better."

Esme thought about that and then nodded. "Despite having my heart broken all over again, I don't regret any of the choices I made with Ryder."

"You'd sleep with him all over again?" her sister asked.

"Oh, I definitely don't regret that."

Bea chuckled. "And you think you can stay platonic with him?"

"I have to," Esme said with a sigh. "Whether he truly loves me and is too afraid to admit it, or his heart was irreparably damaged by his past hurt, I guess I'll never know. But I'm going to do what's right for my babies."

"Let's plan a trip to Remi's Reads soon," Bea suggested. "I think you're going to have a lot of long nights to fill."

Esme groaned and then hugged her sister. "That's the truth."

CHAPTER FIFTEEN

THE FOLLOWING FIVE days were hell for Ryder. True to her word, Esme continued to be cordial and seemingly willing to share the parental duties with him, but that was no comfort given how difficult he found it to be near her without the closeness they'd so recently shared.

It went beyond the physical, although he yearned to touch and hold her. Even more, he felt the loss of the small smiles she'd seemed to save just for him. He missed how he could talk to her about anything, from the details of his day at the office to random bits of news he heard around town.

Gone were the quiet nights of sitting next to her on the sofa, each of them engrossed in their own book, and the nightly ritual of putting the boys down as a team with the two of them joining together to sing their babies a lullaby, either his favorite Bruce selections or the classics she was teaching him.

Although she invited him to dinner each night, it wasn't the same. She usually had some excuse for not eating with him and suggested they take turns handling bedtime for Chase and Noah.

Ryder felt as though he were the one being handled, and he didn't like it one bit. But he kept a smile on his face when he was with her because the alternative of navigating the change in their relationship seemed to be fully disengaging and dividing their time with the boys.

That was the worst thing he could imagine, not just

because of his own experience as a child of divorce. He didn't want to lose the connection he and Esme shared, even though it felt as though the future he wanted was slipping through his fingers.

A knock at the door startled him. It was almost ten in the morning, but he'd called the office earlier to say he was working from home. He hadn't told anyone that he and Esme were now living apart. It would have to come out sooner than later, but he didn't want to see pity or disappointment in the eyes of the people who knew him best. And pretending that everything was okay for the past few days at the office had been excruciating, which was why the work-from-home scenario seemed a viable option.

He got up from the small desk that sat against the back wall of his kitchen and went to answer the door. His mail was still being delivered to Esme's, but it could be one of his neighbors or an errant package.

"What the hell have you done?" his father asked by way of a greeting when Ryder opened the door.

"Hey, Dad." Ryder ran a hand through his unwashed hair and wished he'd changed into something besides the T-shirt and athletic shorts he'd slept in. "This is a surprise."

Chandler wore a bright white oxford and tan wool pants instead of his usual dark-colored slacks, a nod to casual Fridays at the office. "I'm sure it's not as big of a surprise as I had. I stopped by Esme Fortune's house this morning."

"Why were you at Esme's? I thought you were in Dallas and Phoenix until the beginning of next week."

The company had recently purchased a property in Arizona nestled in the foothills of the Sedona mountains. Although his father hadn't been scheduled to oversee the transition to a new management team, he'd decided to parlay an overnight trip to Dallas into a week in Arizona.

Ryder had assumed the trip was partially prompted by

Chandler's avoidance of Esme and Chase. He didn't know why his dad was so reluctant to meet his second grandson and Esme, but the subtle rejection stung, so he'd stopped issuing invitations.

Didn't it figure that his dad chose the week that Ryder's life imploded to show back up like he'd been ready to take an active interest all along?

"Your timing is absolutely perfect, given how my life is going right now."

Chandler raised a heavy brow. "Are you going to invite me in, or am I interrupting you watching the morning talk shows?"

Ryder laughed despite the joke falling flat. "As a matter of fact, I just got off the phone with one of the vendors negotiating a new contract. No need to paint me as an underachiever, Dad. I might not have Brandon's slick manner, but the label doesn't fit."

Esme had taught Ryder that he shouldn't have to change who he was to win his father's approval, and he'd be forever grateful for her faith in him.

His dad walked into the apartment and glanced around. "Her house is a hell of a lot homier."

"Agreed. I've got coffee and some stale muffins from the grocery if you want breakfast."

Chandler patted his trim stomach. "Esme made me an omelet while I visited with my grandsons. It was delicious."

"Of course she did," Ryder muttered. Omelets were her specialty. Their routine had been to take turns cooking breakfast on weekend mornings. Omelets on her day and pancakes or waffles when he was in charge of the meal.

"Chase looks like you," Chandler observed as he sat on one of the leather stools in front of the small island.

"You knew that. I texted plenty of pictures, even if you weren't interested in meeting him."

His father's shoulders stiffened. "I'm not sure if you've noticed," he said slowly, "but I haven't had the easiest time accepting that I'm getting on in years. Being old enough to be a grandfather doesn't exactly impress the ladies."

Ryder wasn't sure if his dad expected him to sympathize, but it had been a crappy week, and he wasn't in the mood to be placating.

"Perhaps it wouldn't be such an issue if you dated women anywhere close to your own age."

His dad laughed and nodded. "You have a valid point, son. Speaking of that, I met someone in Florida a couple of weeks ago. She's a year older than me and out of my league in every way."

"Sounds promising."

Chandler flashed a goofy grin that looked out of place on his serious face. "She is interested in your situation and impressed that I raised a son willing to step up for two children."

A new girlfriend might explain his father's interest in finally meeting Chase and Esme—if the two of them could help him make a good impression on a woman.

"I can see by your face that you don't trust my intentions, and that's also well deserved. But I think it could get serious with Lynda. I convinced her to meet me in Arizona, and I'm hoping she'll come to Texas for bluebonnet season."

"I guess we'll see what happens," Ryder conceded, unsure how to behave with this kinder, gentler version of his father.

"We sure will. In the meantime, the way Lynda talks about the joy her grandchildren bring to her life made me rethink my feelings about being involved in both my grandsons' lives."

Despite the ongoing struggles with his father, Ryder

couldn't deny that he wanted Chandler to get to know Chase and Noah.

"I appreciate you making an effort to meet them, Dad… and I don't know how much Esme told you. But things are strained between us at the moment." He blew out a breath. "The fact is, I'm going to need your support. Now more than ever."

"If that's the case, why did I have to hear about the change in your living status from her? Does your brother know? I haven't talked to Brandon since I've been back."

"I haven't told anyone. It's humiliating."

"Hayes men don't deal well with humiliation."

"I suppose." Ryder grabbed his empty coffee mug from the desk and then went to the counter to refill it. "I make terrible coffee compared to Esme. Can I offer you a cup?"

His father nodded. "I'd love some awful coffee. Esme wasn't exactly forthcoming with details. She simply told me the two of you have decided it would be best to live separately until you find a place that gives each of you more privacy. There's nothing humiliating about making an arrangement you didn't ask for work. However you can."

Ryder poured the coffee, then took the carton of half-and-half out of the refrigerator. He poured a generous dollop into his cup. Chandler took his coffee black —like his soul, Ryder used to think when he watched his father gulp down pots of the bitter brew as a child. Now he could see his dad as human, flaws and all, but not the villain Ryder had made him out to be.

"I asked her to marry me," he said after a long sip. "She said no, just like Steph did, so that's the second time I've proposed marriage and been rejected."

"Third time's a charm?" his father suggested with a wry smile.

"Oh, no. There won't be another time. I've learned my lesson. You always told me the Hayes men weren't meant for love, and I think I've proved it more than once."

"Do you love Esme Fortune?"

Had he inadvertently mentioned love? Ryder's heart pounded in his chest. He hadn't meant to say the *L* word. "I should have said the Hayes men are terrible at relationships."

Chandler lifted the cup to his lips, grimacing after taking a drink. "You weren't kidding about brewing horrible coffee. It reminds me of the kind I make. But this business with Esme is different than the mistakes I made with women. Your mom, in particular. Things got tangled up with her, and I couldn't right them."

"Did you ever try?"

"At first," his father asserted. "You were too young to remember, I suppose. But not as much as I could have or should have. Your mother and I married young. She got pregnant immediately, and your brother came a year later. My business was starting to take off, and to be honest, I wasn't ready to settle down."

Chandler put his cup on the counter and shrugged. "So I didn't. It wasn't right, but I can't change the past. You're not like me, Ryder. Me or your brother. You're built like your mother. You were made for commitment. You're steady and sure."

Heat clawed its way up Ryder's neck. He wasn't confident he deserved his father's praise and wasn't used to receiving it.

"You might think I'm built for a serious relationship, but I can't find anyone willing to commit. I should have learned my lesson when Steph crushed my heart."

"Did she truly crush it all that badly? From the bit I

saw, the two of you had been tumultuous from the start, and weren't you on a break when she found out she was pregnant?"

Ryder inclined his head. "Yes, but everything changed when she got pregnant. No offense, Dad, but I saw what a loveless marriage looks like for too many years. I decided I was going to love her, and I did. It wasn't enough."

"Son, I've made more than my fair share of mistakes with women over the years, but even I know you can't make yourself love somebody if the feelings aren't there."

Ryder started to bite off a peevish retort, then stopped and thought about his father's words. Had he been in love with Stephanie, or had he been in love with the idea of having a family of his own, one that he could show the care and feeling that his parents had never given to their marriage? He'd been absolutely gutted when she died in the accident, but most of that sadness came from her life being cut short and for his son, who would never know his mother.

"Besides, if you are so dead-set against a loveless marriage," his father continued, "then explain to me again why you proposed to Esme. It seemed like the two of you were rubbing along fine without the shackles of a wedding ceremony." Chandler gave a mock shudder. "I don't think you could pay me enough to walk down the aisle again, not that anyone would have me. Anyone worth marrying."

"I didn't want to lose her," Ryder admitted. "Something about walking away from her and Chase when only one parent was allowed to stay overnight at the hospital got to me. I had an overwhelming desire to bind myself to her."

He paused, then added, "But it wasn't done out of love. After Stephanie, I vowed not to let myself love again. I proposed to Esme because I want to build a life together."

"I think you love her," his father said. "And it scares the hell out of you. Which is a trait, unfortunately, that you inherited from me."

"You know, she said something similar. Not about me being afraid but the fact that she thinks I love her and won't admit it. It's ridiculous, and too bad she wouldn't talk about it with you. The two of you could have had quite a laugh at my expense. You tell me I don't love the woman I thought I loved, but I do love the woman I can't allow myself to love."

His father looked pained. "I wouldn't laugh at this situation. I hate that you're hurting and confused. I'm not used to it, Ryder. You always know exactly what to say and do. You're the man with the plan, and we've come to rely on you for that."

"It would appear that either Esme didn't get the memo or that she's unimpressed by my plan."

He lifted the mug to his mouth again, then turned and dumped the coffee into the sink. More caffeine was the last thing he needed. He was already too wired. "It'll work out, Dad. Don't worry about me. I've got my priorities straight."

"I know you do." His father drew one finger along the edge of the counter as if contemplating something serious. "Speaking of priorities, the situation with Esme is not the only reason I'm here."

This was the moment Ryder had been both waiting for and dreading. Chandler had promised to announce his successor at Hayes Enterprises by the end of the month. Despite the weeks Ryder had taken off recently and the fact that he couldn't put in the hours his brother did because being a father came first, he knew he contributed to the company. But he wasn't confident that would be enough to win the CEO position.

"You've made your decision," he said.

Chandler nodded with a smile playing around the corners of his mouth that looked almost smug, which felt unnecessary.

"It's fine, Dad." Ryder rubbed a hand along the back of his neck. "Rip the Band-Aid off. My week can't get any worse."

"Interesting attitude." Chandler's smile widened slightly. "Can it get better?"

It felt like time stood still for an instant.

"Definitely," Ryder answered.

"You and your brother bring different qualities to the table. Your leadership and vision can't be denied, and the staff has complete faith in you."

That sounded promising.

"Your brother, on the other hand, is a gifted negotiator and has the magic touch with our investors. He thrives on travel and meeting new people, so he can function at any of our properties like he's been part of a team for years."

Why did Ryder feel like he was on a dating show he hadn't signed up for, waiting with bated breath to see if he'd be given the final rose?

"Who will make a better CEO?" He didn't bother to clarify that his father was simply making this decision based on his own opinion—because his was the only perspective that mattered.

"I'd like to appoint you as co-CEOs." Chandler held his hands like a maestro directing a symphony orchestra.

Ryder blinked. "You want Brandon and me to work *together*?" He cleared his throat. "Doing the same job?"

"That's the idea behind naming both of you to a CEO role."

"What's the catch? Have you made a deal with a reality show to film us trying to take each other down?" Ryder practically shouted the accusation. He'd just started to repair his relationship with Brandon. He refused to be pitted against his brother once again.

"No." His father shook his head and rose from the chair, pacing to the edge of the kitchen and then back. "Of all the mistakes I made, fostering that inherent competition between you and Brandon is the one I most regret. You remember me telling you that my brother, Tom, died my senior year of college?"

Ryder nodded. "He was killed in the line of duty."

"A true hero," Chandler said with a nod. "He was two years younger than me, and I wanted nothing to do with him. We played different sports, had separate groups of friends and refused to share our toys. It was so stupid, and once he was gone, I realized how much I missed him. I thought we could keep you close by encouraging—and sometimes demanding—that you and Brandon were interested in the same things, even if you were competing."

"It did *not* keep us close." Ryder laughed softly. "You had to see that, Dad."

"I figured the two of you arguing and vying for the same prizes was better than if you ignored each other, but I've never been great with appropriate emotions or ways of demonstrating them."

Ryder searched for the resentment he usually felt toward his dad but couldn't find it, which felt like its own sort of prize, even more than the CEO position. "Me, neither," he admitted. "But I guess we can both learn." He liked the idea of working with Brandon instead of against him.

Chandler moved closer and pulled Ryder in for a hug. "I don't have a lot of room to give advice on women, son, but I have no doubt Esme Fortune is worth whatever it takes. I hope you can work things out with her."

"Thanks, Dad." Ryder smiled, but it felt more like a grimace. He agreed with his father, but that didn't mean he had it in him to be the man she deserved.

CHAPTER SIXTEEN

"YOU DO KNOW that searching for your dream house is supposed to be a happy event?" Lily placed a hand on Esme's arm. "You look like you're about to throw up."

Esme tried for a smile, but it didn't quite take. She'd come to GreatStore to meet up with Lily during her friend's lunch break. They sat in the corner of the café with Esme's laptop open, looking at the two properties she and Ryder were scheduled to tour the following day.

The boys were with him this morning because his father had invited them over for Saturday brunch to celebrate his dad's decision to name Ryder and Brandon co-CEOs of Hayes Enterprises.

Ryder promised that the invitation had also been extended to her, but she'd declined, using the excuse of having plans with a friend. And then she'd quickly had to make plans. It was imperative that she spend as little time as possible with Ryder because every minute they were together chipped away at another piece of her heart.

Not only that, but she also liked Brandon, and more surprisingly, their father. Allowing herself to become close to the Hayes men felt like establishing more bonds that could potentially be broken down the road. She'd taken an immediate shine to Chandler Hayes when he'd stopped by her house. From everything Ryder told her, she hadn't expected to find his intimidating father also charming and sweet, but Chandler had been instantly enamored with Chase, who looked more like his daddy with each passing week.

Chandler displayed the same amount of affection for Noah, and the quickest way to win Esme over was kindness toward both her babies. Maybe she should blame them for the fact that she'd fallen in love with Ryder, although the reason why didn't matter at this point. Her current dilemma was figuring out how to make herself fall *out* of love with him.

"Neither of these is my dream house." She blinked rapidly and tried to pretend like she wasn't on the verge of tears. "The good news is either will be great for raising boys." She tapped on the laptop screen. "One of them even has a barn on the property. Asa has already threatened to get Chase and Noah ponies for their first birthday."

Lily laughed. "That sounds like Asa. He sure does love horses, especially Major. He talks about that animal the way proud parents coming into the baby department talk about their children."

"Yeah," Esme agreed. "Major has been with him a long time. The horse is his best friend and possibly the love of his life."

Lily made a face. "The love of his life, huh? That's interesting, to say the least."

Esme smiled despite her aching heart. "Thank you for spending your lunch hour looking at houses with me. I know I should be grateful that Ryder is such a good father to the boys and willing to go in on a house with me. It will make it easier to share parenting duties."

Lily waved as one of her coworkers walked by. As usual on a weekend, the store was crowded, although Esme was glad the Valentine's Day decorations had been taken down. Every time she thought about the perfect date she'd shared with Ryder at Remi's Reads, it made her wish things had turned out differently.

"I don't think it's necessarily easy to be friends with someone when you secretly want more," Lily said softly, and Esme caught the wistful edge in her friend's voice.

"You're right." Esme kept her gaze on the laptop screen. "But I don't regret telling Ryder how I feel. I heard Wendell say that secrets cause more trouble than they're worth, and I agree."

"But when he didn't know, you weren't hurt," Lily countered.

"I also wasn't happy, not completely anyway. Falling in love with Ryder was a gift, even though it didn't turn out the way I wanted. I thought that a disastrous marriage had ruined my heart." She rubbed two fingers against her chest, covered by the oversize sweatshirt she wore. "But it was still there, bruised but not broken. That's a powerful thing to know about myself. It will take a while, but I'll heal from this heartbreak, too. I have to for the sake of my boys."

"Do you think you'll be ready to date again soon?"

Esme laughed and vehemently shook her head. "Oh, no. I still believe in love, but there's no point in fooling myself. It's going to take a long time to get over Ryder Hayes, if I *ever* do."

"Maybe there's still a chance for the two of you," Lily suggested. "After all, you'll be with him more than you won't." She hit the arrow key to move through the interior photos of one of the potential houses. "Even if you're sleeping on opposite ends of a house. I just wish you could find your dream home. Loving where you live feels important somehow."

Esme drew in a deep breath. "Funny you mention that." She moved the computer's cursor to the browser icon and scrolled to one of her previous searches. "It's not the right house for Ryder and me to share given our current circumstances, but…"

She shifted closer to her friend. "Take a look at this house. It popped up as a new listing yesterday. I'm not sure why it showed up in my search."

Her stomach felt tied in knots as she read the property's description out loud to Lily. Esme had looked at it so many times since the house came on the market the previous day, she practically knew it by heart. "'Turn of the century charm meets modern luxury. This four bedroom, five bath, old homestead ranch stunner has a gourmet kitchen that will welcome family and friends alike. The main-floor primary bedroom has his and her walk-in closets with an en suite bathroom that boasts a steam shower and double vanity. Each of the second-floor bedrooms includes connected bathrooms, high ceilings and window seats perfect for enjoying the view of the open plains.'"

"Is that a library?" Lily asked, grinning at Esme as she pointed at the screen. "It would be perfect for you."

"Can you believe it? If someone had built the house I dreamed of when I was a girl, this would be it. Only I'm not a little girl anymore." She swiped at her cheeks when a few errant tears spilled over. "I know I shouldn't want the fantasy. My heart was frozen after my marriage ended, but it melted for Ryder. I'm not going to close it off again, even if love isn't in the cards for me right now."

"I wish it were," Lily told her with a sympathetic smile.

"It's okay. I should be grateful for the happiness I do have. Chase's health scare showed me that I can't take the good things in my life for granted."

"Of course not," Lily agreed. "You would never do that, but it's also okay to want some things for yourself."

"I wanted Ryder, and that blew up in my face."

"Ryder is an idiot," Lily said simply, and Esme threw an arm around her friend's shoulder.

"That's just what I needed to hear. But I'm in charge of my own happiness and always have been. I've always managed to find a way to be happy." She released a wistful sigh. "And so what if my dream house is for sale in the town that feels like home to me. I'll just use a spare bedroom in whatever house we buy to create my own library."

"That's right. You *are* in charge of your destiny, Esme Fortune."

"What's all this talk about destiny?"

Lily jumped about three feet in the air, and Esme snapped shut the laptop as Asa took a seat across from the two of them.

"What are you lovely ladies doing today?" Asa tapped a finger on the laptop case. "You closed that pretty quickly, little sis. Don't tell me you're setting up your online dating profile already. No, wait. Do tell me because it would serve Ryder Hayes right to have to watch you go out with another man so soon after he mucked up his chance with you."

"Asa, I'm not—"

"I can help weed out the weirdos if you want. Here's a hint, if a guy poses with his guinea pig, both of them dressed in leather chaps, he's probably not the man for you."

Esme and Lily laughed at Asa's silly joke.

"I'm not planning to date anytime soon," she assured her brother. She couldn't imagine any man filling the Ryder-size hole in her heart. But as she'd told Lily, Esme was grateful that these past few weeks had shown her she could love again. She hadn't been sure that was possible but now hoped her heart would eventually mend again.

"Besides, I don't think you have any room to talk. Right,

Lily? Asa would probably make his profile picture a selfie of him and Major."

Lily, who normally had no problem joking with Esme, seemed a bit tongue-tied at the moment.

"Major is a fine horse," she said softly.

Esme groaned while her brother reached across the table to high-five her friend.

"He's the best," Asa agreed. "I'm not joining any matchmaking sites. I don't exactly have trouble finding my own dates, if you know what I mean."

"Just trouble keeping them around," Esme teased, then lightly kicked his shin under the table. *"Love 'em and leave 'em cowboy* would be your perfect online username."

"I always leave them happy." Asa wiggled his brows. "Very happy, for the record."

Lily had lifted the cup of coffee she'd ordered to her lips and choked on the sip she'd just taken.

"Stop that," Esme scolded her brother. "You're going to make my friend upchuck, and my corneas are burning at that mental image."

Asa chuckled and handed Lily a napkin. "Sorry about that."

"No problem," she said, her voice strained.

"On the subject of happy…" Asa pumped a fist in the air. "I think I've finally convinced Val that I'm the ideal buyer for the dude ranch."

Esme felt her eyes widen. "That's great news, but you must be losing your touch if she's not agreed to sell to you already."

"I know, right?" Asa agreed good-naturedly. "But it's going to be worth all the effort I've put in when it's finally mine. The Chatelaine Dude Ranch is special."

"Very special." Lily's smile was tinged with sadness. Esme patted her friend's arm, then shifted her gaze to Asa.

"Did you know Lily's family visited the dude ranch when she was a baby?"

Asa frowned like he was trying to place that conversation. "I think you mentioned that," he told Lily.

"I don't have specific memories," she said, holding tight to the coffee cup. "My sisters and I were only ten months old at the time. But I know the dude ranch was a special place even back then. I'm sure once you make it your own, it's going to be really great again."

Esme felt like there was something her friend wasn't sharing about her memories of the dude ranch. Lily's explanation seemed to satisfy Asa, however, who whipped out his phone and began describing the plans he had for the property to the two of them.

Lily nodded and offered words of encouragement, making Esme wonder once again why some great guy hadn't fallen for this sweet woman. Although she had no basis to act as an expert on love at this point, Esme thought any man would be lucky to have Lily love him.

When her lunch break was over, Lily said goodbye before returning to the baby section, and Esme and Asa walked out to the parking lot together. It was a chilly day, although the sun was out. Esme lifted her head to bask in the warmth of it.

"Are you sure you're okay?" Asa asked, gently nudging her. "I know the situation with Ryder has been tough. I'll still kick his butt if you want."

"No need for that," she assured her brother. "I'll be fine. Chatelaine is my home now, and no matter what happens with Ryder and me, that isn't going to change. I'll manage, and I can't wait to see you and Bea achieve your dreams."

"With significant monetary help from Freya Fortune," Asa added wryly.

"I hope as time goes by she starts to feel close to us in

more ways than just financially. It was nice of her to help with Noah when Chase was in the hospital, although she seemed freaked out in the Grammy Freya role."

"She'll get there, Es. I'm glad you're doing okay, given everything you've been through." He squeezed her shoulder. "For the record, I highly recommend steering clear of love. It's a lot easier."

She patted his cheek. "One day, Asa, I hope you'll see that even the hard parts are worth it." At least, that was what she was determined to believe.

RYDER SAT ON one of the leather recliners in his father's giant family room with Noah nestled against his chest. Brandon sat on the matching couch, bouncing Chase on his knee as the baby gurgled happily.

He and his brother made eye contact at the sound of their father laughing from the kitchen, where he'd excused himself to take a call from his new girlfriend, Lynda.

"He sounds giddy," Brandon said, making a face. "It's not right."

Ryder chuckled and stroked a hand over Noah's back. He knew someday his sons would be too big and rambunctious to nap on dear old Dad's lap, so he was going to savor every moment.

"He sounds happy, which is a definite change. I think it's a good one."

Brandon nodded. "Dad's a lot happier than you, given the recent change in your living situation." He lifted Chase to eye level. "Can you explain to me, little one, why your adoring uncle Brandon had to hear from Grandpa about Daddy royally messing up with Mommy?

"Because Daddy is an idiot." Brandon answered his own question in a childlike voice as if it were Chase speaking.

"Very funny," Ryder muttered. "But no son of mine will call me an idiot."

"Both of them will eventually call you worse if you don't patch things up with Esme."

"Not that it's any of your business, *Uncle Brandon*, or that you have any room to talk when it comes to long-term relationships, but there's nothing to patch up. Esme and I are fine."

"Dude, you look miserable, especially given that we are finally getting a chance to make our mark on Hayes Enterprises and doing it together. I know it's not the thought of working with me that has you perpetually scowling."

Ryder rolled his eyes. "Are you sure?"

Brandon flipped him a middle finger accompanied by a wide smile. "You were always too serious, but she lightened you up, Ry. Esme did a whole world of good in your life. And being my co-CEO is probably the best thing that ever happened to you career-wise."

"So modest, but right back at you," Ryder said with an attempt at laughter that sounded more like a grunt. "Besides, Esme is still a part of my life. It's just different. We're going to look at properties tomorrow, so once we close on a new place, we'll move in, and then it will feel normal again."

"Only *different* isn't good in this case," his brother insisted. "You aren't happy, Ryder."

"I'm fine."

Brandon sat up straighter and pulled Chase close to his chest as he stared at Ryder. "I can't decide if you're just lying to me or if you hope to convince yourself to believe the lie as well. Listen to Dad in there. If he can pull it out after all these years, then you've got a great chance of fixing things with Esme."

He shook his head. "How am I supposed to fix things

with a woman who doesn't want me? I don't know why everybody thinks this is my fault. She's the one who ended it with me. I wanted to marry her."

"She wanted you to love her."

Nerves skittered through Ryder like centipedes crawling over his skin. Unable to sit still, he rose from the chair and started pacing back and forth. Noah made a sound of protest before settling back against his chest again.

"You know I can't do that. I tried to love Steph, and it made things worse. Why would I risk that with Esme? She's too important. I lo..." He shook his head. "Never mind."

Brandon pointed at Ryder, then touched the tip of his finger to his nose. "That's it exactly. You were going to say you love her."

"Was not," Ryder muttered.

"You *love* her," Brandon repeated, "and you don't even have to try. It just happened. You weren't planning on it, and it scares you. I get that."

"How do you get it?" Ryder demanded. "You ever been in love?"

Brandon shook his head and looked uncharacteristically somber. "No, but I'd like to experience it, especially with somebody as well suited to me as Esme is to you. Don't you see? This is the ultimate prize."

Ryder shot him a glare. "Wait. Are you saying that I've screwed it up, so now you're going to try to make a move on Esme? Because that's a terrible idea, Bran."

"First, I'm offended you would suggest that, although I understand my history with your girlfriends isn't stellar. I wouldn't do something like that now, and even if I did, Esme is head over heels in love with you, buddy. I've seen how she looks at you and how giddy she gets when you smile at her. At least admit to yourself that you love her too because it's pretty dang obvious to the rest of us."

Ryder could hardly breathe around the emotion swelling in his chest. "Of course, I love her," he said quietly. "But what good does it do me other than create the potential for experiencing more pain? This can't just be about the two of us. The boys are involved, so if I mess it up, there's way more at stake than my heart. The last thing I want is to hurt her or our sons."

"I hate to be the one to break it to you, bro. But that train has left the station. You did hurt her, but she's willing to put aside her feelings for the sake of Chase and Noah. Imagine what could happen if you took the risk. It's not going to get worse, but it sure could get a hell of a lot better if you tell her how you feel and stop letting fear run the show."

Ryder closed his eyes and let the fear wash over him. His fear of being hurt and being rejected—of being alone. But the biggest fear of all was losing Esme.

What if she met somebody else? What if he had to watch her with another guy?

Noah wriggled in his arms, and he wondered if the baby could feel Ryder's heart thundering in his chest. "Am I the biggest idiot on the planet?" Ryder asked the baby.

"Quite possibly," Brandon answered in his pretend child's voice.

"Rhetorical question," he muttered.

"The better question is, what are you going to do about it?"

Chandler walked into the room at that moment. "What did I miss?" he demanded as his gaze moved between his sons.

"I love Esme," Ryder said quietly.

"Yes, I know, son." His father nodded. "It's about time you figured it out."

And now that he had, Ryder needed to find a way to convince her to give him another chance.

CHAPTER SEVENTEEN

WHEN THE DOORBELL rang an hour later, Esme assumed it was Ryder home with the boys. He'd insisted on returning her house key to her, even though she'd told him to keep it.

"Hi, Esme," Ruby Ashwood said as she held up a hand in a nervous wave. "Is this a bad time? I was hoping to talk to you for a minute."

"This is a fine time," Esme said. She wasn't certain why the hairs on her arm stood on end and a slight shiver passed through her. She took a step back to let Ruby enter. "Ryder took Chase and Noah to visit their grandpa. They should be back soon."

Ruby blew out a breath. "I'm relieved to get the chance to talk to you one-on-one. Ryder is super handsome, but he's kind of intense. The guy doesn't smile much, does he?"

To Esme, it felt like he smiled all the time. Maybe she projected that on him, or perhaps he saved his smiles for her. "He laughs at the boys often enough." She supposed she had no reason to be loyal to him anymore, but it was her nature when she loved someone. That was how she knew her heartache over her late husband had been more about his betrayal than the loss of him.

"Would you like a glass of water? Or I made lemon poppyseed muffins yesterday."

"Water would be great, but I can't eat anything right

now." Ruby wrapped her arms around her waist. "My stomach is tied up in too many knots."

"Is everything okay? How's your grandma?"

Esme walked into the kitchen with the young woman following her.

"She's the one who told me I should come and talk to you."

"Have a seat at the table." Esme took two glasses from the cabinet, filled them with ice and then turned on the tap. "If you're here to apologize, you don't owe me anything, Ruby. We're good."

A horrifying thought streaked a trail across her mind like a firework in the sky, bright and terrible with its whistle reverberating through her chest. "If Ryder reached out to you…"

"Nothing like that. I haven't talked to him since that day when he interviewed my grandma and me. It's probably a blessing that he never called. Honestly, he was a safe guy to flirt with and give my number to. It was clear he only had eyes for you."

"We're not together like that." Esme set the two glasses of water on the table. "Not anymore."

Ruby gripped the glass but didn't take a drink. "Really? I thought the two of you were the real deal. It was cute how you guys kept looking at each other like you were truly together."

"We're partners in co-parenting. There's just—"

"I think I was the one who messed up the ID bracelets," Ruby blurted.

Esme blinked. The young nursing assistant could have knocked her over with a feather.

"I don't understand. You seemed certain it wasn't you when we talked to you and your grandma."

"A lot was going on that night, you know?"

Esme definitely knew.

"I mean, there was the storm, and then the regular L-and-D floor flooded, and we had to move you all down. It was my first week, and moms were screaming, and babies were crying. There was one mom in particular who was so loud. Nana said it was your other baby's mom. I was new, and at first, one of the other nurses was putting the ID bracelets on the ankles. Then she got called out for an emergency."

Ruby took a drink, her fingers shaking. "The thing that jogged my memory is that you and Ryder kept asking about the other volunteer. Not my grandma, but the woman who never came back after that night. I didn't remember her at first, but after talking to you two, it started coming back to me." She released a breath and gave Esme a pained look. "Honestly, after I got off that shift, I went over to The Corral and drank way too much. I didn't remember much of anything the next day, and frankly, I didn't want to. But I can picture that woman's eyes. They were so blue, like the color of bluebonnets. I'd never seen anyone with eyes like that, and she was there."

Esme felt her chest pinch. She placed her hands on the table as if the wood might ground her.

"She wasn't doing the same job as me," Ruby explained. "But I remember her standing in the doorway to the room we were using to do the footprints, bracelets and such. It was more like an oversize storage closet. She was staring like she knew something about me. I got pretty flustered and…well… I'm here to admit my mistake."

After all the worry, Esme had almost no physical or emotional reaction to solving the mystery of who had switched the ID bracelets. It made sense, and Ruby seemed to be telling the truth as she remembered it.

Had the mystery volunteer, whoever she was, seen the

mistake and not said anything? Esme couldn't imagine it, but maybe that volunteer had been as shaken by that night as Ruby seemed to be.

"Say something, Esme," Ruby pleaded. "I'm so sorry. If you and Ryder want to sue me or something, I understand. I don't have much, but—"

"No. We wanted to know what happened the night Chase and Noah were born. Now we do."

"I'm so sorry," Ruby repeated. "I wish y'all could find the old woman. Maybe she'd remember something more. She had a cane and didn't walk well, so she could have had bad eyesight. Likely she didn't even realize what I was doing."

"I appreciate you coming here to tell me. Ryder will, too."

"He's gonna be so mad," Ruby said with a frown. "I hate people being mad at me, but I guess I deserve it."

"He'll be glad we don't have to keep searching for an answer," Esme assured the younger woman.

"Just so you know, I quit my job at the hospital. My grandma was right—I got my CNA license because of a crush on a doctor. I thought if I worked in the hospital, he would see me as a viable love interest. He started dating one of the scrub techs over at County—one of the male scrub techs, so I never had a shot."

"That's a tough break," Esme said, still processing Ruby's revelation as the woman continued to speak.

"My grandma also wanted me to do something meaningful with my life, but after this, she said she just wants me to be happy. So I'm going to nail school."

She held out her hands to display her nails, painted a milky pink. "I'm going to specialize in gel manicures. They're really popular. I like a natural look, but I can do whatever. If you ever want a manicure, I'll gladly give you one for free. In fact, you can have free manicures for the rest of your life because there's nothing I can do to make up for what happened with your babies."

"I swear it's okay, Ruby." Esme realized she truly meant the words. "Maybe the switch was destined to happen because I was meant to be a mother to both of my boys."

Ruby's frown quickly transformed into a smile. "That's a nice way of looking at it. Those two babies are lucky to have you. Ryder Hayes, too. I hope y'all work things out."

Esme had given up on hope, at least for herself.

"Good luck with nail school, Ruby. I know it's not the same as nursing, but you're going to make women feel pretty and pampered. There's not enough of that in the world these days."

The young woman got up and came around the table to hug Esme. "Thank you for being so nice and for saying that."

Esme said goodbye to Ruby, closed the door and then stood in the center of her family room. Her future was the result of an innocent mistake by a frazzled hospital employee. Now she knew the truth, but what did it change?

Not her love for either of her babies or, as she'd told Ruby, the fact that she loved being a mother to both of them. Esme was grateful for her sons and the unconventional family she and Ryder shared.

The front door opened, and she must have had quite the look on her face because Ryder immediately stopped.

"I'm sorry. Do you want me to knock? I know this is all new."

She shook her head and ran a hand over her cheek, surprised to find her body still solid when it felt like she was one million particles floating through the air.

Ryder picked up Noah's infant seat, which he'd set on the porch while he opened the door and stepped inside. "Did I see that nursing assistant we talked to driving away?"

"Yes." Esme stepped forward and closed the door behind him. "Sit down, Ryder. There's something I need to tell you…"

RYDER'S EMOTIONS HAD run the gamut in the past twelve hours, from panic at Esme's wide eyes and serious tone when she'd told him she had something to share, to relief that the mystery of Chase and Noah's switch finally had a resolution.

A thin trickle of hope had followed like a mountain stream in the spring, flowing as the ice and snow above it melted. That was one of the many gifts Esme had given him—melting his heart and allowing him to believe in love again.

Or maybe it was for the first time. He'd wanted things to work with Steph for the sake of their son, but he could see now that trying to convince himself that a sense of duty could transform into love had been naive. Falling for Esme had been easy—they were like two pieces of a puzzle that fit together perfectly.

But he'd hurt her, and any plan he'd had to beg her to try again felt weak and insignificant after she'd explained what Ruby had shared. Although she'd seemed pleased to know the truth, her eyes had remained guarded, her manner distant, like she'd resigned herself to the idea of nothing more between them.

So he'd locked down the declaration he wanted to make, telling himself he needed to give her time.

But another sleepless night convinced him that there was no way he could hold off any longer. He didn't want to wait, even though he had no way of knowing how she'd respond.

Esme had taken a risk in sharing her heart, and he owed her that same courage but had no clue how to prove his devotion until he'd stopped by GreatStore on the way to her house to pick up a few things for the boys.

He'd seen Lily Perry working in the baby department. Whether from lack of sleep, desperation or a combination of the two, Ryder had asked Esme's friend for advice. The request had seemed to shock them both, but one thing Esme had taught Ryder was that he didn't have to handle everything on his own and pretend he had it all together when he was a jumbled mess on the inside.

Lily had fired off a barrage of questions about Ryder's intentions, clearly protective of her friend, just like Esme's sister had been weeks earlier. It made him feel equally grateful and embarrassed. He should be the one to be protecting Esme, and he would for the rest of his life if she'd give him another shot.

His answers must have satisfied Lily because, after a few moments, she'd pulled out her phone and pulled up the site for the realty company he and Esme were working with, assuring him that his best chance of achieving a future with Esme would be to make her secret wish come true.

If Freya Fortune could be a wish maker, Ryder would take a page from the older woman's playbook and do the same. He only hoped it would be enough.

"I think you missed the turn," Esme said with a frown as she pointed to the street they'd just passed.

"There's something I need to pick up at my dad's," Ryder answered. "It will be a quick stop at the gated community."

"Oh." She glanced at her watch. "I don't want to be late for our appointment. The Realtor said there's another family interested in the property."

"We'll be right on time," he assured her, then cleared his throat after his voice cracked on the last word like he was a gangly teenager. He certainly felt as nervous as one, and the fact that Esme had indirectly referred to them as a family made emotion blossom in his chest in the best way possible.

He waved to the man at the guard stand, who recognized Ryder's car and buzzed them in. As he drove through the quiet streets, it felt like ribbons of hope fluttered across his heart.

She watched out the passenger window after turning to check on the boys, each of whom was happily playing with the toys hanging from the handle of their respective car seats.

"I thought your dad lived on the other side of the neighborhood," she said as Ryder turned onto a cul-de-sac with about a half dozen houses. A perfect street for a family.

He heard Esme's breath catch as he pulled into the driveway of the house at the end, a white-washed brick structure with shutters painted black and a wraparound front porch with a view of the lake across the street.

She gazed at the house briefly before turning to face him. "Ryder, where are we?"

He flashed a smile and reached for her hand. "I hope we're home."

ESME CLIMBED OUT of the car, unable to take her gaze off the house she found perfect in every way, and placed two fingers to her heart. If she pressed hard enough, maybe she could force her emotions back into the place where she'd tried to stuff them after that conversation where Ryder offered her the future she wished for as his wife, but in a way that made it impossible to accept.

It felt like an eerily similar situation with the house. She didn't understand how he'd known to take her here, but her dream was in front of her yet still out of reach because there was no way she could make a home there and keep her heart from breaking all over again every single day.

He came to stand beside her, and she could feel him studying her expression. "What's wrong? Is this not the right one? Lily showed me the listing and told me this was the house you loved, so I called the Realtor. If there's a different one—"

"Why are we here?" Esme asked, barely recognizing her own hollow voice. She turned to him, not bothering to hide the tears she felt filling her eyes. His eyes were the color of grass after a spring rain—so full of life and promise that it almost hurt her to look at him.

"I can't live here with you," she whispered, willing him to understand without the humiliation of having to explain it outright.

"I'm sorry," he said automatically.

She turned toward the car, placing one hand on the door handle. "It's okay. Let's get out of here before the Realtor arrives. You can text her and—"

"I'm sorry for being such a fool," Ryder clarified. "I've said it before, Esme. You're better than me in every way, so when you told me you love me, I was terrified."

She turned slowly. "The thought of me loving you is terrifying?"

He nodded, then quickly shook his head. "Yes, but not in the way you think. I know I don't deserve you. I spent my whole life striving to make people happy and earn love. First, with my parents, particularly my father. And then Steph. Nothing I did was good enough. Nothing worked. Then you came along and loved me with no strings, like your heart was mine for the taking."

"It was," she confirmed. "Only you didn't want it. Just

like my parents, who were too wrapped up in themselves to care about being loved by their children, and like Seth, who didn't value what I had to offer him. I can't do it anymore, Ryder. I can't keep giving my heart to people who won't take care of it."

"But I will, Esme. I can't promise I won't be scared, but if you give me another chance, I will hold and cherish your heart. I love you, Esme. I will love you forever."

"You love me," she murmured. The words turned over in her mind—wildflower seeds floating on the breeze until they landed in her heart like they'd found a home. She would nurture his love the way he promised to take care of her heart.

"I do," he said. "Do you think you could love me again?"

She laughed softly. "I never stopped, Ryder, and despite what I told myself, I don't think I ever could. I dreamed of a happily-ever-after but didn't understand the effort it would take. Now I do, and there's no one I'd rather spend my life partnering with than you. I love who you are as a man and a father. I'll give you *all* the chances."

He leaned in and kissed her passionately, sealing their promise to each other. But before she could say anything more, he took a velvet box from his pocket and dropped to one knee in front of her.

"I don't want to hurry you," he said with a hopeful smile. "But I also don't want to wait. Will you marry me, Esme Fortune? You are my life and my love. You and the boys are already my family. My heart. Would you do me the honor of making it official?"

Joy bloomed inside her, bright and fizzy like champagne bubbles. "Yes," she told him as he slipped a brilliant yellow-hued diamond ring on her left hand. "Yes, I'll marry you, Ryder."

He stood to wrap his arms around her. "I never realized I could be this happy."

"Especially not as a result of a mistake like the one that brought us together," she said before he kissed her again.

"Not a mistake." He pulled back and opened the car's back door to reveal Noah and Chase sleeping soundly in their infant seats. "A miracle. Our two miracles."

"Our two miracles," she agreed, knowing whatever adventures life brought their way, she and Ryder would handle them together. Always.

* * * * *

Don't miss the stories in this mini series!

THE FORTUNES OF TEXAS: DIGGING FOR SECRETS

Follow the lives and loves of a complex family with a rich history and deep ties in the Lone Star State.

Fortune's Baby Claim
MICHELLE MAJOR
January 2024

Fortune In Name Only
TARA TAYLOR QUINN
February 2024

Expecting A Fortune
NINA CRESPO
March 2024

MILLS & BOON

The Cowgirl's Homecoming
Jeannie Watt

MILLS & BOON

Jeannie Watt lives on a smallish hay and cattle ranch in southwest Montana with her husband and parents. When she's not writing, Jeannie keeps herself busy sewing, baking and feeding lots of animals. She grew up in north Idaho, graduated from the University of Idaho with degrees in geology and education, and then spent the next thirty years living in rural northern Nevada. Twenty-two of those years were spent off the grid, which gave her a true appreciation for electricity when she moved to the family ranch in Montana after retiring from teaching. If you'd like to contact Jeannie, please visit her Facebook page at Facebook.com/jeannie.watt.1.

Visit the Author Profile page
at millsandboon.com.au for more titles.

Dear Reader,

When I was in high school, my career goal was to be an actress. Real life interfered and instead I studied geology, then graduated during a time when jobs in the field were scarce. Then to make things interesting, I married a fellow geology student. We both ended up with teaching careers, which turned out to be very rewarding.

My heroine, Whitney Fox, exchanged her dream of raising and training horses for a safe career in the city. She never questioned her decision until she got laid off and needed to head back to the family ranch. She assumes that she'll return to the business world, but ranching life appeals to her, as does the cowboy next door, who is also dealing with some life changes and figuring out a path forward.

I enjoy writing books where the characters are certain about what they want, only to slowly discover that perhaps they should choose a different course. That awakening process is so much fun to plot and plan.

The Cowgirl's Homecoming is the third book in my Cowgirls of Larkspur Valley series. I hope you enjoy reading it, and that you'll check out the adventures of Whitney's friends Kat and Maddie in *Home with the Rodeo Dad* and *A Sweet Montana Christmas*.

Best Wishes,

Jeannie Watt

DEDICATION

I dedicate this book to my dad.

CHAPTER ONE

"Do you believe bad things happen in threes?" Whitney Fox pulled a rose-pink satin bridesmaid dress out of its packing material and shook out the folds as she spoke. If things did happen in threes, she was afraid of what might happen next.

"Me? Oh, come on." Maddie Kincaid, one of Whit's best friends and the owner of Spurs and Veils Western Bridal Boutique, made a face as she took the dress from Whit and slipped it onto a hanger for steaming. It was mid-May, and the bridal season was ramping up, one reason that Whit had volunteered to help. The other was that she needed to talk to someone other than her dad and job recruiters.

"Thinking that way sets you up for the next bad thing to happen," Maddie added as Whit opened another giant cardboard box, this time to reveal pale blue dresses.

"Fine." Whit started pushing aside thin plastic. "I'm on the cusp of something good. A new beginning."

An unexpected, scary new beginning. One door had slammed shut and now she had to pry another one open. Which door would it be? And how long would it take to find it? Her stomach tightened at the silent questions.

"That's better." Maddie tended to look on the bright side and right now that was exactly what Whit needed. Someone to tell her things would work out, because for the first time since the trauma of losing her mom nine years ago, Whit was floundering.

She needed to come up with Life Plan Number 3, and so far, she had nothing.

Life Plan Number 1, developed during middle school, had been to become independently wealthy, buy the ritzy Hayes Ranch next door to her family ranch, and raise and train champion Quarter Horses there.

That plan had not panned out.

Life Plan Number 2, formulated during high school while her mother had been ill, had been to get a sensible college degree, save money in a sensible manner and work her way into a lucrative, sensible corporate position. Her dream of becoming a horse trainer had been pushed so far aside that she knew it was never going to happen, although she'd never officially broken the news to her friends Kat and Maddie. The three of them had formed their middle school dream pact together, and Kat and Maddie had achieved their dreams. Kat now owned a small farm and Maddie had her bridal shop. Whit did not have her ritzy ranch and horse training facility. Nor did she want it.

The final few years of her mom's life had taught Whit a hard lesson about ranch economics. Medical bills had sapped them during a time of drought and low cattle prices, and while her dad had been able to pull the ranch out of the red eventually, those nip-and-tuck years had convinced Whit that she needed security. Maybe even some luxury. She needed to become a city girl.

Which she had done. Missoula wasn't exactly a megacity, but it was more urban than Larkspur, and she'd landed a well-paying job there, managing regulations and permitting for a renewable energy company. She'd worked long hours and some months spent more time on the road than she did in the office, but the rewards had been worth it—job security, stellar benefits and a healthy paycheck.

Then the axe fell.

Corporate buyouts were rarely good for the employees of the purchased company. Whit's case had been particularly painful—she'd worked her butt off to get the promotion that (a) allowed her to splurge and pay cash for a luxury car—the symbol of her success, and (b) put her in the direct path of the axe. Her job had been meshed with another position that an employee from the purchasing company now filled. The one bright spot was that the yearly lease on her property was close to renewal, thus allowing Whit to move from Missoula back to the home ranch without paying penalties. It was a pretty dim bright spot, but the only one she had.

"You know," Maddie said, as she began running the steamer over the dress, "you can fill in here until you find something."

"Probably best if I don't," Whit replied before pulling a dress out of the box and removing the protective tissue and plastic. "At least not in the front part of the store."

Maddie murmured something that sounded a lot like, "You make a good point," and Whit laughed as she stripped off the last of the tissue from a blue silk slip dress. Maddie was a master at gently directing people to flattering fits and colors. Whit, not so much.

"I'm going to sell my car." She tried to sound matter-of-fact, but it was hard to keep regret from coloring her voice.

"Sorry." Maddie knew how much Whit loved her first major splurge.

Whit and the Audi TT had seen three thousand miles together before she'd received the layoff notification. They'd been good miles, too, but Whit needed to recoup as much money as possible to provide herself with a cushion until Life Plan Number 3 came to fruition. She'd sunk her entire promotion bonus plus a chunk of her savings into the car. It hadn't seemed risky at the time, but now Whit would dearly love to have a do over. She and her coworkers had not seen the buyout coming or she wouldn't have made her splurge. One day, security. The next day, pink slip.

"After you sell the car, then what?"

"I don't know." A difficult admission, but an honest one. Whit felt like next steps should be obvious, as in, get a new job in her field ASAP, but other factors were coming into play. Like a sense of inertia. She felt freaking paralyzed. Why?

Maddie lowered the steamer head and it spit hot water at the floor before she brought it back up to horizontal. "So your entire plan is to sell the car?"

"Sad, huh?" Whit was determined to put on a brave face while she sorted things out. She hated when people worried about her, having had enough of that after her mother died.

"You need time to regroup," Maddie said sympathetically. "Anyone would, given the circumstances. Maybe you can get something temporary here until you find your next real job."

Whit searched her brain. "I can't imagine what that would be, although—" she made a face "—I can play the banjo."

"Not that well."

Whit tossed a wad of plastic at Maddie. "I'm a great banjo player." Her expression sobered. "I'll figure something out."

"I know you will. Just please—no 'Foggy Mountain Breakdown.'"

"But it is foggy in here." Whit, thankful for the change of subject, fanned the moist air, wondering why the old hardwood floorboards weren't warped, considering the amount of steaming that went on over the years as garments were unpacked and hung.

Maddie turned the dress to tackle the back while Whit

unpacked the rest of the shipment. After pulling the last gown out of the box, she smoothed a hand over her hair. The long blond strands that usually behaved nicely were starting to frizz.

"Have you ever watched *The Fog*?" Maddie shot her a frowning look and Whit shrugged. "Just wondering if anything sinister ever appeared out of the swirling mist back here."

"Nothing sinister, unless you count my former business partner." Who'd secretly hooked up with Maddie's now-ex-fiancé. "Steam is great for the skin."

"So that's your secret," Whitney murmured as she retrieved the plastic wad and tossed it into the trash. Maddie did have beautiful skin.

"Lots of steam and the love of a cranky cowboy."

Whit grinned. "I don't find Sean cranky."

"He tries, but yeah, he's missing the mark more and more." Maddie's lips curved into a gentle smile that made Whit want to smile in return. After breaking up with her cheating fiancé, Maddie had found a guy who truly loved her for who she was, and vice versa. Heartwarming, but not what Whit was looking for.

What are you looking for?

Not a man. She was doing fine on her own, thank you very much. But other than that parameter, she felt uncharacteristically lost and she hated it.

Whit busied herself gathering packing materials and stuffing them into the box for recycling while Maddie emptied the steamer tank. She returned to the room and stood a few feet away from the rack, admiring the shiny, smooth rose-pink satin dresses hanging next to pale blue silk gowns. A few bars of the wedding march played in the main part of the shop, indicating that a customer had entered the store, and a familiar voice called, "Where are you guys?"

"Back here," Maddie replied.

A few seconds later Kat, the third member of their decades-long friendship triad, came into the room carrying a box that made suspicious scratching noises.

"Kittens," she said. "They were giving them away at the grocery store, so I took them all."

"As one does," Maddie said.

"I had to. They're very young, and I'm of the opinion that you can't have enough kitties." Kat set down the box and opened the lid. Maddie and Whit both made an automatic "aw" sound as the three little black-and-white kitties inched their way along the cardboard on their bellies.

"I think they need to be bottle-fed for a while," Kat said. "I guess the mama just disappeared."

"I'd take one off your hands, but I don't know what my situation looks like yet," Whit said as Maddie reached in the box to pull out a kitten. Whit did the same, tucking the squirming baby against the warmth of her neck.

"But you have a plan, right?" Kat replied, stroking her kitten's head with a single finger as it lay in her palm.

Whit's stomach tightened again, but thankfully Kat's phone chimed before Whit had to confess that she had no plan at all. "Oops," Kat said while reading the screen. "Troy is ahead of schedule and waiting in the back lot, so I guess I'd better collect my kitties and go."

"What kitties?" Maddie asked innocently, pulling the collar of her blouse over the kitty she held.

"Livia's kitties," Kat replied, Livia being the one-year-old daughter of Troy, Kat's fiancé.

"I will not deprive her," Maddie said with a sigh. She set the kitten back in the box alongside the other two and Kat gently closed the lid.

"I'll be in touch," she said as she lifted the box, holding it in front of her with both hands. "Good luck with the job hunt," she said to Whit. "Keep me posted."

At a tick after six o'clock, Whit and Maddie stepped out of the shop and into the crisp late-spring air. It appeared that everyone from shop employees to the patrons of the nearby bar whose happy hour had just ended were headed to their vehicles at the same time. Doors slammed; engines started.

Whit led the way across the lot to her car. She'd parked the luxurious dark gray vehicle in a far corner to protect it from parking lot dings and dents. She felt a little pang as she beeped the lock open, then gestured to Maddie to climb inside the plush interior.

"It's beautiful," Maddie said, running her hand over the leather console that separated the bucket seats.

"Nicest vehicle I ever owned." Whit buckled in, then pressed the start button and the engine turned over, purring so gently that it was hard to tell that it was running. Soon she'd be driving the Corolla again, a car so old that she'd parked it on the ranch rather than trade it in for the negligible amount it would have brought.

Thank goodness she had.

A line of vehicles had formed at the parking lot exit and Whit nosed her car in behind a Corolla similar to the one she'd be driving in the future, moving forward a few feet at a time as the vehicles ahead of her waited for breaks in the traffic. When her turn came, a long open stretch appeared and she swung out into her lane, glad to have made a quick escape. She glanced in her rearview mirror and saw a big truck follow her out, its grill just a little too close for comfort.

"Look out!" Maddie cried, and Whit jammed on the brakes, barely missing the dog that had darted in front of her. Less than a second later a crash from the rear snapped her head forward and then back, rattling her brain, but thankfully not deploying the airbag.

She shot a dazed look at Maddie, and then they twisted in their seats to stare out the back window.

"Son of a—" Whit wrenched her door open and stepped onto the pavement. She ignored the passersby approaching from various directions as she strode to the rear of her car. Her bumper and one taillight had been smashed, and there was a big crease in the trunk.

"No, no, no," she muttered, taking in the damage and trying to calculate the impact this would have on her already limited plan. Of course the truck had a deer guard on the front, and the damage to it was negligible.

"Why did you stop so fast?" a deep voice growled from behind her.

She turned to find a tall guy in a cowboy hat staring at her with an outraged look on his face. She was having none of it. She drew in a breath and fired back.

"What were you thinking riding my bumper like that?" The words were barely out of her mouth when recognition struck.

Tanner Hayes. It'd been years since she'd seen the man, but there was no mistaking those chiseled features when he tipped his hat back. He, in turn, gave her the once-over, looking like he couldn't quite place her.

"Whitney Fox," she said drily. "Your neighbor."

"I know who you are."

Maddie cleared her throat and they both turned to look at her. "I'll see if anyone saw anything." She spoke to Whit, pointedly ignoring Tanner.

"Please do," Whit said in a grim voice. She turned back to the man, thinking that her one saving grace was that the Hayes family was swimming in money, so he should have no problem handling the repairs.

But repairs took time and would bring down the resale value of her car. The only concrete part of her plan had just taken a massive blow.

"This is your fault." They needed to get that much straight here and now. Whit gestured at the damage. "You hit me."

"You stopped dead in the middle of a turn." His voice was low and not one bit apologetic.

"Because I didn't want to hurt a dog."

"I didn't see a dog," Tanner said stubbornly.

"Well, a dog ran out in the road in front of me. Anyway, it doesn't matter," Whit replied. "You rear-ended me. The law is on my side."

"Not necessarily."

Whit propped her hands on her hips, noting that a crowd was edging in. Fine. Maybe public shame would do some good.

"Right. Because if you're the guy with the money, then the law tends to be on your side."

"Now wait a minute."

"All I'm saying—" she poked a finger at his chest "—is that you're not buying your way out of this like your dad bought his way out of everything."

His expression went stony, which meant that she'd struck a nerve. Good. She wanted to strike more than a nerve but had to make do with what was legal and available.

"Don't bring my father into this."

Whit felt a small wave of shame. Tanner's father had recently passed away, but the man had never been close to anyone, not even his two sons, who'd left home before

Whit was out of high school. But, yeah, she shouldn't have brought his dead father into this.

She lifted her chin, but didn't mutter the apology that teetered on her lips. Something told her not to and she listened. "All I'm saying is that, often, in cases like this, money talks."

Her head came up as the deputy sheriff's vehicle turned onto the street and parked opposite. Bill Monroe got out of the cruiser and crossed the street. He looked over the damage as he approached, giving a low whistle, then he tilted his hat back as he recognized Tanner.

"Hey, Tanner. It's been some time. Some homecoming."

"It was his fault," Whit said stonily.

"That remains to be seen," Tanner said.

The deputy propped his hands on his hips. "That's for me to decide."

Whit rolled her eyes. Bill and Tanner were old high school buddies, but she knew she was in the right here. "I stopped to avoid a dog. He—" she pointed at Tanner "—was following too closely and smacked me from the rear, and I want that in your report."

Maddie appeared out of nowhere to touch her arm and Whit gave her friend a quick look. Fine. She would allow law enforcement to do their job.

She stepped back and watched as Bill commenced taking measurements and speaking to people who'd witnessed the accident. She gritted her teeth as Bill noted various conflicting eyewitness accounts in his book.

Yes, there had been a dog...

No, Tanner hadn't been following too closely. She'd stopped too abruptly...

Yes, he was too close. She'd done the only thing she could...

They were both at fault...

Neither was at fault...

And all the while this was going on, Tanner stood silently watching the proceedings like the heir to a throne would do—the throne being a sprawling ranch in this case—confident that things would work out in his favor.

And they probably would.

Once Bill had gathered his information and allowed them to move their vehicles, Tanner jerked his head to the side of the street, as if he expected Whit to follow. She frowned at him, and he exhaled and decided to speak where he stood.

"This was unfortunate, but insurance will cover it, and your car will be as good as new—regardless of whose fault it is."

"No," she said grimly. "It won't be as good as new. Its value has now decreased. Some of us don't have the ability to buy a new car on a whim."

"And you think I do?"

Whit sensed Maddie moving beside her, as if trying to signal to her that it was time to drop the matter and leave. Normally, Whit would have done that. She would have taken the hit in stride and moved on. But these weren't normal circumstances. Her vehicle was now worth less than it had been a few minutes ago, through no fault of her own. And the Hayes family had always rubbed her—and most of the community—the wrong way. But money talked and the townspeople listened, regardless of their feelings.

Tanner was watching her, waiting for a reply to his question, which Whit had no intention of giving. It appeared that he had no intention of speaking, either. In the end, Whit was the first to blink.

"I think that when you grow up wanting for nothing, it twists your sense of reality," she said tightly. His mouth went even flatter than it had been before. The crowd that had gathered on the sidewalk was still good-sized, probably because most were patrons from the nearby pub who'd come out to see what the ruckus was about.

And who didn't want to watch a fiery verbal face-off between two people who'd just been involved in a collision?

Maddie gave Whit's arm a yank, and as she gave in and allowed her friend to steer her to the car, she was surprised to find herself guided to the passenger side.

"I'm driving," Maddie said in a no-nonsense voice. "You've had a shock. You can take over after you drop me at my place."

"Fine," Whit muttered, opening the door and getting in without a backward glance—although that part was hard.

Maddie adjusted the mirror and then pulled away before Tanner did. Whit sat back in the ridiculously comfortable seat. "Guess it'll be a minute before I sell my car."

"But you will."

Spoken like the positive-thinking soul her friend was.

"Whose fault was it, Maddie?" Bill had taken witness statements, but so had Maddie in an informal way.

"He was too close behind, but you stopped abruptly. He probably would have hit you even if he'd been farther behind." Maddie stopped at the light. "It was the dog's fault, actually. And whoever allowed him to run."

Whit leaned her head against the window. Her friend was right. It was done, and now it was a matter of mitigating damages, not flinging blame. The blame-flinging had made her feel good in the moment, but it wasn't going to fix her car. It was annoying that she was going to struggle after this, and Tanner Hayes would throw money at the problem and it would, no doubt, go away.

CHAPTER TWO

THE SUN WAS just setting when Tanner pulled his truck to a stop in its parking place beside the barn, out of sight of the main house.

Habit.

His father had been all about appearances, which was pointless because his superior attitude made the ranch an unfriendly place to visit—and to live, which was why Tanner had left home the day after high school graduation, one month before his eighteenth birthday. He'd half expected his dad to insist that he stay until he was officially of age, but Tanner had hurt his dad's enormous pride by making it known he intended to follow his brother Grant's lead and leave home as soon as possible.

They'd eventually worked out a relationship that appeared relatively congenial to the outsider looking in, and he and his brother dutifully returned home for holidays and to help with the larger ranch events, such as branding and moving the cattle to high pasture, but he could never describe his relationship with his dad as anything but strained.

They'd gone through the motions and a part of Tanner wanted their interactions to be genuine, instead of always feeling like they were playacting, and he sensed that on some level, his father did, too. But his dad had been unwilling or unable to drop his pride and admit that there was work to do between them. If there was a problem, it was on Tanner and Grant. Carl Hayes was the patriarch and infallible.

Such was life with a narcissist.

But while his relationship with his dad was troubled, his relationship with the ranch he'd grown up on was not. He loved the land, the work, the animals, which was why, despite the revelation about the state of the ranch finances, he'd disagreed with Grant about selling and they'd worked out a deal. Or so he hoped.

Grant had a tendency to shake hands on an agreement, then attempt to wheedle small changes. Tanner hoped that this time things would play out differently. In return for a healthy sum of money—divided into two payments, a year apart—Grant had signed a paper agreeing to give Tanner three years to turn the ranch around. If he didn't, they would sell.

Coming up with the money had been a stretch for Tanner, who'd never made a whopping salary working for the wheat farm. But he'd managed to secure the funds, so now he'd only be fighting time, instead of time and his brother.

A joyous bark sounded from the yard, and Rose, his yellow Labrador retriever, bounded across the driveway, poking his leg with her nose as he unloaded the groceries he'd bought for his injured foreman.

"Hey, girl." He ruffled her ears and then shut the truck door. He walked around the front of the vehicle, taking in the minor damage to the deer guard, and shook his head. The law probably was on Whitney Fox's side regardless of how abruptly she'd stopped, and his insurance would be the one with the rate hike. Yet another financial worry to add to the stack.

He and Rose headed to the small house across the driveway. Len Anderson, Tanner's ranch manager, had been injured two weeks ago in an ATV accident, and now they were both holding their breath as they waited to see how quickly the old man would regain mobility. Len insisted he'd be good to go with modifications by the middle of June.

That was a fantasy, but Tanner played along, mainly to make the older man feel better.

Len had a daughter who was urging him to come live with her, but Len did not want to go. Not because he didn't love his daughter, but because she lived in a two-bedroom house in bustling Boise, Idaho, and Len was not the bustling city kind of guy. He said he would rather gnaw his foot off than live in a city, and Tanner, even though he barely knew the man, believed him.

Len was a tough old bird. He'd had to be to put up with Tanner's dad. Tanner recalled a long line of employees coming and going from the ranch because of his dad's habit of finding fault with even a job well done, but Len had hired on shortly after Tanner left home and he'd lasted.

Outlasted, actually.

As he and Rose crossed the lawn to Len's front porch, he marveled at how the old man found the time to keep his yard looking so immaculate, in addition to all his other duties. The grass needed to be mowed, which Tanner would tend to, but the flowers along the fence and the honeysuckle vine that climbed the trellis attached to the porch were pruned and well-tended.

Tanner knocked, then opened the door when Len called for him to come in.

"Hey," he said, holding up the bag of frozen dinners. "I got two weeks' worth."

"Let me find my wallet." Len shifted in his chair, reaching for the side table.

"We'll settle up later," Tanner said.

Len gave him a sour look. The guy was clearly unhappy, but he'd seemed unhappy before the accident that had put him first in the hospital, then in the easy chair. Tanner shrugged it off, assuming that only an unhappy guy could have worked with his father for so long. Because any happy guy working for the late Carl Andrew Hayes would have eventually ended up unhappy, unless he was remarkably thick-skinned.

Then again, maybe Len's temperament was the result of a decade of being harangued.

"Any luck finding help?" the older man asked, not quite meeting Tanner's eyes.

"Not yet. It's a bad time of year. But I think that with a little patience we'll get someone temporary to help Wes." He'd sent an email to the local high school guidance counselor to see if she knew of any kids looking for summer work, in addition to posting ads on social media and the local job boards. He was dealing with his father's unfortunate legacy. Carl Hayes had lifted alienation to an art form. It was as if he'd gotten some twisted satisfaction from one-upping people, even if he suffered consequences because of it.

Len let out a huff of breath. "Wes and I can handle things if push comes to shove."

Total lie. Wes was the worst worker ever, needing constant supervision and, according to what Tanner had learned while chatting with the guy at the hardware store, very likely to disappear when the whim struck him, leaving Tanner high and dry.

"Your dad was hard on help." Len spoke bitterly, possibly more bitterly than he intended, because he gave a slight shrug after speaking.

Was he hard on you?

Tanner didn't ask because he didn't know how the answer could be anything but yes. Why would his dad treat anyone differently than he'd treated his own sons?

"That doesn't make the search for help any easier," Tanner agreed.

"Are you riding out tomorrow?"

"I have more bookwork, then I'll get a couple of hours in." Tanner had miles of fence to check, and he was doing it himself instead of sending Wes. He loved being on horseback, allowing fresh air and spectacular views to help him gain perspective, which he sorely needed.

His dad, never one to admit defeat or ask for help, had indulged in increasingly desperate means to keep up appearances. Tanner wondered if Carl had ever acknowledged to himself how much trouble he was in. He'd never done so with Tanner the few times he'd asked about finances—which he'd done only because of a few odd rumors floating around resulting from delays in payment. Tanner had spent the days since taking control of the ranch going over the books. It had been a gut-wrenching experience.

He should have been more cautious and not quit his day job managing a farming operation in central Washington State, but he'd wanted out, and it was too late to change things now. He had to turn the ship around. No easy task, but he had a few sources of income tentatively lined up—water and pasture leases being the most promising, if he could firm up some deals. No one, it seemed, had a clue as to the actual state of the ranch, and for that he was grateful. It made negotiating so much easier when the other party didn't know that they had the advantage, and he wasn't letting on that he was eager for a deal.

He talked for a few more minutes with Len, and when it became apparent that his injured foreman wanted to be left alone, he obliged, heading back to the house to unpack the few groceries he'd bought for himself. Skimping on food wasn't going to save the ranch, but discovering the extent of the financial quagmire he was in made splurging on anything other than the basics feel obscene. His one extravagance, good whiskey, was covered, because his dad had a cellar full of the stuff to impress people he'd done business with.

He'd barely gotten the groceries unpacked when there was a knock on the back door. Wes stepped into the kitchen, looking apologetic.

"Heifers are out again."

An excellent end to the day.

"Did you double-latch the gate?" One of the young cows had figured out how to bang the gate just right to open it. After the second escape, Tanner had determined what was going on, but not who the gate-opening culprit was.

"I did," Wes said stoutly. His demeanor said otherwise. He was young, and green, and bristled at anything that smacked of criticism.

Tanner knew it was a pain to remember to do more than slip the chain into the slot when closing gates, but it didn't take that long to fasten a second latch.

"They're close," Wes said. "And they're not heading for the county road." He cleared his throat. "Yet."

A black cow on a dark road was no fun for anyone, the cow included. And it would be dark in short order, so they had best get the girls rounded up while they still had light.

Rose got to her feet. For a Lab, she was a decent cow dog, but she was getting older, and Tanner didn't want her to get hurt. "You stay here," he told her.

She gave him a sad look, then settled under the table. He grabbed his hat and followed Wes out the door. His errant ranch hand was already aboard his four-wheeler, ready to give his impression of a motocross contestant.

"Be easy with them," Tanner said.

Wes nodded and roared off to get behind the herd while Tanner grabbed a cow-sorting stick and headed to the gate. Thankfully, the heifers hadn't gone far, and Wes soon had them heading to the open gate that Tanner flanked, gunning the ATV engine and generally terrorizing the escapees. Yes, a frightened cow moved faster, but they also sometimes lost it and ran through fences.

Tanner stood several yards away from the gate, in the center of the driveway, creating a barrier. The heifers took one look at him and cut toward the gate. Only one animal refused to go in, but Wes roared up on it and it jumped the fence to get away from the ATV.

Tanner tightened his jaw. Better over than through, but now he had a fence jumper, the worst kind of cow to try to contain.

Tanner secured both latches, then rattled the gate just to make sure it was secure before turning to Wes, who sat beaming on his four-wheeler.

"I asked you to be easy on them."

Wes gave him a hurt look that shifted into indignation.

"I didn't hurt them."

"I don't want them afraid of the four-wheeler," Tanner replied in a voice that was only slightly strained by irritation. Although it might be too late for that. Wes had been with the ranch for four months, having been his father's last hire—and he was very fond of the ATV.

"But you wanted them in. Quick-like, right?"

"Yes, but in the future, don't treat the four-wheeler like a weapon against them."

"Right." Wes tipped back his hat. He looked like he wanted to say something, but ultimately decided against it.

He's going to quit.

Tanner shook off the thought. He couldn't afford to have

Wes quit, but he also couldn't afford to have his heifers riled. Cattle were smart and if they associated the four-wheeler with attacks, then it was going to make his job more difficult in the future, especially if he was trying to move them alone.

"Are we good?" he asked.

"Yeah. We're fine." Wes gunned the ATV engine and headed for the barn. Not long after, as Tanner was on his way to the house, Wes's truck roared by. He shifted down as he crossed the cattle guard, his pipes shooting out exhaust.

Not a good sign. Tanner watched the Chevy barrel down the long driveway toward the county road with a sinking feeling in his gut. If the guy was going to quit because of what had just transpired...well, that was ridiculous. But then again, Wes wasn't the brightest crayon in the box, so there was no telling. Tanner headed on to the house, telling himself that he'd apologize in the morning when Wes showed up for work.

If he did.

WHIT WOKE UP with a headache, which she attributed to Tanner Hayes smashing her car the day before. The crash hadn't hurt her physically, but it had taken a mental toll. She'd tried to put the matter aside and get some sleep, but had woken up time and again wondering how much of an effect it would have on the asking price of her Audi. She was going to lose money. That was a given.

She rolled onto her back and flopped an arm over her face trying to think of something besides her smashed up Audi and the cowboy who'd done the damage. Lying in bed, begrudging reality, wasn't helping matters. She pushed back the covers just as her dad rapped on the door.

"Whit?"

"Yeah, Dad?"

"I'd like to talk to you before I head out for the day."

"I'll be down in a minute." She heard his footsteps receding down the hall and wondered at his tone. It was his get-to-the-bottom-of-things tone, but there was nothing for him to get to the bottom of, unless he'd seen her car and was wondering what had happened.

That was it. Protective father mode was probably kicking in. She'd simply explain that she'd seen no reason to burden him with the mishap when she'd returned home the previous evening. He'd been sleeping in his chair, and she'd retired to her bedroom to do a lot of mental math instead of sleeping.

She headed to the bathroom, showered, changed into her jeans and T-shirt, braided her hair into a single plait that was a touch shorter than the one she'd worn in high school, then headed to the kitchen to explain to her dad how her car had gotten damaged.

When she walked into the room, her dad had two mugs and a carafe of coffee on the table. He always made coffee, then poured it into a vacuum jug to keep it from getting bitter during the day. He loved his coffee, but this morning, he was staring morosely into his mug.

"Dad?"

He looked up and Whit became cognizant of a sinking sensation in her midsection. Before she could ask, he said, "What happened yesterday evening?"

"I got rear-ended."

She expected a look of paternal concern, but instead her father nodded, telling her that he not only knew what had happened, he'd probably already inspected the damage. "And did you happen to say some things to the guy who rear-ended you?"

"Maybe?"

Where on earth was this going?

Whit pulled out a chair and reached for a mug. She filled it to the brim and took a sip as she waited for her dad to explain.

Ben Fox blew out a breath. "I took coffee with the guys this morning at the café."

A regular occurrence since she'd been a little girl. The ranch was only five miles from town, and it wasn't unusual for her dad to meet with his fellow farmers and ranchers several mornings a week at an unearthly hour.

"And?"

"And I heard that you got rear-ended by Tanner Hayes."

"I did." She nodded to punctuate the admission.

"You told him a thing or two after it happened?"

"It was his fault, and he was trying to blame me. I defended myself."

Ben stared at the table between them with a hard expression. "I was in the middle of making a deal with the guy for water rights. It's a tricky negotiation. He's teetering on the bubble between yes and no, and my only child tells the guy that he's not going to buy his way out of the situation the way his dad bought his way out of things." He fixed his daughter with a grim look. "Or so I heard."

Whit's stomach gave a sick twist. There had been a bit of a crowd, and whoever had reported to whoever reported to her dad was pretty accurate.

"I didn't know you were negotiating."

Ben brought his big hand down on the table. "Didn't you want him to buy his way out of it? Fix your car and all?"

Whit pushed a few wisps of hair off her forehead as she tried to come up with the right words to explain herself. "Dad, what I wanted was for him to take responsibility for the accident so that my insurance rates wouldn't go up. And—" her mouth tightened "—I was pretty mad. I was just about to list the car for sale, and he smashes into the back of it and pretends it's my fault, like he expects to weenie out because of who he is. How was I supposed to let that ride?"

Her dad met her gaze in a way that told her that he really wished she had figured out a way.

"I would appreciate it if you would make it better."

"How?"

"Apologize. I can't afford to lose this water lease. If I do, then the expansion we've talked about is not going to happen."

He gave her another long look and Whit swallowed. Her father had wanted to expand his fields to the west forever, had worked so hard to increase the value of the ranch after her mother had passed away, but had lacked the water to do so. Carl Hayes was too much of a megalomaniac to work with, but apparently, his son had been more amenable to a deal.

Of all the people who could have followed her too closely, thus making the accident his fault, it had to be him.

Drat.

"Fine. I'll call him." She had his cell number from the exchange of information.

"See him in person."

"Why?"

Her dad sighed. "So that he can see your face and see that you're sincere. Very, very sincere."

Whit planted her palm flat on the table. "Fine. I'll go see him. I'll make it better." She didn't know that she would apologize, unless she really had to, but she would do what she could to iron this out.

"Whit?" She looked up and saw her dad fighting an inner battle. One corner of his mouth quirked into a rueful grimace. "I get it. Why you were angry. I might have said something along the same lines."

But he still needed her to make it better. Whit reached out and patted her dad's rough hand. "I'll get right on that apology."

CHAPTER THREE

HUMBLE PIE. Her least favorite food.

But Whit was determined to make things better as her dad had asked. Thankfully, she was a fairly good actress, having played the corporate game for many years. In the beginning of her career, there'd been times when she'd done herself more harm than good by pointing out things her bosses didn't want to see or hear, but after a few incidents, she'd learned when to keep quiet and when to speak up. More importantly, she'd learned *how* to speak up in a way that didn't put up backs. Now she was going to draw on her experiences and make this right for her dad.

The Hayes Ranch bordered her family land and had been the ranch she, in her fantasies, had wanted to purchase and use as a horse training facility. Why not? If she was going to dream, it only made sense to dream big. The Hayes Ranch was older and larger than her family ranch, and covered both bottom land and mountainside. Her family had not indulged in fancy gates and archways, thinking such things were a little pretentious, but she had to admit that the gate she'd just driven through, with stone pillars and wrought iron scrollwork, was something to behold.

She rounded a corner, then slowed as a yearling Angus lifted her head from where she was grazing along the roadside. The sound of the engine seemed to startle her because she took off at a dead run, dodging Whit's borrowed ranch truck and heading toward the county road. Not good. Whit looked in the side mirror and saw that the heifer had slowed to a walk maybe twenty yards away, but was still heading for the road. Having nearly hit a cow a few months ago while visiting her dad, Whit wasn't going to be party to that happening to anyone else.

She pulled her truck to the side of the road, got out, closed the door and studied the cow who studied her back, head high, waiting to see what this predator was about to do.

Whit started down the fence line that bordered the opposite side of the road, staying as far away from the cow as possible. Once she eased her way by, she'd start moving the animal in the direction of the ranch.

Easier said than done.

The heifer was nervous. She wanted to eat, but she wasn't going to let Whit get close to her. Finally, Whit crawled through the barbed wire fence and walked in the field, far enough away from the cow to keep from spooking her. Once she was between the cow and the county road, she waved her arms and started the cow running back for the safety of the herd…which had just ambled around the corner where she'd parked the truck.

Holy moly. What kind of outfit did Tanner Hayes run?

Whit waved her arms and continued walking forward. The cow herd stopped as they spotted their leader and Whit coming at them. Heads came up. Danger was assessed, and moments later the herd was galloping back in the direction from which it had come, tails high, bucking comically as they ran. Whit got into her truck and followed behind them. The animals seemed to be afraid of engines, because once hers started, quiet as it was, they ran harder.

Once around the corner, past the trees lining the road, the ranch buildings came into sight. The main house, a rock-and-timber structure with a lot of glass, sat in the middle of what had once been a hayfield. Spruce and pine trees surrounded the house, offering shade and protection from the wind, and the meadow behind was a riot of blooming wildflowers, planted no doubt by some landscaping expert.

Opposite the wide driveway that ran beside the house was a gorgeous wooden barn, a smaller house that probably housed workers or the manager and various sheds and outbuildings, all sided with rough timber to give that true Montana ranch look that Whitney's place, also a true Montana ranch, didn't have.

At the far side of the field behind the barn, she caught sight of a man on horseback heading for the gate near the barn at a fast trot. The heifers milled against the fence that separated the driveway from the pasture and an older man on crutches came out of the small house.

"Hey," she called. "I brought these gals home for you."

"Thank you." The man spoke in a clipped voice, maybe due to pain. "They go in there." He pointed to an open gate.

As he spoke, the guy on horseback arrived at the back of the barn, disappeared from sight, then a moment later reappeared on foot in the corral where the heifers were supposed to be contained. He marched through the corral to the main driveway and then called, "Can you move them my way?"

Tanner Hayes, not the hired man as she'd expected.

She waved her understanding, then circled to get behind the herd. She was a stranger and if there was one thing a cow hated, it was a stranger, and these girls seemed spookier than most, leading her to wonder about the animal husbandry on the Hayes Ranch.

Stranger danger worked, and she'd barely gotten behind them when they raced toward their safe place—the pasture they'd busted out of. Once the last heifer had galloped through the gate, shooting a kick in Tanner's direction, he swung the gate closed, double-latched it, then shook his head as if angry at the herd.

Cows will do what cows will do, and while Whit understood the man's irritation, she once again wondered what kind of rancher Tanner Hayes was. Did he expect his cows to kowtow to him because he was wealthy, too?

"How in the heck?" the old man shouted as Tanner approached.

Tanner shook his head as he walked. He looked different in his ranch clothes. When Whit had confronted him after their fender bender, she'd taken in his expensive boots, expensive hat and perfectly worn-in jeans, which had given off wannabe vibes to her.

He no longer looked like a wannabe. A legitimate cowboy strode toward her wearing worn everything, from the battered palm hat that covered his dark hair to his manure-kicking round-toed boots.

Whit felt a strange little flutter go through her. She'd expected to apologize to the slick rich guy from yesterday. But instead she was talking to someone who looked like he was closer to the land than she was.

She cleared her throat, realizing that she'd studied the man for a few seconds longer than necessary. "I found them on the driveway, heading west."

Tanner gave a grim nod, then shot a look at the old man still balancing on his crutches. "I've got this, Len."

Len's mouth pulled tight before he turned and maneuvered the door open with a crutch, and then made his way into the small house.

"My foreman had an ATV accident," Tanner said when he turned back to her.

"Must have been a doozy."

"He rolled it on a hill. I hate those things," Tanner said.

So did she, but she wasn't going to say that aloud, because it would look too much like sucking up. When she delivered her apology, she didn't want to look like it came from a place of desperation.

"Somebody left the gate open?" She was trying to make small talk, not accusations, but she wasn't sure she'd succeeded.

She was about to explain what she meant when Tanner said, "I think someone opened the gate on purpose."

"Really?" That sounded just plain weird.

"Yeah. I had a guy quit today."

No longer so weird-sounding. "He must have quit at the beginning of his shift," she said.

"He showed up at sunup. Got his tools, pounded on my door and as soon as I answered, he told me he was done."

Whit gave what she hoped was a sympathetic nod. "And you think he opened the gate?"

Tanner ran a hand over the back of his neck. "I'm not making any accusations." But he did think that. It was clear from his expression.

You must be some kind of boss.

Whit pushed the thought aside. Sour thoughts were not going to help the sincerity of her apology.

"I'm here about yesterday."

Tanner cut a look her way, as if he'd forgotten about yesterday.

"Here's the thing." She bit her lip and shifted her gaze sideways before meeting his hazel eyes dead on. "I was about to sell my car. I was literally going to start advertising today, so when you hit me…well, I might have overreacted and—" she sucked a breath in between her teeth "—said some things."

"You're apologizing for comparing me to my dad?"

No…but if that was what had caused his indignation,

then she'd go with it. "I didn't mean that your dad was a jerk or anything." Even though he was. "Just that, well, people fell over themselves to kiss up to him because of his money. He really could buy his way out of most anything."

Whit gave a mental eye roll as she heard the words come out of her mouth. What she'd said just now was almost as bad as what she'd said the day before.

"And he did. You're right."

Tanner stepped closer, hands on his hips and Whit's heart started to beat a little faster as his hazel gaze grew shrewd. He was putting two and two together.

"You think what you said might affect the deal I'm working with your dad?"

"Yes." Why hedge?

Tanner nodded, not speaking, making her wish that she'd been less honest. Maybe she should have remembered to use her corporate-ese and finessed the situation by telling the guy that she'd been unaware of a deal. That she'd simply stopped by to apologize for being a jerk— which she hadn't been, but that was how corporate-ese worked sometimes.

"You didn't know about the deal yesterday, but you know about it now."

The guy was clearly sharp, or her face had given her away. "Dad told me this morning. The rancher coffee club told my dad what happened. He's afraid..." She pushed back the wisps of hair on her forehead.

"That I'll call off the deal."

"Pretty much."

"So you aren't really here to apologize."

Whit squared her shoulders, determined not to let on how easily the man was reading her. "I'm here to make sure that my dad doesn't get dinged for my actions. What happened yesterday was between you and me. He has no control over me. Or what I say in the heat of the moment."

"But you still think I'm in the wrong."

"Don't you?" Whit clamped her mouth shut a split second too late. The words were out. Did she have a freaking death wish?

Tanner stared at her, then, honest to goodness, the corner of his mouth moved. Almost like he was fighting a smile. Whit narrowed her eyes, trying to get a read on the situation.

"Do you want some coffee?"

The first look she gave him was probably rife with suspicion, as in, why invite her for coffee? But she gave a mental shrug. If it helped smooth things over for her dad and got her car fixed, why not?

"Yes. That would be nice."

He jerked his head toward the main house. "I have some left in the pot."

As HE LED the way into the house, Tanner couldn't help but wonder how Whitney's last name—Fox—might have been used to describe her. Sun-streaked blond hair, clear blue eyes and a way of wearing jeans that drew the eye made him fairly certain that she'd heard the "you're a Fox" pickup line more than once. And he imagined that a woman like Whit wouldn't have simply smiled and moved on. She would have straightened the guy out.

He opened the door and stood back so that she could precede him into the spacious kitchen, keeping his gaze above her beltline.

"Wow," she said, taking a turn. "Nice."

"Nothing but the best," he said sardonically. "For my dad, I mean. He liked to surround himself with nice stuff."

"You don't?" The question sounded genuine.

"To a degree," he said. "Who doesn't?"

"My dad. He's pretty happy as long as the dishes are done, the springs don't poke through the cushions on his chair and there's plenty of beer in the fridge."

Ben Fox had struck him that way, too. Just a regular guy who was satisfied with a simple life.

"What about you?" Tanner asked. "That's a fancy hunk of machinery I ran into." He cleared his throat and amended, "After you stopped too quickly." He honestly hadn't been following that closely behind her. He'd simply had the misfortune of being the guy behind her.

"I stopped quickly this morning, too. When I kept your heifers from heading off the property."

"Touché."

He crossed the room to the granite-topped island and poured two mugs of coffee. He kept a suite of clean mugs near the machine, taking them out of the dishwasher beneath the countertop and depositing them on top. When done, he opened the dishwasher and put them back in. Saved cupboard space and steps, he told himself. A manifestation of bachelor life.

"Cream? Sugar?" he asked.

She shook her head. "Like tar."

She'd probably get exactly what she'd asked for, because the pot had been on the heater since he'd ridden out on Emily, a very sweet mare, who was now in the corral behind the barn, enjoying her downtime. "It's not the freshest," he confessed, "but it is today's."

Tanner delivered the cup, then motioned to the table. Or rather one of the tables. There was a table for casual kitchen dining, a breakfast nook table and the official dining room table, visible through the arched side door.

Once she was seated, he took a chair and watched while she sipped, made an approving face, then sipped again.

He took a quick drink and decided that she'd been honest when she said she liked her coffee like tar.

He set down the cup and got straight to business. "I'm going to lease the water to your dad. You don't need to be concerned."

"I...thank you?" The thanks sounded like a question, as if she was waiting to hear what kind of condition he was about to tack on.

He leaned back in his chair, studying her over the top of his coffee cup. "Surprised?" he finally said. Whitney regarded him curiously. Obviously, she had preconceived ideas about him, which quite possibly sprang from his dad's reputation in the area. The acorn didn't fall far from the tree, after all—except in his case it actually did. Far, far from the tree.

"A little. Yes." She set her cup down. "I'm really glad that you're not letting what happened affect your deal with my dad. He doesn't deserve that."

"I guess that's because what happened is between you and me." And he needed the money from the water lease. There was no way that he was letting any source of income slip through his fingers.

Whit appeared to be considering his words, but when she spoke, it had nothing to do with the matter between him and her.

"So, if your guy quit on you, and your other guy is on crutches—" Whitney narrowed her blue eyes "—does that mean that you're it? A one-man ranch band?"

"I have never heard it put that way, but yes. I am. Until the end of May, anyway. I have summer hires coming then."

"Are you having trouble finding local help?"

He debated about how much to confess before finally replying, "Bad time of year."

An *uh-huh* expression crossed her face. She knew exactly why he had to wait for the summer help.

"You can say it if you want."

"Say what?" she asked.

"You can say that no one wants to work on the Hayes Ranch because Carl Hayes was a jerk."

"I wouldn't say that."

"Not to my face?"

Her mouth tightened briefly before she let loose with the truth. "All right. Your dad had a reputation."

"Well earned, too."

She frowned at his honest assessment.

"Why do you think I took off as soon as I graduated?" he asked.

"I guess I figured you went to some Ivy League school, followed by an internship with one of your dad's rich business associates, then, I don't know. A stellar career of some sort?"

"I went to college in Idaho. I paid my own way. I went to work at a career that had nothing to do with my dad."

Whit lifted her mug and took another drink. "What was your career?"

"I managed production for a big wheat farm in central Washington. Basically, I crunched numbers." He turned his cup in his hands. "I missed spending most of my time outdoors. I missed trees, too. Rolling farmland is pretty in its own way, but... I like being around timber."

He had no idea why he'd confessed such a thing, but Whitney seemed to understand. She studied the table for a moment, then lifted her gaze and asked, "Do you need help for a day or two? Because I have some free time."

It was all Tanner could do to keep his jaw from dropping.

Did he need help? He had tens of miles of fence to

ride before turning his steers out on ranch pasture and his cow-calf pairs on the grazing allotment near Old Timber Canyon.

He gave her an assessing look, which she met with an open gaze. She was obviously serious about her offer, but that didn't stop him from wondering about ulterior motives. Why would she offer to help him? He'd already informally agreed to the water lease and would set the wheels in motion as soon as she left. As to the car, their insurance companies were already battling that one out.

Does it matter why she offered?

He had to admit it did not, unless she ended up being more of a hindrance than a help.

"Do you have any skills?" She'd been born and raised on a ranch, as he'd been, but he doubted her father worked her as hard as his father had worked him.

Whitney fixed him with a steady blue gaze, giving him the impression that she was very sure of her skills. "I can probably out-cowboy you."

He couldn't help it. He laughed. Not because he didn't believe her, but because she'd come to apologize, then drew a line in the sand. "That I'd like to see."

"Fine. Finalize the water deal, and I'll be here bright and early tomorrow morning."

CHAPTER FOUR

"YOU'RE GOING TO do what?" Ben Fox asked, tipping back his hat. The wrinkles at the corners of his eyes deepened as he studied Whit's face, clearly expecting her to say, "Just kidding."

"I am going to ride fence for Tanner Hayes for a couple days. Help him out. I start in two days, because he's visiting with his lawyer tomorrow. Something about a water lease."

Ben reached out to pat her knee in a silent thank-you. They sat on the wooden bench under the ancient elm tree that shaded their house, her dad taking a rare midday break. Leaves rustled above their heads in the gentle breeze, reminding Whit of how the sound of the leaves brushing against her bedroom window had kept her from sleeping when she was a kid. Now she found the sound oddly comforting, a reminder of how she'd stayed up late, reading *Western Horseman* and dreaming of the horses she would someday own.

Her gelding, Charley, who had stayed on the ranch when she'd headed off to college, was not the fiery steed of her youthful dreams. He was not coal black. He did not rescue her from threatening situations, nor did he come out of nowhere to win the Grand National or Kentucky Derby. He was a dependable mount with just enough attitude to make him interesting.

"How does this tie into the water lease?" Ben asked.

"It doesn't. He'd already agreed to sign when I offered."

"So it's a thank-you."

Whit considered for a moment. "No. It's a chance for me to get out into open country for a couple of days and help someone out at the same time." She gave a subtle shrug, sensing that he was about to mention that the someone was a Hayes. "It wouldn't hurt to stay on the neighbor's good side if you guys are doing business together, and it'll give me a chance to clear my head. I've got stuff to figure out."

"Like the job search?"

She needed to get on that, but she still felt that odd inertia dragging her down. She was beginning to suspect that it was latent burnout. She'd finally slowed to the point that it had caught up with her. But that didn't mean it would stay with her. She would take some time to center herself, take a mini vacation, so to speak, then hit the ground running.

"Do you like what you do?"

Her dad's question startled her. Was she telegraphing?

"Don't ask hard questions," she joked, but it was difficult to hedge with her father, so after the joke fell flat, she went with vagueness and hoped for the best. "Like any job, there were good points and bad. I gave up some stuff, gained some stuff."

"Your hours were ridiculous."

"Yes. They were." She gave her dad a pointed look. "So are yours."

"But I like what I do."

"I know." He'd lived and worked on the ranch for his entire life and while he had a lot to complain about—unruly weather patterns, drought, the price of commodities—Whit knew that he wouldn't change occupations. Devotion to the ranch had carried him through her mother's illness and passing, and now it was starting to pay off as he was able to expand, thanks to Tanner Hayes.

"You know that you can stay here as long as you want," her dad said gruffly, and when she opened her mouth, he held up a hand to stop her. "Take advantage of free rent until you find something that you *like* to do. Not something you tolerate for a paycheck."

"I can't stay, Dad." She had her pride and that meant not mooching off her father. The ranch was finally in decent shape, so her dad didn't need her help the way he had back when she was traveling home on weekends to ride fence and move cows and swath hay. And he no longer needed the infusions of cash she'd made after landing her job. The only reason he'd accepted her financial help in the first place was because he insisted on giving her a percentage of the profits, when such a thing existed.

"You own a piece of the place outright," Ben pointed out.

Not that she could sell it or anything, so it didn't matter. And if she wasn't bringing in an income, then how could she help fend off the next financial hit the ranch took?

"I'm getting back on the horse, Dad. I'm going to land a job in my field, and I don't think Larkspur has anything to offer there."

It was a discussion they'd had a few days before, and one that her dad signaled he wasn't going to have again by pulling his gloves out of his pocket, a sign that he was ready to head back to work. But instead of getting to his feet, he slapped the gloves on his thigh and focused on the toes of his boots with a faint frown.

"Something else, Dad?"

He looked up. "Thinking about this Hayes Ranch deal. Since you're in the volunteering mood…"

Red flags started waving. "Yes?"

"Will you go to the community board meeting with me? They're finalizing the Hearts of the West event and I might need backup to keep from being suckered into more than I have time for."

Like last year. He didn't say that part aloud, but Whit knew that was what he was thinking. He'd been late to the meeting last year and had gotten wrangled into soliciting prizes, which had been a train wreck. Ben couldn't ask someone for help, much less ask them to donate a prize for a community event.

He cleared his throat. "I would be grateful."

"Are Margo Simms and her minions still at the helm of the board?"

Ben nodded and Whit sighed. Margo Simms, Judy Blanchard and her sister, Debra Crane, ran the community board with a collective iron fist. And because it was a thankless job, they received little pushback, to the point that the three had become a little power mad. The community members grumbled at their dictatorial ways, but played along, because no one wanted to step up to the plate.

"I have your back," Whit assured her dad. They both wanted to do their part for the community, but it seemed as if Debra, Margo and Judy got a kick out of mismatching assignments to personalities—especially if they were late to the planning meeting. "When is this meeting, Dad?"

"Thursday. Six o'clock. Community center."

"I'll add it to my calendar." She smiled wryly. "Don't worry, Dad. I won't let them mess with you."

THE LAST THING Tanner expected at seven o'clock in the morning was for his brother, Grant, who lived hours away in Great Falls, to knock on his door. Tanner crossed the kitchen from where he'd been waiting for a second pot of coffee to brew for his thermos and opened the door. Grant stepped inside, pulled off his hat and hung it on the custom hat rack next to the door.

"Good morning." His brother looked like he'd stepped out of one of those glossy Western magazines, with dark jeans, a white Western shirt, polished boots and an expensive hat. He was capable of getting dirty, but his job in ranch insurance sales rarely called for that.

"What are you doing here?" Tanner asked. Grant had sent a text the previous day concerning an unsolicited offer on the ranch, and since Tanner had been at the lawyer's office working up the water lease, he'd simply texted back *no*, and considered the matter closed. Apparently, it was not, since Grant was now in his kitchen.

"Better question," his brother said. "Why aren't you answering my calls and texts?"

"Because I already gave my answer."

"I have business in Larkspur. I timed it so I could drop by, bring you to your senses, have some coffee and make my meeting."

Meaning that he must have started driving at 4 a.m.

"I'm not selling," Tanner said.

Grant looked around the kitchen. "This place can't be chock-full of good memories for you."

"It's not the same place we grew up in." Tanner crossed the kitchen to the coffee maker, which was finally giving its almost-done gurgles.

Grant looked around again, but Tanner had the feeling that his brother was documenting selling points, not reliving old memories.

"It's not the same house," Grant admitted.

Their dad's second wife, Dena, who'd come into the picture after Tanner had fled home, had done a wonderful job remodeling the house into something that should have been featured in *Ranch Beautiful*. What had been a rather standard sprawling Montana McMansion with log siding and a rock chimney was now a stone, glass and cedar edifice sporting sleek lines that seemed to blend into the rocky outcrop and stand of timber a hundred yards behind the house. The massive renovation had cost Carl a pretty penny, but he'd loved the results. Unfortunately, it now appeared that he hadn't been able to afford the results.

Grant let out a heavy sigh. "It looks different, but it has the same feel."

"I burned sage," Tanner joked darkly.

"Selling would be more effective." Tanner shook his head before pulling a mug out of the dishwasher, and Grant continued, "It's a fantastic offer. Granted, we're not going to see as much profit as I'd like due to the debt, but you can use your half to get a start somewhere else." He cleared his throat. "Some place with better juju."

"I like this place." Parts of it, anyway. The other parts, the memories, he would endure until he replaced them with better ones.

"You're trying to prove something to a dead man," Grant said bluntly.

"That, too."

Grant's mouth tightened as Tanner handed him the cup. It was hard to argue with someone who wouldn't argue back, other than reiterating that a sale was off the table.

Grant tried again. "When Dad said he didn't think you were qualified to take over the place," which Tanner had offered to do when Carl started showing signs of slowing down two years ago, "it was because he was struggling with the finances. He didn't want you to know. It wasn't because he didn't think you were capable. You don't have anything to prove."

Carl had never confessed the financial realities of the Hayes Ranch, not even on his deathbed, but both Grant and Tanner had suspected that all was not well—a suspicion that was verified shortly after Carl's death from pneumonia.

His father was a difficult man in many ways. When his mom had finally fled the marriage during Tanner's sophomore year in high school, Carl had made certain that it was impossible for her to take Tanner with her. Tanner didn't know exactly what his dad had been holding over his mother's head, but he'd told his mom that he understood, that he was good staying with his dad—even though he wasn't. With Grant away at college earning his business degree, the only person left on the ranch to do things wrong—other than the constantly revolving crew—was Tanner.

The thing that saved Tanner's sanity was throwing himself into both ranch work and school, often missing meals as he stayed away from the house, working on a tractor or repairing anything that needed a fix in an effort to stay clear of his dad—which was why he was confident that Whitney Fox wouldn't out-cowboy him, but she was welcome to try.

Then along came Dena, the only person other than Len who seemed to be able to handle Carl Hayes. Tanner believed it was because she didn't love him. If she had, then the old man would have been able to hurt and manipulate her. He tried, but his barbs just seemed to bounce off the woman, who appeared to find Carl's attempts to find fault amusing. Tanner had to give her credit—after watching her operate, he'd learned to take more of that tack himself. He'd started letting the comments slide off his back—or, at least, giving the appearance of letting them slide. The old man had a real gift for getting under the skin.

Tanner eventually learned to find satisfaction in his own opinion of what kind of job he'd done, but there'd always been a part of him that wanted his father's approval. Whenever that part stepped forward, Carl found a way to slap it back. Ironically, it wasn't until Tanner didn't care anymore that Carl began to come around. Tanner couldn't say that they'd had anything approaching a normal father-son relationship, but after Dena had taken her leave, along with a hefty chunk of change in return for her years of letting barbs bounce off her, Carl made an overture to his sons.

They then began a superficial relationship that was as close to normal as they were going to see. Went through the motions of being sons to a distant dad who was probably lonely, but unable to go beyond a certain point in his relationships. Oh, they'd played a great game of pretending. They'd even appeared together at the Larkspur Christmas parade the year after Dena had left, two years before Carl died, the make-believe happy family.

Tanner found himself wishing he hadn't done that, because it seemed to have poisoned his relationship with the community. Carl had burned innumerable bridges with his egotistical ways, and the people of Larkspur seemed to believe that the apple didn't fall far from the tree.

Carl might have brought the town to heel with his wallet, but Tanner couldn't do the same, even if he wanted to, because Carl had not only emptied the wallet, he'd put the ranch into the red with a couple of back-to-back business ventures that had gone very, very wrong.

Morals of the story: Don't dabble in crypto. Don't overextend.

Grant, having taken all the silence he could handle, put his mug on the table with a thump and leaned forward in his chair. "I know we made a deal, but I think you're making a mistake not entertaining this offer."

"There'll be others," Tanner said. And he hated to think that they had to go through this brotherly face-off with each one.

"The more money you lose, the less profit we'll see, and right now that profit is going to be slim. I don't want it to get to the place where it's zero."

Tanner pulled in a long breath, focusing on the table before raising his gaze to meet his brother's. But he didn't say a word. That way Grant had nothing to argue against except himself. The thing was that they'd be better off if he could pull the ranch out of the red and start making a profit again. Grant would get a yearly cut of the proceeds and Tanner would sink his back into the ranch.

Grant pushed back his chair. "How much of an operation do you even have left?"

Tanner figured that his brother knew the answer to that question, but he made a recitation anyway.

"I have the cattle." A hundred cow-calf pairs as opposed to the five hundred they used to run, close to another hundred steers. "I've leased out the farming. I have a summer crew—" the teenage boys who'd worked for him on the farm in Washington "—coming in a few weeks to take care of the fences and cattle." He turned his coffee mug in his hands. "The place is a shadow of its old self, but I think I can bring it back."

"If you fail, I lose, too."

"And if I succeed, you do, too."

Grant gave him a look very much like those his old man had sent his way. "I'd rather have the sure thing."

"We made an agreement," Tanner reiterated. A movement in the yard caught his attention, and he glanced out of the oversize kitchen window in time to see an older truck and trailer pull up in front of the barn. Whitney Fox got out of the truck and headed to the rear of the trailer, her long blond braid swinging from the opening at the back of her ball cap.

"Who's that?" Grant asked.

"My temporary ranch hand," Tanner said, lifting his cup to his lips to drink his rapidly cooling coffee. He felt like smiling at his brother's stunned expression. Indeed,

Whitney Fox in her worn denim and flannel shirt, which seemed to accentuate her femininity instead of distracting from it, was living up to her name this morning. He saw no reason to tell his brother that temporary meant two days, which is what she'd offered, and he'd gratefully accepted.

Grant gave Tanner a look. "She's working for you?"

Tanner drained the cup. "Word has it that she can out-cowboy me."

"Shouldn't be hard. You haven't been on a horse since…?"

"Yesterday." When he'd ridden Emily to check the fences along the hayfields. "It comes back. Just like—"

"Don't say it." Grant looked out the window again, but Whitney was in the trailer, so there was nothing to see. He got to his feet. "I know you have the feels for this place, but we'd be better off out from under it."

"Not happening."

Grant could wheedle and whine, but the bottom line was that they'd made an agreement. Tanner understood that the offer Grant had received on the place was generous, but he wasn't giving up his…white whale?

It didn't matter what it was. In his gut, he knew that he needed to prove something to himself and to a dead man. He needed to hang on to the land that had kept him sane during rough times. And he would.

The horse Whitney Fox unloaded from her trailer was saddled and ready to go, as was the custom with most ranch folk in the area. She was busy tightening the cinch when Tanner and Grant came out of the house. Rose ambled out from under the porch and followed the men down the walk to the fancy gate in the low-lying stone wall that surrounded the front lawn.

"Good morning," Tanner said when Whitney looked their way. "Thanks for coming."

He didn't consider himself an expert in human nature,

but he figured that Whitney would lend him a hand until she got what she wanted—a signature on the water lease and repairs to her expensive car—but all the same, he was grateful for her help. And he rather enjoyed watching his brother try to come up to speed on what was going on between them without asking questions.

"Glad to," she said, settling a hand on her gelding's rump before smiling at Grant. "Hi. Whitney Fox."

"Grant Hayes. I remember you."

Whit gave Tanner a quick look, as if to ask why it was that Grant remembered her and Tanner had not. Tanner had no answer for that, other than Grant recognized the name and was trying to gain points. Whitney couldn't have been much older than junior high age when Grant had graduated and headed off to college.

Grant's phone chimed. "Time for me to hit the road." He gave Whitney one of his patented charming smiles. "Nice seeing you again."

"And you," she said politely, but there was something about the way she watched Grant go that made Tanner wonder if she had a clearer read on his charming brother than most.

When she glanced his way, Tanner said, "It was an unexpected visit, so I'm running behind."

"You're coming with me?"

"I thought we could split up and cover more ground."

"Good idea." Whit crouched down and Rose sidled up into scratching position. Her eyes rolled upward as Whit hit the itchy spot just behind her ears. "We'll wait for you here."

Tanner went back to the house, grabbed the saddlebags containing the lunch he'd made earlier, then headed to the barn. He snagged Emily's bridle off the wall on his way by, then continued through the barn to the back corrals where Emily and Clive, the two remaining Hayes Ranch horses, ate their morning rations. He opened the gate and Emily raised her head and then, sweetheart that she was, took a step toward him. A limping step.

Great.

She'd skidded in the mud yesterday when he'd checked the fences along the fields, and although she'd seemed fine after, it appeared that she'd injured something. He ran a hand down her leg, felt the telltale heat, then straightened and shot a look at Clive. Clive eyed him back.

His dad had once fancied himself a horse breeder, producing some excellent Rocky Mountain Horses. And Clive.

Clive was the last colt born on the property, and while being exceptionally beautiful, with near perfect conformation, a bright copper coat and lots of flashy chrome, he was also exceptionally headstrong. And he hadn't been ridden in two years.

Tanner returned to the barn, hung up Emily's bridle and got Clive's, sighing under his breath as he considered what kind of a day he was about to have with the woman who said that she could out-cowboy him. As long as he had help, he had no problem with her showing him up, but he didn't need Clive working against him.

The one thing he couldn't afford right now was to let pride get in his way. He would ride Clive for better or worse and take advantage of Whitney's help. When he led the gelding out of the barn, Whitney gave Rose a final pat and straightened to her full height, giving both him and Clive a once-over.

"That's a beautiful animal."

"If my father was a horse, this would be him."

"Are you saying he has an attitude?"

"He thinks very highly of himself."

"I'm good with horses," she said. "Want me to tune him up?"

"I think I can handle him, but thanks."

Clive pushed him sideways with his nose, as if to contest the point, and Whitney gave Tanner a slow smile that made him forget the horse. The woman was confident, borderline cocky—or at least her smile was—and her attitude gave him the sense that today, for a few hours anyway, he might escape his own head, where he'd been spending too much time, worrying about how to save the ranch that no one knew was in trouble.

Whitney mounted her bay gelding and when she settled in the saddle, it was obvious that she and the horse were a unit. She barely twitched her rein hand and the horse responded, making Tanner hope that he didn't embarrass himself.

He did. Clive, who was taller than most Rocky Mountain Horses, sidestepped when Tanner put his foot in the stirrup, causing him to hop sideways before pushing off the ground for an awkward mount. He landed with the grace of a partially filled bag of grain. *So cool.*

"Well, that's done," he said, feeling the heat of embarrassment on the back of his neck. But the embarrassment faded as he met Whitney's gaze. She was amused, but in a good-natured way.

"We've all been there," she said. She lifted the reins and her gelding instantly moved toward the gate. When Tanner urged Clive forward, the horse pulled his nose sideways, trying to take command. He came close to winning, too.

"I'm thinking of selling him," Tanner said after riding through the gate that Whitney opened from horseback, "but we need horses."

"Horses people can ride are best," Whit said after closing the gate again.

"Is that where I'm going wrong?"

He hadn't expected to joke, but it made the humiliation of having to fight for control seem more bearable. Needing to change the subject, he said, "I called around about your car yesterday to see if anyone local could do the job. I found a guy if you want his name."

He left out the part about the people changing attitude when he mentioned *his* name. They didn't turn down his business, but there was a noticeable shift in demeanor. Voices grew cold, delivery became clipped. Schedules were suddenly full—until he'd said he needed to get a Fox Ranch car repaired. Suddenly there was an opening.

"That was nice of you."

"Well, not a lot of people work on fancy cars here, so I figured I'd save you calling around for estimates."

She glanced his way. "And the winner is…"

"Clinton Automotive. They have a sister shop in Billings that handles your make, so they can do the repairs in Larkspur. All you have to do is call to set a time. I asked about a loaner, but they said you had lots of rigs on your ranch and wouldn't need one."

Whitney laughed. "True."

Tanner didn't smile, but he felt lighter inside. As they continued across the field, he pushed Clive out of the jolting jog he'd been punishing Tanner with and into a long smooth walk characteristic of the breed.

"Does he gait?" Whit asked.

"He was bred for it, but honestly, I don't know." Tanner was just glad that the horse was no longer doing an impression of a pile driver. By the time they reached the southwest corner of the north pasture, Clive was showing signs of resignation. Tanner was not fooled. He dismounted to open the gate, then spoke to Whit from the ground, fully intending to send her on her way before doing the mounting battle again.

"I'd like you to ride the boundary heading north, then east. I'll do the opposite and meet you somewhere along the way."

"I brought my fencing tools, but they're only good for small breaks. I don't have any wire in my bags, obviously."

Tanner hadn't expected her to come prepared. "If you find a break, just let me know where it is. We'll deal with it later."

"I could do small repairs while I'm out there. It'd be faster."

"I'd like to see what needs fixed." Because he didn't know her skill level and he wanted to make certain that the fences were as tight as possible after a repair...but as soon as he'd said it, he realized it might have been a mistake. Whitney's expression did the same thing that people's voices did over the phone after he'd identified himself. "No reflection on your skills. I just—"

"No." Whitney held up a hand. "It's your ranch. Your fence."

Your need to control things.

She didn't say the words aloud, but her expression conveyed the sentiment quite nicely.

CHAPTER FIVE

DESPITE A RUGGED WINTER, the first stretch of the ranch's north pasture boundary fence was in good shape. The wire could use tightening and Whit would have done it, but she decided to take Tanner's "I want to see it first" seriously. She wondered if he micromanaged his employees on the wheat farm where he used to work, too. Were they glad to see him go?

Or did she just want to assume that since he was a Hayes he was a poor boss? His father certainly had a bad reputation in that regard. And Tanner had ticked off an employee to the point that he may have purposely left a gate open.

Whit arrived at the corner post where the east-running fence made a right-angle turn and headed into the timber. She dismounted and checked the braces that kept the fence tight. Not bad. She mounted once again and followed the fence into the trees.

It was a gorgeous day, exactly what she'd hoped for when she'd signed on to help out at the Hayes Ranch. The sun was pleasantly warm; the wind teased the tendrils of hair that had escaped her braid, but didn't blow hard enough to force her to jam her ball cap farther onto her head. She pulled in a deep breath and wondered for a moment if she *should* be trying to get a desk job.

Was that why she couldn't shake the nagging feeling that she was heading down the wrong path?

It was burnout. She'd researched the matter the night

before, bringing up articles, reading about symptoms, seeing herself in the descriptions. She'd thought she was fine right up until the layoff. Stress was a way of life, as were late hours and not much time for socializing. When she went back to work, she'd have to keep an eye on herself so that burnout didn't interfere with her job.

Maybe she could settle for simply working nine to five?

That didn't lead to promotions...and she didn't know if she could settle for simply putting in her eight, then going home.

Could she?

Hard question, and because the day was so beautiful, it was one that she put out of her mind as she rode into the trees, crossing ground dappled with patches of sunlight. The spring blossoms clustered here and there. Charley stepped over a windfall, his back hooves nicking the hollow log as she crossed, making a low thudding noise. Birds flitted from tree to tree and a critter of some kind pushed its way through the brush twenty feet beyond the trail. Whit stopped, then saw a flash of white as the whitetail doe bounded out of the brush and up the hill.

The first break in the fence showed up at the edge of a small clearing that was bursting with new grass thanks to a slow-flowing spring. The spring itself was fenced with cedar rails, and a pipe led to a tank where livestock could drink without muddying the spring itself. Apparently, for all of his faults, Carl Hayes respected riparian areas.

Whit dismounted and took a look at the fence wire, which had coiled into fat loops after being broken, probably by deer. Judging from the tracks, this was a well-used trail from one feeding ground to another. She took hold of the wire and pulled. It was a clean break and would take next to no time to repair.

Whit debated, then thought, *He'll never know,* and

headed to her saddlebags to get her fencing supplies. The fence had tightening ratchets close to the break, so she was able to let out enough wire to put on a clamp and squeeze it down with the special tool that took all of her strength to operate. Once reconnected, she tightened the ratchet, hammered a missing staple into a nearby post, then re-mounted. Easy fix.

She did two more easy fixes that morning and was pleased that there were no areas where wildlife had tangled themselves up in downed wires, creating major havoc. The sooner the wire was off the ground, the less likely that was to happen.

Whitney stopped for lunch near a small stream that headed down the mountain to join the creek that flowed through the Hayes Ranch. As she sat on a flattish slab of granite nestled among three fragrant pine trees, eating her peanut butter sandwich, it was hard not to appreciate the things that kept her father ranching. He was his own boss, worked close to nature and enjoyed the freedom of setting his own hours, except when the cattle and the hay fields set them for him.

He also froze in the winter, sweltered during the heat of summer and had to figure out how to work around the whims of nature and the commodities markets.

With a small sigh, Whitney closed her sandwich container and stowed it back in the saddlebag. She sat on the rock once again and leaned her back against the pine tree behind her, instantly realizing her mistake as she felt the nasty sensation of pitch sinking into her hair and shirt. Talk about a newbie move.

She put a hand at the back of her head above the place where she was now secured to the tree and gently eased forward, grimacing as the hair pulled free. If she put her hat back on, would it become glued to her head? Whit could honestly say that she'd never encountered a hair emergency while seated at her desk, so score one point for computer work.

After stuffing her hat in the saddlebag, she untied Charley and mounted. There were only a couple more miles to check, and if things continued as they had so far, with the exception of the few breaks she'd fixed, she'd be able to give Tanner the all-clear to release his cattle. And then, unless he had something else on the agenda, she would go home and take the pitch out of her hair.

TANNER AND CLIVE, who'd worked himself into a lather trying to assert control, had stopped near the creek that bisected the Hayes property. After drinking his fill, Clive started playing in the water, then suddenly lifted his head and whinnied, his entire body vibrating as he let out the long call. A moment later Whitney Fox rode out of the timber, the sunlight glinting off her hair as she emerged from between two tall ponderosa pines.

"Where's your hat?" Tanner asked after she'd ridden to a stop.

"I got pitch in my hair and decided I'd just as soon not glue my hat to my head." She patted the back of her head. "Thank goodness for isopropyl alcohol."

"You've done this before?"

"I grew up around pine trees."

"So did I," he said. "Yet I've never gotten pitch in my hair."

"Then you were doing things wrong."

He laughed, then said, "How'd it go, other than the pitch in the hair part?"

"Your fence is in great shape. You can turn out any time."

"No broken wires?"

"The fence is intact," she repeated, folding the reins in her hand. "How's your side?"

"A few breaks. I fixed them as I went."

She cleared her throat. "I did the same."

Like he'd specifically asked her not to. He opened his mouth to mention that small fact, but she cut him off.

"Do you know how many fences I have repaired over the years?"

She gave him a challenging look and Tanner realized that he couldn't afford to alienate either her or her father, but on the other hand, he'd expected her to have an easy day riding the fence and following directions. She'd ridden the fence, but ignored the directions.

He folded his hands on top of the saddle horn to hide his irritation. "Do you know how many people I've worked with who *thought* they knew what they were doing, but didn't?" he asked in a reasonable voice.

The look she gave him told him that he might have just talked his way out of another day of help and his stomach sank.

"Not to say that you don't know what you're doing," he added quickly. "I was just operating in better-safe-than-sorry mode. I don't know your abilities, but I appreciate the help."

"I see your point." She didn't seem to like it, but she saw it.

Whitney turned her gelding toward the ranch without giving a reply, and he had a feeling that she was deciding whether she'd be back. Now that he'd signed the lease, she owed him nothing. Tanner let out a silent breath as he followed her to the timberline and hoped she didn't change her mind.

They rode to the ranch following the creek, a ride through mostly open country. The early spring wildflowers were starting to fade, but later blooming blossoms were taking their place and the lingering dampness from the previous evening's rain brought up scents of grass and earth as the horses made their way home. Tanner had missed these smells. Wheat and dry earth smelled good, too, but these smells brought back the joy of escaping into his own world. The security of being far from the ranch house, where his dad would always find something to judge or complain about. Yes. These were the scents of safety and freedom.

When they arrived at the ranch, Whit dismounted at the gate. Tanner wondered if she no longer had to prove her skill level by opening the gate from horseback, or if she simply wanted to feel the earth beneath her boots. He dismounted an exhausted Clive and followed Whitney through the gate.

They walked side by side to her horse trailer, where she tied her gelding, then pulled off the saddle and stowed it in the tack compartment. She laid the blanket upside down on the floor to dry, then grabbed a currycomb out of the door pocket.

"I'll take care of Clive, then we can talk about tomorrow," he said as she emerged from the trailer. "If you're coming back, that is."

"I am." She spoke to the horse's side as she applied the currycomb, loosening the caked-on dirt and letting air get to his skin.

"Good." Tanner led Clive through the barn, unsaddled him, curried his damp hair, then released him with Emily, who ambled over to see her buddy. She was still favoring the leg, but not as much as she had this morning. He'd give it another day and see how she was before calling the vet. Chances were that it would heal on its own.

When he returned to the trailer, Whitney had just set her

saddlebags in the front seat of the truck. She closed the door and turned to him. "What's on the agenda for tomorrow?"

He jerked his head toward the house. "How about I get us a couple of beers and we can talk in the house?"

She shook her head, and a shaft of disappointment went through him.

She'd already said that she was coming back, so there was nothing to settle there. Was he this hungry for company?

Maybe. It wasn't like Len welcomed visitors. Tanner had left behind a solid group of friends in Washington State, but here, in the place where he'd grown up, he was a pariah. *Thanks, Dad.* He'd looked up his handful of high school friends, the kids who'd helped him ignore his home life, and who didn't hold his dad's actions against him, but with the exception of Bill Monroe, the deputy, they'd moved on. He was like a stranger in a familiar land.

So, yeah. Maybe he was justified in being disappointed.

"I wouldn't mind some cold water, though."

"I've got that."

A few minutes later, Tanner set a glass of ice water on Whit's side of the table and a beer on his own. Whit patted the back of her head experimentally, then said, "Would you mind telling me how bad it is?"

Tanner moved behind her chair, peering down at the silky blond strands that were twisted and glued together in a tangle above her braid. He caught the subtle scent of floral shampoo as he surveyed the damage.

"Do you want me to see if I can take it out?"

Whit's gaze turned thoughtful. "Scissors won't figure into your removal technique, will they?"

He grinned. "Only if you get stuck to the wall or something." She gave him a mock scowl and he said, "I have rubbing alcohol."

"Then, yes. If you don't mind, I'd love to have this stuff gone."

WHIT'S NERVES JUMPED when Tanner touched her hair, his callused fingers gently lifting the gummy knot and then pressing a cotton ball soaked in alcohol onto the strands. She'd been irritated by his assumption that she was some kind of city girl who couldn't handle a simple fence repair, but after he'd explained, she'd seen his point. Grudgingly. She hated being underestimated, but what did he know about her abilities?

"Thanks for doing this," she said as the alcohol evaporated from her scalp, making her fight a shiver. "I don't want to get pitch on the headrest."

"That truck looks like it's seen worse than pitch on a headrest."

She laughed, but it felt a little choked. Tanner was so close behind her that she could feel the heat from his body, the vibration of his chest when he spoke. How oddly intimate it was to have a neighbor she didn't know well dabbing away at her hair.

A neighbor who smelled really good.

She cleared her throat and straightened in the chair. "Just get the worst of it, and I'll do the rest when I get home."

"I can get the majority," he said. He continued dabbing and working the sticky sap out of her hair, wiping his fingers on a paper towel.

"Okay. Not perfect, but it'll do for now."

"Thanks." His hands brushed her shoulders, creating a small ripple of awareness, which in turn made Whit think, *Hmm.*

Tanner Hayes was a handsome guy. And he smelled good. And he had a water lease with her dad that Whit simply didn't feel like jeopardizing. She hadn't read it, so she didn't know what kind of exit clause it might contain.

When he stepped back, she lightly patted the damp area on the back of her head and smiled. "That feels so much better."

"Anytime." Tanner's lips curved before he began gathering up the cotton balls that had tumbled out of the bag onto the table, but his smile seemed somewhat guarded.

"I didn't expect you to arrange for the body shop." She'd thought that she would have trouble finding someone local who would work on an Audi.

"Least I can do in exchange for some help." He capped the rubbing alcohol. "To tell you the truth, I had a rough time finding someone. Every time I mentioned my last name…" He finished the sentence by making a slashing movement across his throat.

"But Clinton Automotive was different?"

"I used your name. Totally different reaction."

"Wow," she said softly, even though she wasn't surprised. Carl Hayes had worked for his reputation of being hard on service people, despite being generous with various causes.

He shrugged. "That's my reality in this town. Guess I'll have to learn to live with it."

Whit drove home with Tanner's words playing in her head. His reality wasn't her concern, but the unfairness of being treated as if he was his father niggled at her. That said, how well did she know Tanner Hayes? Maybe he had his own way of putting people off. He'd put her off that day by stinging her pride.

It wasn't a big deal. Her objective of spending time outdoors before heading back to an office job would have been satisfied by riding the fence and noting where repairs were needed, as he'd asked. But it was difficult to ride by damage that could be fixed in less than ten minutes. Silly, really.

Enough. You're over it.

Whit's dad rode his ATV into the yard as she released Charley into the pasture. The gelding headed directly to the dusty area near the windbreak and had a good roll before climbing to his feet and shaking.

"How'd it go?" Ben shouted over the ATV engine.

Whit cupped her ear, and he turned off the noisy four-wheeler.

"How'd it go?" he repeated.

"It was a nice day out."

"Did you work alone?"

"I did. I rode that fence like I knew what I was doing," Whitney said, and her dad grinned.

"Good. I hope Hayes appreciates a seasoned employee. I did my best work training you."

Before Whit could deliver a comeback, her phone buzzed.

"Take it," her dad said. "I have stuff to do in the alfalfa field. Pivot problem. I'm going to get wet."

"Sorry about that." Whit smiled, then glanced at her phone as it buzzed again. "It's Maddie," she said.

Her dad raised his hand and then the ATV roared away.

"Did your ride go well?" Maddie asked.

"I got pitch in my hair." Which Tanner had taken out. She could still feel the careful movements of his fingers as he'd worked the alcohol into her hair.

Maddie laughed. "Of course you did. Hey, Kat wants to meet for drinks on Wednesday after I close up. Are you in?"

Whit could tell from Maddie's tone that she had more

questions about the day on the Hayes Ranch, but that she would wait until they could talk face-to-face. Her friends would enjoy the part where Tanner didn't think she was capable of fixing a break on her own, considering how much fence she fixed on her own ranch.

"I'm definitely in," Whit said. "But I probably won't stay out very long." Days in the sun were wearing, and her desire to stay out until all hours had declined over the years. Corporate life had cured her of indulging in late nights followed by early mornings.

"We're getting old," Maddie said with a laugh.

"How so?" Whit asked with mock indignation.

"I was about to tell you I needed to be home by nine."

TANNER LEANED BACK in his chair and studied the computer screen as if the numbers would change if he stared at them long enough. The figures stayed stubbornly intact. He ran a hand over his forehead, then reached for his whiskey.

His dad hadn't defaulted on anything, but he wondered what would have happened in another year. Things had been coming to a head rapidly, according to the ledgers, and he'd found a rough draft of a letter to an old business acquaintance in which Carl tried to interest the guy in investing in the ranch.

That was telling, because Carl Hayes sailed his ship alone. He'd had to have been desperate to have written even a rough draft of such a letter. Tanner knew it was only a rough draft, because he'd called the man under the guise of settling his father's estate, and made certain that there'd been no deal in the works.

Carl Hayes had been thinking of asking a friend for help, but hadn't seen fit to let his own sons know the state of affairs. Pride was a rugged thing. Tanner tried to imagine his dad calling his two sons to a meeting, laying out the issues and asking for ideas as to how to rectify the financial situation the ranch had fallen into. Couldn't do it. They might have gone through the motions of looking like a family toward the end of his father's life, but that was as far as it went. Appearances were everything to the guy.

Tanner closed the computer program, stood and stretched, then stepped over his sleeping dog as he left the office and walked into the smaller, more intimate living area on the far side of the stone fireplace where he'd left his phone. The windows of this room, which he preferred to the more ostentatious main living room with its floor-to-ceiling glass panes, looked out over the working part of the ranch.

His ranch.

If he could keep it running.

He walked around the stone fireplace to where the view was devoid of man-made anything. From these windows, it appeared that the house was isolated in a mountain valley, just as Dena had intended. The house was beautiful, yet oddly uncomfortable due to the ghosts of the past, coupled with the fact that he wasn't really a stone, cedar and glass kind of guy.

What kind of house would he build, given the chance? Easy answer. A big old farmhouse like the one his high school friend Bud Perry had lived in. He had great memories of that place, which had since been sold. When Grant had told him the Perrys had moved and that the house was on the market, he'd felt a pang of loss. Not that he and Bud had remained close after high school, but that house, and the Perry family, had been a source of refuge for him.

He hadn't needed refuge for a long time, but returning to his family home had stirred up emotions and memories, and shopping around for a mechanic to fix Whitney's car had reminded him that in the eyes of the community, he was a Hayes.

It was probable that Carl hadn't been able to throw as much money around during the past year or two as the townspeople were used to, and without money to soften his treatment of them, they began responding differently. Why kowtow to someone if you no longer had a reason to?

Tanner got verification of his assumption the next morning, when he woke up to a stream of water heading across the kitchen floor tiles. While he had some rudimentary plumbing knowledge, it soon became obvious that he wasn't up to the task ahead of him, which involved visible pinholes in copper pipes. He could change out PVC, but copper was beyond his knowledge base, so he turned off the water main and started dialing plumbers. He'd already received two "we're too booked to help you" responses when Whitney Fox drove into the ranch. He dialed the third plumber on the list, received the same answer, then went out to tell her they might be a little late starting.

"Unless you're good with plumbing as well as fencing."

She gave him a wry look. "I have many talents. Plumbing is not one of them."

"You want to come in for a cup of coffee while I try to chase one down?"

"I've had my quota of coffee for the day." She pushed a few blond strands behind her ear and Tanner tried not to stare now that he knew how soft her hair was. "Charley and I will wait here." She cocked her head then, as if an idea had struck her. "Do you want me to saddle Clive?"

"I'll manage," he said drily.

"Just trying to save time. What's the problem with the plumbing?"

He explained the holes in the pipes, and she listened with a faint frown.

"Who have you phoned?"

He rattled off the three names and she said, "Really?"

"Yeah?"

"Huh." She pulled her phone out of the chest pocket of the men's chambray shirt she wore over her T-shirt. "Let me try."

"Why not?"

The words came out snarkier than he'd intended, but Whitney didn't seem to notice. She'd already dialed and a few seconds later she said, "Hi, Pauline. It's Whit Fox. I'm in need of a plumber."

Tanner waited, and curiously found himself half hoping that she got the same response he did, even though it was counterproductive.

"It's pretty much an emergency," she said, meeting Tanner's gaze. He nodded. "But here's the thing. It's not at Dad's place. It's on the Hayes Ranch. I'm working here." Whit studied the ground as she listened to the short response, then said, "I'm back home now and lending a neighbor a hand."

Tanner felt his cheeks grow warm as he heard not the words, but the tone of the response on the other end of the line.

Whit laughed. "Honestly. Dad is doing some business with them."

There was another silence on Whit's end, then she said, "Really? No. I can't see that happening." She met Tanner's gaze, a slow smile forming on her face as she listened. "I'm sure tomorrow will work. We can hold things together until then."

The "we" might have been the clincher, because Whit smiled and said, "Pauline, thank you. Tonight would be great. I'll tell him…no, I won't be here. I have an engagement." She rolled her eyes. "No. Not that kind." She ended the call and gave Tanner a cool look, as if she'd never doubted the outcome. "Pauline's son will stop by on his way home from work tonight, if you don't mind a plumber arriving after five."

"I have no problem with that. I'd kind of like to get the water back on."

"You never miss the water 'til the well runs dry," she quipped. "Or you come home from a dusty day's ride and have to bathe in the horse trough."

"Have you done that?"

She gave him a *duh* look. "Haven't you?"

"My experience there is lacking." He settled his hands on his hips. "Which plumber did you call?"

"Superior."

His first call, which had resulted in a quick, "Sorry, we're booked," after he'd identified himself.

"I see," he said with as much equanimity as he could muster. The constant snubs of the community bit more than he wanted to let on. "Thank you. I appreciate your help."

WHIT HAD TO admit to feeling bad for Tanner Hayes after she'd booked the plumber who'd obviously already told him no. She almost explained to him that she and Pauline's son had gone to prom, which was true, but Tanner wasn't foolish. He knew that his father had left a legacy of bad feelings and he was paying for that. She wondered if he knew that his father had been very late to pay his last bill with Superior Plumbing. When Pauline had mentioned that, Whit had been surprised, then realized that it had most likely been lazy fiscal behavior. Carl Hayes wasn't the first wealthy person she'd encountered in her life who didn't seem to understand that small businesses depended on timely payments.

What would it be like to live in that kind of world?

She'd worked tirelessly during college and at her job in an effort to find out. She didn't aspire to be super wealthy, like the Hayeses, but she wanted to be able to live comfortably without worrying about what would happen if the ranch had a few bad years.

Yes, she'd done all the work, sacrificed her free time, and had been laid off for her efforts.

She studied the back of the man riding in front of her on the narrow trail, his sweet dog keeping pace with his gelding. Clive was behaving almost like a normal horse today. He'd tried his sidestep trick when Tanner mounted, but today the cowboy was having none of it and he'd put the gelding's far side against the fence so that there was nowhere for the horse to go when he stepped into the stirrup.

They rode across a meadow strewn with wildflowers to the area Tanner called the south pasture, where they planned to split up to ride their sections of fence. Tanner had seemed preoccupied as they rode through the meadow—possibly due to the plumber incident—but that suited Whit, who was looking forward to a day with the sun on her face and the wind in her hair. The only difference today was that when she ate lunch, she was going to avoid sitting near pitchy pine trees.

"Do you want me to ride the fence and, you know, do nothing else?" she asked as they pulled to a stop at the stream that bisected the property. She wasn't certain where they stood after the previous day's discussion about following orders. Had she prevailed? Had he? Did it matter, since this was her last day, and she could do what she wanted without repercussion?

Tanner responded by riding Clive closer to Charley, who took no offense at the gelding's presence despite Clive bumping his nose against his shoulder. Whit's awareness meter bumped up as she shortened Charley's reins.

"I want you to do what you think is best."

"Right you are." She ran a finger along the brim of her hat in a cocky salute. "It's always good to trust the cowgirl."

"Maybe so," he allowed, giving her another of those looks that made her wonder just what was what. He wasn't flirting…right? So why were her thoughts heading in that direction?

"I'll see you in a couple of hours," Tanner added, his voice all business now, leaving her to wonder what he actually thought of her.

"Yep," she agreed. They reined their horses in opposite directions and a few minutes later, Whit glanced over her shoulder in time to see Tanner disappear into the trees, looking very much the seasoned cowboy. Rose, who'd been snuffling at something in the meadow, raised her head and trotted after him.

After a single day, she didn't know what kind of boss he really was, and she probably never would. Did it matter?

Not unless she or one of her friends were working for the man, and she was almost done with what she'd promised. Now it was full speed ahead figuring out Life Plan Number 3.

TANNER DID HIS best to focus on the job at hand, pushing Clive so that they could cover some miles, but his mind kept straying to the plumbing situation. He was glad to have a plumber scheduled for later in the day, but further proof that the Hayes name was poison in the Larkspur area was gnawing at him.

This was twice that when the Fox name was substituted for Hayes the situation had changed radically. People were willing to help Whitney, while he could whistle into the wind. He didn't have the financial resources to sweeten attitudes with the promise of money, which left him either getting help out of town or convincing the locals that he was okay.

That might take years.

Or longer.

Was he being stubborn by trying to hang on to this ranch?

He'd recently left a small town where people greeted him on the street, to come back to his hometown where he was summarily snubbed. It was obvious now that by keeping to himself in high school and having only two or three close friends, he'd done himself a disservice. No one really knew him. And now they didn't want to.

But he was not his father, and he would not play the victim. There had to be a way around this.

Full-page newspaper ad? Radio spot?

Tanner Hayes is a good guy. He doesn't have a lot of money, but he's cool.

His mouth twisted into a humorless smile, then he made a grab for the saddle horn as Clive jumped sideways, startled by Rose pushing her way through thick brush at the side of the trail. Glad that Whitney wasn't there to see him scramble to stay in the saddle, Tanner pushed Clive forward with his knees. Emily's limp was abating, but he'd already decided to continue riding Clive. The gelding needed miles and he kept Tanner on his toes.

When he met Whitney a few hours later, she reported that the fence was in good condition and she'd only needed to make one small repair. He had not been so lucky, having done some for-now fixes that he'd have to address later in the summer when he had more time for real repairs. The important thing was that he'd be able to turn a herd into this pasture to graze until his start date for the Old Timber Mountain grazing allotment arrived and he'd turn the cow-calf pairs loose on the mountain.

They rode back to the ranch single file on the narrow trail leading through the trees to the meadow below. When they finally hit the grassy expanse, they waited for Rose to catch up, then began riding side by side through the knee-high grass. The air was remarkably clear due to a short rain the previous evening, and with the sun on his back and the scent of earth, pine and sweet grass filling his lungs, Tanner was struck by a sense of rightness that countered the nagging irritation that had stuck with him all day.

What was he going to do to improve public relations?

"About my car," Whitney said, scattering his thoughts of public relations.

"Yes." Tanner shot her a look, but she kept her profile to him, watching as her gelding picked his way over a fallen log half-hidden by grass.

"Do I set things up with Clinton Automotive or does your agent?" She turned to look at him then. "I've never done this before."

"Neither have I." Not until he'd had a close encounter with one Whitney Fox. "Why don't you call the place and set up what's convenient for you. I'll keep my agent apprised."

"Sounds good." She directed her attention back to the path through the deep grass, but even in profile he could see that her brow was still creased. There was no getting around the fact that the damage was going to affect the price of the car when she sold it.

He didn't know how to ask his next question, so he made it into a statement. "You said that you're selling the car."

"I have to." They rode around a residual boulder that a glacier had dumped thousands of years ago in the middle of what was now a field, then she explained, "My circumstances have changed. Temporarily." She added the word as if reminding herself of the fact. "It no longer makes sense to have a car with large insurance premiums and hefty maintenance fees." He said nothing to that, and a moment later she said, "I got laid off not long ago."

That surprised him. He gave her a quick glance, which she met with a what-can-I-say expression.

"Corporate buyout. Pretty much nothing I could have done to save myself."

"What next?"

"I'm taking a little time to settle things in my head, then I start job hunting. I don't have a fully formed plan yet, but I will."

"What kind of company did you work for?"

She explained her job with a renewable energy company, then added, "I want to live close to my dad, but that may not be possible."

After that, Whitney fell into silence, as if talking about her life situation bothered her more than she wanted to let on. And he was good with that because he knew the feeling well. As they approached the gate leading to the ranch, he glanced her way just as she looked at him. Their gazes connected. Held. Whitney was the first to look away.

They arrived at the gate leading to the last pasture before the ranch came into sight. He dismounted from Clive and opened it, allowing Whitney through. Clive attempted to give him a shove with his nose when his back was turned, but Tanner sensed what was coming, turned and stopped the horse with a look.

At least he was making headway on that front.

By the time they reached the ranch, Whitney seemed more her usual self. She untacked her gelding, loaded him then ambled over to where Tanner had just released Clive into his corral.

"Thanks for signing the water deal with my dad," she said.

Her time on the ranch was transactional, regardless of what she'd said before. She was simply making sure that he owed her enough that he wouldn't change his mind. The thought didn't sit well, but what did he expect? He was a Hayes.

For some inexplicable reason, he'd expected her to see him as he was.

Maybe she did…but she was hedging her bets in spite of it.

"Thanks for the help," he said. He thought about extending a hand, then simply didn't. A few minutes later, when he was watching the dust from her trailer settle on the long driveway, a wave of something close to depression washed over him.

The feeling intensified two hours later after the plumber from Superior Plumbing had inspected the pipes and explained how mineral-laden water could react with copper and create the small holes that caused the leaks.

Ironic, really. His dad had wanted the best of the best in his house, so instead of PVC pipe, he'd gone copper. And the best of the best hadn't been suitable for his situation.

Now Tanner got to deal with it, just as he was dealing with the other things his dad had done for appearances, such as overextending.

"Hey, thanks," Tanner said as he walked the guy named Steve to his truck. Steve loaded his tools, then handed the handwritten invoice to Tanner, who glanced at it, then back at the man. "Thanks," he repeated.

Steve lifted his chin. "I'm going to need payment today."

Tanner blinked at the guy. It wasn't the request, but the tone, which sounded like a reprimand.

"Okay," Tanner said. "Is this a policy with your company?" Because he hadn't encountered it in Washington State.

"Not always."

Tanner gave Steve a sideways look. Again, something in the tone. Finally, Steve looked up at the sky for a split second, then said, "Your dad left us hanging for months with a big bill. It caused some problems with our cash flow."

Tanner felt the back of his neck grow warm.

"So the policy is payment at time of service. I'm set up for digital payment." Steve held up the square payment attachment that would connect to his phone.

"Not a problem." Tanner pulled out his wallet, which he always carried, and watched silently as Steve ran the payment before handing him the card back.

"No offense. It's just business."

With a Hayes. Who hadn't paid a big bill on time.

He'd have to take another look at the finances, do some forensic digging to see who else his dad might have offended by late payments after his financial downturn.

After the plumber had left, Tanner started for Len's house, then changed his mind. Yes, the old guy might know a thing or two, but he wasn't ready to be humiliated on all fronts.

One thing was certain. If he was going to continue living in the area, he was going to have to come up with a way to rehabilitate his name.

Right now, he had no way of doing that.

CHARLEY NICKERED AS Whit approached the corral with a wheelbarrow full of weeds she'd pulled from the flower beds near the house.

"I agree," she said to the horse as she wheeled past him to the compost pile. She liked gardening, and the beds needed some serious work, but like her horse, she'd rather be riding on the mountain. The two days she'd promised Tanner Hayes on his ranch had flown by, and even though she'd let herself get caught up in worries about the future on the last day's ride, she'd felt better worrying on the mountain than she would have at home, while staring at a computer and wondering about her next act. She was not yet ready to tackle her future.

She emptied the wheelbarrow and then took a moment to look out over the fields where two tractors were at work, prepping the area where her dad would seed his new crop that would be irrigated with leased Hayes Ranch water. Funny how they had more help than they needed now that she was back home, while Tanner was struggling. He'd leased his farming, but there was still a lot to do with the cattle and the meadow hay he planned to bale.

And that was his problem. She'd lent a hand to be neighborly. In return, he'd arranged her car repair and signed the water lease with her dad.

She'd just started back to the flower bed when the phone in the house started ringing. Since her father rarely got calls, it could well be something important. She abandoned the wheelbarrow and jogged to the house, pulling off her gloves as she went, hoping to catch whoever it was before they gave up.

"Fox Ranch." She cradled the phone on her shoulder as she rubbed soil from her fingers. Her pulse gave a totally unnecessary jolt when the caller identified himself as Tanner Hayes.

"Dad's not here right now."

"I was calling for you."

"Really?" Someday she'd learn not to say the first thing that popped into her head, but that wasn't today.

"I was wondering…" A second or two ticked by before he said, "Could we meet?"

Tanner Hayes was not his usual composed self.

She frowned. "Meet?"

"I want to ask your opinion on something that I think

you have a unique perspective on." He spoke in a low voice, as if he didn't want anyone to overhear.

"You want to put a wind farm on the ranch?"

"No. I need some advice about surviving in Larkspur."

The plumbing incident shot into her head. "Ah." He didn't reply and she said, "I'm not sure what I can do."

"Would you mind letting me bounce a few things off you? Because if not you, then it'll have to be Len or his nephew Kenny, and I don't see either of them being all that helpful."

Whit had to agree. Neither were socially inclined. And maybe she needed to wrap her mind around something else after letting the reality of being unemployed get to her that day.

"Sure. Want to come here? Dad's on the tractor. I don't expect him in until dark, if then." One thing about farm-work—it didn't wait on the convenience of the farmer.

"I'll be there shortly. Thanks."

Judging from the way he said the last word, Whit guessed that this had not been an easy call to make, which piqued her curiosity. She went into the main bathroom and checked herself out in the mirror. A little soil removal from the cheek area, a comb through her hair, some colored lip balm and she was ready for guests.

She opened the fridge and realized that she and her dad needed to up their hospitality game, then told herself that Tanner wasn't coming for hospitality. He was coming be-cause he needed advice.

Would she be able to help him?

To know the answer to that, she needed to wait for him to lay out the problem, which he did less than a half hour later, after declining an expired beer—her dad wasn't much of a beer drinker—and taking a seat across from her at the kitchen table.

"I like your house," he said.

Whit assumed he was being polite, because the house was a sometimes-drafty farmhouse, which had been added onto two times that Whit knew of. It was a hodgepodge type of dwelling that had seemed a touch embarrassing during her self-conscious middle school years, but Kat and Maddie had similar houses, so she'd mostly been okay with it.

"I like it, too," she said, then cut to the chase. "What's up, Tanner?"

He studied the table as if marshaling his thoughts, then tapped his finger on the oak. "I need to figure out a way to redeem the Hayes reputation. I was raised by my old man. I totally get why people avoid anything with the Hayes name on it, but I want to live here, and it's going to be difficult if I can't get a mechanic or plumber or doctor because my dad ticked them off when he was still alive."

Whit reached out to put her hand on top of his, as she would have with a close friend. Then she froze, her fingers hovering just above his.

Holy moly.

She gave the back of his hand a perfunctory pat, then settled both of her hands back in her lap, with the intention of keeping them there.

Tanner's mouth quirked up at the corner. "Did you just there-there me?"

"Maybe," she muttered, knowing that she'd totally there-there'd him. Eager to change the subject, she leaned forward in her chair, allowed her hands back on the table under the condition that they behave themselves, and said, "You're in a tough spot, Tanner. Small towns are notoriously stubborn once a judgment has been made."

"I need to stop having them judge me as if I were my dad."

"How do you propose to do that?"

Tanner met her gaze. He looked uncertain and deter-mined and...uncertain. He cleared his throat.

"I know that you'll be busy networking and job hunting, and helping around this place, but I thought that maybe we could be seen together from time to time. And you could look happy about it, like we're friends."

Whit's pulse jumped. "Like a pretend girlfriend?"

"No."

The word burst out of his mouth and Whit felt instantly relieved. She pulled her hands back into her lap as she stared at Tanner Hayes's handsome face. Twice he'd been turned down for services using his name. Twice those same services had been available to her. She saw where he was coming from.

"Don't you think doing business with my dad is good enough?"

"Apparently not," he said. Whit had to admit that he had recent evidence to prove his case. "If you don't want to do this, I understand. It was a shot in the dark." He pushed his chair back as if he was ready to go.

Whit made no move to stop him as she considered the logic of his idea. All they had to do was appear to be friends.

That would never fly.

The townspeople would assume it was something else, of course. Something more along the lines of a romance. But instead of pointing out the obvious to Tanner, she cocked her head in a thoughtful way as an idea struck her.

"What?" he asked, shifting his weight after the silence had stretched for a few seconds too long.

"Hire me."

"What?"

"I need a temporary job. You need a temporary day

hand. Hire me. Word will get around town that I'm working for you. I'll tell people how great it is being employed by the Hayes Ranch and how different you are from your dad."

Tanner didn't answer immediately, but she could see that he was turning the idea over in his head.

"I'll tell them about the catered lunches, the after-work pool parties…" Her expression sobered and the teasing note left her voice. "All kidding aside, it could work, Tanner."

"It might," he allowed warily.

"Better than if we try to come off as instant friends. That would just turn into a spectator sport. There would be speculation about whether we're dating, and then when we part ways because I get a job elsewhere, some people will assume you did me wrong, which will not help your rep."

"That makes sense," he agreed slowly.

"This gives us a reason to be friendly that the local folk are more likely to buy because of the money aspect."

"Money," he said softly. "Right."

Whit noticed a fleeting shift in his demeanor, but she pressed on regardless. "The only caveat is that I may quit suddenly. If the right job comes along—"

"I understand." His mouth tightened as he glanced down, then he lifted his gaze. "Okay. You're hired. Can you start tomorrow? I'm riding the allotment fence up on Old Timber Mountain."

Whit felt a smile crease her cheeks. This might not be Life Plan Number 3, but it felt right. Just a little detour as she sorted out her future. "I can."

His face relaxed and Whit once again felt the tug of attraction. He was gorgeous, and he was off-limits for the simple reason that Whit needed to figure out Life Plan Number 3 before she started adding to the mix.

TANNER HADN'T GONE to the Fox Ranch with the intention of hiring help. No, he'd gone there out of desperation, getting into his truck and driving to the Fox Ranch before he talked himself out of the idea of asking Whitney to help him with his image in the community. He'd come home with a temporary hire on his books. Whitney Fox was now an employee, and every day that she showed up for work was one day closer to his summer crew arriving and him not trying to sift through the dregs of the cowboy-for-hire world to find someone reliable to work for him.

Tanner spent a few minutes loving on Rose, who'd gone out with him that day to finish some repairs on the south section fence, then fed her and headed out to tend to his horses. When he reached the corrals, Len's nephew, Kenny, came roaring in on his motorcycle, giving a happy salute as he drove by. Tanner returned the gesture, then checked on Emily's leg, which she was now putting weight on, then spent a few minutes brushing her. Clive nosed his way in, demanding equal time, and Tanner, seeing this as a good sign, also brushed the gelding. By the time he finished, the motorcycle was gone, but Len's door was open, so he headed over to rap on the door frame.

"Need help with anything?" he called into the dimly lit interior.

"I'm good." Uneven footsteps followed the words, and Len appeared from the short hallway leading to the back rooms of the house. "Kenny brought groceries."

"Nice of him."

Len gave a small grunt in reply. Tanner had yet to figure out Len's relationship with his nephew, who seemed good-natured but a little squirrelly.

"They're a bit dusty from the motorcycle, but the eggs are all whole this time," the old man said. "How'd the neighbor girl work out?"

The neighbor girl was actually a woman, but he didn't point that out.

"She has skills."

Len grunted again. "Guess it's good that you found someone to help for a couple days."

"She hired on."

Len's mouth fell open in a way that would have been comical if the old guy hadn't appeared so taken aback. "Her? You sure about this?"

"She lives close, seems to know what she's doing and she needed a job." When the old man said nothing, Tanner added, "She's gotta be better than Wes."

Len snorted. "A hot dog would be better than Wes."

And with that, the old man turned and maneuvered his way back into his house, letting the door swing shut behind him.

"You're working for Tanner Hayes?" It was the second time Maddie had asked the question in less than thirty seconds. "You were ready to fillet him when he hit your car and now you're…"

"Neighbors," Whit said firmly. "He needs some help on his place and it just happened."

"Things don't just happen to you," Kat said.

"Not often. But there *was* that surprise layoff." She gave her friend a significant raised eyebrow look as she sipped her drink.

"Touché."

Her dad hadn't been as surprised as her friends were by the news. He'd taken it in stride, simply reminding her that the community board meeting was coming up and he'd appreciate it if she was at the meeting with him. In other words, he'd like it if she wasn't on a mountain somewhere checking a fence when the meeting began.

"It's temporary?" Maddie asked.

"Yep. Tanner has a couple people coming from Washington to work as summer hires, and I'm filling in until they get here. I get a paycheck and I can think about my future while I push cows and fix fences and, you know, enjoy the outdoors before I go back to the desk."

"Maybe you should get something more suited to your personality."

Whit smiled, then stirred her drink, thinking that Maddie made a good point. Unfortunately, the jobs she would enjoy most didn't lend themselves to high paychecks and security. She didn't want to go back to the hardscrabble life she and her dad had shared, to not knowing whether they'd be able to hang on to the ranch when one lean year led into another. Playing cowgirl was fun, but knowing that she had the means to help keep the ranch running, and that she could splurge on things like vacations and cool cars, made being chained to the desk worthwhile. Life was full of give-and-take. She'd chosen security over hardscrabble years ago, and she was making the same choice now.

"Are you attending the community board meeting?" Kat asked, apparently sensing that a change of subject was in order.

"Hearts of the West?" Maddie asked in return. "I am excused."

"No fair." Kat made a sour face.

"Well, if you were busy designing a wedding dress for Debra's daughter, you would be excused, too."

"I'm going to the meeting," Whit said. "Someone has to keep Dad out of trouble. I want to do our part, but I'd like it to be something we can do without losing sleep at night."

Kat laughed. "I remember last year."

"So do I." She'd spent a lot of time she didn't have bailing out her dad, but he was so bad at asking for anything she really had no choice but to help him solicit prizes for the various games and activities.

Maddie nudged Whit's knee and then motioned with her head. "Isn't that the other Hayes brother?"

Whit followed her friend's gaze to the bar where Grant Hayes sat talking to a man she didn't recognize.

"It is. I met him at the Hayes Ranch yesterday."

"I wonder if he's moving back, too."

"I didn't get that impression, but I don't know much about him."

"Do you know much about Tanner?"

I know that he smells good and that he's easy on the eyes. Whit stirred her drink again. "He's not giving off the spoiled rich boy vibe that I expected."

"A point in the plus column," Maddie said.

"Both brothers left home as soon as they could. Rumor has it that they didn't get along with their dad any better than the rest of the community," Kat said.

"I don't know," Maddie said. "The family seemed pretty cozy. Remember them at the Christmas parade? And the women drooling over the Hayes brothers?"

"I don't recall the latter," Whit said, wondering if she'd been able to come home that year. There'd been times when she hadn't been able to get away until Christmas Eve. "I can believe it happened, though. Grant and Tanner Hayes are lookers." She just wished she didn't notice as often as she did.

She debated with herself, then decided to let her friends know the full truth of the matter. "I'm going to help Tanner get a foothold back in the community."

"How?" Kat and Maddie asked in unison. They looked at each other, said, "Jinx," together, then laughed.

"How will you do that?" Kat said, focusing back on Whit.

"By association. I'm going to work for him, obviously,

and I'm also going to make it clear that I like him just fine. Hopefully people will start looking at him differently."

She went on to explain the situation with the mechanic and the plumber, finishing with, "He's not a bad guy, and he should be judged on his own merits, not his father's."

"So—" Maddie glanced at Grant Hayes, then back at Whit "—you think the Hayes brothers are all right?"

There was a cautionary note in her friend's voice, one that Whit paid attention to. Maddie, who worked with the public, was quick to key in to people, often seeing things that others missed.

"I think Tanner Hayes is all right," Whit said. She had no evidence to the contrary, even though, in the beginning, she wanted to find something that painted him as a bad guy. "Do you know something I don't?"

"No," Maddie replied. "My only concern is that because he's doing business with your dad, and your dad really needs that water, you might have a skewed vision of things." She paused for a thoughtful moment. "Before you start paving his way into the good graces of the community, you need to be sure that he really is a good guy."

Point taken.

"He's good with his dog and his horse, and the horse is a jerk, so I think he's okay. But…" Whit's forehead creased. "If I find out he's not that way, I'll abandon ship immediately."

CHAPTER SIX

Whit gave a quick glance at the truck's big side mirror as she waited for Tanner Hayes, who hadn't answered his door when she knocked. Little wisps of hair stuck out in all directions thanks to not having time to properly smooth and braid her hair, but at least the pine pitch was gone.

She was considering undoing her hair and re-braiding it when a movement in the pasture caught her eye. A horse and rider appeared over the top of the low ridge, and she could tell by the way the horse was trying to take control that it was Clive taking Tanner for a ride.

A four-wheeler appeared not far behind him, making Whit wonder how much longer Tanner might need her services. She'd been under the impression that she was his only employee for the interim, but then, as the ATV got closer, she recognized the foreman. He was riding the vehicle with one leg at an awkward angle.

"Hey," she said when Tanner reached the gate. "I didn't unload. I thought you might want to travel with me." Because it made no sense to take two trucks and two trailers for two horses and two riders.

"Sounds good," he said. He held the gate open for the ATV, and the foreman gave Whit a stern nod as he putted by. "Len has figured out how to be of use," he said. "But in a very limited capacity."

"Are you afraid that he's going to hurt himself again?"

"Totally, but some things you can't control."

"Amen to that." If she could, she'd still be working at her old job and driving the Audi with no thoughts of selling. She wouldn't be procrastinating in her job hunt while helping out the cowboy next door who, according to Maddie, may or may not be the nice guy he presented himself to be. Maddie was right—her vision could be skewed. She wanted to believe he was a guy who would continue leasing water to her dad. A guy who would be the good neighbor his father had not been.

After Tanner loaded Clive, he closed the trailer door and said, "Do you mind if I bring Rose?"

"I have a dog-friendly back seat."

"She tends to roll in the mud when she finds it."

She answered with an arch of her eyebrows. "You've seen the inside of my truck, right?"

He laughed. "I'll grab my lunch and my dog, and we can take off."

They drove with the windows down, the fresh breeze and mountain air mingling with the scent of coffee, and Tanner's soap and leather smell.

Tanner was in a lighter mood than he'd been in the day before, and Whit assumed it was because he had his foreman back on the job, albeit in a limited way. His crew was coming at the end of the next month...things were falling together for him, and now all he had to do was convince the community that he and his dad weren't one and the same.

And he might have to convince her friends. Maddie hadn't sounded certain that he was actually a good guy, but who knew what kind of gossip she'd heard about the Hayes family in her bridal shop? Whit told herself that morning that she'd keep an open mind, but so far...yeah. All signs pointed to him not being his dad.

"About my car," she said as they started down the driveway. Tanner shot her a quick look. "Yeah?"

"I got it scheduled at Clinton Automotive, and I'd *really* like for you to pick me up after I drop it off."

"Sure," he said, not understanding what she was getting at.

"Joe Marconi works there. He's a prodigious gossip."

Tanner gave her a confused look, then caught her meaning.

Whit nodded as his expression shifted. "Joe likes me, and if he sees that I'm okay with you, then it'll be a start. You might be able to get a mechanic in a reasonable time."

"Good. I'm living in fear of something else breaking and having to call you to get it fixed."

Whit snorted at his dry response. "I guess that means you need to stay in my good graces, huh?"

Twenty minutes later, after Tanner opened and closed two wire gates on a rain-rutted road, Whit parked in the sagebrush near yet another gnarly wire gate. Tanner let Rose out of the truck, and then, as they were unloading the horses, his phone rang. He glanced at it, then put it back in his pocket.

After they'd led the horses through the gate and refastened it, his phone rang again. This time Tanner silenced it in his pocket. "My brother," he said as if that explained his actions.

Whit mounted her horse. "You don't want to talk to him?"

"Grant has a different vision for the ranch than I do."

Tanner mounted Clive, keeping his focus on the horse, but there was no missing the tension in his shoulders as the cowboy pulled his hat low over his forehead.

"Does he want to expand?" If so, then why wasn't he helping with the place?

"He wants to get out from under it. I want to keep it."

"That is a difference in visions."

Tanner gathered his reins, and she could tell by the shift in his demeanor that they would no longer be discussing his brother, but his voice was agreeable enough when he said, "We'll ride together to the spring, then split up. I just need to warn you that the country can get rough in places. Lots of scree and talus."

"I've been in rough country."

"There are bears and rattlesnakes."

"I know," Whit said, wondering why he was stating the obvious. It wasn't like she hadn't grown up in the area.

"Most importantly, there are pine trees." His expression grew serious as he reiterated, "*Lots* of pine trees."

She sent him an uncomprehending look.

"I'm saying that I don't want to find you with your head stuck to another pitchy tree."

Whit would have smacked him if she'd been close enough. "Did you just make a joke at your new employee's expense?"

A slow smile crossed his face, which in turn caused a spiral of warmth to travel through her midsection.

"It's okay," she said with a dramatic sniff. "If you take responsibility for my car repairs, you can crack all the jokes you want."

"I am taking care of your car repairs."

"Then crack away."

He shook his head. "You've ruined it. Now I have performance anxiety."

Whit fought a smile, and he allowed himself a half smile before his expression sobered.

"I'm serious about the trail. Take care around the slumps and rockfalls. Len got hurt up here trying to use an ATV instead of a horse."

"That's why I prefer horses in the mountains."

"Me, too." He tightened his reins as Clive shied at nothing. "Except maybe this one."

Rose ran ahead of them on the trail, disappearing when she discovered an interesting scent, then reappearing. She beat them to the spring, and when they arrived, Tanner's yellow dog had dark mud encasing her legs and the lower half of her body.

Tanner grimaced. "I'm pretty sure most of it will be gone by the end of the day."

"You've seen my truck," Whit repeated before looking to the east. They'd studied a map of the area before leaving his ranch, and Tanner had shown her the distance he'd wanted to cover that day. If all went well, they'd be done with the area in two days, making minor repairs as they went.

Major repairs would be marked on the map and tended to later. It had been a heavy snow year, so Whit wouldn't be surprised to find long stretches of fencing wire lying on the ground in the areas where snow accumulation would have been higher than the fence posts.

They reined their horses in different directions, Whit heading east and Tanner north. She was almost to the tree line when Tanner shouted, "Hey!"

She looked over her shoulder, and was struck by the picture Tanner, his horse and his dog made in front of a backdrop of granite boulders and aspen.

"Yes?" she called.

"We'll meet back here at five at the latest."

She held up a thumb to indicate that she'd heard him and checked her watch, so that she could gauge time out and time back. Her phone was in the truck, due to lack of cell signal, which meant a day uninterrupted by modern communications.

No way of connecting with other human beings for at least eight hours.

She could already feel her brain begin to relax. She couldn't say that she wanted to do this kind of work forever, because for one thing it didn't pay that well, but for the moment she had to admit that it was perfect.

CLIVE SHIFTED HIS weight under the saddle as Tanner pulled the gelding to a stop in a clearing on a sloping side hill. He drew in a deep breath as he studied the valley several thousand feet below him, dotted with farms and ranches, stretching to the mountains on the west side of the river. And when he closed his eyes, he felt echoes of the same peace he'd felt as a kid when he'd ridden this fence or searched for lost cattle. Or simply hung out, riding a more reliable horse along this same trail.

This was why he was fighting to keep his ranch. This sense of peace and rightness. He belonged here. This particular parcel of land was not part of the Hayes Ranch, but they'd leased it for grazing for as long as he could remember, and it was one of his favorite places to get away from the old man's scrutiny and criticisms. He had similar places on the ranch proper, where he could disappear for a few hours while appreciating the scents, sounds and simple pleasures of being outdoors. Work had been a similar escape. He knew the fences, the infrastructure, the machinery.

Dodging his father had given him a lot of practical skills.

He turned Clive back to the trail and rode on. They'd gotten past the rocky areas and were now on softer ground surrounded by old timber and deep brush. Rose was, of course, in the brush, making noise that Clive had used as an excuse to test Tanner's boundaries and balance earlier in the ride. The gelding was too winded now to try such nonsense, leaving Tanner free to enjoy his ride.

He'd thought that this boundary fence would be the problem child, since snow tended to accumulate in ridiculously large amounts in places, but so far, other than tightening, everything was in order. When he finally found an area in need of serious repair, it was close enough to the rough track that split the property that he'd be able to bring in posts and wire with the side-by-side and a trailer.

That didn't mean there weren't more challenges ahead, but he was feeling good about the day when he checked the time on his signal-less phone for the last time and turned to ride Clive to the rutted mountain road he'd follow back to the meeting area. He whistled for Rose, who pushed her way out of the underbrush and then fell in behind the horse. She was panting happily and covered with little sticky seedpods that he'd have to take care of before she hauled them home on her coat and sowed a new crop of weeds on the ranch. His dog might be getting a little older, but she could still hold her own on the mountain.

His thoughts turned to Whitney, a regular occurrence these days when he let his mind wander. What had she found on her leg of the trail? Was she going to try to fix stuff that needed two people? And was that tug of attraction going to keep growing as he spent more time around her? Or would it dissipate when the novelty wore off?

Tanner didn't see that happening.

He didn't have a firm read on her, but he liked what he saw. Desperation and the need to fit back into the community had driven him to ask for her help, and she'd not only agreed, she'd hired on. Len hadn't seemed too thrilled, but maybe the old man had sexist ideas about ranch workers.

He approached the meeting spot near the spring and felt his spirits lift when he saw her gelding grazing and then spotted her working on the pipe that fed the spring water into a trough.

She looked up as he approached and smiled at him, and the boost to his spirits became something more.

The woman was beautiful. Wisps of her blond hair had escaped the braid she always wore, and he knew when he got closer that he would admire the freckles scattered over her nose and probably study her mouth for a moment too long. She had an effect on him.

She wiped her hands down her pants, leaving green smears, studied the palms, then wiped again.

"I fixed a blockage." She pointed to the rusty clump of mud and algae lying on the ground. The trickle that had flowed when they arrived was now a steady stream.

"You're good at this ranch stuff," he said as he dismounted and pulled the reins over Clive's head. "You should do it for a living."

Her expression shifted just enough to tell him that he'd struck a nerve, which surprised him.

What kind of nerve?

"I think I'll stick with what I trained for."

"I don't know how you could go back to working in an office," he said. "Look at this workspace."

"I love it," she agreed, but there was a guarded note to her voice.

"Any adventures today?" he asked, changing the subject to the reason they were there.

"I'm not stuck to a tree. I did see a cougar."

"Really? I've never seen one in the wild," he confessed as she picked up her gelding's lead rope, which was dragging on the ground as he grazed. Her reins were wrapped around his neck near his throat and secured so that he could eat without breaking them. "I've seen my share of bears and elk and badgers, but never a cougar."

"It was pretty much a streak in the distance. Charley took offense, but other than that, no adventures."

"The fence?"

"Nothing to address."

They fell in step, leading their horses to the trailer parked fifty yards away. Rose was already there, lying in the shadow cast by the truck.

"Amazing," Tanner said as they neared the trailer. "No flat tires."

"Were you expecting one?" Whitney asked curiously.

"I haven't had an uneventful day in weeks, so, yes, maybe I was."

She tightened her mouth grimly as she gave her head a solemn shake. "Now you've done it. Jinxed yourself."

"I don't think so." He took a chance and dropped Clive's lead rope to the ground, tempting fate while simultaneously proving Whitney wrong as he allowed the gelding to graze while he loosened the cinch. Clive played along for once in his life, and Tanner pulled the saddle off the horse's sweaty back.

Whitney knew exactly what he was doing and gave him a gentle smirk before doing exactly the same thing. The difference was that she was dealing with Charley.

After Tanner brushed the seedpods off Rose's coat, he loaded her into the back seat of Whitney's truck and then they drove down the dusty track to the main road, taking turns opening and closing wire gates. They were almost to his ranch when he said, "When we were talking about the water lease, your dad mentioned that you are part owner of the ranch."

"I am, but he has the majority. He makes the decisions."

Interesting. He knew he shouldn't pry, but her guarded response earlier had hooked his curiosity. "Is there a reason you don't work the place with him?"

"Money."

The immediate answer surprised him. It was logical, yet somehow disappointing.

"I like security and I like nice things," she said, as if sensing his thoughts. "Money helps with both."

"Nothing wrong with either of those, but what about the things money can't buy?" he asked. The cliché had merit in his book.

"I think life is better when it's well funded."

He couldn't argue with her, but was still aware of a niggling sense of disappointment at her reply. He wasn't in a place to talk about nice things, living in Dena's zillion-dollar house and trying to keep his dad's showpiece ranch running, but the Fox Ranch was nothing to sneeze at. It was well kept and orderly.

You want money, too.

He did, but it was to keep his ranch, not to indulge. A shoestring budget was fine, and while he'd been comfortable enough working for the wheat farm, he'd learned good lessons in money management during the lean years when he'd put himself through college. Money was good, but living and working in a place that brought you peace was better.

Tanner shifted in his seat and tried to force his mind elsewhere. Whitney saw things differently. It was her life.

But he still wished she hadn't said that.

THE NEXT MORNING, Whit was woken by her dad knocking on her door. "I thought you needed to be out of here by six."

She grabbed her phone, then let out a groan. Twenty minutes to get ready, catch and saddle her horse, and make lunch. She rarely overslept, but it had been a long day yesterday and it had been a minute since she'd spent the entire day in the saddle.

"I caught Charley for you." Her dad looked up from his coffee as she came into the kitchen wearing yesterday's jeans and a navy flannel shirt over a pink T-shirt, and carrying her boots.

"Thanks," Whitney said, sitting in her chair and pulling on the boots.

"I saddled him, too."

Whit raised her gaze. "Thanks." Her dad never coddled. Everyone saddled their own horses—unless they were going to be late to the job, apparently.

"Made your lunch."

Whitney narrowed her eyes. This was not normal Ben Fox behavior. Something was up.

"Why?" she asked bluntly.

"The meeting is at six tonight." He spoke as if that explained everything, which it did as soon as she recalled the threat of the community board. "If you don't show, I might end up in charge of concessions or something."

"Dad. Don't worry. I have your back. And if I don't, the word you need to practice is *no*."

"Say no to The Trio? Ha. Good one." Ben drilled her with a look that had a pleading edge to it. "Don't be late, okay?"

"Okay." She pulled on her jacket, then fastened the flaps on her saddlebags, which had a fully packed lunch in one side. After slinging the bags over her shoulder, she gave her father a reassuring pat on the arm. "I won't abandon you."

"Thank you. I don't need to be fighting these battles at my age."

"I'll be there," Whit repeated as she headed to the door. The Trio had terrified her as a teen, but she was older and wiser and not so easily buffaloed. Yes, she would do her part for Hearts of the West, as would her father, but neither of them was going to be ramrodded into doing more than they could handle. Not on her watch.

When she arrived at the Hayes Ranch fifteen minutes late, Tanner was waiting at the turnaround spot with Clive, who was saddled and ready to go. As soon as she came to a stop, he opened the rear truck door, tossed in his gear, and then led Clive to the back of the trailer.

"I overslept," she said when she caught up with him at the trailer.

"It isn't like you have to clock in." He spoke in a light voice, but she sensed a reserve and wondered if he'd encountered an event after proclaiming yesterday an uneventful day.

"I have a thing about being on time. Years in the office, I guess," she said as he tied Clive and then exited the trailer, closing and latching the door behind him.

"We were a little more free-form on the wheat farm."

"But you probably worked all night sometimes."

"Oh yeah," he agreed. "Ready?"

"I am."

And she was also concerned about his distracted attitude. Should she ask?

No. She was there to ride fence, not to suss out her boss's personal issues. But Tanner didn't feel like a boss, and they'd made an agreement, which involved his personal life, so...

"Everything okay?"

He gave her a surprised look, as if she was infringing on his business, which in turn made her feel self-conscious. Whit didn't do self-conscious and the fact that she felt that way both irritated her and shut her up, so when he said, "Everything's fine," she turned her mind elsewhere.

Or tried to.

Definite change of energy between them.

She could live with that, but…she didn't like it. When she thought back to how many times she'd worked alongside difficult people on a project, the fact that she didn't like the shift gave her pause. It was almost as if she missed him.

A man she hadn't known for that long.

But with whom she felt an affinity.

There was no denying that, but maybe, as Maddie had suggested, she'd misread him. Her perceptions were skewed by his business dealings with her dad and the fact that he was wickedly attractive. And he was fun when he played.

Today Tanner opened all the gates and Whitney let him. When they arrived at the turnaround point, they unloaded their horses in mutual silence. It wasn't a petulant silence or a punishing silence, it was more of a Tanner-getting-a-grip silence and she couldn't see how that could possibly involve her. In fact, when he caught her mid-stare, he gave a reassuring smile, telling her that whatever had made him go quiet wasn't personal.

Had he encountered more blowback because of who he was? Possibly so, because after riding the rutted road together for a mile or so, to the place where they'd both left off the day before, his expression relaxed as he lined out the plan for the day, which was pretty much ride fence, meet in the middle. No mention of not getting stuck to a tree.

She missed that. It made her want to…what?

Reach out and touch him? Reassure him?

Instead, Whit touched the brim of her hat and she and Charley made a right-angle turn to head through the brush to the fence line half a mile away.

TANNER SUCKED IN a deep breath of pine-scented air. It was good to be on the mountain, feeling the echoes of his teen years. His taut mental muscles began to relax. He'd made two mistakes the previous day. The first was asking Whitney what motivated her and getting the last answer he wanted to hear, and the second was accepting the phone call from his brother.

Grant, being Grant, wanted the second payment Tanner owed him in return for keeping the ranch off the market. He had a business opportunity that he needed to jump on. Tanner had taken a long hard look at the books, and his savings, and figured he could scrape it together with the understanding there would be no more to come. And that Grant would stay off his back about it.

He wouldn't, but the deal would be done, and his brother would have no recourse.

He'd yet to answer Grant, but if he could swing the deal, he would and he would pray that he had no big equipment repairs and that the pivots remained operational, and Len didn't hurt himself again, so that when Whitney signed off, he was paying one salary instead of two.

Clive picked his way over rocky ground, taking greater care than usual. If the gelding didn't watch himself, he was going to become a dependable mount. Usually when Tanner thought such things, Clive brought him back to his senses in short order, but the horse kept picking his way along the trail. Once they reached flatter ground, Tanner dismounted, giving the horse a break and stretching his legs. The fence, which had to have been a challenge to build in the rocky area, was in decent shape. Saints be praised!

Rose took advantage of the stop to find a nice boggy area to roll in and reappeared at his side sporting a faintly green tinge to her yellow coat. But a lot of the seedpods were now drowning in the bog, so he was good with that.

And Whitney had no trouble allowing a smelly, muddy dog into her back seat, so all was well.

Except that part where he'd judged her.

If she was motivated by wanting nice things, as his dad had been, so be it. She'd given him an honest answer and it wasn't her fault that it touched a nerve. Money complicated things. But so did lack of the stuff.

He let out a breath.

Money concerns were controlling him at the moment, and he didn't like it one bit. He reached the end of the east-west fence line half an hour later and turned to the south. If things went according to plan—which wasn't a frequent occurrence lately—then he should run into Whitney soon.

As he did.

She lifted her chin when she saw him, smiled in a way that made him forget money worries and found himself nudging Clive to move faster over the soft earth of the trail. The gelding obliged and he and Whit reined up at the same time, the two geldings touching noses in greeting.

"Good day?" he asked.

"You have remarkable luck in fences. I replaced a bunch of staples, but there was nothing broken, no rotted posts."

He raised his eyebrows. "Did you just jinx me?"

She wrinkled her nose. "I did it on purpose."

They worked their way back to the dirt track that split the allotment and disappeared over the mountain to another rancher's allotment on the other side of an official Forest Service gate. He glanced at Whitney as she moved past him to take the lead on the narrow, rutted road. There was no getting around his attraction to this woman who wanted what he didn't have, and didn't really aspire to have.

If he could make enough money to hang on to his property, he would be a grateful man. He didn't need a lot of nice things. He simply wanted peace of mind.

TANNER WAS MORE talkative on the ride back to the trailer. They decided on a cross-country shortcut, and as they left the trail, Tanner gave a whistle. Rose did not appear. Tanner whistled again.

"That's odd," he said. He pushed back his hat and scanned the area around them.

Whit had to agree. The Lab enjoyed exploring, occasionally giving a squirrel or chipmunk a good chase, but she never went too far from her human, since it was her job to make sure he was all right.

"The last time I saw her, she was chasing the ground squirrel around the big boulder near the line shack." She'd made two circles before the squirrel had headed off in another direction.

Tanner pulled Clive to a stop and whistled again.

Birds sang, a chipmunk scolded them, but there was no sound of a Labrador retriever crashing through the brush.

"This doesn't feel right," Tanner said.

There had been wolves spotted in their area, but surely they would have heard something had the sweet old girl gotten into a rumble.

"Let's head back the way we came," Tanner said.

Whit's stomach knotted as they turned the horses. Like Tanner said, this felt wrong.

The corners of Tanner's mouth were tight as he urged Clive back down the trail the way they'd just come. Whit followed behind as Tanner called Rose's name and whistled. They'd gone close to a half mile when a sound caught Whit's ear.

"Hold up," she said. Tanner's gelding stopped, the clatter of rocks beneath his hooves mingling with the low whimper.

Tanner dismounted, folding his reins over the gelding's neck. Clive lowered his head to shake off the reins and then stepped on one as Tanner walked to the edge of the deep gully behind the shack.

"Rose!"

Another whimper.

"She's down there," Tanner said before he disappeared over the side of the gully. Whit took a few seconds to tie Clive and Charley to sturdy tree branches, then jogged to the edge of the gully where she could see Rose at the bottom, struggling to get out from between two angular rocks where she'd gotten herself stuck. Despite his careful movements, Tanner's feet went out from under him on the steep slope and he skidded the last couple of yards. Pushing himself upright, he rubbed Rose's head, and she licked his hand.

"It's okay, girl," he murmured.

Whit swallowed as she watched the pair. It was obvious how much he cared for the dog and how much the dog cared for him, and Whit was a sucker for such things.

"She must have fallen," Tanner said before trying to get a hold on her to ease her out from between the rocks. The dog yelped and he immediately released his hold.

"Bruised or broken ribs, I imagine." Whit started down the slope to join him, talus rolling beneath her feet.

"Yeah." Tanner analyzed the situation, sitting back on his heels as he stroked the Lab's head and told her things would be all right. "We need to move that rock. She's really wedged in."

Whit knelt next to the dog and gently felt beneath her. "I'll find a pry pole."

Tanner nodded and spoke to the dog again while Whit took off to find something to wedge between the smaller of the two rocks and the rock next to it. She returned with a sturdy windfall. Tanner took the branch, broke off a few lower limbs, then jammed it into place. The rock moved when he pushed down, then slid back into place.

"I'll hold it and see if you can get her out," he said.

"Let me hold it." She didn't want to hurt Rose and simply wasn't strong enough to lift an eighty-pound dog.

They switched places. Tanner got his hands situated and then said, "Go."

Whit used all of her weight to pull down on the branch. The rock moved and Rose gave a sharp yip as Tanner lifted her free.

He fell back on the talus, holding the dog on top of him as Whit let go of the branch and the rock settled into place. He ran his hands over Rose's side. She had an oozing wound where she'd torn her hide on the tumble down the hill, and she winced and cried when Tanner felt along her ribs.

"It's going to be tricky getting her back to the truck."

"I'll ride Charley back, unhitch the trailer, then drive up here."

"Windfall across the road," Tanner said. "We'll have to get her out on horseback."

Tanner carried Rose up the hill, no easy task with the loose scree moving under his feet. Whit mounted Charley, who was the more reliable of the two geldings, and Tanner eased the dog up in front of her, across her thighs. Whit gave the dog a gentle pat.

"She knows we're not hurting her on purpose," she said.

"Yeah." Tanner's features remained tight even though the first part of the rescue had been successful. He mounted Clive and they made their way down the mountain, following the rutted road that cut the allotment in two. When they got to the trailer, Tanner eased the dog off the saddle and laid her on the ground. Rose tried to get to her feet, but he put a gentle hand on her, stopping her.

"I'm worried about internal injuries if she broke ribs."

"Our ranch vet is good," Whit said. "I'll call her."

"Thanks," was all he said, but there was no mistaking how much his dog meant to him.

Whit headed to the truck to open the back door to allow Tanner to set Rose on the rear seat. The Lab closed her eyes, but her tail gave a few reassuring thumps before he closed the door.

Whit drove faster than normal as they headed for town, watching Tanner out of the corner of her eye as she drove. He stared straight ahead.

"I know she's going to be okay," he said to the windshield.

But she was hurting, and no one wanted to see that. Whit reached out to touch his arm and he shifted his gaze. She met his hazel eyes and felt a rush of compassion tinged with something deeper before dragging her attention back to the road.

"You might want to slow down," he murmured.

Indeed, the last wire gate was fast approaching.

"My brakes are good," she replied in the same low tone he'd used.

She sensed the look he gave her as she slowed the truck, but she wasn't setting herself up for another flash of discomfort. The guy put her off her game. She didn't want to react to him the way she was, but what could she do?

WHIT MADE IT to the vet's office in record time. The office had just closed, and the waiting room was empty. Tanner left Rose on the back seat of the truck where she was comfortable and followed Whitney into the clinic. Whitney greeted the receptionist by name—Callie—and then Dr. Leonard, a harried-looking older woman, came from the back and followed the two of them out to the truck. Rose lifted her head and thumped her tail again as the doctor ran her hands over Rose's sides.

"Let's bring her in, get an X-ray," she said.

Whit headed to the clinic door to hold it open while Tanner eased Rose off the seat. A moment later, he surrendered his girl to a vet tech and then followed the canine gurney to the examination room. Whit hung back and Tanner wished that he could tell her it was okay to go, but she was his ride, and it wasn't like he could call an Uber or ask Len to pick him up.

When Tanner rejoined Whit half an hour later, he had what he considered good news. "Bruised and cracked ribs, no breaks. They suspect a concussion, so they're keeping her overnight for observation. They stitched up the gash, and other than being sore, she's going to be fine."

"Poor girl," Whit said as Tanner sat beside her on the hard wooden bench. "She's so sweet and trusting. You hate to see her hurting."

"It's tough," Tanner agreed. "She wants to go wherever I go, but she'll be ten this year, and isn't as agile as she used to be. But when I leave her at home, it breaks her heart."

"She'll be back on the trail before you know it," Whit said, leaning her shoulder into his in a reassuring way.

And wasn't it funny that it was a shoulder bump that made him realize how much he liked this woman?

She was fun, tough, empathetic. Ridiculously attractive. A ranch girl who'd made it in the corporate world and had every intention of going back. There was so much about her that he liked, which was why he needed to step back.

It was plain to see that despite this odd little interlude, with her helping him find a foothold in the community and his hiring her to work on his ranch, they had different goals and motivations. They had little in common in that regard. She was going to leave the area and land a high-powered job because she liked the security that money brought. There was nothing wrong with that. He, on the other hand, wanted to pull the place he loved out of debt and squeak by. Yes, that was about money, too, but he was willing to sacrifice financial security in order to keep his ranch.

He was about to speak when the receptionist said, "Mr. Hayes. I have some forms."

Whitney suddenly got to her feet, as if remembering something, then said, "I'll meet you outside."

When he stepped out of the building a few minutes later, he found her texting.

"Am I keeping you from something?"

Her head came up. "There's a meeting I was supposed to go to with my dad. I was just telling him what happened and that I'm taking you home."

"Is it important?"

"He should be able to hold his own." Tanner cocked his head at her dubious tone, and she explained, "It's a community board meeting. They're making plans for the Hearts of the West event and Dad's deeply afraid of being strong-armed into doing more than he has time for. He's kind of a pushover when it comes to these things and, unfortunately for him, people know it."

"I'll go with you."

"I don't think you know what you're getting into."

"How so?"

She let out a breath. "You're fair game."

"I don't understand," he said slowly.

"Go to this meeting with me and you will. When it comes to assigning tasks, the women who run the community board are... How shall I put this?" She folded her arms over her chest as she gave a quick glance skyward. "Like wolves stalking sheep. The sheep being the community members."

"They can't be that bad."

She studied him for a moment, as if giving him time to change his mind. Finally, she said, "I guess you can find out if you like. My dad will appreciate it."

Tanner jerked his head in the direction of the truck. "Let's go."

A faint it's-your-funeral smile curved her lips, making him wonder if he should heed her warning. But there was no way he could do that. Not after she'd helped him get his dog to the vet.

"If you insist," she said in a grim voice. "We'll consider it another step in the Hayes reputation rehabilitation."

CHAPTER SEVEN

THE LARKSPUR COMMUNITY HALL was located in the original Larkspur High School, a 1920s-era brick building that had been converted into offices. The gym now served as a meeting room and when Whit and Tanner stepped inside, the maple boards squeaked under their feet. Immediately, all eyes turned toward them—and, Whit noticed, her dad's eyes held a hint of desperation in their depths. Glancing up at the massive whiteboard behind the table where The Trio and their minions held court, Whit understood why. There was her father's name next to—Whit gave a mental groan—Prize Solicitation. What were The Trio thinking?

One look at Debra's face answered that question. They were thinking that Whitney was home and would take over for him. But what if she got a job before Hearts of the West, which was a month away?

Tanner and Whit took seats behind her dad, and Whit patted one of his stiffly held shoulders. "I'll handle it, Dad."

"You couldn't have saved me," Ben whispered over his shoulder. "I even said no. It didn't help."

"Whitney," Debra Crane said brightly. "Can we also put you down for the solicitation of prizes?"

"That won't work for me." The words came out sharply, but Whit didn't care, even though she'd clearly heard a gasp from the audience. She had had a day, and she wasn't about to be ramrodded into something she didn't want to do. Not when she could help with other assignments more efficiently. She was tired of allowing the fear that, if crossed, The Trio might resign the board, to allow them to continue to push people around.

Debra was in the middle of writing Whit's name on the board when she stopped and turned toward the room. "Excuse me?"

"I don't want to ask for donations and neither does my father. We'll help in another capacity." Whit spoke firmly, causing Debra's eyebrows to approach her hairline.

"I'm sorry, but we've already—"

"I'm happy to volunteer for the setup committee. It's closer to my skill set and certainly closer to Dad's."

Whit felt her father shift in his chair, but she didn't look at him, fearing that if she broke eye contact with Debra, the woman would finish writing her name on the whiteboard.

"It only makes sense to match people to their skills," Whit continued as if schooling the woman, which she was, in a public forum no less. But it was time to rein in The Trio. "We might hide it, but my dad and I are not public relations people."

"Obviously," Margo muttered from her chair at the front, but she spoke in a low enough voice that she could deny saying anything at all. Behind her, people were starting to murmur and Whit wondered if she might have started a low-key uprising.

"I appreciate all the work that the board puts into this, and I want to help," she said. "Please put us, my father and me, on the setup committee. You have openings."

Debra, obviously not used to having her steamroller tactics questioned, made a quick goldfish impression, opening and closing her mouth, then she turned to erase Whitney's and Ben's names from the prize solicitation committee with a slash of the erasing cloth. She then added them to the setup committee, forming their names with vicious strokes, and dotting the *i* in Whitney's name with a stab that flattened the marker head.

Margo let out a sigh and stood. She held out her hand for the marker, which Debra passed over before sitting.

"Would *anyone* like to procure prizes?" she asked. "Anyone here with that *skill set*?"

Whit let the verbal arrow bounce off her and was gratified to see that two people raised their hands, albeit tentatively. Both names were erased from other committees and added to prize solicitation.

And so it went for the next ten minutes, with people resigning from assigned committees and being added to others. The Trio was no longer having fun. People had struggled against them in the past, and a lucky few had gotten their way, but tonight had played out differently. Whit wondered briefly if they would abandon their positions, then decided that they loved power too much. They'd come up with other means of control.

Which they did in short order.

Margo's forehead was shiny by the time the committees were all sorted out. She let out a breath, drew herself up and turned a smile toward Tanner, whose chin came up, and when Whit glanced sideways, she saw a clear deer-in-the-headlights look on his face.

"Mr. Hayes, how nice to see you. We appreciate you volunteering for the setup committee. Can we also count on the usual generous donation from the Hayes Ranch?"

Whit guessed that Tanner had no idea what that donation might be, since she felt him shift in his seat beside her.

"The facility rental," she said out of the corner of her mouth. The community did not own the historic barn and grounds where Hearts of the West was held, and it was the only place suitable for the event, which had expanded every year.

"How much?" he murmured back.

"A few thousand, plus the insurance."

Tanner went still and Whit had to fight not to turn to him. He cleared his throat but before he could speak, Debra gushed, "We are so grateful for your family's continued support. It means so much to the community. When you didn't reply to our letters, I was concerned, so…again, thank you for showing up personally."

Whit's quick sideways look took in a stony profile.

Was he not a charitable guy? Or was it simply the way Debra assumed that the donation was a done deal that rubbed him the wrong way?

Whit decided to go with the latter. It certainly put her back up, even as she was basking in the afterglow of her victory.

"I owe you that chocolate cake you like so much," Ben murmured as they walked out of the meeting fifteen minutes later. Tanner had gone to speak with Debra, then caught up with them at Ben's truck.

"How long have those three been in charge?" he asked.

"Forever maybe?" Ben said.

"No one wants the job," Whit added, "so that allows them to go mad with power. They know they're bullet-proof."

Ben glanced Whit's way. "Maybe you and Maddie and Kat should take over."

"That'd be grand, Dad." She mock-punched his shoulder. "I appreciate what Margo, Debra and Judy do. I would just like them to soften their tactics."

"I'd be careful," Ben said. "They'll be gunning for you next year." He turned to Tanner. "How's your dog?"

Tanner filled him in on Rose's condition, then said, "By

the way, everything is squared away on the water lease. Stop by Harris and Sons offices anytime to add your signature. After that, I'll have Len handle the details of the diversion."

"Great." Ben smiled at Tanner, then turned to Whit as he pulled his keys out of his pocket. "Guess I'll see you at home?"

As Whit and Tanner headed to her truck and trailer, she murmured, "Sorry about that. I can truly say I didn't see that coming. I thought at worst they'd assign you to a committee that you were ill suited for."

"I ignored the letters. They're on my desk. I didn't open them, because I assumed they were for some community event I wouldn't partake in."

They stopped next to the trailer and Tanner climbed onto the running board to check the patient geldings waiting inside, then lightly jumped back to the pavement.

He looked down at Whit and said, "That'll teach me."

She gave a perfunctory smile.

The ride to the Hayes Ranch was accomplished in silence, but it wasn't the oddly uncomfortable silence that they'd traveled in that morning, when Tanner had been preoccupied. Apparently, he'd worked out whatever that issue had been, only to be presented with a new one.

When they arrived at the ranch, Tanner suggested that Whit leave Charley there rather than hauling him home and bringing him back again in the morning when they headed back to the mountain.

"Unless you need a day off."

"I do not," Whit said. She didn't want to kick around the house, waiting to hear from the recruiter she'd contacted the day before via email. Yes, she had to go back to work, but she wasn't in a hurry.

"I'll drive tomorrow." He gestured at the trailer where

the horses were starting to shift restlessly now that they were on the ranch and familiar smells were coming in. "The boys can have a sleepover."

"Sure." Charley and Clive had bonded. They weren't ready to share a feeder, but they could share a corral.

They unloaded the horses, and released them into a good-sized pen that already had sweet-smelling hay in the feeders. Tanner's mare was in a separate pen, so Whit felt secure leaving Charley for an overnighter.

When she headed back to her truck, Tanner fell into step with her but there was something in the way he carried himself, the energy he exuded, that told her something was up. Something beyond his dog and the results of the board meeting. Instead of opening the truck door, she turned to him. The night air was soft on her face and the breeze teased the wisps of hair that had escaped her braid. She pushed them back in an almost impatient gesture.

"Is something wrong?" It was more of a statement than a question, which Whit had discovered long ago usually gave her a quicker answer. Simply assume something is wrong and state it as a fact.

Tanner's chest rose as he pulled in a deep breath. His eyes seemed darker than usual in the artificial light shining down on them from the overhead pole fixture. Dark and troubled.

"I can't afford what they're asking for."

The stark statement sent a minor jolt through her. "You can't?"

If he had told her that he was flying to the moon that night, she wouldn't have been any more stunned.

"No." He dropped his chin, then shook his head and lifted it again almost immediately, as if he wasn't going to let life defeat him. "The ranch is in the red and I'm fighting to get it out."

"How?" Whit immediately regretted the question. "None of my business."

"Dad made some financial mistakes." His lips twisted in a cynical way as he said the last words. "And he was too proud to tell us." The twist became a full-on smirk. "Classic Carl Hayes."

Whit pressed her lips together. She couldn't find words. Didn't want to find words. So instead she lifted a hand to touch his face, causing a swirl of warmth to flood through her as she stroked the stubbled plane of his cheek before she casually dropped her hand.

His gaze had darkened at her touch, and he started to lift his own hand, only to let it fall again.

He was fighting something. Maybe reality. She had no way of knowing, but her heart, which she considered dependable in most circumstances, did exactly what she didn't want it to do. It started twisting. She wanted to be empathetic but…distant. Was that even possible?

This wasn't a dog she was dealing with. This was a man. So much more dangerous.

But when had she ever stepped back from danger? Except for that one time at the alligator farm…

"No one knows?" she asked.

He shook his head. "And they won't. Right?"

Whit's gaze snapped up. "If you don't trust me, then why—"

The look on his face stopped her cold. He did trust her, or he wouldn't have told her the truth.

"Okay," she said. "When are they expecting the check?"

"I put them off, told the tall lady that I had to talk to my accountant. I doubt that Dad funded them last year, because things were tight according to the books, but appearances meant a lot to him, so maybe he scraped the money together somehow. I don't know."

"Okay. Let me think on this."

"I'm not asking for you to get involved." There was a fierce note in his voice. He cleared his throat and said, "Since I asked you to help me with my reputation, I thought you should know that there's a reason for my apparent stinginess. And that you may soon be released from that duty." He spoke unironically, as if working for him had been a duty.

Whit cast about for solutions, as she always did when confronted by a problem.

"I don't need to be paid for helping you." It would have been nice to bring in a paycheck to help tide her over, but she had free rent, as her dad had mentioned yet again that morning, and when she was done on the Hayes Ranch, she could take another temporary job that paid. She wasn't going to cause her neighbor, whom she was beginning to like more than she probably should, additional financial difficulties.

Tanner had other ideas. "You will be paid."

She thought not, but she wasn't going to have an argument under a yard light that turned them both blue. Instead, she gave him the same look she'd given her dad upon finding out that they were in similar circumstances. "Thank you for telling me. It helps me understand a few things."

Like the moment on the mountain yesterday where she'd probably come off as money hungry and he'd clammed up all of a sudden.

"When you come to work tomorrow, I want things to be as they were this morning. In other words, I'm paying you."

They studied each other in the oddly blue light.

"We'll figure something out," she said softly.

"We?"

Her chin came up. "I took you to that meeting."

"But you are not responsible for what happened there."

She begged to differ. She was responsible for some people being more comfortable in their Hearts of the West work assignments. She was also responsible for bringing him into harm's way, and putting him into a situation he had no way of getting out of while saving face.

Tanner took a step closer, and Whit became aware of the fact that his nearness only made her want to close the space between them even more. Suddenly she wasn't thinking about paychecks or getting Tanner off the hook for the venue rental. She was thinking about the guy in front of her who smelled so good. Whose hazel eyes were searching her face for answers.

If only she knew the question.

Whit broke first, but probably not in the way Tanner expected.

"We've got to be unified on this," she said in her corporate team-leading voice.

He frowned at her. "In what way?"

"In a you and me way. You can use my help. You may as well accept that I'm going to give it."

"Okay." The word came out grudgingly. Tanner was not a man who was used to being forced into teamwork. And there was still something in his expression that part of her wanted to answer. When his gaze dropped thoughtfully to her lips, Whit knew it was time to de-escalate.

"We'll handle this together," she repeated firmly.

"I'm not—"

Whit put a hand on his upper arm, effectively cutting him off before rising onto her toes to gave him a quick, casual kiss. So casual that he had to get the message that she was putting whatever it was that they were feeling into the friend zone. If she was romantically interested, she wouldn't have given him such a chaste little kiss. And she wouldn't have stepped out of reach so quickly after delivering it.

At least she hoped that was the message she sent.

"The deal is sealed," she said as if she couldn't still feel the warmth of his mouth on hers.

He touched his mouth with the side of his index finger. "Good sealing," he said.

"I'll see you tomorrow." She walked the few steps to her truck and pulled the door open. "Take good care of Charley."

TANNER POURED HIS second cup of coffee at 5:30 a.m. to his surprise, he'd fallen asleep almost instantly the night before, then awoken at 4:00 a.m. and lain staring at the ceiling, worrying about his dog and wondering if he'd made a mistake telling Whit the truth about the ranch finances. Wondering if that quick kiss had been a gesture of understanding or pity or what. Or perhaps it was exactly as she'd said—a gesture to seal the deal. It wasn't the first time she'd touched him. He knew because he remembered every instant that she'd made contact. A hand on the arm, a pat on his cheek. A kiss on the lips.

Whatever had prompted the kiss, it had stirred a longing in him that rivaled his concern for his dog and his indecision as to how to make the community donation that was so obviously expected. The quick little kiss made him realize that he was alone, which was not a healthy state of being.

He turned his mind back to the donation. He could change his yes to a no. He may have to, although it would have to be soon, because at this point the community board was counting on him to provide the venue rental fee. He should have opened the letters from the board, but had considered them the mail equivalent of spam. He'd have to watch things more carefully in the future.

Say no or come up with the money?

Saying no was not going to help him get future plumbers and mechanics. It might not hurt, but he didn't know. That was the problem with returning to the small town he'd only known as a kid. He wasn't familiar with the players or the unspoken rules. Whit was guiding him.

Whit, who'd offered to work without pay. As if.

He got to his feet to pour a third cup of coffee. The light was on in Len's house, but that was not unusual. Sometimes Tanner wondered if the old guy slept with his lights on, but kept the thought to himself. Len was an efficient manager, but he wasn't exactly warm and fuzzy. He liked to be left alone, and frankly, Tanner liked leaving him alone. Unlike the foreman's relationship with Carl, which Tanner would have called a friendship of sorts, theirs was more of a professional relationship. Tanner had grocery shopped for the old man a time or two while he was recovering from his injury, but Len had recently told him that his nephew Kenny—a kind of squirrelly kid who seemed resentful of Tanner—had volunteered to take over the job.

But Len knew the ranch, and Tanner could depend on him. So what if he didn't want to be friends, too? Tanner had his own friends…who lived seven hundred miles away in the middle of Washington State. And it looked like Whitney might also qualify, if he could put his growing feelings aside.

After finishing his third cup of coffee, Tanner headed down the hall to shower, only to be stopped by the landline ringing—at 6:00 a.m. He reversed course and answered on the third ring.

"Is this the Hayes Ranch?"

"It is."

"Your steers are in my grain field."

"My steers—"

"Are in my grain field. I'd appreciate it if you'd get them out of there. Now."

"Where are you located?"

"I'm your neighbor to the east. Stevens Ranch."

"I'll get right on it," he said. Because his neighbor's next step would be to call the brand inspector, who would confiscate his cattle. He was kind of surprised that hadn't already happened, given the way his dad liked to fight with the neighbors. That would be a nice bit of payback.

He went to his room to change out of his sweats into jeans and the first shirt he put his hand on. He yanked on his socks, jammed his feet into his boots and headed down the hall. The house seemed empty without Rose showing him the way to the kitchen, but at least he knew she was in good hands.

He grabbed his jacket off the hook by the side door and headed to Len's house. The old man yelled for him to come in after he knocked, and Tanner opened the door to find Len seated at his table, an old-school game of solitaire laid out on the table in front of him.

"The steers are out. Stevens's property."

Len's head jerked back. "I thought you had that girl ride the fence."

"I did."

"Doesn't look like she did too good a job of it."

Tanner let the comment slide. "Right now, I just want to get the steers out of trespass." Thereby hopefully shoring up his relationship with the neighbors. Unlike his dad, he recognized the value of getting people on your side, which was one reason he was going to come up with a way to make the usual Hayes Ranch donation to the Hearts of the West event.

"I'll go with you."

Tanner shook his head. "Whitney should be here soon.

I'll take her with me." Len looked like he wanted to argue, so Tanner added, "I want to check the fence with her. Find out what the problem was."

Len made a silent "ah" and then Tanner heard the sound of an engine in the distance. "She's here. I'll keep you posted."

Tanner went behind the barn to catch Clive and Charley. By the time he led the geldings out of the corral, Whitney had pulled up next to his truck and trailer.

"Change of plans," he said, tamping down the part of him that lit up upon seeing her. She might have given him an I've-got-your-back kiss, but she was still his employee and they had work to do.

"How so?"

"The steers are in the Stevens Ranch grain field."

A frown brought her eyebrows together as the realization struck that she'd ridden the fence the steers had to go through to get to that grain field.

"No way. That fence was tight." She spoke with such indignation that, despite having to spend the morning rounding up steers instead of doing the work on his agenda, Tanner found himself fighting a smile. Not that he was going to let her see.

"I guess we'll find out," he replied in a neutral tone.

"Guess so," she said. She set her hands on her hips and looked out across the field to where she'd ridden the first day, then brought her gaze back to him, a flash of challenge lighting her eyes. "If the fence was breached at one of the spots where I fixed it, I'll eat my hat."

"WOULD YOU LIKE ketchup for your hat, or will you eat it plain?"

They'd driven to the Stevens Ranch, spotted the steers in the grain field before the ranch buildings came into sight, stopped the trailer and unloaded the horses. The first step was to find the breach in the fence and see about pushing the steers back through it. The break was at Whit's repair.

She picked up the wire with the metal sleeve that had clamped the two broken pieces together still hanging on one end. One of the wires had slipped free.

She gave a defeated sigh and let her chin fall to her chest in a very un-Whitney-like way.

Tanner pushed back his hat. "The sleeve failed. It happens."

"Easy for you to say. You didn't get all egotistical about your fence-fixing abilities. Now I have to eat crow for the second time this month."

"The first time being...?"

"When I came to you to ask you to please continue the water lease with my dad after you messed up my car."

"Which as you now know, I would have done anyway because I need the money. You didn't need to eat crow."

"Argh." Whit raised her fists to the sky. "Wasted crow."

Tanner couldn't help but smile. He loved it when Whit did Whit, and if he wasn't careful, he was going to fall in love with this woman. Which in turn made him glad that they'd talked about what they wanted in life so that he wouldn't make any mistakes in that regard. Whitney wanted a comfortable life with nice things, and he wanted to hang onto a debt-ridden ranch. That put them firmly in the just-friends zone.

But with Whitney looking at him the way she was now, with that sassy smile on her lips, he had to admit that he wouldn't mind making a few minor errors with her.

"Let's push them through."

They remounted their horses and circled the steers, who were spread through the grain field, bringing them into a bunch, then pushing them toward the opening. Once the lead steer figured out where the break was, he dashed through, and the rest followed.

"I'll get the tools," Tanner said.

The steers began to scatter, working their way through the trees, seeking out the tender grass that grew in the sunlit areas. Whit guarded the break, in case one of the steers decided fresh grain shoots were better than young grass, but none of the cattle seemed interested in returning to the field.

Tanner fixed the fence the exact same way that Whit had, but he used two sleeves instead of one, crimping them with extra force. Maybe she wasn't the only one who was egotistical about her skills.

"By the way," he said conversationally, "I'm still waiting for you to out-cowboy me."

"Maybe that's already been done. Maybe you don't know defeat when you see it."

"That makes no sense."

She laughed, unconcerned, and started packing tools.

"Any news on Rose?"

"Not yet. I plan to call when we get back."

They rode back to the barn side by side through the uncut meadow grass. Tanner explained how he'd leased out part of his farming for the same reason he'd leased the water, but that he still had hayfields to tend to once his crew showed up.

"Until then, I'm hanging on as best I can. Len will be on his feet before long and then I should be able to spend time maintaining equipment and other fun things."

"You have corrals to clean," she pointed out.

"I know."

"I'm good with a tractor," she said as she leaned down to open the gate from her horse.

"Show-off," Tanner muttered.

"This is part of out-cowboying you. It's the small skills that win things."

"Yeah, yeah, yeah," he groused as he rode through the gate. "Stand back."

Whit did as she was told and was impressed that Tanner managed to maneuver Clive so that he was able to close the gate. The gelding jumped forward when Tanner tried to drop the latch, almost unbalancing him, but overall, it was impressive.

"Bravo," she said. "Clive is coming along."

She began leading Charley to the trailer, thinking they'd put some work in on the tangled stretch of fence on the mountain that Tanner had told her about, and be done with it, but he stopped her.

"It's late. We'll work around here today, go to the mountain tomorrow."

She gave him a sideways look. "If the steers don't get out, that is."

"Are you questioning my fencing skills?"

"Just curious to see if they stand the test of time."

Tanner seemed lighthearted today, which made her wonder if he was trying to distract her from his confession the night before. Deflection by banter.

The guy needed breathing room after telling her the truth about his ranch.

Maybe she did, too. Maybe banter was the way to handle their relationship from here on out. It would simplify matters, but it wasn't like they could banter their way to a solution for the venue rental issue. She'd meant what she'd said about being a team, but it was up to Tanner as to whether to enlist her help.

She thought about that as she unsaddled Charley and then released him into the corral. Tanner took his time with

Clive, brushing him down before leading him to the pen. Whit rocked back on her heels, hands in her back pockets, waiting for orders when he returned to the horse trailer.

"Since you're good with the tractor, let's see what you can do with those corrals."

"Happy to," she said.

And so she spent the afternoon cleaning corrals and stacking the compost in piles to be spread on the fields after breaking down. It was a tiring job, and a dusty one, but she'd made some decent progress when Tanner waved her to a stop. And by some miracle she'd managed to spend most of the time thinking about her future—her real future. She needed to get busy with her job search, up her networking game and call her former coworkers to see where they'd landed.

Tanner appeared at the gate of the corral she was finishing and made a slicing motion across his throat, followed by a gesture to indicate that she should leave the tractor where she was working. Whit lowered the bucket, popped the lever into Neutral and shut down the machine.

"How'd you spend your day?" she asked as she joined Tanner at the gate.

"You don't want to know."

The grease marks on his shirt and arms told her that maybe she didn't, but she took a guess. "Baler?"

"When isn't an older baler fighting back?" He held up a bottle of water, damp with condensation, and she took it gratefully. "The vet phoned, so we're calling it a day."

She lowered the bottle from her lips and wiped the moisture off her mouth. "I can work without you, you know."

"Or you could come along."

"The vet already knows you're a good guy. She saw you with your dog."

"Right."

They continued toward the area where Whit was parked, walking side by side.

"About yesterday," Tanner said.

She took a stance, water bottle gripped in one hand. "We aren't going to argue about pay again."

There was something about the way he met her eyes that caused her to shift her weight. No. This wasn't about pay.

"You kissed me," he said simply.

That. Yes. Whit launched into a Crocodile Dundee impression. "That wasn't a kiss," she drawled. "*This* is a…" Her voice trailed off and her lips unconsciously parted as she met his eyes.

So much for deflection by humor.

"You were saying?" he asked in a much better Australian accent than her own.

She cleared her throat. "I was saying that was just a deal sealer." So much for her tactic a casual kiss putting them in the friends lane.

"Okay." He glanced down, toeing the gravel with his boot in a thoughtful way. "My lawyer never does that."

Whit gave up trying to save face—as if she had a chance.

"You want a kiss?" she asked, expecting him to back off after she'd drawn her line in the sand.

"Wouldn't mind." There was a light of challenge in his eyes.

Whit rarely let a challenge go unanswered, so even though her heart was now pounding, she stepped forward to put her palms on either side of his face. She slowly drew his mouth down to hers so that there was no question of consent. He could step back at any time.

He did not step back.

Their lips met in a kiss that was warm and sweet and promising. Maybe a little too promising.

Whit's breathing was ridiculously uneven when she dropped her heels back to the ground. She met his gaze as if seeking reassurance that she wasn't the only one who felt that way, then found herself back in Tanner's arms as their lips met again in a deep, heady kiss. And when the kiss ended, Tanner gathered her against him in a way that felt so right that it was scary.

Really scary.

Whit jerked back.

"Whoa," she said.

Tanner moistened his lips. "Agreed."

"I can't afford to... I mean..." She cleared her throat and stopped with the embarrassed schoolgirl act. "That was hot."

Tanner nodded.

She shook her head. "We can't do that again."

"That might well be a mistake."

"Bad timing," she continued as if he hadn't spoken. "I'm job hunting. I work for you." *I'm not ready for another complication in my life.* She put her hands on her thighs and let out a breath.

"Totally bad timing."

When she looked up at him, she could tell that he understood. He was not insulted by her retreat.

She could have kissed him.

She didn't.

He reached out and brought her in for a gentle hug. A brotherly hug. Maybe if he gave her a noogie, she'd believe it was truly brotherly, but it made his intentions clear without having to hash things out. Thank goodness. So much better than her own attempt to make her intentions clear.

Whit stepped back and for a moment, they considered each other from a safe distance. "Yesterday was so serious," she said. "The vet, the meeting, the..." She didn't have to say the-ranch-is-broke-confession because he understood. "And now today—"

"Is a different day."

She gave a choked laugh. "Yes, it is." She let out another whoosh of breath, then brought her hands together. "What do you say we go get your dog?"

WHIT DIDN'T KNOW who was happier during the reunion at the veterinary clinic—Rose or Rose's dad. The Lab's midsection was bandaged, but Dr. Leonard said she foresaw no issues now that the danger of concussion had passed.

"Take the stitches out in seven days," Dr. Leonard directed. "Call me if there's any change in behavior. She had a good dose of antibiotics, so the wound should heal just fine. You can take off the covering tomorrow. Keep an eye on it."

"Thank you." Tanner leaned down to stroke his dog's head inside the cone of shame, then straightened again as the door opened and Margo Simms from the community board came in carrying a lopsided cat carrier in one hand.

"Mr. Hayes." She beamed at him, but Whit knew that the beaming was all part of the control process. "I was going to call you."

Tanner gave her an uneasy smile.

"You have been generous in your support."

"It's a good cause."

"Indeed, and we have had a small hiccup."

"A hiccup."

She set down the carrier and the cat inside gave a plaintive yowl as she took Tanner by the sleeve and led him to the side of the room, far enough away to make it look like she was seeking privacy, but not far enough away that Whit and Callie the receptionist couldn't overhear the conversation.

"Today we got word that the venue rental fee has increased," Margo said in a stage whisper. She gave him an expectant look.

"I'm sorry to hear that."

Obviously not the answer that Margo had expected. She waited for more, but Tanner remained silent. The message was clear, but Margo refused to accept.

"And your father *generously* footed the entire venue rental in the past, but I want you to know that we *can* cover the overage from the community fund." But it was obvious that Margo did not want to go that route.

Callie met Whit's eyes, her own widening at the little drama playing out in front of them.

"Right."

An awkward silence followed the single word. Tanner smiled tightly, Callie shifted her position, and Whit decided it was time to intervene before the receptionist made popcorn to eat as she watched the action.

"Tanner, I hate to interrupt, but I have that appointment. I'm going to be late if we don't leave now."

"When would be a convenient time to call you?" Margo asked Tanner.

"I'll be on the mountain tomorrow," he said. "No service." He made no offer to call her back, which wasn't going to help with his reputation rehabilitation plan.

"Tomorrow evening, then." Margo made it sound like a done deal.

Tanner nodded rather than reply and took the leash from Whit. They left Callie to deal with Margo and made their way to the truck. Rose whimpered when Tanner helped her inside, then licked his hand after curling up on the rear seat.

They drove out of town in silence, then Whit said, "Just

because your dad footed the bill for Hearts of the West, it doesn't mean that you have to."

"I think it does. If I want to get help on the ranch, I need to follow through on the one thing that put my dad in good graces with the people of this town."

"Don't let pride—"

Tanner shot her a look.

"Okay. Do let pride stand in your way." Whit lifted her gaze skyward before refocusing on the road ahead of them.

"I'll figure something out," Tanner said. "We're good."

CHAPTER EIGHT

No harm, no foul.

But no matter how often Whit repeated the mantra, she couldn't shake the feeling that she'd just started going down a slippery slope by kissing Tanner Hayes. It wasn't the first time she'd impulsively kissed a man, or shared a hot kiss, but it was the first time she'd done it with a man she worked for. Or a close neighbor. Or her dad's business associate.

So many reasons not to have done it, but while Whit questioned the wisdom of the kiss, she couldn't bring herself to regret it. Tanner Hayes had a way with his lips, so her only regret was that the man had enough worries without adding her to the list.

That said, what a kiss.

When she got home, her dad was still in the fields, so she retired to her command center at the dining room table, which was rarely used for dining, and pulled up her job search information. She wasn't settling for just anything, and between selling her car and living rent-free, she had time to find the best fit instead of taking the first thing that came along, as many of her colleagues had to do.

She skimmed the list of openings on several sites, answered an email from a recruiter, then put the laptop to sleep. But she didn't move away from the table.

Something was off. She'd been slow to start her job search, but that was because of the latent burnout she'd suffered, coupled with the shock of being axed. Honestly? She'd thought she'd be safe in a layoff situation.

She didn't want to find herself in that same situation again.

No guarantees. You know that. In other words, it was time to get it together and take her chances on a new job. Just as in the corporate world, things on the ranch could change on a dime, and she wanted her family ranch to have a security blanket. She wanted to be able to afford nice things. She didn't want to scrimp and make do, as she'd done for most of her life.

Did that make her shallow? Whit didn't think so. She liked the life she'd built in Missoula. Liked having money to burn, and liked the prestige of her position. Taking a backward step, having her safety net pulled out from under her and moving back home had been difficult.

So why wasn't she actively doing more to find the perfect job?

Because she had the luxury of time, and because there was no real reason not to be momentarily distracted from her goal by doing some ranch work and hanging out with a guy who was unexpectedly witty and caring and—

Stop it, Whit.

It was time to stop thinking about Tanner Hayes.

She leaned back in her chair, stretching her arms over her head. The truth was that she didn't want to obsess over her future, as had been her practice in the past. There truly was no reason not to enjoy these early days of summer, because she'd have a job nailed down by autumn. She would work on the Hayes Ranch for a few more weeks, ride Charley in the mountains, help her dad set up for Hearts of the West.

But she wouldn't be sharing any more kisses with Tanner Hayes.

WHITNEY'S TRUCK PULLED into the driveway at exactly the same time as it had yesterday. And the day before. Whitney was punctual and serious in her work ethic, which were the traits Tanner told himself he would dwell on. Good employee traits.

He couldn't keep a straight face as he lied to himself. Whitney was a beautiful woman who would spend a few weeks in his life, then move on. She knew her own mind, made plans, stuck to them.

Rose lifted her head when Whitney knocked on the door.

"Got any coffee?" she asked after he called for her to come in.

"Always." Tanner felt a whisper of relief. They were post-kiss cool.

Whitney went straight for Rose, crouching down to offer commiserative words concerning the collar of shame and injuries. She gave the dog a few gentle rubs on her chest, probably one of the few areas that didn't hurt, then stood.

"Has Margo hunted you down yet?" she asked as Tanner set a mug on the table. It wasn't the tar she preferred; for that she'd have to wait a few hours.

"I turned off the ringer on the landline and she doesn't have my cell number."

"Oh. I gave it to her," Whit said innocently. "Was that wrong of me?"

"Not funny," Tanner said as he took his chair. "I have never ducked someone like this in my life. I hate feeling like a weenie."

"You were never in the sights of The Trio before."

"I'm calling Margo tonight and telling her that…" His voice trailed as he rubbed a hand over the back of his neck. "I don't know what I'm telling her."

"Tell her that you'll provide the venue."

His gaze came up. "I think you're missing the point."

"Hold Hearts of the West here. On your ranch."

"Here?"

She nodded. "Here." She leaned forward. "The idea came to me as I was driving over. You're not that far from town and I know for a fact that there are people who want to get a closer look at the place. Particularly this house."

Tanner realized that he was staring. So did Whitney. She smiled as if waiting for him to come up to speed, which he was.

"What do you think it would entail?"

"A few weeks of headaches—some major, some minor—but think about it. You would get yourself in solidly with the community—"

"And you wouldn't have to parade me around town like a prize sheep," he pointed out.

"No. I'm still going to do that." Whit gave him a reassuring pat on the arm. She met his gaze as she did so, as if to say, "See, we can touch in a friendly way."

She was setting the tone, helping to keep them in the friendship zone without things feeling weird.

"Do it," she urged. "Call Margo and give her your offer, and tell her that due to your finances being tied up after your dad's passing that it's the only solution that you can offer. You did put her off earlier by mentioning your accountant, so…"

"I wish you would have come up with that finances being tied up thing earlier." Why hadn't he thought of that simple solution?

"I was trying to save my own skin at that meeting. And back then, I thought you could afford to write a big check."

Strange how it felt good to have someone in on the secret other than Grant. Even Len was in the dark, as far as Tanner knew. The only way the foreman would know that the ranch was in trouble was if Carl had told him, and Carl hadn't even told his own sons the true state of affairs.

"Well?" Whitney asked.

"I need more coffee." Tanner got out of his chair and crossed the kitchen to the island. He brought the pot back to the table, poured, then put the pot back.

"I've never been to a Hearts of the West event. What would it involve?"

"Okay. A little background. It started while I was in college. The money goes to the community fund, which does a lot of good deeds. They used to hold the event in February as a Valentine's Day celebration called Hearts of Winter, but after three blizzards in a row caused three cancellations in a row, they moved it to June and changed the name."

"It's a Valentine's event in June."

"They don't call it a Valentine's event, but they use hearts as a theme for everything. And it is a little romantic, what with the cow flop contest and all."

"Cow flop?" Tanner gave her an uncomprehending look.

"Surely you…" Whit looked at the ceiling as if he was hopeless. "They make a big grid on the ground with chalk, number the grid, people buy squares, then they turn out a cow and the square that she goes on wins."

"A cow poop contest."

"Exactly."

"I hope there are other events?"

"There are. That's the only one that involves a cow."

"Good."

"There are vendors, kids' events, dinner and dancing. It's lots of fun. And if you held it here, all you'd have to do would be tolerate people coming and going. Think of how many people you'd get to know again."

"I didn't know that many before I left. Just a few close friends." He could see now that he'd isolated himself during high school, with the exception of that small handful of friends he'd mentioned.

"Time to rectify that."

Tanner studied the table as he considered just what he was getting himself into. He loved the idea of not writing a big check. Loved the idea of changing the Hayes reputation.

He looked up at Whitney. "This won't get in the way of the ranch work?"

She shook her head. "Shouldn't."

"Are you going to lead me down this path, then get a job and abandon me?"

"It's a possibility."

He considered, then gave a slight nod as he came to a decision. "I'll call Margo."

Whitney touched his sleeve and gave him one of her fascinating slow smiles. "This will be fun."

"I'm glad you think so, because you will be my right-hand in this endeavor."

"I don't know about—"

"Right hand."

She smiled. "Got it."

"I LOVE BEING able to meet regularly." Kat stirred her cocktail, giving Whit a satisfied look. "All three of us. Just like old times."

"We're going to milk it for all it's worth until you take off on us again," Maddie added.

"It might be a while before that happens," Whit replied. Both of her friends perked up, and she let out a sigh. "I mean, I am getting a job elsewhere, but it won't be instantaneous."

Maddie stabbed her straw into her drink a few times, then she looked up with a cheeky grin. "I heard that you caused quite a commotion at the board meeting."

"That you broke the bonds of tyranny," Kat said.

Whit rolled her eyes, but had to admit to some truth to the words. "I got tired of cooperating with uncooperative people."

"I heard rumors of a statue in the town square," Maddie said in a hushed voice.

"If only we had a town square," Kat added.

Whit laughed and leaned back in her chair, giving a quick look around. The pub wasn't very full, so they could talk without anyone overhearing. Tonight she didn't have much to say, preferring to listen to Kat tell stories about the latest wild scheme her rambunctious brothers had come up with and the challenges of co-parenting a young toddler.

Maddie soon had them in stitches, telling stories of her guy, Sean, helping out at the bridal boutique.

"You're quiet tonight," Kat said to Whit.

"Nothing to report," she replied easily. Fixing a broken waterer wasn't news, and the actual news she had, she couldn't share until Tanner had firmed up the details of holding Hearts of the West on the Hayes Ranch. Once things were settled, they'd discuss.

Kat launched into a story about her fiancé Troy trying to shoe a noncooperative pony, and Whit had to admit that the affection in her friends' voices when they talked about their partners stirred a touch of envy in her.

It was a good kind of envy, she decided. The kind where you don't begrudge your friends, but hope you can have what they have someday. She'd like to eventually experience raising a toddler and coming home to someone dependable. She could see it happening in the distant future.

But at the same time, she liked the solo life she'd built. Liked providing for herself and having the security of her career. Yes, it involved a desk and computer rather than people and the outdoors. She may be missing out in some areas, but life had a way of balancing out. Her mother had shared that message many times when things in Whit's young life had taken an unfair turn, and she hung on to those words.

Things would balance out.

"Earth to Whit?"

Her chin snapped up. "Sorry. I was…thinking about Mom."

Kat tilted her head and raised her glass in a silent salute. Maddie followed suit and they all drank.

"I have a proposal for you," Whit said after a beat of silence. It was one of the reasons she'd suggested drinks tonight.

"Yeah?" Maddie pushed her glass aside.

"Given proper notice, would you like to help push Hayes's cattle to Old Timber Mountain?"

Kat raised her hand. "I would."

Maddie grinned at Whit. "A day on horseback? Count me in."

"I'm not sure when, but we've ridden the fence and it's almost ready to go."

"All you have to do is to say the word," Kat said, "and you'll have two enthusiastic day hands."

"It'll be like the old days," Maddie added.

Kat lifted her glass again. "To reliving the good old days." She gave Whit and Maddie a wicked grin. "So, you want to go tip some cows or something?"

"WHAT ARE YOU DOING?" Tanner asked Len. He'd knocked on Len's door after Whit had gone to work in the corrals and was surprised to get no answer because Kenny's motorcycle was parked outside. Then he'd heard the sound of a tool dropping in the shop.

Len gave him a guarded look. "I'm fixing the carburetor on the Weedwacker. I'm still useful around here."

"You are," Tanner said matter-of-factly. "Just don't push things."

"I was thinking that I could also maybe work on that float in waterer number 2. It's still high and I—"

Tanner shook his head. "Whitney will do it."

Len let out a frustrated breath and stood straighter, holding the wrench against his palm. "I'm just gonna ask. Is she a danger to my job?"

Tanner gave a surprised laugh. "No. She's here to help until she finds a job."

"And if she doesn't do that?" Kenny asked.

Kenny didn't seem to be a bad kid, if one overlooked his tendency to be as defensive as his great-uncle. His distressed jeans hung low on his skinny hips, and the oversize T-shirt had seen better days, but that was all just a fashion statement. The kid took good care of his uncle.

"She's not a permanent hire." Kenny and Len exchanged looks and Tanner asked, "Is there a reason you don't believe that?"

"I heard that she likes this job, which might make her want to keep it."

"News to me," Tanner said, and if Kenny had heard such a thing through the grapevine—well, he didn't put faith in grapevines. "Where did you hear this?"

The kid shrugged. "One of the guys who works for Joe at Clinton Automotive."

Gossipy Joe speculating. He met Len's gaze. "You have seniority. You will not be replaced."

He was also injured and may never be 100 percent again. It was easy to read the older man's concern.

"Len. You have my word."

"The word of a Hayes. Huh."

With that, Len went back to his carburetor and after a brief glance his way, Kenny joined him, leaving Tanner just this side of mystified. He almost asked why Len, who'd stuck with Carl Hayes until the end, would say such a thing, then decided he didn't want to know what might have gone on between Len and his father. If Len wanted him to know, he was free to tell him. If not, then he and Len would work out their own relationship over time.

Tanner left the barn and headed to the house to make that phone call he'd been dreading. He poured a cup of tar, turned off the coffeepot heater, looked up Margo's number and dialed. She answered on the first ring.

Tanner took a quick sip, grimaced, then said, "Tanner Hayes, Ms. Simms. I wanted to talk to you about a possible venue change..."

After outlining his offer, which would literally save him thousands of dollars he didn't want to spend, he was rewarded with a long silence. Knowing The Trio's contrary way of thinking, he half expected the offer to be summarily rejected.

"This would be a way to help introduce myself back into the community. To...give back." Tanner rolled his eyes. He did want to give back, but it sounded so hokey when he said it aloud.

"I can't speak for the board," Margo replied after a thoughtful silence. "But I can call an impromptu meeting to discuss."

Tanner used the opening to explain that after his father's

death, there were still some financial issues being ironed out and he couldn't be depended on for that big check.

Margo perked up like a bird dog on a scent when he mentioned financial issues.

"I'll get back to you," she promised.

"Do that," Tanner said. He hung up the phone thinking that no matter which way things went, he was in for some headaches. Either his reputation would suffer in the community because he'd broken his father's tradition of buying community support, or his ranch would be the site of a major event with lots of comings and goings, setups and cleanups.

Grumpy Len was going to love that.

Margo called that evening. The board had indeed held an emergency meeting and they would like to visit the ranch tomorrow to see if it would do for the event.

"That large meadow of yours would be perfect for the tent," Margo gushed, "and the views…"

They planned for a midmorning get-together the next day, which meant that Whit would be working alone, at least until he could catch up with her after the meeting. If this worked out, he would save face and he wouldn't lose money he couldn't afford to spend just yet. He wouldn't be the jerk Hayes Ranch heir who refused to continue his father's attention-getting traditions.

Next year at this time, he'd make certain he had enough money in the bank to pay for the usual venue, thus leaving his ranch in peace. And he would do it for the good of the community, not so that he could exert some sort of control over people.

He was a different kind of Hayes.

"How did it go?" Whitney asked the next morning after arriving for work. The sun was just topping the trees when she pulled in, creating little streaks of sunlight across the driveway and encouraging the songbirds to give it their all as they greeted the day.

He pushed his boot toe into the gravel. "I'm not sure whether I'm delivering good news or bad."

"They approved."

"And asked for a tour of the house."

Whitney grinned. "Nosy, aren't they?"

"Curious. They did say that they missed Dena."

"I never knew her."

"She kept Dad in line. Her secret weapon was that she didn't care." Whit sent him a look and he explained, "She just ignored all the stuff that sent me over the edge."

"What kind of stuff?"

"Judgment, I guess. Let's just say it was hard to live up to his standards. And if I did—"

"He raised the bar."

"Yep."

"That couldn't have been easy."

"It made it easy to leave home," he said.

"That's sad."

"We made up later."

"For real?"

He hesitated, as if not wanting to address what was real and what wasn't. "As much as was possible. We pretended, hoping that if we pretended long enough, it would start feeling real."

Whit absorbed the words, but said nothing. It broke her heart, to be honest. She and her folks had been the epitome of land-rich, cash-poor as they scraped by year after year. That scraping had been the reason she'd given up her silly dream of becoming a horse trainer—not to mention buying the Hayes Ranch—and gone into renewable energy production instead, a field where she could flirt with upward mobility.

She'd lived like a college student for the first few years of employment, funneling money into the ranch in return for a percentage of eventual profits. Thankfully, her dad managed to turn the ranch around. With Whit's help, he paid off the last of her mom's medical bills and was able to sink some money from his second job into the place. Now the Fox Ranch was holding its own, with a full crew and, surprisingly, more head of cattle than the Hayes Ranch had. The fields were in good shape, and thanks to the water lease, they would soon have more land under production.

At this point in time, the Fox Ranch was doing very well after two decades of struggle. The Hayes Ranch was not, but no one, save for her and the Hayes brothers and their accountant and lawyer, knew the true lay of the land.

Strange how things played out.

"Are you still on board to help me drop off my car tomorrow? Clinton Automotive called to remind me."

"How about I meet you in town?" he said, leaning back on his heels. Whit met his gaze, told herself not to be drawn into those hazel depths.

"Great," she said in an upbeat voice. "We can grab breakfast. My treat."

"I might not be able to afford a venue for a major event, but I *can* afford bacon and eggs."

She almost said something about receiving graciously, then decided that given the circumstances and personal pride, he didn't need a lesson in etiquette.

"We'll split the check."

Tanner rolled his eyes, but he didn't argue.

"I have good news," she said.

"Yeah? Shoot."

"Maddie and Kat are game to help move the cattle whenever we drive them to Old Timber, so one less worry there."

"I should pay them."

She gave him a *really?* look. "No. You shouldn't. That isn't how things are done and you know it." When neighbors helped neighbors, the only payback was the promise of reciprocation in the future. And maybe a big lunch or dinner on the ranch.

"I guess I'm used to more transactional relationships."

Whit shook her head as if dealing with a difficult student and took a slow, swaggering step closer to the man, with the intention of making her point—neighbors don't pay neighbors. The proximity effect was immediate. An instant recollection of how it had felt to be wrapped in his arms.

You're close enough, her small voice shouted.

Whit had to agree with her inner warning system. It would be easy to step out of the friend zone, to replay that hot kiss and really muck things up. She wouldn't do that. She might be impulsive, but not in the life plan area.

"You were about to say something?" he prompted. Whit could see that he was aware of her inner battle. Was it possible he was fighting the same fight? Because his hands were curled into loose fists, as if he was trying to keep them under control.

She lifted her chin and said, "Yes. I was about to say that if you're going to become part of this community, you're going to have to let that idea go. Transaction worked for your dad. It's not going to work for you."

"I'm going to have to take my chances being a good guy and hope that people notice?"

Whit nodded. "You're playing the long game, Tanner."

And she would keep playing it with him, until she found that she couldn't.

CHAPTER NINE

THE NEXT MORNING, Kenny rode his motorcycle into the ranch just as Tanner was heading out to feed the horses and do a few quick chores before meeting Whitney in town at Clinton Automotive. Kenny usually showed up in the afternoons with his deliveries to his great-uncle, so Tanner ambled over to ask why he was there so early.

"Taking Uncle Len to the Zoo. Doctor's appointment," the kid said as he got off his motorcycle. Len came out of the house and worked his way down the steps.

"Going to Missoula," he called to Tanner in a gruff voice, calling the city by its proper name rather than the Zoo.

"Hope you get good news."

"It might happen."

But Len didn't sound convinced that it would.

While Tanner was feeding Emily and Clive, Len and Kenny drove away in Len's truck, leaving the motorcycle parked next to the foreman's house. Tanner hoped that Len heard something that would cheer him up, although it was possible that the guy was simply negative and morose by nature. That said, he was still haunted by that "the word of a Hayes" remark.

He was going to broach it, but he would wait until Len was less guarded. The way things were going between them, they might discuss the matter in a year or two.

He was due to meet Whitney in town at Clinton Automotive in forty-five minutes, which gave him time after feeding to open the gates and move the steers into another pasture. He headed out on the ATV, because it was fast. The steers knew the routine and followed behind. Tanner opened the gate, and a few minutes later, the leader, seeing an opening in the fence, began to gallop. His buddies followed and soon fifty Angus flew past Tanner, only a few of the fat, sassy steers feeling the need to throw a playful kick his way. He closed the gate, then glanced toward the waterer fifty yards down the fence line.

The thing was surrounded by a lake, created by a leak at the back of the unit. He rode the ATV to the waterer and took off the cover to investigate. Not an obvious fix, so he'd tackle it later. That meant heading back to the shop to get tools to shut off the water supply, which was going to make him late, but he wasn't going to have water flowing for the hour or so that he would be gone. By the time he'd finished, he was wet and cold and had just enough time to change his jeans and make sure Rose was comfortable before heading to town.

"THIS IS A BEAUTY," Joe Marconi, the head mechanic at Clinton Automotive, said after Whitney handed him the key fob to her fully loaded Audi TT RS. "You're lucky that we were able to get the parts from the Billings store." His eyes strayed to Tanner, then to the damaged rear end, then back to her. "What a shame."

Whit gave a careless shrug. "These things happen," she said. "The important thing is that I'm able to get it fixed locally."

"I guess so," Joe allowed with another accusatory look at Tanner, who fought an exasperated look as he shifted his weight to his opposite leg. "This was a pristine vehicle."

"What's the time frame?" Whit asked, and after getting

an open-ended answer—"depends on if we find other issues"—she turned to Tanner. "You said something about
breakfast before going back to work?"

"It's on me." He gave her a *touché* look. "You're on the
clock after all."

The guy was good. She hoped they didn't have to arm
wrestle for the check after eating. She turned back to Joe.
"I'm helping out on the Hayes Ranch while I look for another job in renewables."

Joe bounced a look between them. "I heard you were
working there." The wheels were turning in his gossipy
head. *Why* was she working there?

"Len's still healing from his accident, so it's neighbors
helping neighbors, you know. And Tanner's a good boss."

Tanner cleared his throat, obviously concerned about
Whit overplaying her part. "Everything is cleared with the
insurance company?" he asked Joe.

"We're good," Joe said.

A few minutes later, when they were seated in his truck,
Tanner turned to Whit and asked, "Do you think he suspected that he was being played?" Joe lifted a hand to wave
as they backed out of the parking space, then turned to run
a reverent hand over the hood of Whit's car.

"No."

"You're that certain."

"Yes."

"'Neighbors helping neighbors,'" he quoted. "Tanner
is *such* a good boss."

"You can't be subtle with Joe. And I wanted to be sure
he knew it was professional, not romantic. Therefore I emphasized the boss thing."

She was impressed at how offhand she sounded, because thinking about Tanner and romance was becoming
a guilty pleasure. It wasn't going to happen. His reaction

after the kiss assured her of that, so no harm in the occasional venture into fantasyland.

Especially because, *again*, it wasn't going to happen.

They found a parking spot on a side street and walked to the café across the street from Maddie's bridal shop.

Holly Freely, the red-haired motherly dynamo who owned the café, approached with a coffeepot. "Hey, you two."

And although Whit knew for a fact that Holly was not judgmental, she could tell she was curious about Tanner Hayes. Whit had been acquainted with Holly for a long time. The café had been a favorite high school hangout, and she and Kat and Maddie had their own favorite booth in the back, which was now occupied by an elderly couple.

"You know Tanner, right?"

"I haven't seen you since you were in high school," she said, pouring coffee in both cups. "I guess I did see you from a distance," she added musingly, holding the coffeepot in front of her, "with your brother and father, but I don't think you've set foot in here for a decade, at least."

"I was one for quick visits home. There and gone." He smiled, making Whit's breath catch. He wasn't holding back with Holly. "But I'm back for good, and you'll be seeing me on a more regular basis."

"That would be nice," Holly said in a tone that even Whit couldn't read.

"I'm working for Tanner while I job hunt."

"Well, isn't that nice?" Holly said. "You living close and all."

"It is." Whit beamed at the woman. "I get to spend my time doing things I love while looking for a job...doing something else I love." Internally, she grimaced at that. She didn't love working in corporate. She loved the security it provided and the sense that she had the means to weather storms and to help the Fox Ranch do the same.

"So it all worked out," Holly said, adding, "Good for both of you," before continuing on with her coffeepot, checking tables.

Tanner pulled the menus out of the holder and handed one to Whit. She opened it, even though she knew the contents by heart. Little had changed since her high school years of eating fries and drinking cola and laughing until she was in danger of it coming out of her nose. She closed the menu and set it on the table.

"You know what you're having?"

"Fries and gravy."

He side-eyed her and she reached across the table to touch his hand. "Try it."

He closed his menu without seeming to notice that she'd touched him. Again. "Sold."

Whitney settled her hand back in her lap—but not before Holly, who was pouring coffee at a nearby table, noticed.

"JUST A COUPLE more stops," Whit said when Tanner tried to head to the truck after an excellent breakfast. She was taking this project thing seriously.

But, on the plus side, Holly at the café had treated him with more genuine warmth upon his exit than his arrival. She'd been all professional smiles when she'd seated them, but when he paid for the ticket, she'd made a little joke when handing him his change and her smile had touched her eyes. He had tipped generously and promised to come back soon.

He and Whitney visited several other businesses for minor purchases, with her introducing him at each one as if no one in town had ever heard of the Hayeses, then they stopped at the bridal boutique that her friend owned.

When they walked into the shop, the wedding march sounded, startling him, and a man sitting in a brocade chair looked up from his phone and grinned.

"Yeah. It just comes out of nowhere. You aren't the first to jump." He got to his feet and held out a hand. "Sean Arteaga. Proprietor."

Tanner gave Whitney a quick look. He'd been under the impression that Whitney's friend was Maddie, who'd been with her when he'd rear-ended her car.

"Sean owns half the boutique," Whit explained. "Long story."

"Maddie had errands, and no fittings until this afternoon, so I'm holding down the fort. I have a bride arriving in half an hour. Hopefully Maddie will show up before the bride does, but if not, it's all on me."

He spoke without irony, and Tanner fought a smile. He recognized Sean as a bronc rider he'd watched ride in some of the richer Washington State rodeos. Seeing him surrounded by tulle and lace and talking about meeting with brides was, well, interesting.

"I sold a prom dress a few minutes ago," Sean continued. "Lilac number." He looked at Tanner. "I'm supposed to be a silent partner, but every now and again I am called upon, which means I have to get my hands all gussied up." He held up his hands, which were nicked and scarred but clean as could be.

Tanner did the same and Sean gave an appreciative nod. "Same line of work? Ranching?"

Sean was not a local, and it was refreshing to meet someone who hadn't already formed an opinion of him. "Wheat farming before that."

"I'm heading off to diesel mechanics school in a few

months, and after I graduate, I don't think my hands will be allowed in the shop."

"Good hand talk, guys, but since Maddie isn't here, I think we'll be on our way. No offense, Sean." Whit adjusted the two small shopping bags she carried on one arm.

"None taken." He gave Tanner a humorous look. "If you ever need a wedding dress, I'm your man."

Tanner laughed. "I'll keep that in mind."

And he didn't see it happening any time soon.

THE FINAL STOP before they were finally able to leave town was at the grocery store.

"What's it like to cook in that amazing kitchen of yours?" Whit asked Tanner.

"I don't cook a lot."

Whit gave him a disbelieving look. "That's criminal." She let out a breath. "I have no choice but to call the kitchen police."

"I've never been much of a—"

"Whitney! Mr. Hayes!"

They turned to see Dr. Leonard, the veterinarian, coming up behind them pushing a cart overloaded with paper products. "We go through a lot of paper towels," she said.

"I can imagine."

"How is Rose?"

"The stitches look good," Tanner said. "She's resigned to the cone. I don't think she'll disturb the wound, but I don't fully trust her."

Dr. Leonard laughed. "Labs are really good at appearing innocent. I'm looking forward to seeing her again at Hearts of the West. I heard you're hosting this year."

"I am. The committee thought it would be good to change things up this year."

"Test run," Whit said, as if the ranch would be up for hosting the next year if things went well.

When the vet turned her cart around and headed back the way she'd come, Whit said to him, "This hosting thing is gold."

"I'm just surprised how quickly the word spread."

"Are you?" she asked. "Really?"

He made a noise in his throat, acknowledging the speed of small-town grapevines. They could work for you or against you, and in this case, he was hoping for the better outcome.

They continued through the store with him throwing instant food into the cart and Whit rolling her eyes even though she was putting almost the same stuff in her basket. "For my dad," she said when he'd given her a particularly pointed look.

"Your dad likes Marshmallow Crunchios? He looks like more of a cornflake guy to me."

"Appearances are deceiving."

All in all, he'd had a decent day in Larkspur—much better than he'd anticipated—and he had enjoyed parts of it, like breakfast, and walking around with Whitney, being amused and sometimes touched by her insights into their former classmates.

The former star quarterback, now employed by the local service station, had gone the way of the cliché, peaking in high school, but Whit explained that he was better off for it. "His parents were so pushy that I'm surprised he didn't have a nervous breakdown. He's happy now."

Tanner wondered if he needed to look up former quarterback, Dakota Reese, and arrange to have a beer. It appeared they had something in common.

And then there was shy Amber Lee, a woman who'd graduated a year behind Tanner and was known for spending every free moment in the library. She had, in fact, become a librarian, but she moonlighted as a mounted trick rider during the summer months, traveling from rodeo to rodeo.

"That's something I could see you doing," Tanner said.

She shook her head. "I was set on becoming a horse trainer."

"What happened?" he asked.

"That thing called life."

When they got to the ranch, Whitney set her groceries in his kitchen so they wouldn't get hot in the truck, then fired up the ATV and rode around the pastures, checking the waterers while Tanner worked on the flooded unit. His phone rang just after he finished the repair and was drying his hands on the shop towel he kept in the toolbox.

"Aiden. Good to hear from you." *Please don't tell me you can't make it this summer.*

"Hey, boss. Just checking in to give you a definite ETA. Looks like two weeks on the nose and Coop and I'll be there."

One less battle. Between him and the boys, he'd be able to keep the cattle managed and get the farming done on the acres he'd kept for himself. Whit would move on, and his ranch would be emptier without her, despite having his crew on board.

Such was life. His life, anyway.

He'd just do what he always did and push on.

"I'M NOT SURE how long the Audi repairs will take." Whit dug into her ready-made pasta bowl, twirling the spaghetti onto her fork. "When we left it at the shop, Joe said it would be about a week, but he couldn't say for sure. It depends on whether he finds other issues."

She and her dad had been discussing the wisdom of

rebuilding the engine on the old hay truck as opposed to finding a "new" used truck, when Ben had brought up the matter of her car.

"Just make sure he doesn't charge you storage while he waits for parts." Ben smiled grimly. "I heard he did it to Carl Hayes once."

The townsfolk did have their ways of getting back at people who disrespected them.

"I'm hoping that by Tanner being there and being friendly, Joe might look at him through a different lens and not do things like that to either one of us."

"That reminds me," her father said, a slightly cagey note to his voice. "I heard a rumor while at coffee this morning."

"Imagine that. A rumor at the ranchers' coffee klatch."

"It's not a coffee klatch," Ben said gruffly.

Whit set her chin on cupped hands. "What rumor did you hear?"

"You and Tanner Hayes are dating." Her dad gave her an expectant look, and for the life of her, Whit couldn't tell if he wanted her to confirm or deny.

She denied.

"Crap." Whit closed her eyes for a beat, then sat back in her chair. "That was what I *didn't* want them to think."

"Because it's not true?"

"Of course it's not true." She scowled at the table. "I purposely made a point of saying that I was *working* on the Hayes Ranch. I mentioned it at every place we stopped."

"How many places did you stop?"

"Six or seven. I wanted to make good use of my time and I had things to pick up here and there." With Tanner tagging along, looking like a good beau. Had he been carrying bags for her?

Of course he had been.

Shoot.

"Then you aren't seeing him?"

"Are you really asking me that question?" Whit leveled a dark look at her father. "I mean, *when* would I be seeing him? I do my job there and then I come home." Surely her dad didn't think they were flirting with each other instead of working. He knew her ethic better than that.

"Right."

Whit bit her lip as she considered the situation. "Do me a favor?"

"What?" her dad asked warily.

"Tell your coffee kl…" She caught herself. "Tell the guys that we're not dating. Convince them that we're just friends and that I'm working for him."

"Telling and convincing are different things, but yeah. I'll make it a point."

"Just don't make too much of a point, so that they think you're covering something up."

Ben gave her a look. "Like I don't know how to manage my own crew."

"You can distract them by mentioning that Hearts of the West is being held on the Hayes Ranch this year."

"Everyone knows that."

"The Trio is coming to the ranch tomorrow afternoon to take a look. I'll probably be there, you know, to witness the event."

Her dad's eyes widened at this tidbit. "Really? Are you going to keep to the background, or give them what for again?"

"Background. Totally."

Her dad feigned disappointment.

"I did my part at the meeting. I think it's best to stand back for a while."

Ben got to his feet, ready to begin his evening of sports TV. "This reign of terror needs to end."

"You could always run for the board this fall. Bump one of The Trio off her throne."

Ben gave her a wide-eyed look. "Are you out of your mind?"

Whit laughed. "I've got to go job hunt, Dad. I'll see you later."

"THANKS FOR THINKING of me, but it's not what I'm looking for."

Whit ended the call from a recruitment contact who excelled at finding jobs that were below her experience level. Her cell signal disappeared, and she tucked the phone in her front jacket pocket.

"Not a good fit?" Tanner asked conversationally. The call had come just before Whit and Tanner turned onto the road to Old Timber Mountain on their final day of fence repair, following a scramble on the ranch proper as they made it presentable for the all-important visit from Margo, Debra and Judy. The ranch looked good; now the real business of cattle grazing was back on the agenda.

"Nope. And I'm not going to waste anyone's time." Particularly her own.

It was the second offer for an interview that Whit had turned down. She'd worked her butt off to get to the level she'd achieved at Greenbranch Renewable Energy, and she wasn't going to take a position that was several rungs down on the ladder. Not unless she got desperate, and she didn't see that happening, since she'd had several pings already about potential jobs. She'd agreed to one interview the following week, but so far none of the other jobs had met her parameters.

"I'm not taking just any job." He gave her an ironic look and she added, "*This* job doesn't count. I'm doing this as favor to a neighbor."

"Who has a contract with your dad."

"That might have gotten me into this, but it isn't what keeps me coming back."

"What does?"

There was something in his expression that made a red flag go up, but just a little one, so Whit continued. "The scintillating work environment, of course."

"I hear that the boss is an okay guy." He gave her an amused side-eye.

"So some say." She side-eyed him back. "I'm not necessarily one of them."

He growled and she laughed. The guy who people avoided because of his dad made her feel good.

"I'll give you this," she said as she swung the truck and trailer in a big arc at the last gate. "I didn't laugh as much at my old job. It was a put-your-head-down-and-work environment."

"That sounds…efficient."

"I laughed after hours. When I was at work, I worked." Which was why she'd gotten the promotion that had ultimately been her downfall when the buyout occurred.

They unloaded the horses and led them through the wire gate. When Tanner mounted, Clive stood still, even though the reins were loose on his neck. A big change from the first mount she'd witnessed weeks ago.

"I've been working with him," Tanner said as he picked up his reins. "Don't want to embarrass myself in front of your friends."

Maddie and Kat had agreed to help move the cow-calf pairs to the grazing allotment in a few days' time. "They've seen their fair share of gnarly horses," Whitney assured him. "And we've all hit the ground a time or two."

"Clive isn't gnarly. He's…calculating."

Whitney had to agree. The gelding seemed to wait for

the most opportune moment before indulging in an act of control, such as sidestepping or shying at nothing. But lately Clive seemed to be feeling mellow. He followed Charley without bumping him with his nose as they rode the trail, and despite working his tie rope loose when they'd stopped for lunch after fixing the final stretch of downed fence, he'd stayed put instead of disappearing into the timber at a gallop.

Yes. Clive was being a good boy and he continued his good behavior on the ride to the trailer—right up until the grouse flew up out of the underbrush at his feet. He was several yards ahead of Charley when he took to the sky, and Whit had to give Tanner credit for riding him out through a series of serious bucks and crow hops, as the horse took advantage of the clearing where the grouse assault had taken place.

Charley snorted and danced, but trusted that Whit would keep him safe from horse-eating birds. Clive gave one last buck, landed spraddle-legged and blew snot with a loud whistle. Tanner held his position, sitting deep in the saddle, shoulders back, waiting for the gelding to give an encore, then a crash sounded in the underbrush behind Charley, and Whit's trustworthy gelding reached his breaking point. He launched himself sideways at the unexpected noise and went down in the muddy bog just off the trail.

He hefted himself to his feet, leaving Whit sitting in the muck, then gave a full body shake, flinging mud in all directions. Whit wiped the muddy splatters off her face as Charley started picking his way out of the bog, his feet making gross suction noises.

Whit looked over her shoulder to see Tanner standing on the bank, holding Clive's reins. He offered Whit a hand and she took it, allowing him to pull her to her feet.

"Thanks," she muttered.

"What is it about you and gooey substances?" he asked.

"I'm only muddy from the waist down. It could have been much, much worse."

"I'll give you that." The words were barely out of his mouth when Clive hit Tanner with his nose, sending him stumbling forward. He let go with a colorful curse, but somehow managed to keep his feet as he windmilled his arms and sank into slimy mud up to his knees.

He gave Whit a weary look, started to take a step, then stopped abruptly. "My boot is coming off."

Clive started to amble away, his duty done for the day, but Whit snagged his loose reins. A moment later, after Tanner had made it to dry ground with both boots still on his feet, she solemnly handed him the reins.

"I need a new horse."

They walked the last half mile to the truck, water sloshing in their boots. After loading the horses, they made their way to the cab. As soon as Whit sat on the protective canvas seat cover, her pants felt even wetter. She wrinkled her nose as Tanner reached for the key.

"This stuff smells funky," she said.

"And could present a laundry challenge." Tanner put the truck into gear, then glanced her way. "Is this the kind of stuff you were trying to avoid when you said no to full-time ranch life?"

"Not at all," Whit said on a surprised note. "This was the part I liked."

Tanner lifted his eyebrows in a questioning expression. "What part didn't you like?"

"The part where I felt guilty whenever we had to spend a penny. Even a school field trip could be a challenge."

"The ranch wasn't doing well when you were young?"

"My mom got sick just before I went into middle school. Cancer, and the medical insurance was bare-bones. We were squeaking by before her diagnosis, but after...it was awful, and it stayed awful long after Mom passed away."

Tanner didn't say anything, and she appreciated the way he waited until the lump that always formed when she talked about her mom gave way, allowing her to speak normally again.

"I hated going into crisis mode every time something went wrong, and you know how often something can go wrong on a ranch. We had to sell most of the cattle to meet expenses, and we got to the point where we weren't even close to breaking even while I was in college. Dad took on a side job, and he thought he was going to have to sell, which was really hard because the land has been in the family since the turn of the last century."

"That's rough," Tanner said. When she glanced his way, she understood that recent events in his own life made it possible for him to relate to what she was talking about. So she went on.

"I decided that I wasn't going to live like that. If my refrigerator blew up or I needed a car repair, I wanted to be able to handle it without figuring out what to give up. I didn't want to scrimp for the rest of my life, so I said no to ranching, no to horse training and went into something where I could indulge in the occasional luxury."

The result was that when her fridge had broken down, she ordered a new one. She had a closet of nice clothes, a suite of stylish furniture that was now in storage and a great car. The car was going, but she'd get another. Someday.

"Your ranch is doing better now."

"I helped save it," she said matter-of-factly. She gave Tanner a quick warning look. "Don't ever say that to anyone. I don't want my dad's pride hurt."

"I know something about keeping a secret," he replied easily.

Touché.

She directed her gaze forward, watching the clouds move over the mountains across the way. "I lived bare bones in the beginning of my career, funneled cash into the ranch, and we eventually got to a place where we were earning money instead of bleeding it and Dad was able to quit his side job and go back to ranching full time. That's why I don't have as much of a savings cushion as I would like." She let out a breath. "I thought I was safe careerwise and had time to build my savings. I was not."

"Which is why you're selling the car."

"Even though the ranch is doing well right now, all it takes is a couple bad seasons in a row, a few disasters and it could be right back where it was."

Tanner frowned at her, and she realized how doom-and-gloom her attitude sounded, but that was indeed how she felt about ranch life. She loved the work, loved the out-doors, but the risks were not worth the reward.

"I won't live that way," she concluded.

"You mean the way I'm living now?"

"No offense."

"None taken."

But she had apparently given him something to think about because he was quiet for the remainder of the drive home…or maybe he was thinking about Debra, Margo and Judy, who were due to arrive an hour before Whitney went home for the day.

Her dad would be disappointed that she had nothing to report on The Trio's Hayes Ranch tour, but her clothes were a wreck, and she wasn't about to borrow some from Tanner.

TANNER HAD BECOME oblivious to the scent of decaying organic matter and mud by the time he drove under his father's fancy archway, and his wet jeans had warmed to body temperature, but he was pretty excited by the prospect of cleaning up. Whit had at least another half hour before she'd be able to get out of her muddy clothes.

Tanner took the turn off the drive that led behind the barn, and as he did so, he caught a glimpse of a sedan parked in front of his house.

"What the...?"

Whit craned her neck as the barn blocked her view. "I'd say that Debra, Margo and Judy are an hour early. I wonder if they've been in the house?" she asked in a thoughtful voice. "At the very least, they've looked in the windows."

Tanner glanced down at his muddy, funky-smelling jeans and boots. "When you show up early, you get what you get."

"No apologies," Whit said firmly. "If they sense weakness, you're toast."

"Agreed. Two against three. Can we take them?"

"We have to try."

Tanner held up his fist and Whit bumped it before they simultaneously reached for their door handles.

They debated about unloading the horses, decided that it could wait until they were done with The Trio, then made their way through the barn to the main driveway, where three women wearing neat mom jeans and cardigan sweaters were waiting near the front walk.

"Mr.—" Debra's voice faded as she took in Tanner's appearance. Then she swept her gaze over Whitney and her eyebrows inched even higher.

"We had an incident," Whit said calmly.

"We thought we had time to shower," Tanner said, then realizing the way the woman's expression changed, amended his statement. "I thought *I* had time to shower. Whitney is going home."

She gave him an *I am?* look. He nodded.

She turned back to the women. "Yes. I'm going home to shower and do laundry. I'll see you tomorrow morning, Tanner."

Sending Whit on her way was not easy, because Tanner, who could face down an angry drunk in a country bar, was at a loss as to how to handle these three fifty-something women.

Whit headed for her truck, little clumps of mud coming off her boots as she walked.

"Would you like a moment to change?" Margo asked Tanner.

"I'm good if you are."

"We are perfectly fine," Judy said. She cast a sweeping view around the property. "This will actually be quite lovely for the event. We have to rent a large tent for the dinner, and we were hoping that perhaps, if finances were not *too* tied up…"

"I'll spring for the tent. The one thing I can't do is to spend a lot of time here managing setup because I am running a ranch." Shorthanded, at that.

"That's perfectly fine, Mr. Hayes." Debra sniffed. "It seems that Whitney has that skill set."

"And I'll have my foreman Len Anderson keep an eye on operations while she's working."

"Len Anderson?" Margo said, as if she wasn't aware that the man was employed by the Hayes Ranch.

For a moment, Tanner thought that the ladies might change their minds. They exchanged glances, made a few unusual faces at one another and then, without a word being spoken between them, nodded in unison. The silent exchange was borderline spooky, and the opening scene of *Macbeth* shot into his head.

Tanner pushed the thought aside and said, "Great. Perhaps we can meet and discuss liability and those types of issues."

"That sounds marvelous, Mr. Hayes."

"Tanner." He held out a muddy hand, then pulled it back again. "We'll have to pretend," he said.

Judy's smile was genuine, and he thought maybe he'd made a breakthrough.

"We'll be in touch, Mr.—Tanner," Margo said before leading the way to the sedan. The women climbed inside and a moment later drove away.

The dust from Whit's truck was still settling when they left, because she'd lingered near her truck for a while before pulling out. It slowed the ladies down, but Tanner waited until they were out of sight before letting his muscles relax. Those women had a gift for putting people on edge.

He stood in place for a few more seconds, debating whether to tell Len about his new duties—which he truly hoped the older man would agree to—then decided to clean up instead.

Rose came out from under the porch, where she'd been sleeping and perhaps hiding from the community board, and greeted him by pushing the edge of the cone she still wore against his hand. Tanner ruffled her fur, apologized for not being able to take her with him that day and noted that she'd made a trip to a faulty waterer. Her underbelly was almost as muddy as his clothing.

He'd chase that down after he changed his clothes.

When he went into the house, he instantly noted little bits of mud that hadn't been there when he'd swept the floor that morning.

No wonder the ladies, who'd been curious before, hadn't asked for a tour. It appeared that they had welcomed themselves into his home, or at the very least had opened the door. Rose had joined them, flaking mud as she went.

"Yeah. I watched them," Len said when Tanner visited the man a half hour later, with his hair still damp from the shower. "They just opened the door and kind of yoo-hooed. Only one of them went inside and it wasn't for long. Your dog followed her in." He gave a small snort that might have been a laugh. "She had a hard time getting her out again."

Which explained the scrape of mud he'd noticed on Judy's slacks.

"So they didn't riffle through drawers or anything?" Tanner was being facetious, but he had to admit he didn't think such a thing was impossible.

Len considered. "I don't think they had time." He gave Tanner a sideways look accompanied by an almost smile, and Tanner sensed his second breakthrough of the day. He hated to ruin it, but he did, by explaining to Len that he would soon be the grand overseer of the Hearts of the West setup.

"Me?" Len scowled. "And why here?"

"Community relations," Tanner said. "Dad burned so many bridges that I have to do something."

"He did do that," Len said.

Len had worked for his dad for longer than anyone, but apparently had no warm feelings for the man.

"I don't want anyone screwing things up," Tanner said.

"Yeah. I can keep an eye on things. It'll feel good to be useful again. Doctor said it'll be a bit until I can operate a clutch."

"Len, if you handle the community board, you don't need to worry about clutches."

In fact, if Tanner had any kind of windfall in the near future, he'd give the man hazard pay.

CHAPTER TEN

Ben was stuffing jeans into the top-loading washing machine when Whit let herself into the mudroom. He did a double take, then said, "Tell me you weren't trying to catch ducks again."

"I haven't tried to catch a duck since I was ten." She grimaced as she looked down at her filthy jeans, stained with black organic-rich mud.

"It smells like you were in the duck pond."

"Nope," she said cheerfully. "It was a bog on the mountain. Charley dumped me."

"Charley?"

"There was a lot of excitement at the moment." She motioned toward the door, indicating the need for privacy. "I'll finish loading your clothes and throw my stuff in."

"No. I don't want that nasty mud all over my clothes. Leave yours on the floor and we'll do them later."

"Fine." Her dad had always been better at laundry.

He finished loading his clothing, started the machine, then left the mudroom, pulling the door shut behind him. Whit grimaced again she kicked off her boots and water dribbled out, then she eased out of jeans that insisted on clinging to her skin. Gross, gross, gross.

But again, all in a day's work. Things like this were *not* the reason she didn't want to go partners with her dad and work the ranch. It was her outside job that allowed her to infuse enough cash to become a silent partner owning 20 percent of the ranch. Twenty percent of the ranch profits wasn't going to support her, and even if it would, she didn't trust that the operation would remain solvent. Her dad was a rancher to the bone and accepted the whims of markets and weather as the price he paid for living the life he loved.

You love it, too.

She did. But she was a realist. Not everyone got to combine their job and lifestyle. It was better to go with the sure thing: a monthly paycheck instead of semiyearly lump sums at sale time, company-paid benefits, a retirement plan.

Then why aren't you hitting the job search harder?

Because she was being picky. She had that luxury at the moment, and although she had yet to flesh out Life Plan Number 3, she knew what she didn't want. So far that had been everything the recruiter had thrown her way.

When she went into the kitchen, wearing the chenille robe she kept in the mudroom for emergency strip-downs, her dad was sitting at the table with a printed spreadsheet in front of him.

"I got some donations for Hearts of the West," he said proudly. "Not by myself, but I was there."

"What? Really?" Whit sat across from him and turned the spreadsheet so that she could read it. Sure enough, there were businesses marked off. She gave him an incredulous look. "I fought to get you onto the setup committee."

"And don't think for one minute that I'm not grateful. Harold got put on prize procurement because he missed the meeting, so the guys and I had mercy and went with him. He needed moral support."

Whit went over the spreadsheet, dragging a finger down the first column. "Let's see. L&M Construction. Good one. Daisy Lane Daycare. Okay. Walt Stenson." She raised her gaze, then read on. "Littlegate Farm. Uh-huh." Whit looked up again. "Gee, Dad. Did Kat help you?"

Because every one of those businesses had a link to Kat or her fiancé, Troy Mackay.

"Troy joined our ranch meeting group."

Definitely not a coffee klatch.

"He comes a couple times a week while Kat watches the baby. It's good for his farrier business to make contacts."

Whit nodded at the spreadsheet. "Did Troy make that?"

"Harold got it from Margo. Anyway, I thought I'd let you know that I sucked it up. It's easier when you don't have to do it."

"I'm proud, Dad. It's good to expand your skill set." She grinned as she mocked her own words. "Just keep it secret, okay?"

"I'm not foolish. I know what would happen if you-know-who found out." Ben folded the spreadsheet in half and put it on top of the stack of papers near the landline. "What do you do on the Hayes Ranch?" he asked.

"Today I bog surfed."

Her dad didn't even crack a smile. "And…"

"I'm still riding fence and checking waterers. I dug out a ditch the other day. After we put the cows on the mountain, I may do some range riding. Tanner is going to have to get busy in his fields in a bit. First cutting is coming up, so I'll handle things until his crew arrives in a few weeks."

"Do you like what you're doing?"

"Well enough," she said, recognizing the potential for a fatherly ambush.

Her dad knew not to push when she spoke in that tone, but he wasn't able to keep himself from saying, "You seem happier. More relaxed."

"It's the mud baths, Dad."

He pressed his mouth flat, his way of acknowledging a

touché, then slapped his cap on his leg. "I gotta head out. Dinner is every man for himself."

"My favorite kind," Whit replied.

Ben put on his hat at the door, then stopped and turned back. "The Hayes Ranch is still pretty nice?"

"You'll get to see for yourself when we set up for Hearts of the West."

"Guess I will." Ben drew in a breath. "What made him do it? Hosting the thing, I mean?"

"Community relations. Tanner is trying to overcome his dad's reputation."

"He doesn't want to control everyone with his check-book?"

Whit felt guilty as she said, "I think he would prefer to have people respect him because he's a decent human being."

Ben's gaze became thoughtful, then he said, "Looking forward to seeing the place."

With that, her dad stepped outside, closing the door after him, leaving Whit to wonder if she really was more relaxed. If so, what had she been like before?

Stressed from work.

Who wasn't? She managed her stress just fine, thank you very much. She'd simply have to make an effort to leave the job, whatever and wherever it might be, behind when she visited her dad in the future.

THE NUMBERS WERE not looking good.

Tanner leaned back in his chair and closed his eyes. He'd been laying out hypotheticals and yes, he'd squeak by this year and the next, as long as they got rain, paying off the debt as he went, but would he be able to bring the place out of the red in three years, in order to avoid having to sell?

It was going to be nip and tuck. If cattle and hay prices held…he set the pencil on the table and rubbed his eyes, then stilled as he heard a noise outside. It was daylight, but too early for Whitney to arrive for work. He got to his feet and went to the window. It was quiet outside except for the early-morning bird songs, and he was cognizant of an empty feeling as he went back to the table where he had his calculations spread out.

The ranch felt better when Whitney was there. He didn't want to think about what that meant, because frankly, it was threatening to his peace of mind. He didn't trust easily, didn't get attached and when he hit a point in a relationship where he had to bare his soul, he stepped back. Always.

Yet he'd told Whit about the ranch being insolvent.

Different kind of trust, he assured himself. It would hurt his pride if people knew what shape the ranch was in, regardless of the fact that he hadn't been the one to put it there. But it wouldn't ruin him emotionally.

Different kind of trust.

Whit understood his issues because she was allergic to scraping by, and would eventually take a job that gave her the security that was so important to her. She needed a secure job. He needed his ranch. He didn't care if it scraped by as long as he had it. He would rebuild it. Make it his. Pay his brother a yearly dividend.

Maybe burn down this house.

He regarded the beautiful room in which he worked and wished that his dad and Dena hadn't sunk so much money into renovating the house. Poor use of resources, but appearances were all-important to Carl Hayes.

As they are to you, or you wouldn't be keeping the finances a secret.

Maybe he was like his dad in that regard. No one wanted to be seen as a loser. He might have inherited his losing hand, but he found himself unable to share his father's guilty secret—except with Whitney Fox.

WHIT WAS PEELING a hard-boiled egg for her Sunday lunch when her phone pinged with a notification for a video call. She quickly rinsed her hands and pushed Accept when she recognized the name on the screen. Her relationship with Rob Ketchum had been close to love-hate. The guy had great ideas but was terrible when it came to execution. As he'd laughingly put it, he was the brains and Whit was the brawn. He never seemed to notice that Whit never laughed at his joke.

"Hey, cowgirl," he said with a laugh when Whit came on the screen.

"Hey, yourself. How's the new job?"

He gave her a coy look. "That's why I'm calling. They have an opening at Tullamore Wind and Solar and they've yet to fill the position. If you're interested, they'd be happy to interview you. I sang your praises."

"Would I be working with you?"

"We're a great team, you and me. I'm the—"

Whit couldn't handle hearing that she was the brawn yet another time, so she cut him off. "Is it in New Mexico?"

"Albuquerque."

She liked Albuquerque.

"I'm gonna cut to the chase," he said in an upbeat voice. "Are you still in the market for a job, and would you like to interview for TWS?"

"Tell me more about the position."

Whit took a seat at the table and jotted down notes, then asked Rob to send her the details via email.

"So, should I tell them you'll do an interview?"

"I'll take a look at the information you sent, and I'll get

back to you tomorrow. One question, though—will I be working under you?"

His tone grew serious. "We might have the occasional project together, but this place is set up differently than Greenbranch. This is a great opportunity, Whit. Excellent people. A real team environment."

"I'll let you know after I look everything over."

After ending the call, Whit went to the sink and continued peeling her egg, then rinsed it, salted it and took a bite. She smiled as she chewed.

A job had just come looking for her.

"What's up?" Tanner asked as Whit waltzed into the shop where he'd been blowing the dust out of the riding lawn mower Len had made good use of the previous day, preparing the big lawns for the Hearts of the West setup.

"I have an interview."

His stomach sank, which was silly. And telling. "Do you need time off?"

"It's a video interview. I could do it here between chores."

"Is it a job you'd consider?"

"It's a good one," she said. "It's in New Mexico."

"That's a bit of a distance."

"The company is working on some serious renewable energy opportunities and needs someone with my expertise in federal regulations and permitting. The pay is good, the potential for advancement is good. I could keep my car. One of my former colleagues landed there and recommended me."

"Sounds promising. New Mexico is beautiful." It was the most positive thing he could think of to say. It wasn't like he could say that losing the closest thing he had to a confidante was going to leave a hole in his life, but the truth was, he was going to miss having someone to talk to. He was going to miss Whit.

You knew this was coming.

He did. And it hammered home the fact that he was about to be alone. Ally-less. His brother wasn't on his side regarding the ranch. Len was about as warm and fuzzy as an iguana. He'd become dependent on Whit to bounce things off of.

"I went to the hot-air balloon festival in Albuquerque a few years ago and could totally see myself living there."

"Good."

An awkward silence fell, then Tanner said, "When is the interview?"

"Tomorrow. Short notice, but my former colleague just got wind of the position and managed to get me into the system."

"Sounds like a good friend."

Whit laughed. "I did a lot of his work for him. I did it so that I wouldn't look bad when we worked together, but now it has paid off, I guess."

"If they hired someone who slacked, they'll hire you."

"He looks really good on paper. Not at all like the slacker he is. And I do owe him a solid for this." She glanced at the table where he had his papers spread out. "Taxes?"

"Ranch math."

"And?"

He was struck by how easy it was for him to say, "It's going to be a nail-biter."

"Ranching can be that way." She spoke flatly, as if reminding herself of why she was job hunting. "Unpredictable."

"You're making the right move."

"Why did you just say that?"

He hesitated, then spoke his mind. "Because you're questioning yourself."

"Not at all." He lifted an eyebrow, and she tightened one corner of her mouth. "You're right," she confessed. "I am. And I shouldn't be. Other than the distance from home, this is exactly what I'm looking for." She held his gaze. "You'll keep my secret?"

"The interview?"

"The doubts." She pushed her hands into her hair. "I hate doubts. I fought them in college and thought I was done."

"Come here." He motioned with his head as he spoke, indicating that she needed to come closer, just as he'd said.

"Do I look like I need a hug?"

"Totally. And I happen to be in a hugging mood."

"Aren't I the lucky one?"

"Yes, because I don't hug just anyone. Only those people who can do something for me. I'm a transactional hugger."

Whit let out a choked laugh and moved closer, even as a small, cautious part of her warned against following instinct. But the instinct was strong, and Whit didn't feel like fighting. She felt like filling her lungs with Tanner's scent and feeling his heart beating beneath her cheek.

"You do know how to sweet-talk a girl," she said as she came closer, feeling a touch awkward.

"Years of practice." He folded his arms around her, and she breathed deeply, thinking she'd never encountered a guy who smelled better than Tanner, and then laid her cheek on his chest, closed her eyes and listened to his heart.

"Doubts are normal. Healthy, even."

She wasn't thinking about doubts any longer. She was thinking about the trouble she could get herself into if she stayed. The need to settle herself, to get back into the professional groove, was strong.

But what if she could grow something meaningful with this man?

His lips touched her hair in a light kiss and Whit shivered. *Do not fall in love. Don't do it.*

He nuzzled her ear, brushed her neck with his fingertips, and when she raised her head to look at him, to try to get some clarity as to what the situation was between them, she found herself without words. So what could she do but kiss him?

And kiss him she did. Short, sweet kisses. Long, deep kisses. Lose-herself-in-the-moment kisses.

Finally, she eased away from him, but kept her hand on his chest as she said, "What are we to each other?"

"Allies." He watched her as he spoke, gauging her reaction.

She didn't know if she believed him, but appreciated that he knew what she needed to hear.

"I like that," she said softly. "Allies."

"NEW MEXICO IS a long way away." Maddie closed the back door of Spurs and Veils, and a moment later the muffled sound of the UPS truck starting up drifted into the room.

"I haven't made the cut yet." But the interview had gone well, and she'd know if she would be asked for a second interview in two days. Whit picked up a box and headed back to the steaming area. The biweekly dress unpacking was an excellent opportunity for the friends to bounce things off one another, only today Whit was doing all the bouncing.

"You will." Maddie put her box on the one Whit had just set on the ground.

"How are things going on the Hayes Ranch?" Kat asked as she lugged in the last of the UPS delivery through the back door and set the box on top of the other three.

"They're going good." Whit waited for Maddie to open the top box and then start moving plastic aside.

"You're dating the man, you know." Maddie gave Whit a solemn nod when she raised a disbelieving gaze. "I have it on good authority."

"Bridal shop rumors?"

"My clients are all about happy endings," Maddie said, shaking out a short cocktail-style dress in a delicate apricot color.

It was Whit's turn with the steamer and again her hair was frizzing up.

"Keep me posted. I'm curious as to what Tanner and I will be up to next." Maddie laughed and Whit looked at her over the top of the steamer head. "He really is a good guy and I hope that the community comes to understand that before I leave."

"You sound pretty sure that you'll get this job."

"Nothing is ever sure, but I have a ton of experience and I was recommended by someone they've already hired from my old firm."

"It's just too bad that it's so far away."

"The company has a generous vacation plan. I'll be able to come back several times a year." She'd spoken to her former colleague the previous evening. Her sense that he wanted her there to help him with his job grew stronger as they talked, but everything else about the job met or exceeded her parameters.

"So other than labor issues, Tanner is doing okay?" Whit frowned and Maddie explained, "Gossip. After they decided to change the venue from the Gallagher Barn to the Hayes Ranch, people are talking. And there's been rumors that he can't get help because he can't afford it."

Whit willed away the guilty flush that threatened to give her away. She never lied to her friends and rarely kept anything from them, but she'd promised Tanner, which meant that for all intents and purposes, she knew no more than her friends did about the Hayes Ranch. The secret was in the vault.

"He can't get help because his dad was a jerk and people assume he is, too."

"But he's okay to work for?" Maddie asked.

Whit thought she'd made that clear, but maybe she hadn't.

"I have no complaints," she said.

"Well, you are dating," Kat pointed out.

Whit made a face and went back to steaming. "I like working there. I like Tanner. We're allies."

She ran the steamer head over the dress as she spoke, giving extra attention to a stubborn crease until she realized that her friends had gone quiet.

"Allies?" Kat asked.

"It's hard to explain, but it's not romantic."

Why had she mentioned romance?

Better question—why did she feel so cagey about having said the word *romantic*?

Confession was good for the soul, and keeping things from her friends was not her style, unless it involved other people's finances.

"We've kissed a few times." She gave a casual shrug. "Twice. Three times if you count a quick brush of the lips."

Whit looked up in time to see her friends exchange looks, then quickly busy themselves.

"It's nothing." When her pants didn't spontaneously catch on fire, Whit continued, "The man has a force field around him. He's not the trusting kind."

He had trusted her with certain secrets, but only after they'd shared some trauma and he realized that they had stuff in common.

Whit handed the silky apricot dress over to Maddie and took another, in the same color but a different style. "I know his limitations and he knows mine." They were allies.

"I did hear that things weren't great on the Hayes Ranch after his mom and brother left."

Whit met Maddie's gaze. "How so?"

"Bill Monroe—you know, the deputy on the scene of your fender bender—and I were standing in line at the bank and got talking about the accident. And the Hayes brothers. He said that Tanner changed after his brother went to college. Kept to himself more and more."

"That sounds like he's an emotional abuse victim," Kat murmured.

The steamer head spit as Whit held it at the wrong angle, but no water spots appeared on the dress. She righted the head and continued steaming. "I don't think his dad treated him well, but Tanner fought back. Left home as soon as he could, established a relationship with his dad on his terms. He might have suffered emotional abuse, but he isn't a victim."

If her friends were surprised at her flat statement, they didn't show it. Of course, Whit didn't look at them, either. Tanner had become a touchy subject with her.

Not a good sign, girl. You need to do something about that.

CHAPTER ELEVEN

PUSHING THE CATTLE to the grazing allotment on Big Timber Canyon would have been a much shorter trip if Tanner's neighbors to the east had allowed him to move through their scrubby pasture, but when he asked, he got an unequivocal no.

Good old Dad.

He wanted to ask what Carl Hayes had done to them, but decided against it. The less time the neighbors spent thinking about Carl, the better for him. He just had to somehow convince said neighbors that he was different, and that was where Hearts of the West came into play.

There were already people visiting his ranch, taking measurements, scoping out locales. Everyone seemed pleased with the new venue, and he'd had to give a total of four house tours. People may not have liked his dad, although they seemed quite fond of his checkbook, but that didn't keep them from wanting to see what Dena had done to the place.

Everyone, including The Trio, who finagled the first official tour—not to be confused with their unofficial tour led by Rose—told Tanner how lucky he was to live in such a house.

He was. Now all he had to do was hang on to it.

The cattle filled the county road from ditch to ditch as they headed toward new grass.

A hundred cow-calf pairs were not that big of a cattle

drive, and other than the occasional car or truck needing to slowly work its way through the herd, which was blocking the road, it was a quiet trek to the first wire gate.

Len's leg and hip had healed to the point that he could straddle the four-wheeler, and he'd agreed, with a surprising show of cooperation, to allow Rose, who was now cone-free, to ride on the rack on the back. Tanner had worked up a box with low sides so that she wouldn't tumble off when Len gunned the engine, and the Lab was quite content riding drag with Len at the back of the herd.

Maddie Kincaid and Kat Farley rode flank on one side of the herd and Whitney and Tanner rode flank on the other.

Tanner opened the gate and held it while Len pushed the cattle through and Whit brought Charley to stand near him, out of the way of the herd.

"Don't let them spread," Tanner called, and Kat and Maddie expertly brought the cattle back into a line.

"I have a good crew," Whit said.

He smiled at her. "So do I."

She pressed her hand to her chest in a gratified way, and he grinned at her.

After closing the gate, Tanner remounted Clive, who was becoming more trustworthy by the day. But he still swung his head back and hit Tanner in the knee. Tanner moved him forward and Whit fell in next to him. The cattle were no longer trying to spread, so they were able to ride side by side.

"I made the cut for a second interview," she said conversationally. After receiving the call that morning, she'd been alternately excited and uneasy. She needed a job. This was a good one. She wasn't ready to leave. She liked being closer to her dad and and—she shot a quick look in Tanner's direction—she was going to miss working with this man.

"Congratulations."

"It's not a done deal and the one caveat *if* I get offered the position is that I'm staying with you until your mini crew arrives."

"Aiden and Cooper will be here early next week."

"So I can just…leave?"

"I'm in no hurry to see you go."

There was something in his tone that caused her to give him a sideways glance, but he kept his profile to her. In fact, he appeared not to have spoken at all.

"I'm in no hurry to go," she replied. "But life happens."

They rode in silence, the only noise being the beat of the cows' feet and the *putt-putt* of the ATV behind the herd.

As was customary, Tanner fed his crew after they'd ridden home from the cattle drive. Len waved off his invitation, saying that he needed to rest his leg, but the old guy was pleased with how much he'd been able to do that day. Tanner spent a pleasant hour with Whit and her friends, eating takeout from Holly's Café and being entertained by the three women telling tales of their high school days.

He learned that Whit and Maddie had not started out as friends, but instead had been the youngest at a riding camp and grudgingly paired up for mutual protection, which is how they ended up being lifelong friends. Kat had been Maddie's friend and had also bonded with Whit, and they'd become a solid trio from middle school on.

"This is a beautiful house," Maddie exclaimed as she and Kat helped clear the table.

"Only the best for Carl Hayes."

He spoke matter-of-factly, because it was the truth, and Whitney's friends took it that way. Carl had loved nice things, and that love had ultimately been his downfall. Whit liked nice things, too, but not in the way Carl had. And the woman was not afraid to work hard and get dirty.

Or gooey. The incidents with the pitch and the bog still made him smile. She was so easygoing about things that might set other people off.

Whit saw Maddie and Kat to the door, then after her friends had driven away, she crossed the room to where her sweatshirt lay over a chair.

"I should go."

"One drink to celebrate interview number two?"

She considered it, then said, "Why not? Got rye?"

He got up and poured, then handed her a glass of WhistlePig.

Whitney sat in a custom-made oak chair and held the drink on the arm. "I could get used to only the best," she said.

"There used to be more artwork, but Dad sold a lot of it before his death."

"Trying to make ends meet?"

"He pretended he was tired of looking at the same old stuff, but it was one of our first inklings that all was not well. Each piece of art was like a treasure hunt to my dad. I couldn't see him letting his finds go to someone else."

"But he did."

Tanner nodded.

"Did he have to mortgage the place?"

"He secured a private note with a business associate, which allowed him to keep operating." Tanner swirled his drink. "I'll be paying on that sucker for a while. Dad was also in the process of trying to get a friend to invest in the ranch, despite having the loan. I found the rough draft letter outlining the idea, but it never got off the ground."

"It must have been shocking to find out that your inheritance had been compromised."

"I suspected, but Dad was tight mouthed about it. I'm

sure he thought he could pull the ranch out of the red. He was Carl Hayes, after all."

Whit's mouth curved as she regarded her drink, but she wasn't smiling. "Life plays out in funny ways."

"Amen to that."

Rose padded into the room and fell to the ground at his feet, letting out a sigh as she rested her chin on his boot. Tanner smiled down at his girl, then looked up in surprise when Whit came to sit beside him on the sofa.

"Ally time," she said.

"Yeah?"

"Your financial issues, my job search...yes. Time for some mutual moral support."

"Your job search has taken a positive turn," he pointed out.

She sat close enough to him that it felt natural to slide his hand along the back of the sofa as he spoke. When his fingers brushed her shoulder, she moved even closer, leaning her head against his arm. It felt companionable and right and when she said, "So why aren't I more excited about making it to the next interview level?" His arm tightened around her.

"You don't want to be that far away from your dad?"

"That's part of it. He's not getting any younger."

"And of course, there's me." He meant it to sound facetious, but it came out sounding way too serious. Whit shifted the position of her head to look up at him.

"Which kind of boggles the mind," she murmured.

His lips twitched and so did hers—just before they met. He could get used to this, cuddling with a beautiful woman with his dog at his feet.

"You know what?" Whit murmured.

"Nope."

"I could get used to this." She pushed herself to a sitting position, unaware that she'd just spoken his thoughts aloud.

A half dozen responses sprang to his lips one after another and he choked every one of them back. Whitney was a special woman, but he wasn't that special a guy. He had trust issues that had obliterated every serious relationship he'd attempted to embark upon. Sometimes a guy just had to accept reality, and his reality was that he'd protected himself for so long that he didn't know how to stop.

"I'm not going to get used to it, however. We made a deal."

"I must have been absent that day."

"We agreed to help each other out and I don't think complicating our lives falls into that category."

"You classify me as a complication?"

She got to her feet, downed the last of her drink, then raised the empty in a toast. "More than that, Tanner Hayes, you are a danger."

He wanted to point out that from his standpoint, she was a threat, but there was no sense arguing about who was more dangerous. They knew their paths forward and all they had to do was to keep to them.

WHIT WAS IMPRESSED with how she sounded like she had the whole attraction thing under control before parting company with Tanner. Like she had a choice about the matter. She didn't. She didn't want to be drawn to the man, but she was. An ally was a good thing. One that disturbed one's equilibrium, not so much.

Yet she kept kissing him.

New Mexico will save you.

Yep. She could run and hide in the name of financial security, and no one needed to be the wiser. But her plan took a hit later that evening when she got a phone call from

Lacy Tom, a friend who, along with her husband Buster, had been laid off with Whit.

"Have you guys landed anywhere yet?" Whit asked.

"I did. Right here in Missoula. The accounts department in the hospital. Buster is looking, and he's found a job that he might be able to do remotely, so fingers crossed we'll be okay."

"Great to hear."

"How about you?"

There was an edge to her friend's voice that made Whit reply cautiously. "I'm helping a neighbor with his ranch while I job hunt." She wasn't going to jinx her new job possibility by talking about it.

Lacy stopped being coy. "Rob called Buster trying to track you down." She hesitated. "Rob doesn't have your contact information?"

"Not since I turned in my company phone and quit using my work email." She'd wondered how he'd found her.

"He told Buster that you guys were the best team and that he's really hoping to welcome you aboard at his new company."

"Really?"

"Rob is a charming work leech and he needs you to leech off from." Whit knew that was a danger, but he'd assured her during the interview that if they worked together, it would only be on the rare occasion.

"He told me he didn't think we would be working together that often. Just the occasional luck-of-the-draw project."

"He told Buster that he'd been given the opportunity to bring someone on board as his second."

Whit pressed a hand to her head and muttered a few words she didn't say in front of polite company. It would have come out eventually, because Whit did not go into things unaware, but the fact that Rob had tried to blatantly misrepresent their professional relationship fried her. She wasn't that naive, and it ticked her off to have Rob think she was. And it ticked her off that she'd been so excited about the job possibility.

"Lacy, thanks for the heads-up. I could work for the same company as Rob, but there's no way I'm putting myself through the stress of working *with* him again."

"Glad I could help," Lacy said. "If Buster finds something, I'll let you know. There might be something else there for you."

"Thanks. Actually, I'm doing okay now. And thanks to you, I've dodged a bullet."

"WHAT'S HAPPENING HERE?" Aiden Book asked as he got out of his car. Tanner had seen his help's distinctive orange Ford Ranger from the barn where he'd been working on the swather, and emerged to meet the kid before he was swept up into the crowd and put to work.

The Hayes Ranch was buzzing with activity as the community board and various committee members milled about the place, placing stakes that Tanner had been admonished to be careful of and arm waving as they decided how best to use the area.

"I'm hosting a community event," Tanner said. "Good to see you." As in really, really good. It'd only been a matter of two months, but it looked like Aiden had grown at least an inch in that time. Tanner hoped he could afford to feed him.

"Young man," Judy called as she hurried over. "Please move your vehicle. We have a delivery coming in."

Aiden met Tanner's gaze and Tanner nodded. "Behind the barn is good. I'll show you." Tanner got into the car and directed Aiden around the granary to the place where he parked out of the way.

Aiden parked and then spent a few seconds taking in the fields, the pastures and the mountain that rose up at the far edge of the north field. "Nice place. How's the fishing?"

Tanner pointed to the creek that cut through the pasture. "It had fish when I was a kid. You can check it out later." He jerked his head toward the house. "I'll help you cart your stuff in. I assume Cooper's not far behind you?"

"Girlfriend issues. He'll be here in about an hour."

Aiden pulled two duffel bags and a computer case out of the trunk and Tanner took the last grip bag. They walked through the barn and out the open bay door, then crossed the driveway to the flagstone walk leading to the house. Rose emerged from under the porch and gave Aiden a joyous greeting.

"What happened to you?" he asked. "I heard you had an accident."

Rose made happy whining sounds and shifted her weight from side to side as she gave Aiden a big canine grin. He ruffled the hair between her ears, then stood back up.

"She recovered okay?"

"She did, but her feelings are hurt when we go without her, so I'm letting her come along next time."

"Holy...cow..." Aiden stopped just inside the door, gaping as he took in the interior of the house. "And you voluntarily lived in a single-wide instead of working out of this place?"

Tanner never mentioned his family to his friends and coworkers at the wheat farm.

"My dad and I didn't see eye to eye."

"My dad and I get that way sometimes." Aiden spoke

with the assurance of a kid who knew that even if he got sideways with his dad, things would work out.

Tanner smiled and then led the way down the hall to one of the many guest rooms. It was going to be good to have some company around the place. "Your room. Coop's room."

"Good. We can stay up all night giggling."

"Right." More likely they'd be up all night cutting hay.

"So tell me about this event."

"Not much to tell. It's a fundraiser and their original venue didn't work out, so I volunteered my place."

A knock sounded at the door and Tanner instantly tensed, hoping it wasn't Judy again, only to relax again when Whit called his name.

"Come in!" he yelled.

When he and Aiden emerged from the hall leading to the bedrooms, she was standing in the living room.

"Whitney Fox, this is Aiden Book."

"Someone else in the single syllable surname club."

Aiden grinned appreciatively. "Are you part of this community event thing?"

"In a small way. I'm also part of the ranch operations for now."

"Aiden, meet my range rider."

"Nice to meet you," she said.

Tanner could see that Aiden was as impressed with his range rider as he'd been with the house.

"Nice to meet you," he echoed.

Whit turned to Tanner. "Len is having a bit of a meltdown out there. I didn't feel like intervening."

"Right." He turned to Aiden. "Settle in. The fridge is full."

"Excellent." Aiden gave Whitney a polite nod then headed back down the hall.

"He worked for me for two summers. This is probably his last. I'm glad he could come."

He and Whitney headed across the lawn to the sound of raised voices. They rounded the corner of Len's small house and found him facing off with an older blonde woman dressed in creased jeans and a starched long-sleeved pink oxford shirt.

"You were a pain in high school and you're still a pain," the woman said to Len as they approached.

"Now listen here—"

"No. You listen—"

Tanner stepped between Len and a woman he didn't know, something he wouldn't have normally done, but both parties were getting red-faced. He turned to the woman. "Is there a problem?"

She pointed at Len.

Tanner gave Len a look and the older man said, "You told me I was in charge."

And since telling him that, Len had been in a better mood.

"You are." He turned to the woman, thinking that since hosting this event was an exercise in bettering community relations, he needed to tread lightly. He didn't know who she was, but she seemed to think she was in charge. "Perhaps you could—"

"We are setting up the tent there." She pointed to where a corner stake had been driven into the ground.

"It'll block my morning sun."

Tanner refrained from rolling his eyes, but it took effort. "It's temporary."

The woman gave a victory sniff. Tanner needed Len to understand—he needed the community to believe he was a good guy.

"We have to set up the vendor booths there." She pointed. "And the flattest, largest spot for the tent is there and it allows us to hook into the power source."

Tanner gave Len a help-me-out-here look and the old man scowled deeply, then broke.

"Fine, Leticia. That looks like a great place for the tent."

Leticia gave him a smug look and strutted back to the group that was staking out sites and arm waving.

"I hate letting her win. She was always pushing the envelope, that one." Len glared after her and Tanner rubbed the side of his head. Apparently, age didn't change mindsets.

"If there are any other problems, I'll be servicing the swather. I'll introduce you to the new crew later."

"About time we got that hay down."

Len limped off. Tanner watched him go, then turned looked at Whit, who shrugged. "I have to fix some windbreak boards."

"Aren't you and your dad supposed to be part of all this setup?" Because she hadn't said a word about it, instead working her usual hours on the ranch.

"Only on the morning of. We're doing all the last-minute stuff, setting up games and helping vendors. I had another talk with Judy, and I must have made an impression at the meeting, because she agreed."

She gave him a quick smile then, before heading off in the direction of the corrals.

He and Len might never be friends, but he found that he didn't mind the guy. If he and his dad had had the same conversation, it would have ended entirely differently. But Len seemed to accept that he wasn't going to get his way and move on.

No wonder the cranky old guy was growing on him.

SMALL CREWS SHOWED up on the ranch every couple of days, and after the first visit, Tanner told Margo Simms that the volunteers didn't need to check in, but if they felt that they had to, then Len was the man to talk to.

He did his best to steer clear and let the workers do their jobs, so he was surprised when, as part of his steering clear, he went through the barn to saddle Clive for a quick fence check while Whit mowed ditches, and found a middle-aged woman studying his horses through the rails of the fence.

"Oh. Hello," she said when he appeared from the back of the barn. "I was just admiring your Rockies."

He smiled, then she floored him by saying, "That gelding was supposed to be mine, you know."

Tanner gave the woman a surprised glance. "Clive?"

She nodded. "I owned the stud he's out of. Your father and I had a deal. In exchange for the stud fee for three mares, I got the pick of the get. Your dad had great mares." She pointed to Emily. "Good example there. Anyway, after the foals were born, I picked Clive. Your father changed the deal and insisted that I take one of the two fillies. He wanted the gelding for himself."

The word of a Hayes.

Len's odd statement shot into his head.

"I'll trade you back," he said.

The woman laughed. "The filly worked out just fine. I have a new stud and she threw an excellent little stud colt last month."

"Are you *sure* you don't want him?" Tanner asked. "I could have Clive's bags packed before you go."

The woman gave him an appraising once-over. "You look like your father...but I'm sensing you're cut from different cloth."

"There were things we didn't see eye to eye on." He wasn't going to bad-mouth his dead father, but he wanted the woman to know that they were different. "And Clive here…he's headstrong. You came out on the better end of the deal."

She smiled. "I was angry at the time because I wanted a gelding to ride, but I've heard rumors that he wasn't the mount your father had been hoping for."

"Sounds like karma was at play here."

"I think so." She held out a hand. "Mary Bledsoe."

He did the same. "Tanner Hayes. Nice to meet you."

WHIT HAD JUST parked the tractor and was thinking about heading home for the day when the phone rang in her pocket.

Rob Ketchum.

She stepped into the shop through the open door, saw Tanner working on the ATV and quickly stepped out again before he saw her. The phone buzzed again as she opened the main door of the barn and stepped into the cool interior.

Her mouth flattened before she accepted the call and said simply, "Rob."

"Whitney. I just got word that you canceled your second interview. Did you get a better offer?"

"No."

"Then what happened?" Rob sounded affronted.

"I decided that I want to work closer to home. My dad isn't getting any younger, and I need to be nearby."

Besides that, she'd rather get tossed into a bog than "team" with Rob again.

"You're not going to find a better job. I went out on a limb for you, and with a little finessing we can still schedule the second interview. It's not too late."

"Rob, I appreciate you thinking of me, but I'm not going forward."

Rob put forth another sputtering argument, but Whit cut

him off and hung up the phone. She leaned back against a grain barrel. One bridge burned.

"You plan on working here full-time?"

Whit nearly jumped out of her skin when Len's gruff voice sounded. She turned to find the man standing at the door to the tack room.

"Why do you ask?"

"Because I won't have you pushing me out." He made a frustrated noise as he moved closer. "You'll tire of this place and leave, and I have nowhere else to go."

Whit studied the man as a thought took root. "Is this why you're so cranky with Tanner?"

Len gave her a startled look, as if he thought he was the only guy on the ranch allowed to speak freely. "I'm worried about my future. I got lied to by one Hayes, and it's going to take me a while to trust the other." As soon as he finished speaking, he let out a harsh breath and turned to go.

"Wait a minute."

The man slowed. Turned. Gave her a malignant look that held an edge of…fear? And despite herself, Whit felt for the guy.

"We need to talk to Tanner."

"Don't go pushing your nose into my business."

"You're the one who opened the can of worms. Are we going to see Tanner, or do I have to bring him over here?" When the old man didn't reply, she called Tanner's name. She had good lungs, and he wasn't that far away.

The alarmed look on Len's face concerned her; she didn't want him having a heart attack or something, but he'd started this, and she was going to finish it. For his own good. She didn't for one minute believe that Tanner would push him out, and it seemed the guy needed major reassurance.

Tanner opened the barn door, looking alarmed, as well.

His expression shifted to bemusement when he saw Len standing a few feet away from Whit.

"Len has a concern. I think you should hear it."

"A concern." Tanner hooked a thumb in his belt as he waited for his foreman to speak.

Len swallowed, looking patently uncomfortable.

"Tell him," Whit urged the man.

"I had a deal with your dad."

Not what Whit had expected. She'd brought Tanner in for job reassurance. Now she was a witness to something different.

Tanner's face instantly tightened. "What was the deal, Len?"

"I had a job offer from an old friend a few years back. Good job, too. Your dad told me that if I stayed on here, that I would always have a place. And if he passed on before me, that I would inherit that five-acre plot near the main road."

"Do you have anything in writing?"

Len gave his head a shake. "He told me he'd made an addendum to his will, but when the time came, there was no mention of me."

His father had named neither son to be executor of his will, tapping his attorney for the job. The bequeathals had been straightforward—a fifty-fifty split between sons. There had been no amendment made for Len.

"Word of a Hayes?" Tanner asked softly.

Whit frowned, but Len simply nodded and then his mouth flattened. "He even told me he had the plot surveyed."

"I'm not selling the ranch, Len. You have a home."

"Until your brother forces a sale."

"I'm not going to let that happen."

Len's expression remained mutinous, as if he was afraid to believe the truth.

"I'll have my lawyer work something up. We'll sign it." Tanner held the older man's gaze until he looked down.

"No need."

"There is if you have issue with the word of a Hayes."

Len lifted his gaze. "Your dad was good to me in a lot of ways, but this hurt."

Tanner shifted his weight. "I'll have papers drawn up, and we'll agree to some terms. I think you deserve that and we'll both sleep better knowing we have a deal."

The older man didn't reply, but Whit read the relief in his face. He needed the papers and Tanner understood that. Tanner was a good guy, and if he continued as he was, he would be fine with the community. He didn't need her help, even if he thought he did.

Whit had fulfilled her commitment to the ranch, and to him.

So why was it so hard to think about leaving?

CHAPTER TWELVE

IT'S TIME TO MOVE ON.

Whit reached into the soapy dishwater and pulled out a coffee cup, hoping to lose herself in a mindless task, but failing as the events of the day continued to play on a loop in her head.

She needed to move on, because Tanner Hayes had her thinking about *not* doing that.

Life plans were important, and surprisingly easy to forget when the guy warmed her heart by guaranteeing an old man that his living situation was secure. Or when he wrote "Wash Me" in the road dust on the back of Judy Blanchard's otherwise pristine car. Or when he did a hundred other small things that made her laugh or squeezed her heart.

Camaraderie, she told herself as she scrubbed a bit of baked beans off the plate her dad had used at lunch.

Baloney, her small voice answered.

But she would continue to play that game. She would be Tanner's sounding board and workmate, while at the same time keeping her emotions under control.

She'd try, anyway.

She put the plate in the drain rack and reached for the skillet.

It was time to put new energy into finding a job—one that did *not* include Rob Ketchum. The guy had almost played her and that ticked her off. Had she gone soft during her time at home? She knew better than to fully trust the guy. She'd had a few blips of doubt, but had brushed past them.

Just like you're brushing off your attraction to Tanner. Except in that case it made sense. If she couldn't play the long game, then it wasn't fair to anyone to play at all.

After she'd finished the dishes and wiped down the counters, she stood for an uncertain moment, listening to the reassuring sound of the baseball game playing on the television in the living room. Her dad was probably asleep.

On with the job search, but her first move was to call her former workmates, Lacy and Buster, to let them know that their insights about Rob had been dead-on.

This time Buster answered, and Lacy was out.

"Thanks for giving me the heads-up about Rob," Whit said as she walked into the kitchen so as not to disturb her dad. "He did indeed plan on us having another one-sided partnership."

"Are you—"

"I am not."

Buster hesitated, then said, "FYI, I hear there have been issues with our former company and the merged positions. Rumor has it that they may be contacting former employees in the near future. Sounds like they got pink-slip happy and shot themselves in the foot and ended up with their own employees in roles they aren't prepared to handle. Typical case of thinking they knew what they were getting into, but didn't."

"Interesting."

"Would you go back?" he asked.

Whit closed her eyes. Thought for a moment. "They'd have to make one heck of an offer to compensate for laying me off."

"I don't know what I would do, either. I tried to tell them

that a guy trained in human resources wouldn't be able to do my job, but they assumed I was just trying to keep my job. Which I was, so…"

Whit gave a small laugh. "I hope they do contact you, and I hope you get double your old salary."

And what was she going to do if they contacted her?

THE HEARTS OF the West crew had finished setting up for the day, but there were still a few stragglers loading tools into their vehicles as Tanner and Whit sat on the steps of his house sharing a beer before Whit headed home. It had become something of a routine for them over the past week. Work on fences, check the cattle on the mountain, feed the steers, have a beer before parting company.

"Big day tomorrow," Whit mused.

"And won't it be grand when it's over?" he said. Whit nudged him and Tanner made it a point not to smile. He was not looking forward to having his space being invaded more than it already had been, but he approached the matter with good humor, because he wanted to forge better relationships with his neighbors. Rebuild some burned bridges.

He wasn't certain how well that was going, but no one had keyed his truck or anything, so maybe it was going okay?

The frame tents were up—one for dining, one for games—and the generators to supply electricity for the food booths were in place. The area for the kids' activities was decked out, and the dance floor was in position. There was a slight chance of rain that evening so the folding chairs had been left in their racks, and the raffle committee members had yet to draw the chalk grid inside the panel enclosure for the cow flop contest.

"Last one," Whit said as a pickup with a lumber rack pulled out of the drive. "I'd better follow."

He didn't want her to go.

It'd been that way for the past few days. Whit would say she was leaving, and Tanner would feel a stab of disappointment.

Aiden and Cooper were still on tractors, mowing hay. Tanner could hear the faint drone of the engines in the distance. They'd be back in an hour or so, and then the house wouldn't be as lonely, but what really bugged Tanner was realizing that he'd never felt lonely like this before. Alone was his state of being. Alone was his protection, his strength. He didn't fear it.

But he no longer embraced it.

You're setting yourself up for a fall.

He got up and offered Whitney a hand. After pulling her to her feet, their fingers clung for a moment, then drifted apart, and they walked down the flagstone path to the low stone wall. Rose lifted her head from where she still lay on the porch, loath to move from her spot of early-evening sun, but wanting to keep a close eye on Tanner, just in case he needed her assistance.

"You get the day off tomorrow."

"Thanks." She gave him a wry smile.

"You're coming to this thing, of course."

"If I don't, who are you going to hang out with?"

Tanner smiled. "I'm glad I'm only the venue guy. I don't think I could handle running this thing."

"You ran a major farm."

"Where Margo, Debra and Judy were not employees."

"Len has had a great time bossing them around."

"But he steers clear of Leticia."

The old guy had met his match there. Leticia, whom Tanner had discovered via Margo was in charge of the layout committee, won the tent location contest and several other minor skirmishes.

"I think he enjoys doing battle," Tanner said as he set his beer aside. "Speak of the devil…"

Whit raised her gaze to see Len crossing the gravel drive, his cane slipping every now and again as it came down on a larger piece of gravel.

"Can you help me out?" The words came out in a burst as he stopped a few feet in front of where they stood at the gate.

"Of course," Tanner said.

"It's Kenny." Len's face hardened as he spoke, as if he expected an instant backlash when he said his nephew's name. But Tanner said nothing, and after a brief hesitation, the old man continued. "He was on his way out here with the groceries and had some kind of wreck. His phone kept cutting in and out, but as near as I can figure, he can't get his motorbike out of a gully."

"Is he hurt?" Whit asked.

"I don't think so. He kept talking about the motorcycle." But the worried look on the old man's face made Tanner's insides twist. Had his dad worried about him that way? He didn't know. Would never know.

"Any idea where the gully is?"

"I'm guessing that it's the one on the big corner past the Fairfield Ranch."

"I'll go take a look."

"I'll go with you," Whit said. "My truck or yours?"

"Mine's hooked to the horse trailer. In case we need to load the bike."

"Yours it is."

"I appreciate this," Len said gruffly.

"It's what people do for one another," Whit said. She

glanced over her shoulder at Tanner, then started for the truck.

She made a good point.

"LEN'S HAVING A rough spring," Whit said as they drove over the cattle guard, the empty trailer rattling behind them. "Do you think your dad intended to alter his will to give him the five acres he promised?"

Tanner gave her a weary look before fixing his gaze back on the road. "I'd like to think that he did. That he treated other people better than family. Especially the guy who remained loyal to him."

Whit thought of the few times she'd seen Carl Hayes out and about. He'd been a handsome silver-haired man with a ready smile that didn't reach his eyes. He drew people in with natural charisma, then surprised them by turning cold when he no longer needed them. She'd heard her dad and friends talk about the man and how they avoided dealings with him. But he'd been a steady source of revenue for the community, giving generously and writing it off on his taxes. *He has more money than he knows what to do with*, was the common refrain.

Come to find out he didn't.

"There are only a few corners," Tanner said, punching the gas after they turned from the driveway onto the county road. They sailed along the washboard road, then Tanner slowed as they approached the first big corner. He stopped the truck and Whit got out to take a look. The creek ran close to the road there, but it was slow and lazy. The gully wasn't deep. She called Kenny's name, then got back in the truck.

"Not here."

The next corner was less than a mile away and as they

approached, a solitary figure came into sight, walking along the edge of the road.

Kenny.

Tanner pulled up beside him and the kid gave them a mutinous look.

"We're here to help. Your uncle sent us. Where's your bike?" Tanner asked.

The kid jerked a thumb over his shoulder and Tanner said, "Let's go get it."

Kenny got into the back seat of the truck and Whit turned to give him a quick once-over. He had scratches on his face, but other than that seemed no worse for wear.

"It wasn't that bad a wreck," Kenny said stiffly, wiping a hand over his cheek. "The bike's too heavy for me to get up the bank."

"What happened?"

"Gravel got me."

Whit almost said, "You need to drive more slowly," but held her tongue.

The motorcycle lay on its side at the bottom of the gully, which wasn't so much deep as steep-banked on the roadside. After skidding down the bank, with the dirt and gravel shifting easily beneath their boots, Tanner and Whit made a plan to roll the thing down the creek until they came to a place where the bank was more manageable and secure.

"Just around that corner," Tanner said as he and Kenny started pushing the bike. Whit climbed back onto the road and turned the truck and trailer around in a nearby field. By the time she got to the low spot Tanner had pointed out, Tanner and Kenny were trying to wrestle the heavy motorcycle onto the road.

"I couldn't have done that alone," Kenny said after the bike was on the road. He swallowed. "Thank you."

"Can you start it?"

He tried, but the engine wouldn't take hold, so Whit backed the trailer to a low spot, and between the three of them they managed to load the motorcycle, setting it on its side.

The ride to the ranch was quiet, until they turned onto the driveway.

"My uncle was worried that you were going to replace him," Kenny said abruptly. He didn't need to explain who the "you" was, even though he didn't speak directly to Whit.

She exchanged a quick look with Tanner, then said, "I'm not."

"We know about that," Tanner said. "Len and I talked."

Kenny blew out a breath. "He's, like, all proud, you know."

Whit watched as Tanner met the kid's eyes in the rearview mirror. "Listen carefully. I'm not letting Len leave the ranch unless he tells me he wants to go."

The kid's chin came up. "Really?"

"As long as I have the ranch, your uncle has a home."

"Okay."

It might have sounded like an inadequate response on the surface, but Whit heard the relief in the kid's voice. She gave Tanner a sideways glance, but he kept his gaze straight ahead, then his chin came up.

"Are you kidding me?" he muttered.

Kenny took hold of the seat back and pulled himself forward to get a look at the Land Rover parked in front of the gate where no one ever parked.

"This keeps getting better," Tanner muttered.

"Your brother?" Whit asked as they drove past the Land Rover to the turnaround area.

"Appears so."

Tanner pulled behind the barn and turned off the engine. "Grant can cool his heels. I'm going to see Len." He looked over the seat at Kenny. "First I'll help you get your bike on its wheels."

"I'll entertain Grant," Whit said.

Tanner gave a curt nod in response, and after getting out of the truck, she heard Kenny say to Tanner, "You don't like your brother?"

"I like him fine," Tanner said as they walked to the back of the trailer. "We just don't agree on some stuff."

"Like what?"

Whit headed into the barn before Tanner could answer, but she had to admit that she wanted to hear what Tanner said to the kid. Ironically, he, the community pariah, seemed to have a knack with people.

Although he wasn't so much of a pariah anymore. The people working on the Hearts of the West setup were treating him like any other community member, not like a guy who might stab them in the back at any minute, just because he could. They were moving closer to trust.

Would Tanner ever be able to trust others back?

WHIT HAD ALREADY ushered Grant into the house by the time Tanner got done talking to Len, explaining once again that no matter what, the guy had a home there.

"More business in the area?" he asked as he came into the kitchen.

"I'm talking to the folks on the Fairfield Ranch about insurance. But I have some disturbing news and thought it would be best if I delivered it in person."

Grant seemed to have a lot of disturbing news of late. Tanner sank into a chair across the table from his brother. "Shoot."

"Bert Wallace had a heart attack."

"I'm sorry to hear that," Tanner said. Bert was one of their father's oldest acquaintances, and possibly the closest thing to a real friend that Carl had, because they were cut from the same cloth. Appearances and money were numbers one and two in their lives. Relationships a distant third. He'd given Carl the personal loan to keep the ranch afloat, but he hadn't done his friend any favors when he'd set the interest rate.

"He's okay?" Tanner asked.

"So they say. He's in the hospital in Billings," Grant replied offhandedly, before leaning forward and asking, "What if he sells the note?"

The private loan Carl had taken out to keep up appearances until he recouped losses could be sold. All Bert Wallace had to do was to give six weeks' notice to allow an opportunity for refinancing. Until this point, Tanner hadn't worried about the note. But now that Grant was on the job, all bets were off.

"Isn't that exactly what you want him to do?"

Grant blinked at him. "I'm here to warn you that trouble may lie ahead."

"Okay." Tanner wasn't certain he believed him.

"Selling the ranch makes sense, Tanner." Grant spoke adamantly, then seemed to remember that Whit was there, and changed his tone. "I want top dollar. I don't want to be scrambling to sell in order to get out from under this debt." He tapped the table with his index finger, emphasizing the words as he said, "That kind of knowledge tends to bring down prices."

"I'll worry about the note when and if it comes due. It's *my* worry, Grant. For the next two years and nine months it's my worry. So…do you want to spend the night?"

Grant got to his feet. "I have a room in Larkspur."

"I can offer you a drink or—"

"Thanks, no." Grant picked up his hat from where he'd left it on a chair back and held it with both hands. "I need to head back. I have a late dinner meeting with another client. What kind of circus are you setting up here?"

Grant knew exactly what the circus was, but Tanner explained what he assumed his brother already knew, since he was doing business in Larkspur. "I'm hosting Hearts of the West."

"So you don't have to write a big check. Brilliant." Grant sounded sincere.

Tanner walked his brother to the door while Whit hovered near the table. He was glad she wasn't taking this as a cue to leave, because for once in his life he felt like talking. He poured two whiskeys, handed one to Whit, then sat on the cream-colored leather sofa. Rose immediately moved from where she lay to settle at his feet.

"And this is where I am," he said to Whit. "My brother is not my ally."

She perched on the sofa arm next to him and ran a hand over his tense shoulder muscles.

"He pointed out a legitimate concern," she offered. "The guy selling the note after a health scare. He might want to have more ready cash."

"It is a concern, but I'm guessing that this was my brother's way of warning me before he goes to work on the guy, trying to talk him into selling the note."

"You think that he would do that?"

"I think that he wants more than yearly profits from this property—once I start turning a profit, that is."

"You need to buy him out."

He gave her a *duh* look. "You think?"

Instead of being insulted, she smiled and ran her hand over the back of his neck. Her fingers were warm and soothing and just what he needed—a momentary distraction from the reality of his life. "We need to think outside the box."

"Uh-huh." He noted the way she'd said "we" and the way it made him feel. Like they were a team. Allies. Like someone had his back and not just for a convenient moment.

"Did I sound like I just came out of management training?"

He pulled her down onto his lap and wrapped his arms around her. "You did."

"Mr. Hayes," she said in a prim voice, but she leaned into him instead of easing away. He felt her let out a soft breath and he settled his cheek on her hair, no longer worrying about what was right or wrong. Whit would keep them honest.

He wrapped his arms around her more tightly, holding her close and breathing in the fresh scent of her hair. There were so many things he wanted to say to her, things he wanted to discuss. Things he was half-afraid of discussing because he was fully afraid of the answer.

"Whitney—"

The sound of the front door opening interrupted him, followed by the noise of two teenage boys entering the house. Boots and other things hit the floor, then the fridge door opened and one of them called, "Dibs on the potato salad!"

Whit eased herself off Tanner's lap. He started to speak, but she touched her fingers to his lips to silence him.

"Let's leave things as they are."

The faintly pleading note in the voice of a woman who rarely pleaded was enough to decide him. Whitney had to make the next move.

The question was, would she?

CHAPTER THIRTEEN

BECAUSE BUSTER TOM had warned Whit about the possibility of a call from the Greenbranch human resources department, she was mentally prepared when it came. One of her former bosses had already returned to the company, which green-lighted Whit's return if she so desired. The fact that Shandra Johnson was willing to risk a second go with the newly formed Greenbranch-Lowell Renewable gave Whit reason to hear them out. Which she did.

She liked what she heard, but after ending the call, the wave of uncertainty hit, and she had to talk herself down. Her dad didn't need her on the ranch. That had been proven a dozen times over since her return. Unlike in years past, she wasn't called up for emergency fence repairs, or to take her turn on the tractor in the hayfields.

And as Len continued to heal, and with his temporary crew now at work, Tanner didn't really need her, either.

What *she* needed was to get back out there and start focusing on her career again. The Greenbranch-Lowell HR representative had laid out all the possibilities for advancement in the newly formed company, and although Whit still had a bad taste over being let go to begin with, she understood that the way things looked on paper and the way they played out in real life were often miles apart. She could have told the Lowell executives that coming up to speed on federal regulations was no easy task, but why bother after getting booted?

As it turned out, they'd figured it out on their own and they wanted her back. The offer included a bonus and a raise. A new title.

And, she assumed, the long hours that went with that new title.

Her dad was going to think that she was a fool to leave the ranch and go back to a desk, and she could see his point, but she appreciated the security of her career. She'd worked hard to build it, and had received many perks because of it.

Once her bank account was back up where it belonged, and she had poured enough into her retirement fund to feel secure, she would be in a position to rethink her options. She had a feeling that she would stay right where she was, working with people she knew and a company that appeared to be better because of the buyout.

Life Plan Number 3 was taking shape.

She only wished it wasn't making her chest ache as she chose practicality over dreams that wouldn't pan out any better than Life Plan Number 1.

"Let me get this straight." Ben frowned at the paper Whit laid down in front of him with the offer that had come in less than two hours after the call from Shandra. "The company that bought your old company wants you back?"

"The person whose position merged with mine isn't working out. They need someone who knows the ropes, fast."

"You'll be in Missoula."

Whit set a hand on her dad's shoulder. "That's the bad news…they've moved their executive operations to Portland. But it's closer than New Mexico."

"Still a distance." He gave her a long look. "There's more to life than money, Whit."

"I'm not chasing money, Dad. I want security. Don't

forget that you might have lost the ranch if it wasn't for the money I earned at this same job."

"And if I had lost it, I could have dealt with it."

"Really?"

"It would have eaten at me, but that's how life works, Whit. Doors close and open. The only reason we have the ranch to begin with is because your great-great-grandfather's business in Butte went bankrupt and he decided to try his hand at ranching. I bet it killed him to lose his business, but he found something that made him happier." His voice gentled. "You have been happier."

"These past several weeks have been like a big vacation. That's why I'm happier."

"Or maybe you're doing something you like better than clacking away at a keyboard all day."

"That clacking provides security."

"I can't deny that. But…"

Ben obviously had more to say, and Whit wanted to hear it. "Life goes by fast, Whit. I don't want you to wake up one morning and realize that you've sacrificed good years to a career that doesn't let you see real sunlight as often as you should."

"I'll take vitamin D."

Ben didn't crack a smile. "Why are you really taking this job, Whit?"

He knew. He knew that she was running scared. When was she going to learn not to make jokes when she was afraid? It was her tell.

"I'm taking this job because I'm afraid to stay here."

And there it was. The honest truth that she had been dodging.

"Does that have anything to do with Tanner Hayes?"

She flattened her mouth and let her dad draw his own conclusions from her silence.

WHIT KNEW THAT she'd done the right thing taking the Greenbranch job.

She was occasionally impulsive in her personal life, but she always made safe and sane career decisions, which was what she'd done when she'd said yes to Greenbranch.

So why did she feel so torn about leaving the ranch, and Tanner, behind?

Do you really have to ask yourself that question?

As much as she tried to convince herself that what she and Tanner shared was the equivalent of a short summer romance, her heart begged to differ, whispering that she should take a chance, stay on the ranch and pursue the life she loved. Then her brain stepped in to complicate matters by bringing up financial security and adult responsibilities. The battle between logic and emotions had kept her up for a good part of the night, so when she rose in the early morning hours to drive to Hayes Ranch for the Hearts of the West event, she drank two cups of coffee in an attempt to jump-start her tired body.

Her dad walked into the kitchen just as she was about to head out the door.

"You're already leaving?"

"I have to help with final details. The event starts at ten, and you know something will explode or somebody will melt down before then."

"Last year the cow went AWOL."

"And I promised Debra that wouldn't happen again."

"Good luck with that," her dad said. He crossed the room to the coffee pot, then shot her a curious look when he saw that there was only about a cup left.

"I didn't sleep well," she admitted. Whit was not a huge coffee drinker, so by almost emptying the pot, she'd given herself away.

But her dad had mercy and didn't ask questions. Instead

he said, "Making a big life move is never easy, even when it's just going back to your old job."

Whit smiled, then crossed the kitchen to give her dad a kiss on his weathered cheek.

"I appreciate that you understand why I need to go."

"I may not understand the why," he said, gruffly, "but I can see you have the need."

Whit took what she could get and headed out the door to start the old ranch truck she was driving that day.

When she got to the Hayes Ranch it was abuzz with activity. Someone called her name and soon she was on the chalk machine, making the squares for the cow flop. The cow was corralled nearby, so there would not be a repeat of last year's, "Has anyone seen the cow?"

She spotted Tanner after she'd finished the grid, standing near a vendor's booth, deep in conversation with Len. For once the older man did not look defensive. It was good to see the two of them conversing freely after everything that had gone on between them, thanks to Carl Hayes's empty promise. Tanner was going to be all right. He had his summer crew, his foreman was now on his side, and the community was warming up to him.

Her job here was done.

You have to tell him you accepted the offer.

She would and she didn't need to feel shifty about it. They'd laid out parameters, and one of those was that she could leave at any time to take a job. That was exactly what she was doing.

The vendor booths had just opened for business and the local musicians were tuning up when Whit found Tanner standing near the barn, watching the stream of cars pulling into his ranch. High school kids in orange vests directed the parking in a newly mowed hayfield. When he heard her approach, he turned, his expression reminding her of a cartoon of an expectant father.

"Nervous?" she asked.

Tanner's cheeks creased as he smiled, and Whit's heart did a little stutter. Was she ever going to stop reacting to that smile?

Not today, apparently, which made delivering her news all that much more difficult.

"I am nervous," he confessed. "I'd like the event to go well." He shifted his weight as he looked over the vendors' booths. "I feel like if it doesn't…" He made a slashing motion across his throat.

"This isn't on you." Whit came to stand in front of him so that the toes of their boots were a few inches apart. "All you did was to graciously let the community use your property."

"I feel responsible."

"You shouldn't."

"Says who?" he asked in a mock challenge.

Whit tossed her hair and moved a half step closer to the man. "I do."

He settled his hands on her shoulders, fixed her a long hard stare. Whit made a face at him, and his challenging look melted away.

"People are being friendly with me. I owe you for that."

"They're getting to know the real you."

"I am pretty awesome."

His smile was infectious, and Whit felt the corners of her mouth tilt up. She needed to tell him that she was leaving, but she wasn't ready to see that gorgeous smile fade from his face. He looked so open and relaxed, so totally different than when they first met. So much had happened since he'd rammed her car from behind and she felt a bond with the guy that went beyond a few shared kisses.

Were they more than allies?

Yes, her small voice whispered.

But she wasn't going to put a name on anything. What was the point when she was about to leave?

Tanner's grip tightened on her shoulders, and she sensed that he was about to kiss her, right there in front of anyone who happened to look their way. And she wasn't going to stop him. Instead it was Kenny who stopped him, calling Tanner's name from where he stood behind a vendor's booth with a cartload of folding chairs.

"Better go and make a command decision," he said, reluctantly releasing her shoulders from his warm grip. "I'll see you later."

"Yes, you will." Whit brushed a few windblown strands of hair from her face.

I have news.

She let out a breath as she watched him walk away. Telling him that she was leaving was going to be harder than she'd thought.

Tanner was enjoying the Hearts of the West event more than he'd expected, although he had to admit that he was looking forward to having peace and quiet on his ranch again. He was also looking forward to having some time alone with Whit.

She'd been on the property since early that morning, managing the final setup and tweaks of the game and vendor areas. Then she'd volunteered at the children's games and for the cow flop contest—both morning and afternoon sessions. She'd also lent a hand with the pet scramble, a favorite with the kids as they scrambled to catch ducks, chickens, piglets and baby goats that they were allowed to keep.

If he didn't know better, he would think that she was dodging him. But that wasn't Whit's modus operandi.

A steady stream of music drifted from the gazebo where local musicians took turns playing, and a few people were taking advantage of the portable dance floor that he was assured would be crowded by the late afternoon.

A hand touched his shoulder and he turned to find Whit standing behind him. He tried to ignore the fact that his heart rate bumped up at the sight of her, as it always did, but it was getting harder and harder to do that.

"Another three hours and you'll have your ranch back." She handed him a beer as she spoke. "I thought you could use one," she said when he took the cold bottle from her. "Hosting can be exhausting." She tilted her head as she surveyed the people milling around the vendor booths, sitting on the grass listening to music, playing various games. "Even when it is going remarkably well."

"Actually," he replied slowly, "I haven't minded hosting." When she looked at him incredulously, he added, "Okay, the days leading up were rough, and I was nervous earlier, but like you said, it's going well. And it's nice to have people talk to me, instead of glaring because of something Dad did to them."

"They like you, Tanner. You've proven yourself."

"Maybe I can get some help on the ranch after my summer crew leaves." He raised his chin in the direction of his new hire who was in the process of chugging a liter bottle of Pepsi in front of an admiring crowd of teenage boys. "Besides Kenny."

"You hired Kenny?"

"It seemed like the thing to do."

Now that Whit was about to leave—with a paycheck, whether or not she wanted one—he'd started thinking about the kid, and wondered if he might like to work closer to his great-uncle. Come to find out, he did, so now Tanner had someone on the payroll who knew how to deal with Len's impatience.

"Nice," she said. "I'm sure you'll be able to find day hands when you need them. I've taken great pains to let people know that the Hayes Ranch is a good place to work."

Her speech sounded oddly perfunctory, and the smile that followed didn't bring the usual light to her eyes. When Tanner gave her a curious look, she fixed her gaze back on the crowd. Whit was not acting like Whit. Tanner wasn't a body language expert, but he could read trouble.

"Tell me," he said.

She turned to him and let out a breath that made her shoulders drop a good inch. "I'm going back to work for Greenbranch. The new incarnation."

The abrupt announcement surprised him, but then again it didn't. "I guess we knew this was coming." But now that it had, he realized how much he'd been hoping that Whit would decide that she wanted to stay in Larkspur.

"You understand, right?"

The fact that she'd asked that question meant that what he thought mattered. So he spoke a simple truth.

"Frankly, I don't want you to go."

She opened her mouth to reply, just as Judy and Margo waved at them, then crossed the front lawn to join them. "We just want to thank you for volunteering your ranch," Margo said. "We've had our largest turnout ever."

"Glad to help," Tanner said.

"We'll have to talk about next year." Judy gave him a coy look, then a jet of fire at the barbecue caught the ladies' attention.

Margo took hold of Judy's arm. "We'd best see what's happening over there."

"Have they never seen a barbecue flare?" Tanner asked once they were out of earshot.

Whit said nothing and when he looked at her, he could see that telling her he didn't want her to go might have been a tactical error. But it was also the truth.

"You know that I have to go," Whitney said, as if they hadn't been interrupted.

He nodded, not trusting himself to speak just yet. His thoughts were jumbling, and he didn't want to say something he regretted later.

"I *like* being with you," she continued. "I can't deny that we share something." She let out a soft huff of breath. "Something I did *not* see coming."

"Join the crowd," he muttered, torn between agreeing that Whit needed to follow her original plan for her sake, and confessing that his feelings for her were growing stronger by the day. He'd known that this was coming, but had hoped it wouldn't. And in an odd way he felt betrayed—by his own heart.

"Maybe after I…" Her voice trailed as if she didn't want to continue the thought.

"Get more money in the bank?" he asked.

Her gaze flashed up to his face. "There's that."

Part of him regretted uttering the words, but another part pressed on.

"How much, Whit? How much before you can let yourself take a chance?"

"I don't know," she said in a stony voice.

"Gotta stick to those life plans."

"They've kept me secure so far."

And security was important to her. Her job had helped her save the family ranch and she was afraid of not having the means to stave off another emergency.

Which meant that she had to leave. And that he needed to be understanding even if it was ripping his heart out.

"I care for you." He chose the word *care* because it was safer than saying that he was falling in love with her. He didn't want to risk Whitney's reaction to a sudden declaration.

"I know." She whispered the words, as if they were a guilty confession. "I care for you, too."

Tanner became aware of the sound of an altercation near the gazebo. Someone had started yelling, but he kept his gaze pinned to Whit's face.

"You don't want to do the scrape-by thing, and that's what you'd get if things grew between us."

Whit's chin jerked up. "Being poor wouldn't stop me from loving someone."

His mouth opened, then he closed it, feeling like she'd just hit him square in the chest. Finally he said, "I guess that's my answer."

"Tanner!"

Whitney jumped at the unexpected voice, and they turned together to see Grant heading toward them, walking with a rolling gait.

"I didn't know he was here," Whit said in a low voice. Neither did Tanner, but it would have been easy to arrive unseen given the crowd and the parking situation.

"Tanner!" he yelled again, even though he was only two or three feet away from him.

"I'm right here." Tanner winced at the smell of alcohol on his brother's breath.

"I've been talking to people."

"I'm sure you have."

"And the consensus is that you should *sell* this place. You're broke and everybody knows it."

Tanner simply stared at his brother, then a moment later

he became aware of Whit putting a reassuring hand on his sleeve.

"How many people have you talked to?" Tanner asked, setting his beer on the porch rail next to him and steadying his brother, who was listing from side to side.

"He's going to pass out," Whit said. "I worked at a bar in college. I know the signs."

So did Tanner, and he didn't want his drunk brother ruining the Hearts of the West event. He put a firm hand under Grant's elbow and Whit took hold of his other arm.

Together they led him up the steps, having to stop once because he almost sent them over backward. "I can take it from here," Tanner told Whit when they'd made it inside.

"Are you sure?"

He met her gaze. "Positive."

"I thought that…" She lifted her chin. "Fine. I'll leave you to it."

"ARE YOU OKAY?"

Whit's gaze jerked around as Kat touched her shoulder from behind. She was headed toward the food booths and hadn't realized that her friend was following her, shaken as she was by the double whammy of Tanner saying he didn't want her to leave and his brother announcing the ranch's financial status to the world.

"I'm not." Now that her friend was near, Whit allowed herself to feel the full impact of what had just gone down.

"Troy has the baby," Kat said, pointing to where her fiancé stood with his little daughter near the petting area, allowing Livia to watch the action. "Let's duck out."

"Let's," Whit agreed.

Somehow, Maddie caught up with them before Whit opened the barn door, and they stepped into the cool interior. A giggle from the dark told them that they weren't alone, and Whit called out, "This building is off-limits." Because apparently teens couldn't read the neat sign on the door.

Four middle school-aged boys appeared from behind the straw bales, and then sheepishly marched to the door.

"Is that all of you?" Whit asked.

The last boy mumbled an affirmative just before the door closed behind him.

"That was something," Kat said, and Whit knew she wasn't referring to middle school boys.

"Did Tanner's brother make a major scene?" Whit asked as she sank down onto a straw bale, glad to be away from prying eyes. She'd heard the ruckus begin while she and Tanner had been talking, but had been so focused on their conversation that she'd ignored the yelling until Grant accosted them.

"It was pretty spectacular once he got rolling. He was shouting about Tanner being a fraud and the ranch being broke."

"Poor guy," Maddie said, obviously referring to Tanner. "I mean, you know how many ranches are in the red, so that's not a big deal."

"Except that it's the Hayes Ranch."

"Yeah, that is a big deal. How the mighty have fallen and all that." Maddie blew out a breath as she sat beside Whit. "But I was thinking more about the embarrassment factor of having your own brother turn on you in front of everyone."

"Yes." Whit was certain that stung as much as having private business aired publicly.

Kat took a seat on a different bale, pulling it around so that it was at an angle to Whit and Maddie, and then the three of them sat in silence, allowing Whit to gather her thoughts.

No easy task.

"Tanner will have to deal with this matter without my PR skills," she said. "Such as they are."

"Why is that?" Kat asked, her gaze narrowing shrewdly.

Whit attempted an upbeat look. "Because yesterday I accepted a job at my old company. I'm leaving soon."

"Whoa," Maddie said. "Your old company?"

"It's a real opportunity." Whit explained about the restructuring and her hope that she could once again start climbing that corporate ladder and make the final jump to management.

Except her heart wasn't in it. Her voice was stiff, but other than a quick exchange of glances, her friends didn't call her on her forced enthusiasm.

"I was going to take you guys out for drinks and announce."

"Congratulations," Maddie said. Kat nodded and patted Whit's knee. "You can owe us the drinks."

"Here's the thing…" She swallowed and rather than giving them a big lead up, simply said, "Tanner doesn't want me to go."

"Okay," Maddie said, her tone gently encouraging Whit to go on.

"But I have to." Whit spoke the words in little more than a whisper. She did, right?

Kat left her bale to squeeze in on the one that Whit and Maddie shared, so that the three sat shoulder to shoulder to shoulder.

"I'm glad you're taking the job," Maddie said. "It'll give you some distance. Help you settle on what you really want in life without being distracted by…" Her voice trailed off as Whit met her gaze, then she forged on. "Distracted by a hot guy who's a pretty decent person."

"He is a hot guy. And I am distracted."

She made it sound like a minor thing when it was anything but. She told herself that she already knew what she needed and wanted—the security of her career—but the truth was that she had just enough doubts to make her uneasy.

"I need time to get a perspective," she admitted, then she gave Maddie a sharp look. "What did you mean by *what I really want*?"

Maddie hesitated, then said, "I mean that you've been glowing since you came home. You love the life here. I know that your career is important, but I'm wondering if once you get back to it, it'll seem *as* important as it did before."

"I agree with Maddie," Kat said. "But if you stay here, you'll always wonder if it was because of the hot guy. And maybe your career *will* be exactly what you need once you get back to it."

Whit raised her eyes to the ceiling high above them. A small bird was perched on the rafters, looking down at her and she felt a pang of envy. What a simple life, flying, eating, drinking, nesting. She looked back at her friends.

"You guys figured things out. Your lives, I mean." Whit smiled wistfully. "But we don't all need the same thing, do we?"

"We—you—need whatever makes you happy," Maddie said.

"Right." Whit got to her feet. "I love you guys."

"Are you going somewhere?" Kat asked.

Whit nodded in the direction of the door. "I'm going to see how Tanner is faring with his brother."

"Are you sure?" Kat wore a concerned look as she stood up.

"I want to talk to him before I leave for the day."

"You're going home early?" Maddie also stood, absently brushing straw from her jeans.

"I am. I'm done here. My commitments have been fulfilled and I want to go home."

Where she would not be forcefully reminded of things she was choosing to leave behind.

"Do you want us to wait around until after you talk to him?" Kat asked.

Whit shook her head before holding out her arms to hug her friends. "If I need support, I'll ping you guys, but I think I'll be fine." She attempted a smile. "Thank you for talking me down."

She and Maddie and Kat exited the barn, only to find another group of kids considering possibilities there. "Off-limits," Kat said sternly, and the kids scattered, laughing as they ran.

"Good luck," Maddie said to Whit. "Sean and I will also be taking off soon. If you *do* need to talk, any time day or night—"

"Thank you." Whit gave her friends another quick hug, then turned and headed for the house, having only a vague idea of what she was going to do once she got there.

If Tanner and Grant were talking, she'd slip away. If they weren't, she'd wing it.

Her heart started beating faster as she mounted the steps to the wide porch, and when she looked in through the tall windows of the double doors, she saw Tanner standing near the stone fireplace and his brother's boots resting on the arm of a sofa. Grant appeared to have passed out.

Time to wing it.

Screwing up her courage, Whit knocked and Tanner's head came up. His expression barely changed at the sight of her, but he waved her in. She stepped into the beautiful house, hesitating on the threshold as the door closed behind her, muffling the sounds of the festivities.

"It's okay," Tanner said with a glance at his brother.

It probably wasn't, but she crossed to where Tanner stood near the leather sofa where Grant Hayes lay with an arm over his eyes, gently snoring.

She was both curious and concerned as to how matters had played out between the brothers, but wasn't about pry into Tanner's family affairs. Not when things were so shaky between them. To her surprise, he answered the question she wasn't going to ask.

"I think my brother and I understand each other," he said with a grim twist of his lips.

"What do you understand?"

"That he has no hold over me. No way to make me sell the ranch. People know the truth now. I don't have to pretend."

"Will the truth bring in the real estate people?"

"I imagine I'll be dealing with some unsolicited offers. I'm good at saying no."

"And the private note?"

He smiled humorlessly. "If it comes in, I'll start leasing out the house and grounds for short stays and events, like say, the one going on now."

"You don't want to do that."

"I'd rather stick a fork in my eye, but a fork in the eye is better than having to sell."

Whit propped her hands on her hips, glancing down at the expensive wool rug at her feet.

"Sometimes," he continued, "we have to make temporary sacrifices to keep the life we want. I want this ranch."

She understood.

"There's other things I want, too." The look he gave

her left no doubts as to his meaning. "But if it's not the right time—"

"Tanner..."

"Then it's not," he said firmly. "I jumped the gun. I'm not certain about my feelings, either. I guess I thought if you were, then we could figure things out, but now it's a moot point."

Whit's instinct was to argue, even though it was counter to her goal. Like Maddie said, she needed time, and she needed distance. So did he.

"Kenny is going to start work immediately," Tanner said.

An indirect way of saying he didn't need her any longer. Whit ignored the painful twist of her heart and brought her hands together.

"I have to see about renting an apartment in Portland."

Grant stirred on the couch, and they simultaneously glanced his way. He settled again and Whit took advantage of the moment to say, "I should go."

Tanner nodded, but he didn't say goodbye, and Whit didn't move. She couldn't leave things as they were. She studied the rug for a brief moment, then met Tanner's gaze.

"What I said about being poor not stopping me from loving someone...it didn't come out as intended." She pushed her hair back from her forehead. "That said... I need time to think."

"We both do."

"Right."

He hooked his thumbs in his pockets as if trying to keep from reaching for her. Whit knew the feeling, but if she gave in now...she couldn't.

Time and distance.

"Goodbye, Whitney." Tanner's voice was rough, but firm. "Good luck in Portland."

"Goodbye, Tanner."

She swallowed as she turned. Stupid tears burned the corners of her eyes as she crossed the room to pull open the heavy door. She stepped outside into the sounds of celebration. The community members were having the time of their lives indulging in food and music and games, thanks to Tanner. He was now part of the community, thanks to her. Everything had worked out as planned.

Except for the things she hadn't planned.

She glanced over her shoulder as the door swung shut, but it was too late to catch a glimpse of the man she might very well be in love with.

The latch caught with a quiet yet definitive click.

This part of her life, the fun easy days on the Hayes Ranch, was over.

CHAPTER FOURTEEN

TANNER WOULDN'T LET his mind linger on Whitney, or the fact that his life had a pretty good-sized hole in it now that she was gone. That was the plan, anyway. They'd had fun, they'd grown close. She'd been his ally and his sounding board. He'd fallen in love; she hadn't gone that far. That was something he had to learn to live with.

Kenny was working out well as an employee, helping his uncle get around and lending a hand when Len needed it. He was familiar with Len's short fuse and knew when to hand him a tool and when to let the man get it himself. In fact, Kenny was pretty impressive in that regard. And he had a genuine fondness for Len.

Tanner just hoped he'd be able to continue paying Kenny and Len if the note came in. Just in case he couldn't, he'd talked to his attorney about fulfilling his dad's promise to Len. There were issues to work out, but Len would get his parcel of land.

After coming to that decision, he'd taken yet another hard look at his finances—or lack thereof—and had come up with a plan that wasn't optimal, but was probably inevitable, since every bank he'd approached for a loan had turned him down due to the money already owed on the property. If push came to shove, he would turn his house into a glorified bed-and-breakfast, or whatever they called the short-term rentals, but while it was a good bluff with his brother, further research had shown that it wouldn't bring in enough to handle the note.

Still, good bluff.

Property was gold in Montana, and he could get some gold by going against his gut and selling off a parcel, something his attorney told him he had the right to do, as long as he split proceeds with Grant. He hated to sell anything, especially since a neighboring ranch had done the same the year before, and it was now a cozy subdivision advertised as country living at its finest, but he also hated wondering if Grant's announcement at the Hearts of the West was going to result in people looking to take advantage of his circumstances. There were plenty of vultures out there and Grant was trying to send them his way.

He had to do something, and the only piece of property he could reasonably carve out to sell was next to the five acres that his dad had promised Len. The problem there was that it contained the diversion point for the water he'd leased Ben Fox.

He could change the diversion, but it would take time and he needed to alert Ben. He'd given the man his word that he'd have water for the next three years and he was standing by that.

When he pulled into the Fox Ranch later that afternoon, intent on explaining to Ben that even though he was going to list a piece, it would not affect the water lease, he had to slow to avoid the chickens that had been pecking in the gravel, filling their craws. Rose remembered her roots as a bird dog and pressed her nose against the passenger-side window, whining her desire to show Tanner exactly where those birds were.

"I see them," he said as he pulled to a stop in front of the house.

The Fox Ranch looked prosperous with its freshly graveled driveway and neatly painted outbuildings, and if he hadn't known better, he would have assumed it was always so.

Ben Fox came out of a shop-like building as Tanner got out of his truck, after rolling the windows down so that Rose would be comfortable. "Do not get out of the truck," he said to the dog, who gave him an easy canine grin. In her younger days, she might have sprung out the window, but her old bones couldn't handle much of that anymore.

"Hey," Ben Fox called.

"Hey. Sorry to drop in unannounced." He'd tried to call the landline, but it had remained busy, so finally he decided to stop by on his way to town and the county assessor's office, where he would inquire about plat map changes. "I'm looking at changing some things, and wanted to give you a heads-up."

"Come on in and have a cup, and you can tell me about it."

Five minutes later, Tanner was seated at the kitchen table, with a deeper understanding of why Whitney liked her coffee like tar. Ben casually tossed out the fact that she was coming home to pick up her car in a week or two, and Tanner asked if she was doing well in a polite kind of way that had her father giving him a speculative look.

"She likes the changes in the company."

"Good." Tanner sipped his coffee without grimacing and then explained that he was thinking of parceling off some land to sell. "I will make absolutely certain that your water lease is not affected, but frankly, this is my only option in case of the unexpected."

"Yeah. I heard about that unexpected," Ben said. "Your brother puts on a good show."

Tanner didn't mention that he half suspected that his

brother might be in contact with Bert, urging him to call in the note.

"Do you want to sell the piece?" Ben asked.

"No. I'll lose production and I'm afraid of chipping away at the place." Total honest truth. It felt good not to hedge.

Ben thought for a moment, then said, "I think you need to talk to the rancher crew."

"I don't understand."

Ben focused on a tattered patch on the knee of his coveralls. "No one would do business with your dad because there was that possibility of being burned."

"I had the same experience."

"Things are different now," Ben said. "Stop by Holly's Café tomorrow morning. It won't hurt, and some of the guys are pretty creative when it comes to getting out from between a rock and a hard place."

Tanner gave him a dubious look. "Okay…"

Ben gave Tanner a stern look. "But be warned."

Always a catch.

"Yes?"

Ben grinned. "You may find yourself becoming a regular."

GREENBRANCH-LOWELL RENEWABLE was a different animal than Greenbranch Renewable had been. Whit returned to work her first day ready to hit the ground running and dive into the backlog of work created by her predecessor's lack of knowledge and practical skills. It was shocking to discover then that employees were discouraged from working overtime. Being chained to one's desk was not considered a positive. Calling in sick was encouraged when one was actually sick.

She had security. Her new salary allowed her to keep

her car, which she had yet to retrieve from Montana. She lucked into an affordable sublease on an apartment. She was working with some familiar faces that Greenbranch-Lowell had brought back. Shandra wasn't her boss, but she was in her department. She felt valued.

And secretly miserable as she battled an emotional state of flux. Why couldn't she settle?

You know why.

"Are you okay?" Shandra asked over Friday drinks on Whit's one-month work anniversary.

"I'm still getting used to working a sane number of hours," Whit said, leaning back to allow the server to place a glass of rye in front of her—a drink that reminded her of Tanner.

Everything reminded her of Tanner.

"But since I'm not being interrupted at every turn with an emergency this or that, I'm actually catching up during normal working hours."

Shandra lifted her drink, her bracelets sparkling against her dark skin. Whit used to wear jewelry to work, but she'd yet to unpack hers. A lot of her belongings were still in boxes, and she knew how telling that was. One day soon, she'd hang pictures, put out mementos, make her little apartment a home.

"I was wary, too," Shandra said. "I didn't think this new model would work, but it does."

"It seems to." Whit ran her fingers over the condensation on the side of her glass. "Why did they cut so many positions in the first place?"

"They made a mistake—the new broom sweeps clean, and all that—but you have to give them credit for realizing quickly what was and wasn't working, rather than persevering with a bad decision out of pride."

"Yes. Persevering out of pride." Whit was persevering, but she could truthfully say she wasn't doing it out of pride. Nope. She was all about security. But what good was security if she wasn't happy?

Whit drew in a breath to speak, then changed her mind.

"Go ahead," Shandra said.

She was getting as bad as Tanner when it came to discussing personal matters.

You're worse. Tanner started letting things out and you started shutting them in.

"I left a cowboy back home."

Shandra's chin dropped and she studied Whit from under perfectly shaped eyebrows. "Why would you do such a thing?" Whit was about to reply when Shandra added, "Seems to me that an unsupervised cowboy could get himself into a lot of trouble."

Whit laughed even as her stomach twisted. Tanner might get himself into trouble, but she wouldn't be able to stop that.

"He needs to come here, where you can keep an eye on him."

That wasn't going to happen.

Whit gave her former boss a weak smile. "It felt like a holiday thing. I was only going to be home for as long as it took me to find another job. That was my mind-set. Then I got a job and I left, and I miss him."

"Okay."

She opened her mouth to say, *But, of course, I have my priorities straight and I know the feeling will fade.* Instead, she said, "I really miss him."

"And he's not the kind to move here?"

"He has a ranch there. Responsibilities."

Shandra put a hand on top of Whit's. "I don't know what to tell you."

"Tell me that it's smart to stay with a company that's

doing so much to create a great work environment for their employees."

"There's that, for sure."

"Tell me that it's important to build retirement and sock-away savings, because you never know when you might have to pump money into the family ranch."

"Okay."

"*If* I went home and got a job there, where I'm closer to..."

"Your cowboy?" Shandra said.

"I'd make half of what I'm making now. If my dad's ranch got into trouble again, I wouldn't be able to help." He'd made noises about accepting the loss, and figuring out a way to forge a new life, and Whit had no doubt that he could...but why would she let that happen if she could help avoid it?

Shandra swirled her drink, her bracelets catching the light. Then she looked up and said, "If."

Whit blinked at her.

"What if the ranch *doesn't* get into trouble?" Shandra continued patiently. "Being here because of what *might* happen when you'd rather be there seems kind of...dumb?"

Whit had to agree, but there were things that Shandra didn't know—like the trauma of almost losing the ranch. Having difficulty affording books when she went to school. Little things that carved deep trenches of worry back in the day.

"We barely squeaked by for a lot of years. I don't want to experience that again."

"How old were you when this went on?"

Whit frowned. "It started when I was in middle school and continued through my college years until I got the job with Greenbranch."

"Frontal lobe." Shandra lifted her glass to emphasize the words.

Whit also lifted her glass. "Frontal lobe to you, too."

Shandra smiled as she set the glass down. "Your frontal lobe doesn't fully develop until your early twenties. Your amygdala is hanging on to the bad memories. Creating a fear reaction."

"Is there a cure?"

"Conscious thought and logic." Whit raised her eyebrows at the seemingly simple answer and Shandra leaned forward, setting her palm on the table. "You need to overcome the thought patterns that are sabotaging good decision-making. When Lowell took over Greenbranch, they got rid of everyone above a certain level because they *thought* that the current employees wouldn't be amenable to change."

"They had a point."

"Then they realized they had a problem, and changed course, carefully bringing back people who could benefit the company."

"That is a good model, but—"

Shandra shook her head. "Lowell didn't start out with that plan. They *changed* to that plan, hoping for the best. They took a chance and it worked. People were starting new, instead of shifting gears and grumbling about change. They had a fresh attitude."

"You're saying…?"

"I'm saying that maybe you should take a look at your reality. What's steering your course, and are you going in the *right* direction for the *right* reasons?"

"Are you trying to get rid of me?" Whit asked, only half kidding.

"Never. But I want you to be happy." Shandra's expression was very, very serious as she asked, "How can you get to that place? Is it a matter of time? Or a matter of change?"

"OVER HERE, TANNER." Ben Fox raised a hand as Tanner walked into Holly's Café, as if he might miss the two tables pushed together, surrounded by six people wearing flannel and canvas.

Tanner lifted his chin in acknowledgment and started across the room to the empty chair next to Ben. He'd gotten there at 6:15 a.m., fifteen minutes after opening, and judging from the coffee cups closest to where he'd taken a seat, most of this crew was ready for their second cup.

"Tanner, I think you know everyone?" Ben then went through brief introductions, just in case. "Martin Fairfield," a neighbor that Tanner knew by reputation only, "Joe Johnson, Liz Forgone, Walt Stenson, Max Tidwell. Troy couldn't be here."

Tanner smiled and nodded, feeling very much as he had during the brief job interview phase of his career. He'd only participated in two interviews before he landed the wheat farming job, so the feeling wasn't a comfortable one.

After Holly gave him a warm hello and topped off everyone's coffee, talk centered on how to get the county commissioners to grade an unimproved road, and if they could not manage that, whether the volunteer firemen would offer their water truck if they were able to rent a grader.

Tanner started to relax as the road maintenance talk continued. He didn't know what he'd expected, other than the usual—to be snubbed or lambasted for the sins of his father, despite making headway with the townspeople since he'd teamed up with Whit.

But Ben Fox hadn't invited him to the klatch to be lambasted. Logically, Tanner knew that, but knee-jerk reactions were hard to control, and his nerves jumped when Max Tidwell, owner of a local guest ranch, abandoned the topic of road maintenance and turned to him. "Ben tells us that you're in need of some creative solutions to a problem."

"Yes." Succinct, and the sum total of what he was willing to put out until he understood his audience better. He assumed that they were there to help, but why?

"Can you tell us what you're facing?" Walt Stenson asked in his gruff voice.

I don't want to.

Tanner sucked in a breath and fought against his ingrained instinct to handle his issues on his own. To not put himself out there to be judged.

"The ranch is in debt. There's an operating loan and a private loan. I'm concerned that the private note will be called in, and I'm looking for a solution that doesn't involve selling off land that I need to operate."

Tanner studied the faces of the ranchers after he'd finished, trying to read reactions and wondering if he'd just made a huge error in being honest with them. It was a relief to no longer have to guard his secret, but he'd just let out information that opened up the possibility of people using it against him. People who wanted to profit from his bad luck.

"Welcome to the club," Liz Forgone muttered, and then gave him a weary smile. "These guys helped me out two years ago."

Tanner felt a small surge of hope. "How?"

Max spoke again. "We don't want to see viable farmland taken out of production. A parcel here, a parcel there, it adds up, and agriculture takes a hit as houses spring up on land that could still be growing crops."

Tanner agreed, but instead of speaking he waited, expecting red flags to crop up at any moment.

"If you want to talk in a more formal setting, bring us the numbers, what you owe, your projections for the future and all that." Max gestured at those around the table. "If it looks doable, we can help you refinance."

"You're kidding."

The words popped out before he could stop them. He'd been expecting offers to buy pieces of his ranch, or perhaps lease opportunities, but not to get out from under the note that his brother wanted to have called in so that he could force a sale.

"We're serious," Ben said. "We work with the Cattleman's Bank."

"They already turned me down. The ranch has a traditional loan in addition to the note." His dad had covered all of his borrowing bases.

"But they won't turn us down," Martin said.

"Why do you say that?"

Joe Johnson chuckled. "Because I'm the president of the bank and I trust these guys."

"We have a lot of money in Joe's institution, including an emergency fund that we use to make loans," Martin said. "We put this together a few years ago, when Lizzie here needed some help, and the fund has grown nicely thanks to decent investments and interest, of course."

"Refinancing is the first step," Max said.

"And we can help you find a crew that sticks with you," Walt added, "if you want to go back to full operations. I know that your dad cut back in recent years." He made a tsking noise. "I just didn't know why."

Tanner looked around the table. "What do you get out of this other than saving farmland?"

"Satisfaction," Liz said. "It could happen to anyone."

Half an hour later, Tanner left the café feeling dazed. He had neighbors who were going to help him. Granted, they were going to get their money back and interest to boot, but the offer alone was enough to humble him.

He walked with Ben to his truck, which was parked near Tanner's.

"I don't know how to thank you for this opportunity," he said to the older man.

"It's not a done deal, but I have a good feeling about it."

Ben got into his truck but before he pulled the door shut, he said, "You're not your father, and I think you've hit a point where you don't have to keep proving that."

"I'm beginning to believe it."

"I think my daughter has feelings for you." Ben tossed his bomb, then waited for Tanner's reaction.

"I think we both know that she's not coming back to stay." Tanner tipped his head to the side as a thought struck him. "If your ranch got into trouble, you obviously have some options for help."

"As long as the fund isn't being used."

"Does Whitney know this?"

"Yes. I'm no psychologist, but I think her career is her way of dealing with the aftermath of her mom's death. She had no security during that time other than me and her two best friends. We almost lost the ranch. Now she makes her own security in the form of money in the bank."

Tanner glanced up as two women walked past on their way to the café, the only business open at this hour. One of them smiled at him and he smiled back, thinking that it felt good to no longer be an outcast, before turning his attention back to Ben.

"Next moves?" Tanner asked, referring to Whit rather than the loan. He guessed from Ben's expression that he got the drift.

"We wait."

CHAPTER FIFTEEN

LIFE PLAN NUMBER 4 was shaping up in an open-ended kind of way. Whit had left it that way on purpose, even though it was a tad unnerving not to have all the i's dotted and t's crossed. Every now and again she had to pause and assure herself that open-ended was fine. Sticking to an obsolete plan out of fear was not.

Life Plan Number 3 had served her well. It had helped her save the ranch. It had put money in the bank and allowed her to buy nice things.

Now, thanks to her weeks with Tanner, she was in a been-there-done-that frame of mind.

She didn't need the security her corporate job provided any longer. She liked it, because it allowed her to be impulsive in other areas, but she didn't need it. She'd get by.

Shandra had asked if getting to a place of contentment was a matter of time or change.

The answer had come so much more rapidly than Whit had anticipated. Change. It was a matter of changing her outlook, of reassessing what security really meant. Of knowing that she could scrape by if necessary, and that if she was scraping by with a guy she loved, it would be a shoulder-to-shoulder venture.

Structure and money had been her security, but she was strong enough now to take risks. She'd been strong enough before, but hadn't recognized the fact. Deep down, she'd been the frightened teen who'd given up so much, only to lose her mom. She'd equated lack of money with loss, only to set herself up so that pursuit of money meant loss.

Loss of a possible relationship with Tanner.

But that loss was not carved in stone.

She hoped. They hadn't parted company on the best of terms, and they hadn't been in contact. She told herself she was brave enough to do this, to give up everything she'd thought she wanted to head back home and start a new life.

Maddie and Kat would probably laugh if they saw brave Whit shaking in her shoes, so she wouldn't. She would head home, get a job, live on her ranch and see if it was possible to salvage things with Tanner.

If not, then they'd be neighbors. And it would hurt to see him, to know what she'd given up in a mistaken effort to keep herself and her family ranch safe and secure.

She'd be lying if she said she wasn't nervous about the whole situation, but she also had no intention of changing her new course.

Not unless she was forced to. The only person who had that power was Tanner.

THE LOAN WAS in the works. Two weeks after the coffee klatch meeting, papers had been signed and the check was being sent directly to Bert Wallace, much to Grant's chagrin. Now he had no choice but to wait to see if Tanner could pull things out of the red.

Tanner was going to do just that. As he'd once told Whit, he was good at making ends meet, and now that he had some breathing room, he needed to see about finding a used cultivator to replace the one that was now beyond repair due to simple wear and tear.

He scrolled through the community marketplace on social media, hoping to find what he needed, flipping past furniture, tools, trailers, cars—

He abruptly reversed the direction of his thumb and went back to the car he'd just scrolled by.

Whitney's car.

As in, the car she was supposed to have picked up that weekend. He'd spent Saturday and Sunday jumping when the phone rang, then being disappointed when it wasn't her calling to ask about his new business deal with the coffee klatch ranchers. Maybe her dad hadn't told her.

Maybe if he wanted her to know, he had to tell her himself.

He read the listing, then sat back in his chair. She was selling the car after all.

It could mean nothing.

Or everything.

He reached for the phone and dialed the number on the ad. A few rings later, Ben Fox answered.

"Hi, Ben. Tanner Hayes. I see that you have a car for sale."

"Then let me hand you off to the owner." Tanner's heart rate bumped up as he heard Ben walking through a room, his footsteps echoing. A moment later he was back on the line. "She's not here."

"Would she want to talk to me if she was?"

"I can't answer for her, Tanner. I can just tell you that she's gone, the car's gone and the dust is settling in the direction of your ranch."

TANNER WAITED A good hour for Whitney to show, then decided that Ben was wrong. She didn't want to see him. If she did, he would have known that she was back in the area. Selling her car.

Why was she selling her car?

He went to the barn and started the tractor, warming the oil so that he could change it. Cooper was supposed to service the tractors, but Tanner felt the need to keep busy. If he focused on the ranch and rebuilding, he spent less time thinking about what he wished could have been.

Actually, he was going to do more than wish.

While the tractor idled, he readied his supplies, then after ten minutes he turned off the machine and reached for his phone instead of the wrench. He wrote a short text and pushed Send. His head came up a split second later when a texting chime sounded from outside the shop.

No way.

The door opened and Whitney stepped inside. "So much for surprises," she muttered.

"How much of a surprise did you want to give me?" he asked, somehow managing to get words out of his tight throat.

"I was going to stand outside the door for a bit while I gathered my courage," she muttered. "I got all of five seconds before your text came in."

Tanner's heart started thumping against his ribs. Slow, steady thumps that still didn't seem to be getting enough oxygen to his brain.

Whit lifted the phone with his text message on the screen. "Apparently, you'd like to meet?"

"I thought I'd have time to prepare."

"That would make two of us."

Barriers were rising on both sides and Tanner knew that he couldn't let his barriers get in the way yet again.

"If you were willing to try…" He looked past her to the door she'd just come through, trying desperately not to screw up.

"Try…" she echoed.

His gaze shifted back to her as she started toward him with slow, measured steps, her boots echoing off the walls of the barn.

She stopped just out of touching range and pushed her thumbs into her front pockets. "I quit my job."

"Whit—"

She cut him off with a look, which was just as well, because he had nothing other than a flickering sense of hope.

"It's been a rough month."

"On the job?"

"In my head." She studied his boots as he studied her. "I've never been in love." She lifted her gaze. "Not like this. It's ripping me up, but it's also making things so much clearer."

She loved him. His heart swelled, but he waited for her to continue. He needed to know everything she was thinking. Every problem she had with them being together so that he could counter it.

She let her gaze travel around the interior of the barn. "Maybe I wasn't so far off the mark with Life Plan Number 1."

"The one you made in middle school?" The one she'd told him about when they were riding on the mountain.

"When my mom was sick, yes. Maybe I was meant to be on the Hayes Ranch, training horses. Or a horse." She gave him an unreadable look. "Clive is still a menace."

"Not as much of one as before."

Everything in Tanner's being cried out for him to take this woman in his arms. Hold her. Tell her how much he needed her in his life. Instead, he found the strength to say, "I got out from under the private note."

"I know," she said quietly. "Dad is very proud of that."

"I still have a lot of financial worries."

She lifted her chin. "Here's what I think about financial worries." She closed the distance between them, took his face in her hands and kissed him. A long, slow kiss that melded into another long, slow kiss, which ended with Tanner backing her across the barn floor until she came up against the tractor tire. Then he kissed her again.

When he finally lifted his head, he pushed his fingers into her hair, then dropped one last light kiss on her beautiful mouth. "Since when don't you care about security?"

"Since I started doing battle with my amygdala."

Tanner blinked at her. "Uh…"

"Long story. Bottom line, I'm facing my fears. And then I'm beating them into submission. I was trying to do that outside the door when your text came in."

He laughed and pulled her closer. "You're really quitting?" He wasn't sure how he felt about that, knowing how important her job had been to her, but maybe some of those reasons no longer applied.

"First, I'm going to give the powers that be a pitch about working remotely. This company doesn't have a policy in that regard, so I'm hoping to force them into making one. If they say no, then I'm quitting. I own part of the ranch next door. It may not support me, but I'll have a place to stay while I find a local job." She frowned up at him and he realized he was staring at her as if expecting her to say, "April fool."

"What's wrong?"

He smiled. A genuine, nothing-to-hide smile. "Everything is right."

She touched a finger to his lips, and he kissed it. "Get used to it. With me around, things are going to go right a lot."

"You think?" he asked, dropping his hands to link behind her waist and pulling her closer.

She gave him a sassy smile. "I don't think. I know."

EPILOGUE

"FOOD'S NOT READY YET." Tanner settled on the grass beside Whit, stretching out his legs and leaning back on his hands.

"How long?"

"According to my stomach, too long."

Whit laughed and leaned into his shoulder. The summer had flown by, and it was time for Aiden and Coop to return to college for the fall semester, so Tanner had arranged a going-away party, which was now in full swing. Len and Whit's dad sat at a picnic table, playing cribbage. Kenny, Aiden, Coop and a few of the local ranchers were playing volleyball, which was something of a spectacle. Whit had to admit that it was amusing to see some of the guys in their go-to-town clothes instead of dusty jeans and plaid shirts. They'd brought wives and kids, and the summer picnic on the Hayes Ranch was shaping up to be a good time for one and all.

Tanner's stomach growled and Whit gave the hard muscles a pat.

"Good things come to those who wait," she said, turning her attention to little Livia, who was toddling around the lawn hanging on to Kat's finger. Her friend was a natural-born mother and after a quick elopement—she was afraid of having a real wedding due to the tendency for unexpected things to happen during Farley events—she and Troy were now trying for a brother or sister for little Livia.

"I don't want the kids to be too far apart in age," Kat had confessed to Maddie and Whit.

"How many kids do you want?" Maddie had asked.

"Open-ended," Kat had replied, and then been mystified when Whit laughed.

The volleyball sailed their way and Whit slugged it back into the game.

"Good one," Tanner murmured.

"I have skills," she said.

"Next you'll be saying that you can out-volleyball me."

"In a heartbeat."

He smiled into her eyes. "In your dreams."

She raised a hand to his cheek and smiled into his eyes before he took her lips in a quick kiss.

"Deflection will not work," he growled into her ear.

"Experience tells me otherwise," she replied, turning her attention back to the action.

She had to go to work the next day at her new job with the Natural Resources Conservation Service. She wouldn't be buying sporty roadsters, but she didn't need one. What she did need was the man sitting beside her. The man who'd sworn he'd love her forever.

"I'd like to get married someday," she murmured as she watched Maddie set out plates with her fiancé, Sean. Her friend looked so happy, as did he. She and Tanner had discussed the big step, even though they were only months into their relationship. Discussed it, tabled it. And now Whit was bringing it up again.

"To me?" he asked.

She ran a critical gaze over him. "I don't think I could do better."

His smile made her forget to breathe for a moment, and the next thing she knew her hair was touching grass as he leaned over her, kissing her deeply.

A wolf whistle sounded, and they pushed themselves back to sitting positions with sheepish grins, then Tanner stood and held out his hand.

"I like your plan," he said as he pulled her to her feet. "It's Number 5."

Tanner laughed and pulled her close. "That might soon be my favorite number."

* * * * *

WESTERN

Rugged men looking for love...

Available Next Month

Maverick's Secret Daughter Catherine Mann
The Rancher Resolution Viv Royce

....

Fortune In Name Only Tara Taylor Quinn
Reunited With The Rancher Anna Grace

....

LOVE INSPIRED

United By The Twins Jill Kemerer
The Cowboy's Secret Past Tina Radcliffe

Keep reading for an excerpt of a new title
from the Western Romance series,
SWEET-TALKIN' MAVERICK by Christy Jeffries

PROLOGUE

NEARLY EVERYONE IN our small Montana town had attended some sort of event in the newly renovated Bronco Convention Center. But only one other couple had thrown an actual party inside of it. Of course, the last weekend in January wasn't exactly the time of year for a large outdoor gathering, and the crowd tonight was definitely a large one.

Everyone knows that when the beloved mayor invites the whole town to celebrate his thirtieth wedding anniversary, it's not a question of *if* you'll go. It's a question of what you should wear and who else is going to be sitting at your table. Sure, you could miss the annual Christmas tree lighting or a rodeo on occasion. Those types of events brought in enough tourists that your absence might go unnoticed. However, tonight's party celebrating Rafferty and Penny Smith was strictly for the locals. And anyone who was anyone in Bronco, Montana, had RSVP'd yes before the invitations were even printed.

"Thank you all for coming out to join me and Penny on this momentous occasion," Mayor Rafferty Smith began his speech welcoming everyone. The man was a great speaker and an even better storyteller. It was no wonder he kept getting reelected. "You know, when I first asked Penny to marry me, I wasn't sure she'd say yes. In fact, I don't think *she* even knew she was going to say yes. But we were just a couple of young kids in love back then, flying by the seats of our pants. We had no big plans other than making it through each day and having as much fun as we could. Nobody tells you how much work a marriage takes... I mean, nobody except all the boring adults who know better than you. But you ignore them because you've got too many stars in your eyes. Then, as time goes by and you begin to look back on all the ups and downs, all the good times and the bad, you begin to realize what you've actually accomplished. Personally, my biggest achievement is sharing the past thirty years with the woman I love."

Everyone oohed and aww'd as the mayor pulled his wife onto the stage beside him. "Penny, you've stuck by my side all this time and there is nothing I could give you that would even come close to everything you've given me these past years. But I couldn't show up here completely empty-handed." The crowd chuckled politely, then applauded as Rafferty presented his wife with a black velvet jewelry case. "They say pearls are traditional for the thirtieth anniversary, but if you ask me, there is nothing traditional about you, Penny Smith. Like this necklace, you are one of a kind and I can't wait to see what the next thirty years have in store for us."

Rafferty made a big show of fastening the stunning heirloom pearl necklace around Penny's neck, causing the guests to cheer uproariously when he hauled his wife into his arms for an over-the-top kiss.

Everyone in the crowd agreed—the party was already off to a fabulous start.

CHAPTER ONE

Dylan Sanchez forced himself to come tonight because he didn't want to be the only business owner in Bronco who refused the mayor's invitation. Oh, and because his parents and siblings would've never let him hear the end of it if he'd skipped.

At the rate the Sanchez family was growing, though, it wasn't just the opinions of Dylan's two brothers and two sisters he had to contend with, either. He'd assumed that when his sisters got married and his brothers got engaged, they would find better things to do with their time than remind him that he was now the odd man out.

Clearly, he'd been wrong about that.

Not that Dylan wasn't proud to be the last Sanchez standing. Growing up in a competitive family, if he wasn't going to be the first one to do something, then he sure as hell was going to outlast everyone else. It was just that being surrounded by so many happy couples, talking about anniversaries and upcoming weddings, could start to wear on a happily single guy.

Plus, he hated crowded events.

"Aren't these tables only supposed to seat ten people?" Dylan muttered to his father. "How did we manage to get thirteen chairs crammed around one tiny space?"

"Thirteen chairs *and* a stroller," his brother Dante said as he rocked his and his fiancée Eloise's daughter back to sleep in her little buggy. Merry, Dylan's eight-week-old niece, was officially his favorite family member, and not just because she kept her opinions to herself.

A few minutes later, when Dylan mentioned the lack of elbow room, his sister Sofia replied, "Boone and I are going to sit with the rest of the Daltons once they pass out the cake. You can put up with being squished for that long, Dylan."

"Yeah, but I don't know how long I can put up with Felix stealing my beer." Dylan snatched the pint glass from his older brother's hand. "The bar's right over there if you want to go get your own."

Felix had the nerve to smile unapologetically. "Shari and I are going to head that way for another round as soon as she and Mom get done talking about bridal shower themes. In the meantime, you can share."

Uncle Stanley returned from the buffet line with two full plates and his fiancée, Winona Cobbs. As the older couple took their seats, there was even less space to move.

Dylan turned toward his sister Camilla. "I think your in-laws are looking for you."

"No they're not," Jordan Taylor, Camilla's husband, replied. "My dad and uncles are busy holding court with the mayor."

"If you need to get away from us, Dylan," Camilla said as she nodded discreetly at a table with several young women, "there's room over there."

"Stop trying to set me up. Between the car dealership and the new ranch, I don't have time for a girlfriend right now."

"When have you ever had time, Dyl?" Sofia asked. "Aren't you getting tired of the dating scene? You're not getting any younger."

"Uncle Stanley is eighty-seven and *he* just got engaged. So there's not exactly an age limit for someone getting married. In fact, I don't have to get married at all." Dylan knew he sounded defiant, possibly even stubborn. But the more his family talked about weddings, the more determined he became to stay single.

"Don't forget, kiddo, that I was already married once and there's nothing better than sharing your life with someone." Uncle Stanley, who'd been a widower for some time, turned to Winona. "Speaking of which, we should probably be setting our own wedding date soon."

Winona, a ninetysomething-year-old psychic who was prone to mystical statements, shrugged noncommittally. "We will when the time is right."

"You're not having second thoughts, are you?" Uncle Stanley asked, concern causing the wrinkles around his eyes to deepen.

Winona shook her head, her messy white bun tipping to one side. "Of course not. But love cannot be rushed. It *will* not be rushed." Then she pointed an age-spotted hand covered with several rings at Dylan. "But it cannot be avoided, either. Love always finds a way."

Dylan opened and closed his mouth several times, unsure of how to respond. Or if he should. He reclaimed his beer once again from his brother and drained the glass before changing the subject.

"Anyway, the ranch has me so busy lately, I hired two new salespeople for the dealership to cover for me. But January is normally a slow month for car sales. I need to think of something to get business moving again."

"You could try not spending so much time at Broken Down Ranch," one of his sisters suggested.

"It's called Broken *Road* Ranch," he corrected. His family had always been supportive of his dream to own land, but several of them had recently questioned his decision to own *this* particular property. The place was a bit of a fixer-upper and most of the buildings had seen better days. But it sat in one of the best spots in the valley and, hopefully, the grass would return this spring and make it look not so...well...run-down.

"What about a car wash?" Dante, the elementary school teacher, suggested. "My school did one before summer break last year and made a decent amount."

Dylan frowned. "I don't need a onetime fundraiser. I need to get more people on my lot. But without being one of those cheesy salespeople who resort to gimmicks or corny commercials just to make a buck. You know how I hate public speaking."

"What about a game of hoops?" Their father had raised his children with a passion for sports. "We could do a tournament, like we do with the rec league. I'll be the referee."

Several people at their table groaned, including Dylan's mom, who had attended more than her share of basketball tournaments over the years.

"That would take an awful lot of time for people to form teams and have practices," their mom said. "You need to put something together sooner and you need a theme."

"Valentine's Day is coming up," Sofia said a bit too casually and all the women were very quick to agree. Suspicion caused the back of Dylan's neck to tingle.

"You guys want me to do something on a commercialized holiday created for the sole purpose of selling romance to people? What am I going to do? Have a Valentine's dance?" Dylan snorted at the absurdity. "No wait, maybe I should send everyone who wants to test-drive a car on a ride through a tunnel of love."

Uncle Stanley raised his hand. "I vote for the tunnel of love idea."

Dylan needed another drink. "Buying a vehicle is a big decision, you guys. When someone comes to my dealership, it's to make a practical purchase. They're not there for all that mushy stuff."

And neither was Dylan. He didn't do mushy. He certainly didn't do grand gestures like Mayor Smith had done up on the stage a few minutes ago when he'd given his wife that necklace in front of the whole town.

"Valentine's Day is one of the biggest nights of the year in the service industry," Camilla, who owned her own restaurant, pointed out. "Trust me, when it comes to gifts, some people want more than flowers and chocolates."

Dylan grimaced. "So I just get some big red bows and hoist up a new banner? Maybe dress up as Cupid and shoot arrows at the potential customers?"

Winona lifted her wineglass. "Lots of gals in this town wouldn't mind seeing the Sanchez brothers dressed up like Cupid and wearing nothing but a tiny white toga."

Thankfully, that suggestion got a resounding set of *noes* from Felix and Dante. Several more ideas were offered and rejected before Dylan excused himself to go to the bar while his family wore themselves out discussing the most absurd concepts that would never come to fruition. He told himself that he'd grab another beer, maybe a plate of food, and by the time he got back to the table, his family would have moved on to another subject.

However, Dylan got sidetracked talking with a few buddies about the upcoming baseball season, speaking to one of the city council members about a permit application for some electric vehicle charging stations and checking the score on the college basketball game. When he returned to the party, he ran into Mrs. Coss, the older lady who owned the antiques mall next door to his dealership.

"I think it's a great idea, Dylan. I'll even be willing to lend you a few pieces from my 1920s rolling pin collection as long as they're just used for display purposes."

He smiled politely despite his confusion. "What's a great idea, Mrs. Coss?"

"The bake-off. Maybe I'll put out a shelf of my older cookbooks and a rack of mid-century aprons to do a little sidewalk sale." The band began playing their rendition of the "Cha Cha Slide," and before Dylan could ask her what she meant, Mrs. Coss said, "This is my song. We'll talk more about cross-promotion tomorrow." She patted him on the arm and dashed onto the dance floor before he could say another word.

Dylan heard the word *bake-off* several more times on his way back to the table. By the time he arrived at his seat, most of his siblings and his mom were already gone, blending into the crowd. His dad was still there, though, holding baby Merry and serenading her with the off-key lyrics of the line dancing song.

"Where'd everyone go?" Dylan asked his dad.

"They're spreading the word about the bake-off."

Dylan's temples began pounding. "Please tell me that this doesn't have anything to do with my dealership."

"Hey, Dylan," LuLu, the owner of his favorite BBQ joint, called out from two tables over. "What's the prize for the bake-off?"

His dad responded before Dylan could. "A year's worth of free mechanical service. Oil changes, new brakes, tire rotations, that sort of thing."

All the color drained from Dylan's face as he stared at his dad in shock. "I was gone for thirty minutes."

Apparently, thirty minutes was all it had taken for Dylan's entire family to come up with a harebrained idea to hold a Valentine's Day–themed bake-off at his place of business. Oh, *and* promise the winner a prize valued at potentially thousands of dollars. But it was too late to call the thing off. Gossip spread like wildfire in Bronco and Dylan was officially on the hook for a contest he hadn't authorized.

"Nobody even asked my permission," he told Dante, the first sibling who returned to the table.

"Have you met Mom and our sisters? You walked away midconversation. That's practically giving them your blessing to proceed however they see fit."

Dylan rolled his eyes. "It's a car dealership, not the set of some cooking show. You've seen my break room. I have an old microwave and a toaster that sets off the smoke alarm anytime I want a bagel. How do they think they're going to hold a bake-off there?"

"I don't know. Something about a giant party tent and one of Camilla's suppliers who rents out restaurant-grade ovens." Dante took his baby from their dad. "I wasn't really paying attention, man."

Could this evening get any worse? The pounding at Dylan's temples revved into a full headache and he was about to call it a night. But if he left the party now, what other crazy schemes would his family come up with in his absence? Needing to ward off the gossip and do damage control, he rose from the table.

Unfortunately, he didn't get more than two feet when the mayor thwarted his plans.

"Dylan!" Rafferty Smith reached out to enthusiastically shake Dylan's hand. "I hear we're holding an exciting town event at the dealership next month. Penny loves that British baking show, by the way. Obviously, I'd be honored to help judge the contest. I'll tell my assistant to clear my schedule for that day."

Okay, so having the mayor make an appearance at his dealership could actually be good for business. Plus, Dylan was in the middle of working on a bid proposal to supply the city officials with a fleet of vehicles. Since he didn't want to risk losing that contract, he had no choice but to clench his jaw, smile and act as though this ridiculous bake-off plan could actually work. That it wouldn't be nearly as embarrassing as him running around dressed like Cupid. "Great. It should be a lot of fun. I look forward to having you join us."

Mayor Smith then took a step closer and lowered his voice. "Just between us, any chance you happened to see a pearl necklace around here?"

"You mean like the one you gave your wife less than an hour ago?"

"Shh. Keep your voice down. Penny had it on when we were on the dance floor, but it must've fallen off somewhere. I'm trying to ask around discreetly because I don't want to cause a—"

"Attention, ladies and gentlemen," the lead singer of the band interrupted as he spoke into the microphone. "We have an announcement to make. If anyone finds a pearl necklace, please bring it up to the stage so we can reunite it with its owner."

The crowd's hushed murmurs quickly grew louder as everyone realized whose necklace had gone missing. Rafferty Smith muttered, "So much for doing anything discreetly in this town," before striding away.

Dylan couldn't agree more.

Surely someone would find Penny's necklace soon. Dylan doubted his own reputation as a serious businessman would be recovered as easily.

ROBIN ABERNATHY WAS better on the back of a horse than she was in front of an oven. But she'd been known to have a few tricks up her sleeve when it came to the kitchen. Or at least a few recipes.

Okay. Two recipes. One of which, fortunately, was a

batch of cookies. Besides, she didn't want to actually win the Valentine's Day bake-off. She just wanted to get one of the judges to notice her.

She parked one of the ranch trucks at the curb in front of Bronco Motors, then stared at her reflection in the rearview mirror. Her summer tan had long faded, and her complexion could benefit from a swipe of blusher. Too bad she didn't own any makeup. She dug around in her purse and came up with a tube of colorless lip balm. Oh well. She yanked the elastic band out of her hair, ditching her usual ponytail. Maybe she'd look more feminine with her hair down.

For the first time in thirty-one years, Robin asked herself why she couldn't be better at the whole flirtation thing. Probably because she spent too much time with her brothers and the other cowboys out on her family's ranch. If she couldn't find the time to go out on many dates, then she certainly didn't have the time to put much effort into her appearance. If a guy didn't appreciate her for being herself, what was the point in bothering with a second date?

But that was before Dylan Sanchez had smiled at her during Bronco's annual Christmas tree lighting event. She hadn't been able to stop thinking of the man since then.

She'd planned to casually run into him at the Smiths' anniversary party, but a last-minute emergency with one of her client's horses had kept her away. Maybe it was better this way since his recently announced bake-off might prove to be a better opportunity to talk to the man without such a huge crush of people around.

As if on cue, she saw him striding across the dealership lot and heading into the office. Robin wasn't used to the feeling of butterflies in her stomach because it was rare that her nerves got the best of her. Before she could overthink what she was about to do, she exited the truck and slammed the driver's door, closing off any doubt and leaving it behind her.

You can do this. Gripping the printed flyer tighter in her fist, she entered the building that served as a couple of offices and a showroom for a brand-new 4x4 truck. She'd purposely picked a time when she thought the dealership wouldn't be busy and, from what she could see, it appeared she'd planned well. Nobody else was around.

Dylan's voice made its way through an open door and then a second voice responded from what sounded like a speakerphone. Not wanting to interrupt his call, she casually walked around the vehicle on display, reading the information on the back window sticker.

It wasn't that she was trying to eavesdrop, but it was hard not to hear him in his office ten feet away. It only took her a few moments to figure out the extent of the conversation. His small herd had been overgrazing in the same spot for years and he couldn't move them until he had time to repair some fences. The other voice clearly belonged to a fertilizer salesman trying to convince Dylan to invest in an untested anti-erosion soil product. The last phrase sent a warning bell to Robin's brain and she found herself inching closer to the office.

Dylan was pacing back and forth in the small space, the lines on his forehead deeply grooved. When he caught sight of her, she immediately took a step back, but not before she saw his face transform from concern to a veneer of charm and grace.

"Let me call you back, Tony," he said as Robin pretended to be absorbed in reading about all the off-road features listed on the truck's sticker price.

"Welcome to Bronco Motors," Dylan told her with that same smile and those same cheek dimples that she'd been seeing in her dreams the past several weeks. "Are you interested in trying this out?"

She almost said yes, then realized he was talking about the car between them. "Oh, um, not today. I came to sign up for the bake-off."

She held up the flyer, as if to prove that was her sole intention in coming here.

If Dylan was disappointed that she wasn't there to buy a car, he covered it well. "Right. So full disclosure, my mom and sisters did the flyers this past week and posted them all over social media before I even got a chance to create any sort of official sign-up or even come up with contest rules. I wasn't really prepared for the amount of interest I've already gotten." He walked over to an empty reception desk and retrieved a clipboard. "So I've just been having people put their contact information on this sheet. We'll reach out when we have all the details finalized."

Whoa. Up close, the man smelled even better than he looked. Trying not to let the scent of his cologne go to her head, Robin took the clipboard from him and it only took a quick glimpse at the other names on the list to see that it was all women. Apparently, she wasn't the only one in town who wanted an excuse to get up close and personal with the last single Sanchez brother.

She paused with the pen in her hand. This was so foolish. What was she even doing here? Someone like her wouldn't have a chance of winning a baking contest or attracting a guy like Dylan. But as he stood there watching, another thought occurred to her. He'd just asked her if she wanted to go for a test-drive. Her parents bought all their ranch vehicles from this dealership, including several of this exact same model. If Dylan knew who she was, then he would know that Robin wouldn't need to test-drive a car she often used at work.

Which meant he had no idea who she was.

Robin wasn't sure if she should be relieved or offended. Until he added, "I should probably warn you that the bake-off is on Valentine's Day. In case you're already busy that day. Or, you know, have plans."

She looked up quickly and was rewarded with the sexiest smile and the most smoldering pair of brown eyes she'd ever seen. At least this close. Was he suggesting that she might have some sort of date for the most romantic day of the year? Her sister, Stacy, teased her about being oblivious to men flirting with her. Was this one of those times?

Since Robin couldn't just stand there staring at him in confusion, she mumbled what she hoped sounded like, "No, I'm available." Or at least it would've sounded like that if her tongue wasn't all tied up in knots.

She scribbled her name on the list, along with her cell number and email address. Her face was flushed with heat by the time she returned the clipboard to him, but he didn't give it so much as a glance before tucking it under his arm.

His phone rang from his pocket and he pulled it out long enough to glance at the screen and then silence it.

"I should probably let you get back to work," she said, jumping on the excuse to get away before she did or said something else that made her seem like a lovesick fool.

"Only if you're sure I can't interest you in a test-drive."

No, Robin wasn't sure at all. But her whole goal in coming here today was to meet the man in person and see if this crush she'd developed on him from afar was just as foolhardy as she'd been telling herself. And the answer was yes.

"Nope, I'm all set," she said, pivoting to leave. Before she executed a full turn, though, she stopped in her tracks. "Actually. I know this is none of my business, but someone needs to stop you from making a huge mistake."

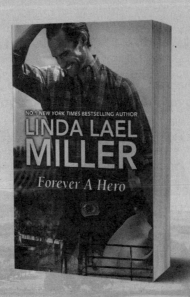